Beyond Betrayal

A Story of Heartbreak,
Healing, and
Redeeming Love

A Novel by
DANNA DEMETRE

Praises for *Beyond Betrayal*

Beyond Betrayal is the book we would have handed ourselves during the hardest season of our own marriage—a story that doesn't flinch from the devastation of betrayal or the pride that leads a spouse astray yet extends the kind of grace that makes repentance feel possible and redemption real.

Danna writes both Grant and Kate's journeys with such honest tenderness that husbands and wives alike will find themselves convicted, moved, and quietly asking God what He might be doing in their own unraveling. Every couple who has ever held a broken marriage in trembling hands, or sat with friends who have, needs this book.

~ Mark and Jill Savage, authors of ***No More Perfect Marriages, I Really Messed Up***, and ***My Heart is Broken***

Beyond Betrayal by Danna Demetre is a captivating novel filled with realistic characters, authentic relationships, and profound spiritual insight. Demetre's compelling storytelling draws readers so deeply into the lives of her characters that they may find themselves praying for their futures and cheering for their redemption.

More than an engaging story, this novel offers rich, godly wisdom for marriages in every season. Beautifully written and deeply moving, *Beyond Betrayal* draws readers closer to the God of love, grace, forgiveness, and restoration while inspiring greater honesty, wisdom, and hope in their own lives.

~ Pam Farrel, author of 60+ books including bestselling ***Men Are Like Waffles, Women Are Like Spaghetti*** and ***Red Hot Monogamy.*** *Together with her husband, Bill, they Co-Direct Love-Wise Ministries.*

Advance Reader Reviews:

What a joy to preview Danna's beautifully crafted Italian romantic adventure. It resonated in so many ways. I pray this heartfelt story touches the lives of everyone that reads it in one way or another.
~ Lezli Powers, Advance Reader

With her vivid characterizations and gorgeous settings, Danna Demetre tells a story that is gripping, raw, and real. Beyond Betrayal is a page-turner; I couldn't put it down and read late into the night, laughing, crying, and cheering Kate on. This powerful, hope-filled story truly does stay with you long after you have turned the last page. ~ Susan Grygier, Advance Reader

Beyond Betrayal is a beautiful blessing! It walks you through life's heartache into a place of healing and sharing friendship in Italy along the way! God's grace and love truly shine through this faith-filled story! ~ Laurie Fletes, Advance Reader

Beyond Betrayal is a beautifully written Christian fiction novel that kept my attention from the beginning to the end. The story is engaging and filled with individuals you find yourself really caring about. I appreciated how faith is woven naturally through the story and look forward to reading more fiction novels from Danna.
~ Cas Strouse, Advance Reader

Published by Danna Demetre

First Edition

Beyond Betrayal is available on Amazon in Paperback, Hardcover, Kindle and Audible.

Printed in the United States of America

For information about books, speaking engagements, or other resources, visit: www.DannaDemetre.com

Dedication

To my husband and best friend, Lew

You have been my greatest encourager through every dream, every challenge, and every step of this new journey of writing a story of redeeming love. Thank you for believing in me, supporting this book, and helping create a legacy of enduring love for our family and for others who may need hope that God still restores broken things. Forever and a day, my love.

To my dearest girlfriends: Sharon, Sheri, Gwen, Patti, Debi, Robyn, Diane, and Charity

Your friendships and lives have encouraged me over the past 15 to 35 years as we've "done life" together much like the women in this book. Your own difficult experiences and faithful prayers and support in my deep valleys inspired me to create characters and friendships in this book that I hope resonate with many women. You are each a true gift from God.

To my Savior and Lord, Jesus

You alone redeem what feels beyond repair. You bring beauty from ashes, hope to the hopeless, and healing to wounded hearts. Thank You for Your grace in my own story and for the countless ways You continue restoring what the locusts have eaten. This book was written prayerfully and with deep dependence upon You. May it encourage hurting women, strengthen marriages, point readers toward forgiveness and truth, and ultimately bring glory to Your name.

PROLOGUE
Thirty-Five Years

Austin, Texas

Grant still reached for her in his sleep.

Even after thirty-five years of marriage, his hand found her in the dark as if trained by instinct, resting against her waist, her hip, sometimes tangling in the soft cotton of her nightgown. It was a small thing, but it always made Kate smile. Many nights she lay still, savoring the quiet evidence that some parts of love only grew more certain with time.

Their bedroom in their Austin home held the life they had built together. A worn leather chair sat in the corner where Grant read every morning with his coffee. Framed photos lined the dresser, three grown children captured at graduations and weddings, and one chaotic Christmas when everyone wore matching pajamas and Grant insisted on taking selfies like he was twenty-five.

Jesse, their oldest, now thirty-one, stood tall in one photo beside his bride, Rachel with California sunshine stretching behind them while their almost two-year-old son twisted in his arms, already trying to escape.

Emma, twenty-eight, beamed in another frame, her engagement ring catching the light, the Dallas skyline faintly visible through the restaurant window where her fiancé had proposed.

Nathan, twenty-four and forever thoughtful, leaned against a brick building on the East Coast, graduate schoolbooks tucked under his arm, looking more like a professor than the youngest child who once refused to sleep without the hallway light on.

The house had once been noisy – backpacks dropped by the door, cleats kicked off, piano practice drifting down the hall. Now it echoed differently. Quieter. But not lonely.

Kate was sixty-two now her long, thick auburn hair had very little gray thanks to her faithful stylist every six weeks. She looked and felt a decade younger than her driver's license claimed, the fine lines at the corners of her eyes earned more from laughter than sorrow.

She stayed active, lifting weights a few times a week, walking briskly through her Austin neighborhood most mornings, occasionally adding Pilates when she felt ambitious. Years as a labor-and-delivery nurse had trained her to move with purpose, to steady young mothers through crisis and joy, through loss and miracle. That same resilience had steadied her own children through teenage rebellion and early heartbreak.

She often joked she had to stay in shape to keep up with Grant, who still went to the gym three to four times a week. Grant had aged well. He was handsome in the grounded way men become when they've been loved for a long time. His hair had gone mostly gray at the temples, but his hazel eyes were unchanged, the same eyes that had undone her decades earlier. If anything, his face looked better now than it had in their thirties. Less restless. More settled. He complained about a few new aches with dramatic flair, as if she had never spent twelve-hour shifts on her feet delivering other women's babies.

Grant and Kate Bennett were the kind of couple who still held hands in parking lots. The kind who shared dessert. The kind who had weathered raising three children across two decades of soccer games, college move-ins, wedding rehearsals, and tearful airport goodbyes and had come out laughing on the other side. They had built something real. Not a showpiece marriage. Not flawless. But anchored.

On warm Austin evenings, they often sat on the back patio with glasses of wine and talked about growing old together. The patio itself was nothing fancy, stone pavers Grant had installed one summer, convinced he could do it without watching a single tutorial. Kate had teased him while he sweated and swore and refused help. Now the pavers were uneven in places. They laughed about it.

"That's our patio," Kate would say, tapping her glass against his. "Not perfect, but solid."

"We'll be that couple," Grant had said just a few months ago, bumping her knee with his. "The ones still flirting at eighty."

She laughed. "Eighty? And you'll still be chasing me around the kitchen?"

"I am and I will be!"

And he had been.

Theirs had never been a passionless marriage. Even now, in their early sixties, there was heat between them—familiar and easy, like a well-tended fire. Some nights, when the world quieted and they were back in the place where all their days began and ended, Grant would look at her with the same boyish admiration that had once made her blush.

"You know," he had told her, tracing the inside of her wrist as they lay in bed, "I still can't believe I get to be married to you."

She rolled her eyes, because she didn't trust tenderness without teasing. "Stop it. You sound like you're trying to get out of taking out the trash."

He laughed and kissed her shoulder. "I'll take the trash. I'll take all the trash. Just don't leave me."

She smacked his arm lightly. "I'm not going anywhere."

She believed that. Because thirty-five years makes you believe certain things are unshakable. Because she believed covenant meant something—not just the word spoken in vows, but the life practiced afterward. The staying. The forgiving. The choosing each other again and again.

There had been seasons when she didn't like Grant very much—years when he worked too much and she felt like a single mother even with a husband in the house, juggling hospital shifts, homework, orthodontist bills, and three wildly different personalities under one roof.

But even then, they came back to each other. They always came back.

That was long before Italy.

Before the fracture.

Before the line that would divide their life into two parts Kate would never forget.

Before Italy … and after.

PART ONE

The Life She'd Planned

CHAPTER 1
Up, Up, and Away

Somewhere over the Atlantic

They had talked about this trip for nearly ten years.

It lived in the margins of their conversations between church events and family obligations, over hurried lunches and late-night phone calls. A dream they returned to when life felt too predictable.

“My family’s villa is calling us,” Claire would remind them.

“Someday,” Evelyn would say.

“When things slow down,” Marianne would add.

“When we finally have time,” Kate would finish.

Time, it turned out, never simply arrived. It had to be taken. And now, somehow, they were here, four women in the dim cabin of an overnight flight, suspended between the life they knew and the one they had only imagined.

The cabin lights had dimmed, but none of them were sleeping. Evelyn sat upright, flipping through a magazine with exaggerated seriousness, though she hadn’t turned a page in several minutes. “I still cannot believe this is actually happening,” she said. “We’re crossing an ocean at our age. Voluntarily.”

Marianne smiled, her voice calm as always. “You say that like we stowed away.”

“It feels like we did,” Evelyn replied. “Like someone’s going to tap us on the shoulder and say, ‘Ladies, that’s enough adventure. Time to go home now.’”

Kate laughed but said nothing. She understood the feeling.

Across the aisle, Claire had her seat reclined halfway, gesturing with a plastic cup of ginger ale as if the entire Atlantic needed to hear her. “This was never just a trip,” she said. “You know that, right?”

They did.

Kate studied the women around her, these women who had become something deeper than friends over the years.

Marianne, who had buried her husband and learned how to carry grief without letting it harden her faith. She was close to her two adult daughters, but they lived in another state with their families and her four precocious grandchildren.

Evelyn, the youngest of the group at sixty-one, had never married and yet loved fiercely—her family, her friends, and her independence without apology.

Claire, who had walked through the fire of a nasty divorce and rebuilt her life piece by piece with a strength that never needed to announce itself. She had never had children which allowed her to be the most adventurous of the four friends.

And her. Thirty-five years of marriage. A life built steadily, faithfully. Children grown. A home filled with memories that no longer needed her in the same way.

When had they all become women with histories instead of plans? They had grown up together in church basements and hospital waiting rooms. They had passed babies between them, shared recipes, buried parents, and survived entire seasons of life by leaning on one another. And now, they were crossing an ocean together.

Evelyn set the magazine down. "Okay, but seriously … it took an actual handwritten letter to make this happen."

"That's because nobody ignores Zia Rosa," Claire said.

Marianne smiled. "There's something sacred about paper. You can't just swipe past it."

Claire leaned across the aisle, her voice softer now. "She's been there almost a decade on her own. Since my grandmother passed."

"Alone?" Evelyn asked.

Claire shook her head slightly. "Alone in the house. Not in the world. In Italy, nobody is ever truly alone." She hesitated, then added, "Zia Rosa—*Zia* means aunt in Italian—has always been a part of the foundation of our family and the villa."

Kate watched her closely. There was something in Claire's tone she didn't hear often, less edge, more memory. Claire leaned back, her gaze drifting for a moment as if she were no longer on the plane but somewhere much farther away.

"The villa has been in my family for generations," she said. "My father grew up there with grandparents, parents, and children all under one roof. That's how it worked. Meals together. Life together. Everything shared."

Her voice softened. "There were always voices. Always movement. My grandfather planted many of the olive trees the year my dad was born. My grandmother used to say they were planted 'for the future.'"

A small smile touched her lips. "And after my grandfather died, the house didn't fall apart. The women held it together. My grandmother and Zia Rosa worked, adapted, made what they needed with their hands. The villa stayed alive."

Kate felt something settle in that word. Alive.

"When my dad came to the States," Claire continued, "he brought us back every couple of years. From the time I was little, I knew that place. The gravel path. The smell of olive oil and sea air. The way everything slowed down there."

She paused, then added, "It wasn't anything fancy, but it was grounding. Like stepping into something that had been there long before you and would still be there after."

Evelyn studied her. "And now it's just her?"

Claire nodded. "Just her. In a house built for generations." Her voice caught slightly, then steadied. "She keeps it going. Still cooking, still tending the trees, still opening the shutters every morning like someone might be coming."

A quiet settled between them. "That house…" Claire said, "it's not just property." She shook her head. "It's a legacy."

She paused and then added, "Did I ever tell y'all that I can stay in Italy as long as I want."

Marianne raised both eyebrows, "What?"

"Dual citizenship, since my grandparents and parents all were born in Puglia. After years of paperwork, Italy finally admitted I belong there."

Evelyn stared. "You've been holding that information back this entire time?"

"I was waiting for the right dramatic moment."

The women looked at each other curiously … each one wondering just how long Claire would stay a Villa Santoro.

Kate reached for the unfolded letter on her lap, smoothing the crease with her thumb. She had asked Claire if she could read it again herself. It had been months since Claire first read it aloud during one of their long lunches.

Something about it had felt alive then… and now. After hearing Claire speak, it carried even more weight. As Kate began to read, the words felt less like an invitation and more like a calling.

Cara Claire,

Now I am too old to stay alone in the villa. The house is too quiet. It is not good for a house to be quiet for so long. You must come home, cara mia. Bring your friends with you. This house was made for voices, for laughter at the table, for women talking in the kitchen.

The rooms remember when you were little. They are waiting again. Even the olive trees outside, they are still standing, like always, patient. Come soon. A house needs vita.

Ti amo,

Zia Rosa

Claire watched Kate as she read. "The house remembers," she said quietly. "That's exactly how it feels."

Kate looked up, her throat tightening slightly rereading Rosa's words, "a house needs life." She folded the letter carefully and rested it in her lap.

Claire lifted her cup. "To Monopoli."

"To Zia Rosa," Kate added.

"To Villa Santoro," Marianne said.

Evelyn raised a brow. "To three months of carbs."

"And to staying awake long enough to see the sunrise over the Adriatic," Kate replied.

They touched plastic cups in the dim cabin light.

Outside the small oval window, darkness stretched endlessly beneath them. Somewhere far below, the ocean moved in its slow, ancient rhythm. As the cabin finally settled into quietness and her friends drifted toward sleep, Kate reached into her bag and pulled out a small leather notebook.

She had bought it impulsively at the airport bookstore; a soft, cream-colored journal with a stitched spine and blank pages waiting patiently to be filled. It felt like the right moment to begin something new. The engines hummed steadily as she balanced the notebook on the tray table. For a moment, she simply looked at the first empty page. Then she began to write.

Lord,

Thank You for this moment.

The words came slowly at first, then more easily.

Thank You for the countless blessings in my life. For my family. For the love Grant and I have shared for so many years. For children who have grown into good, strong adults.

She paused, a faint smile touching her lips.

For friends who feel more like sisters.

Claire's laughter echoed in her memory. Marianne's steady wisdom. Evelyn's fearless spirit.

Thank You for the gift of these friendships and the chance to spend this time together in such a beautiful place. I pray that these weeks will refresh my spirit.

The pen hovered briefly.

Help me slow down. Help me notice You more clearly in every moment. In the morning sunlight, in long conversations, in laughter around a table.

Her handwriting slowed as the prayer deepened.

Teach me to live each day with greater awareness of Your presence. Help me celebrate life with gratitude instead of rushing past it.

For so many years, her life had been busy with children, work, church responsibilities, schedules layered upon schedules. This trip felt different. A pause.

Let this be a season of joy.

She underlined the word, joy.

Not a joy that depends on circumstances, but the kind that comes from knowing You are near.

Kate leaned back and reread what she had written. Then she added one final line.

Whatever these days hold, help me receive them with open hands and a thankful heart.

She closed the journal and rested her hand lightly on its cover.

Somewhere ahead, across thousands of miles of dark water, waited sun-warmed villages, winding streets, and the laughter of women who knew her story almost as well as she did.

Kate leaned her head back against the seat and closed her eyes. For the first time in months, she felt something she had almost forgotten how to recognize. Anticipation. Not for what she might accomplish or what she might fix, but for what she might simply experience.

Outside the window, dawn was beginning to gather beyond the horizon. And far ahead, though she could not yet see it, the coast of Italy was waiting.

CHAPTER 2
Buongiorno, Italy!

Puglia Region, Italy

If anticipation burned calories, the four women would land in Italy ten pounds lighter.

The plane dipped low over a sweep of silver-blue water, and Claire pressed her forehead to the window as the coastline curved beneath them—white stone towns, flat rooftops, olive groves stretching inland in disciplined rows. Puglia did not rise dramatically like Tuscany. It unfolded, wide and sunlit.

Claire brushed a loose strand of her chin-length blond hair behind her ear, her sunglasses perched on top of her head, her posture alert with anticipation. Even after years away, something in her seemed to recognize the land below before her mind could catch up.

When they stepped out of the Bari Airport, the air felt warmer but softer than home, carrying the faint salt of the nearby Adriatic Sea.

"Welcome to the heel of Italy," Claire said, slipping her sunglasses back into place with practiced ease.

Adjusting the strap of her leather bag, Kate followed the others toward the pickup area. She wore a soft linen blouse over faded blue jeans, comfortable strappy sandals, and the hopeful exhaustion that comes from arriving somewhere long imagined.

Beside her, Marianne moved with quiet composure, elegant even after a long overnight flight. Her navy knit top and white cropped pants looked effortless, her posture naturally upright. Her dark hair was glossy and smooth, pinned loosely at the back, the striking silver streak at her part catching the morning light. There was something grounded about her presence, the calm steadiness of a woman accustomed to listening deeply, a skill honed both in life and in her part-time work as a social worker.

Evelyn followed just behind them, tugging her carry-on with easy strength. Lean and athletic, she moved with the natural confidence of someone who had spent decades on tennis courts. Her short brown hair framed her face simply, practical but flattering, and her sun-kissed skin somehow perpetually tan, made her look more like she had just returned from vacation than begun one. Dressed in fitted travel pants and a soft athletic top, she managed to look both sporty and distinctly feminine. Her friends often joked she had the best legs south of Dallas, and she had long ago stopped arguing.

A quiet man named Marco, who spoke just enough English, loaded their luggage into a black Mercedes van that looked far too sleek for the countryside roads ahead. As the van pulled away from the airport, Claire twisted around in her seat, slipping easily into her role as guide.

"The Puglia region is different from other parts of Italy. It's not polished like Tuscany or dramatic like the Amalfi Coast. It's agricultural. Many families have lived on the same land for generations. And Monopoli …"

A smile softened her expression.

"…Monopoli is a very special city."

As the car merged onto the coastal highway, flashes of turquoise water appeared between old stone walls.

"Monopoli isn't tiny, but it feels intimate," she continued, warming to the story. "About fifty thousand people in the city and surrounding area. It has a working harbor, not just tourists. Real life fishermen who still go out at dawn and church bells ring all day. It's big enough that no one asks too many questions, but small enough that if you visit the same café twice, they remember your name."

They passed groves of ancient olive trees; their trunks twisted like arthritic hands gripping the red earth.

Lowering her voice slightly, Claire added, “And Zia Rosa’s place is about a mile from the Centro. Close enough to walk, far enough that it’s quiet. The villa is on almost two acres with olive and fig trees and an amazing garden. And if we’re lucky …” A small grin appeared. “Chickens. I’m hoping she still has them. There is nothing like fresh eggs in the morning.”

The road narrowed as they turned off the main highway, the sea disappearing behind limestone walls and hedges of oleander.

“She’s proud,” Claire said. “And strong. Very strong. You don’t tell Rosa Santoro what to do. You suggest. Carefully.”

The women laughed and Claire’s gaze drifted back outside the car window.

“She stays in one of the two downstairs bedrooms. The rest of the house is ours, five rooms upstairs, and two baths. We’ll share the kitchen with her, of course. She’ll be in heaven if we let her cook for us.”

Turning with a grin, she added, “So, ladies, you will be learning to cook and eat like you never have before. I haven’t seen her in over three years.” Claire’s voice softened. “I know she says she’s fine. She always says she’s fine. But she sounded thinner on the phone, if that’s possible. She hesitated. “I just hope she’s still as strong as I remember.”

Ahead, a low limestone wall appeared, sun-bleached and draped in bougainvillea the color of spilled wine. A wrought-iron gate stood slightly open, and carved into a weathered stone pillar.

LA VILLA SANTORO

The tires crunched on the narrow gravel road as the car slowly rolled around a large curve before revealing the old villa, an impressive white limestone structure glimmering in the sunlight. Flowering vines in vibrant colors of pink and purple grew unrestrained from trellises anchored to its old walls.

"Here we are!" Claire announced with the excitement of a child.

A quiet breath filled Kate's lungs. "This is not real," she whispered.

Marianne's hand found hers. "It feels ancient."

"It *is* ancient," Claire replied. "Parts of it date back to the 1700s. Zia Rosa says the stones remember everything."

One of Evelyn's eyebrows lifted. "Well, let's hope they forget all the food and wine we're about to enjoy like there's no tomorrow."

Reunion with Zia Rosa

Zia Rosa was not the soft, flour-dusted nonna people often imagined.

She stood tall for her generation, her spine straight as a board, shoulders set back from decades of real work. Her frame was lean, almost wiry, the strength of someone who had lifted soil and stone longer than most people lift grandchildren.

Her hands told the truest story: broad-palmed, veined, strong, her nails kept short and clean, faintly stained near the cuticles from crushed tomatoes and grape skins.

Once dark as espresso, her hair was now bright silver, twisted neatly at the nape of her neck. Her skin carried the deep honeyed bronze of southern Italy, sun-earned and lined more by light than worry. Her eyes were sharp, clear, and assessing. They missed nothing. She wore a dark cotton house dress, sturdy leather sandals, and an apron that had likely seen forty summers completed the picture.

Before the van came to a full stop and the driver killed the engine, the front door of the villa flew open and there she was. Zia Rosa stood squarely in the doorway, one hand gripping the frame as if steadying herself against a sudden rush of emotion, her apron tied firmly at the waist as her dark eyes swept across the courtyard.

"CLAIRE!"

Claire had barely stepped onto the gravel when Rosa rushed forward, cupping her cheeks and kissing them once, twice, three times, her laughter breaking into something dangerously close to tears.

"You are here*! Finalmente*! At last!"

Holding her at arm's length, Rosa studied her as if measuring the years that had passed. "Mamma mia! You cut your hair! It brings out your blue eyes."

Laughing, Claire ran a hand through her chin-length blond bob. "I retired. It felt symbolic."

"Retired!" Rosa threw her hands into the air. "From real estate? Finally! Now you are footloose and fancy-free, yes?" She winked proudly at her English.

"Something like that."

Leaning closer, Rosa lowered her voice conspiratorially. "You look wonderful. Strong. Younger than when you left."

Then her attention shifted to the others, beginning with Kate. Her brows lifted as she spoke rapidly to Claire in Italian, hands already dancing through the air.

Pressing her lips together to keep from laughing, Claire warned, "Shhh! They might understand you!"

Rosa gasped theatrically. "Do they speak Italian? Do I need to be careful what I say?" Her eyes flicked suspiciously back to the women.

Not understanding a word, Kate smiled politely.

Claire translated. "She says you're beautiful."

"Ah!" Rosa waved dismissively. "Of course, I say you are beautiful."

Stepping closer, she took both of Kate's hands. "And what do you do?"

"I'm a labor and delivery nurse," Kate said. "Parttime. And I mentor women at church and sometimes speak at conferences."

Instantly, Rosa's expression softened. "Babies." She pressed a hand to her heart. "You help bring life into the world."

Kate nodded. "I love it."

"Ahhh." Rosa squeezed her fingers warmly. "A woman who works because she loves. That is good."

Her attention moved to the others with the same scrutiny. "And you … very elegant," she said, nodding toward Marianne. "The one who keeps things organized, yes? The one everyone depends on."

Marianne laughed. "That sounds about right."

Then Rosa turned to Evelyn, head tilting slightly, eyes narrowing with curiosity. "And this one …" She studied her a moment longer. "Strong spirit. She will say exactly what she thinks."

Evelyn lifted an eyebrow. "I've been accused of that."

"*Bene*. Every table needs one woman who tells the truth."

Rosa clapped her hands once decisively, as if the reunion itself had officially concluded. "*Basta*. Enough standing in the sun like tourists," she declared. "Come inside before you melt."

Still smiling, she ushered them through the open front door with the authority of a woman fully in charge of both the house and everyone inside it.

The heavy wooden door opened into *il salotto*, the main gathering room of the villa and the temperature shifted immediately. Thick limestone walls held decades of coolness, carrying the faint scent of lemon oil, espresso, old wood, and something savory simmering deeper in *la cucina*—the kitchen.

Kate stopped just inside the doorway. "Oh…" she whispered.

The room felt less decorated than accumulated … layer by layer, year by year, generation by generation. High vaulted ceilings stretched above dark wooden beams softened with age. Sunlight filtered through tall, shuttered windows, laying warm golden rectangles across faded terracotta floors worn smooth in the center from countless footsteps.

A massive stone fireplace anchored one wall, its mantel crowded with framed photographs of weddings, baptisms, babies balanced on hips, stern-faced ancestors beside laughing ones. Deep linen-covered sofas faced each other near the hearth, softened with embroidered cushions that clearly prioritized comfort over matching colors. A carved wooden armoire leaned slightly with age beside the staircase, while shelves overflowed with books, candles burned low, ceramic bowls, and small religious icons tucked naturally among everyday objects. Nothing matched perfectly, but everything belonged.

Beyond a wide archway, the kitchen glowed with late afternoon light. Copper pots hung from iron hooks above a long farmhouse table scarred by decades of rolling dough, chopping vegetables, and conversations that had likely lasted far into the night.

Evelyn dropped her bag beside one of the sofas with dramatic exhaustion and kicked off her sandals. "I would like everyone to know," she announced, stretching her long legs out in front of her, "that I'm prepared to spend the remainder of my life in this room."

Rosa pointed toward her approvingly. "This one understands rest."

Claire chuckled, setting her own bag down more slowly as she looked around the room. Her expression had changed since stepping through the door, as if she were pondering a memory.

"It looks exactly the same," she murmured.

Marianne traced her fingers lightly across the back of a weathered chair. Elegant even after the overnight flight, she moved through the room with calm appreciation, taking everything in quietly. "It feels so much different than staying in a rental house," she said. "It feels loved."

Rosa reappeared carrying a large tray lined with tall sweating glasses. "Of course it is loved," she replied as if the answer were obvious. "A house knows when people love it."

She handed out fresh lemonade infused with mint and slices of lemon floating near the surface. Another pitcher held iced tea darkened with citrus and lightly sweetened with honey.

"Drink," Rosa instructed firmly. "You all look dehydrated and how you say … exhausted."

Evelyn blinked. "I already love her."

Rosa ignored this completely and disappeared back toward the kitchen muttering something in Italian about hungry Americans. The women settled deeper into the furniture, glasses clinking softly as sunlight drifted through the room. For a few moments, nobody spoke.

Then Marianne lifted her glass slightly. "All right," she said. "One thing. What's the one thing each of you is most looking forward to on this trip?"

"Easy," Evelyn answered immediately. "Eating pasta without guilt and pretending walking through Italy counts as cardiovascular excellence."

"It absolutely counts," Claire assured her. She leaned back against the sofa cushions, her chin-length blonde hair still wind-tousled from travel. "Honestly?" she said. "Sleeping with the windows open again. Hearing church bells in the morning. Fresh bread. Olive oil that ruins you for all other olive oil."

Marianne smiled. "I think I'm looking forward to slowing down. I don't remember the last time I went a full day without checking the time."

Their eyes drifted toward Kate. She looked down into her lemonade for a moment before answering. "I think…" She smiled. "I'm looking forward to remembering who I am when nobody needs something from me."

The room grew quieter after that. Not awkward. Just honest.

Claire reached across the sofa and squeezed her hand lightly. "Well," she said, glancing around the old villa, "this seems like a pretty good place to figure that out."

La Prima Sera—The First Evening

The first evening unfolded without ceremony. Rosa insisted on something simple for dinner. “Nothing heavy the first night,” she declared.

By the time the women wandered back outside, the courtyard had begun to glow beneath the soft gold of early evening. An overhead arbor draped with twisting grapevines stretched above the long wooden table, its leaves filtering the last light of the day into shifting patterns across the stone. Strands of tiny café lights had been woven overhead between four ancient olive trees planted at each corner of the courtyard long ago, their thick, gnarled trunks silvered with age and time.

Large earthen pots overflowed with rosemary, lavender, basil, and trailing geraniums that softened the limestone walls surrounding the space. Nearby, jasmine climbed along an iron trellis, its sweetness lingering faintly in the warm air.

Soon the old wooden table held thick slices of crusty bread, tomatoes dressed in olive oil from Rosa’s own trees, shaved pecorino, olives wrinkled from curing in brine, and a platter of grilled vegetables still warm from the pan. Small bowls of marinated white beans, roasted peppers, and paper-thin slices of prosciutto appeared almost magically beside them. A bottle of local Primitivo breathed between the women, deep garnet against the fading light.

“This,” Evelyn announced, leaning back in her chair, “already feels better than therapy.”

“Cheaper too,” Claire added.

Their laughter drifted upward into the vines overhead.

They sat beneath a sky slowly surrendering to sunset as the string lights flickered on one by one, casting a warm amber glow across the courtyard. Beyond the olive grove, the Adriatic lay unseen but present, the faintest scent of salt riding the breeze. Cicadas hummed steadily in the distance. Somewhere farther off, a church bell rang the hour, softened by space and evening air.

For a long moment, no one reached for a phone. No one checked the time. Surrounded by old stone and familiar laughter, Villa Santoro no longer felt like a destination. It felt like the beginning of something.

Soon, jet lag tugged at their eyelids. Their laughter slowed and their words softened. No one wanted to say it first, but all of them were thinking the same thing.

"We could talk all night," Marianne murmured, lifting her glass.

"We will," Claire replied with a smile. "Just … not tonight."

Nodding approvingly, Rosa added, "*Si*. Sleep. Tomorrow, we begin properly."

For a moment, they sat quietly, each woman absorbing the miracle of being there in Puglia, at Villa Santoro, together. Then, mustering energy, each rose, chairs scraping quietly against stone and walked back into the ancient villa.

Upstairs, the rooms were simple but airy with white walls, shuttered windows, and iron bed frames. Kate's room held a narrow twin bed dressed in crisp cotton, a small wooden crucifix above the door, and a lace curtain flowing in the night breeze.

After changing into a soft cotton sleep shirt, she brushed out her auburn hair and sat on the edge of the bed. Through the open window came distant laughter from the harbor, a scooter somewhere along the road, and the low murmur of the sea.

Reaching into her bag, she pulled out the journal she had started on the flight. At the top of the next blank page, she wrote:

First night in Monopoli.

Then she smiled and began.

Lord, what a day.

Thank You for safe travel and for the warm welcome waiting here. Seeing Rosa felt like stepping into something sacred. Tomorrow we'll walk the old town, drink too much espresso, and probably talk for hours. Help me be present for every moment.

Please watch over Grant and the kids while I'm away. Keep everyone safe and help me notice You everywhere here—in the sea, in laughter, in small surprises.

She closed the journal and set it on the bedside table, then folded her hands in her lap. "Thank You, Lord," she whispered. "For this place. For these women. For Rosa."

Her thoughts drifted homeward to Grant, to familiar rhythms, to the comfort of shared evenings that suddenly felt very far away. She lay back against the pillow, exhaustion finally claiming her. Outside the window, the calm rhythm of the sea echoed quietly in the dark as she quickly sank into a relaxed and blissful sleep.

CHAPTER 3
The Calm Before the Storm

Monopoli, Italy

Kate woke before the others.

For a moment she didn't remember where she was. The ceiling above her was white and unfamiliar. The air felt lighter somehow. Then she heard a rooster's uneven crow, the sound of car engines shifting from the city center a mile away, and the faint rhythmic hush of the sea carried inland on the breeze and remembered. Italy.

Stretching her arms overhead and taking in a deep breath, she slowly sat up and swung her legs over the edge of the bed and felt her bare feet touch the cold tile floor. She rose and walked to the window, pushing open the wooden shutters. Sunlight poured into the small room, turning the iron bed frame gold. The sky was already a brilliant blue—unapologetic and endless. Downstairs she could hear movement. The scrape of a chair. The clink of porcelain. Rosa.

Kate slipped into a white T-shirt and faded jeans, then padded barefoot down the narrow staircase. The kitchen was bright and alive. Windows stood open. A small moka pot bubbled on the stove, its soft hiss signaling coffee was moments away.

Rosa stood at the counter, cracking eggs into a ceramic bowl. "You are awake," she observed without turning around.

"I didn't want to miss the first morning," Kate answered.

Rosa glanced back, approving. "*Bene*. Yes, good. First mornings matter."

The *cucina* felt less like a room and more like the heartbeat of the house. Morning light cast a gold glow on the walls and the worn limestone floors. Open shelves held mismatched ceramic bowls, hand-painted plates, jars of dried herbs, and neatly folded linen towels softened by years of washing.

Near the back door, small baskets overflowed with tomatoes, lemons, onions, and figs gathered from the garden, while a cluster of basil plants crowded the windowsill beside bottles of deep green olive oil pressed from Rosa's own trees. Nothing matched perfectly. Yet everything in the kitchen radiated warmth, abundance, and the quiet confidence of a place where people had been fed and loved well for a very long time.

Soon the others filtered in. Claire barefoot and wearing a loose striped shirt and white cotton pants, her short blond hair tousled from sleep; Marianne tying her dark hair into a low knot, silver glinting at her part; Evelyn blinking against the light in a pale blue sleep shirt under a cardigan she had thrown on with reluctant dignity.

On the table sat fresh bread warmed in the oven, fig jam, slices of pecorino, and a small bowl of brown eggs.

"My chickens are lazy," Rosa declared. "But not useless."

The moka pot gave one final sputter. Espresso was poured into small porcelain cups, rich and dark. They stood for a moment with cups in hand, letting the bitterness wake them properly.

"This," Evelyn said after her first sip, "is not Starbucks."

Rosa sniffed. "*Grazie a Dio.*"

They laughed in unison surprised Rosa knew about Starbucks.

Claire unfolded a small map of Monopoli on the table. "We can walk into town this morning. It's just about a mile. We'll see the harbor. Maybe the cathedral."

Rosa nodded. "You must see it in the morning light. The stones glow."

Kate traced the rim of her cup with her finger, smiling at the familiarity of the ritual—strong coffee, simple food, women in conversation. "I've always loved Italy," she said quietly.

Her friends looked up. They had heard pieces of the story before, but never here. Never while sitting in Italy with the Adriatic breathing in the distance.

"It feels like coming full circle," she continued. "I first came here in my early twenties. I was visiting my best friend Susan from high school. Her father was an Army officer stationed in Vicenza, halfway between Verona and Venice."

She smiled faintly. "They moved to Italy during our senior year and I missed her terribly. A couple of years later, she wrote and invited me to visit. I saved for a full year from my student-nurse earnings just to afford the ticket."

She paused, glancing out the window toward the hills beyond the villa as if she could still see northern Italy with river light, pale bridges, and vineyards stretching toward the horizon.

"During my four-week visit, we took a weekend trip to Verona," she said. "And that's where I met Grant."

Marianne leaned forward. "You've never told us the whole story."

Kate let out a girlish giggle. "We were so young. He was traveling through with a friend. I first saw him at Juliet's Balcony, the *Casa di Giulietta*, where visitors, mostly tourists, leave letters to Juliet and ask her for relationship advice and how to find true love."

The women smiled and Evelyn exclaimed, "Oh yeah, I saw a cute rom-com movie some years ago all about those letters!"

"Well, there I was, standing in that little courtyard, looking up at the balcony like it held answers. I was twenty-two, dramatic, and absolutely certain my romantic life was about to begin."

"And then?" Evelyn prompted.

"And then I turned to say something to Susan and ran straight into him."

"Literally?" Evelyn asked.

"Literally," Kate said. "I dropped my purse, a shopping bag, everything. Lipstick, coins, receipts, all over that ancient stone."

Marianne winced. "Embarrassing at that age."

"Completely. Grant dropped to his knees so fast you'd think he'd rehearsed it. Apologizing. Gathering my things. His friend Dave had already started talking to Susan, of course."

Claire smiled knowingly. "Naturally."

Kate shook her head, smiling at the memory. "Grant kept handing me my things like they were breakable. And when I finally looked up at him …" She paused. "He was just so present. His eyes were kind. Curious."

She traced the rim of her espresso cup again. "There were no violins. No lightning bolt. Just this quiet sense that something in my life had shifted a few degrees."

She grew quieter. "The four of us met up every day for the next ten days. We talked for hours about faith, family, what we wanted from life. We were both still becoming who we were. But something about that city …" She shook her head. "Verona felt like a beginning."

She smiled. "Grant lived on the East Coast and I was from California. It should have been impossible. But somehow, it wasn't."

Her voice softened. "Every time I come back to Italy, I remember that girl who was so idealistic. Before mortgages and routines and responsibilities. Before I understood how complicated life could become."

Her eyes lifted toward the open window. "Italy always reminds me that new beginnings are possible."

Rosa, who had been listening while wiping her hands on her apron, nodded thoughtfully. "*L'amore nato in Italia*," she said. "*È forte*." Love born in Italy is strong.

Kate smiled. "It was," she said softly. "And it is."

Claire clapped her hands once, bringing them all back into the present. "So, shall we head to the harbor first?"

Rosa nodded. "Yes. You will see Monopoli properly. Then we eat again."

"Again?" Evelyn asked, laughing.

Rosa lifted her chin. "Always again."

Outside, the chickens clucked lazily, and a mile away the city center was coming to life and ready to be explored. Inside, coffee cups emptied and plans for the day began to take shape, the first full day of many.

Exploring Monopoli

The streets of Monopoli curved unexpectedly, narrow and sun-washed, revealing laundry strung between balconies, potted geraniums and old men arguing about football outside a café.

Claire walked three steps ahead of them, narrating everything.

"This is where Zia Rosa used to buy produce. And, that bakery over there …" She pointed across the piazza. "They used to let me sit in the back and watch them braid the bread. And here, at this corner, this is where I scraped my knee when I was nine."

"You scraped your knee in Italy?" Evelyn said. "How tragically romantic." Claire spun around and walked backward.

"You don't understand. I felt different here. Even as a child. Like I belonged to something very special."

A woman stepped out of a doorway and froze mid-motion. "Clairetta?"

Claire gasped. "Signora Lucia!"

The rotund older woman embraced Claire in a flurry of Italian, tears, and hands on cheeks.

"Sei cresciuta! Ma guarda te! La tua zia mi ha detto che venivi …"

Kate leaned toward Marianne and whispered, "I love how you can hear affection in a language even when you don't understand it."

Claire turned back, eyes shining. "She says Zia Rosa talks about me constantly."

"Of course she does," Marianne replied.

They wandered toward the harbor. Fishing boats bobbed in the small port, painted in chipped blues and reds. Nets lay coiled like sleeping animals. The air smelled of brine and espresso.

Claire insisted they sit at a café overlooking the water. "Four *cappuccini*," she told the waiter confidently. "*E ... quattro cornetti*."

"You sound legit," Evelyn admitted.

Claire grinned. "I know just enough to be dangerous."

The *cornetti* arrived warm, powdered sugar drifting across the plate. Foam left white crescents on their upper lips.

Kate closed her eyes as she tasted the coffee. "This is what slowing down tastes like."

"No," Evelyn corrected. "This is what carbs taste like."

They laughed.

Later that afternoon, Zia Rosa joined the women as they wandered along the old city walls discovering the unique beauty of Monopoli. As they entered a tiny cobblestone piazza, the sound of children laughing echoed off the buildings while several boys kicked soccer balls wildly through the open space, weaving effortlessly around startled tourists and elderly residents who barely looked up anymore.

Near a weathered fountain, three elderly women—clearly local *nonne*, grandmothers—sat shoulder to shoulder on an old wooden bench, talking animatedly in rapid Italian while keeping sharp eyes on everything happening around them.

One wore a black floral dress with sensible shoes and silver hair pinned into a tight bun. Another had on a faded navy housedress beneath a cream cardigan despite the warmth, thick reading glasses sliding down her nose as she gestured emphatically with one hand. The third, plumper than the others and clearly the loudest, wore a crisp apron over her dress as though she had only stepped away from cooking long enough to monitor the neighborhood properly. All three paused mid-conversation to study the American women openly.

Claire lowered her voice dramatically. "There they are. The official town gossips of Monopoli."

The women laughed.

"I'm serious," Claire continued. "That's Teresa, Nenita, and Maria. If someone gets engaged, divorced, pregnant, fired, or caught kissing somebody they shouldn't be kissing…" She shrugged. "These women know before the priests do."

As if on cue, the loudest of the three narrowed her eyes toward Claire and called out something in Italian that made Zia Rosa laugh under her breath.

"What did she say?" Kate asked.

Claire grinned. "She wants to know if I finally brought home a husband after all these years."

The women burst into laughter again as the *nonne* shook their heads knowingly, entirely unoffended by being discussed. The loudest of the three pointed toward Claire and said something else in rapid Italian. Zia Rosa rolled her eyes.

"Oh no," Claire said. "What now?"

Rosa translated reluctantly. "Teresa says if you are still unmarried at your age, perhaps your standards are too high."

The Americans laughed.

"Tell her my standards are perfectly reasonable," Claire said. "I simply haven't found a man who meets them."

Teresa folded her arms and replied with another sharp comment.

"What did she say?" Marianne asked.

Rosa sighed dramatically. "She says that after sixty, a man only needs three qualifications."

The women waited. "He must love God, have all his teeth, and still remember where he parked the car."

Evelyn nearly choked laughing. Even Kate laughed harder than she had in days. Rosa turned back toward the bench and called something to the women.

Teresa answered immediately.

"What did you say?" Claire asked.

A mischievous smile tugged at Rosa's mouth. "I told her that with standards like hers, she should have married a saint instead of Giuseppe."

The three *nonne* erupted in loud protests. "Giuseppe was no saint!" one shouted.

"Exactly," Rosa called back. "And neither are the men you're recommending for Claire."

The Americans laughed all the way across the piazza while the *nonne* continued arguing good-naturedly behind them.

As the afternoon stretched on and the sights, sounds, and scents of Monopoli flooded their American senses, Kate felt something inside her slowly begin to loosen. No schedules. No demands. No endless pressure to hold everything together. Just women walking slowly in the light beneath a foreign sky.

Il Mare—The Sea

Claire woke them early the next morning. "Beach day!" she announced, throwing open the shutters with unnecessary enthusiasm.

"You are not eight," Evelyn muttered from beneath a pillow.

But they went. Enthusiasm for a new adventure propelled them out of bed despite lingering yawns and muttering about needing more sleep.

The Adriatic was impossibly clear, the water so translucent it seemed lit from beneath. Pale limestone cliffs curved around small coves like protective arms.

They found a small crescent of beach tucked between the cliffs, where smooth white stones gave way to a narrow stretch of pale sand. A few weathered umbrellas stood like quiet sentinels, their canvas faded by years of sun and salt. It felt private and sheltered from the wider world as if the cove itself had been waiting for them.

Claire ran straight into the water, her red one-piece already half soaked before anyone else had even set down a towel.

"*È perfetta*!" she shouted back at them.

Marianne waded in more cautiously; her dark hair tucked under a wide-brimmed straw hat. Her one-piece navy and white stripped bathing suit exuded the classic style she naturally wore even in the most casual settings.

Evelyn gasped dramatically at the temperature, then marched in anyway, looking like a resort advertisement in oversized sunglasses and a moderate, black two-piece swimsuit that suited her firm, fit body that her friends constantly reminded her was unfair for her age.

Kate stood for a moment at the shoreline in an emerald, green one-piece, watching the light fracture across the surface. She'd left her auburn hair loose this day and the sea breeze blew it back into what looked like a dark flame of fire behind her in the late morning light.

She stepped cautiously forward. The water was cool but welcoming. It wrapped around her waist, her shoulders, her heart. She floated on her back and closed her eyes. For the first time in months, maybe years, she felt weightless.

When she emerged, Claire was already chatting animatedly with two elderly women perched on the rocks nearby.

"What are you telling them?" Evelyn called.

"That you are all famous American actresses on holiday."

Evelyn blinked. "I knew this trip would expose us."

Claire laughed. "Relax. I told them you were teachers."

They stayed until their skin warmed and pinked. On the walk back through the village, they stopped for gelato—pistachio, lemon, stracciatella.

Kate licked melting lemon from her fingers and felt absurdly alive.

"You're glowing," Marianne told her.

"It's the sun," Kate replied.

But it wasn't. It was something else. Possibility, maybe. Or simply the absence of noise.

Quella Notte—That Night

The villa was quiet in a different way that evening. Contented. After another simple but delicious meal, the women drifted to their rooms one by one, tired in the best possible way. Kate remained alone in the courtyard for a moment.

The trees cast long shadows in the moonlight. She loved the sound of the sea always murmuring just beyond the grove, the pungent scent of jasmine in the air. She pulled her phone from her pocket and noticed a message from Grant earlier that afternoon.

Hope you're having the time of your life. Miss you already.

She smiled. Then typed back:

It's beautiful here. I wish you could see it.

She lingered another moment, breathing in the cool evening air and something that felt very much like peace. Then she went inside.

CHAPTER 4
Joy Disrupted

Monopoli, Italy

Kate had no way of knowing that she was living the final hours of her old life.

Lying back against the narrow pillow, listening to faint laughter drifting from somewhere in the village, Kate replayed the highlights of the past two days. Monopoli had already exceeded every expectation. The beauty, the warmth, the easy rhythm of life—it all felt like a gift. She drifted off imagining the adventures still ahead, certain the best moments of the trip had yet to come.

The last remnants of jet lag tugged at her eyelids. Now, her body was more than ready to surrender to sleep. She was sure she was dreaming when her phone buzzed faintly on the bedside table just after midnight. The sound startled her even though the volume was low. At first, she ignored it. Then she realized it was not a dream. On the sixth buzz, something inside her stirred and a quiet instinct made her reach for it.

She glanced at the screen.

Hubby.

The name she had typed into her phone years ago and never thought to change. Grant had probably forgotten the time difference.

"Grant?" she answered tentatively.

"Katie," he said. Then he hesitated. It sounded as if he were clearing his throat. "Kate," he repeated.

His voice sounded different. Distant. Thirty-five years of marriage teaches you to understand the language beneath a man's words.

Kate sat upright in the narrow bed, her heart tightening. "What is it?"

Silence. Then quietly: "I need to tell you something."

Outside the open window, church bells began ringing in the distance, marking the midnight hour. Kate would later remember that sound and the cool air brushing her skin. The way something deep inside her seemed to brace itself before her mind fully understood why.

"I didn't mean for it to happen," Grant said.

For a moment Kate said nothing. Decades of marriage collapsed into a single sentence.

The room suddenly felt smaller. The whitewashed walls that had seemed charming earlier now pressed inward. Moonlight spilled across the tiled floor, turning everything silver and unreal.

"Kate?" Grant said cautiously. "Are you still there?"

"Yes."

Her voice sounded steady, almost calm. She barely recognized it.

"I've been seeing someone," he said finally.

The words hung between them.

"It started a while ago. I tried to stop it, but … I didn't."

Something fragile seemed to crack in the quiet room. Kate swung her legs over the side of the bed and stood. The cool tile beneath her feet grounded her, though the rest of her body felt strangely detached.

"How long?" she asked.

There was a pause. Too long to be comforting. Too short to be innocent. "A few weeks."

A few weeks. Kate's mind began moving backward through recent memories. Dinner with friends. Sunday morning church. The night they had lingered in the kitchen laughing about nothing at all. The way he had pulled her close before they went upstairs. The text he had sent earlier that day telling her he missed her.

A few weeks.

"Who is she?" Kate asked.

Her voice remained controlled, though something deep inside her had begun to tremble. Before Grant answered, her mind searched instinctively for something she might have missed.

A recollection materialized in her mind like a movie reel. A crowded donor reception. Soft music. Candlelight reflecting off glasses. Grant standing beside a dark-haired woman she didn't know. The woman had smiled warmly when they were introduced. *"I've heard so much about you,"* she had said.

At the time it had meant nothing. Now the memory hovered at the edge of recognition.

"Lydia," Grant said quietly.

The name hung in the air before anything else made sense.

"You met her once," he continued. "At that donor reception. She works with the foundation. It just started as conversations."

Conversations. Kate almost laughed. Not because it was funny. But because it was so painfully ordinary.

Lydia.

The name unlocked the memory completely. The reception hall glowing with candlelight. Lydia's dark hair falling over one shoulder. The fitted black dress. The easy confidence of someone who belonged in every conversation. And the way her eyes had lingered on Grant just a moment longer than necessary.

At the time it had meant nothing. Now the memory rearranged itself. Kate turned slowly toward the open window. Lydia.

How old had she been? Mid-forties perhaps. Maybe early fifties. Certainly younger. Not young-young. But younger in the quiet, measurable ways that suddenly mattered. Smoother skin. A body not shaped by pregnancies and decades of shared life. Energy that still belonged closer to the middle of the story rather than its later chapters.

The first sting of comparison rose before she could stop it. Had Grant noticed her immediately that night? Had Kate been standing there smiling politely while something invisible had already begun?

"Kate?" Grant said cautiously.

"I'm here."

Her voice sounded calm even to her own ears. Detached. As if someone else were speaking. Conversations. That word lingered.

Conversations had always been *their* strength. Late-night talks about faith and calling. Long discussions about parenting, finances, dreams for retirement. They had been the couple others came to for advice. Now conversations had undone them.

"Do you love her?" Kate asked, surprising herself.

Silence followed. The kind that carries its own answer.

"I don't know," Grant said finally. "I think I might."

The tremor inside her widened. Thirty-five years. Three and a half decades of shared history. And now the word *love* could be divided.

Kate pushed the window open wider and inhaled deeply, wanting to feel the movement of air into her lungs and to validate she was really having this conversation. It was not a bad dream.

Somewhere below, laughter echoed faintly in the wind. Life continued. People were drinking wine and telling stories. Laughing in the way Italians seemed to always celebrate life. And thousands of miles away, her marriage was breaking apart.

"Why are you telling me now?" she asked quietly.

"Because I couldn't keep pretending," Grant said. "You deserve the truth."

Truth. The word hovered between them. But Kate already sensed the truth was larger than what he was saying. If this had truly begun with "conversations," it had not begun yesterday. It had been growing in the shadows for a while.

She pressed her palm against the stone windowsill. The surface felt solid. Ancient.

"Is it over?" she asked.

Another pause. "I don't know."

That was the moment the floor disappeared. Not the confession. Not even the possibility of love. The *not knowing*.

"I still love you," Grant added quickly. "You must believe that. I love you. I just … I don't understand what's happening to me."

Kate closed her eyes.

For thirty-five years she had believed marital love was more than deep affection and attraction. It was a lifetime covenant reinforced by a daily decision to show up and choose your spouse over all others. It was a promise strengthened by practice. Something you guarded. Now her husband sounded like a stranger explaining the weather.

"I need time," he said. "I need to figure out what this means."

Time. As if time were neutral. As if time did not favor the one who was already leaving. Kate realized then that this conversation was not simply a confession. It was a request. He wasn't just telling her. He was asking her to live inside the uncertainty.

The church bells finally stopped. In the quiet that followed, something inside her shifted. Not anger. Not yet grief, but a morsel of clarity.

"Grant," she said quietly, "while you're figuring it out, I will not compete."

He inhaled sharply. "That's not what I'm asking."

"It's exactly what you're asking." Her voice did not rise. It didn't need to. "I won't share you," she continued. "Not emotionally. Not physically. Not spiritually."

"I'm not asking you to share me."

"Yes," she whispered. "You are."

The truth settled between them like dust after a collapse. On the other end of the line, he sounded smaller now. “I never meant to hurt you.”

She almost said *I know.* Because she did know. Grant was not reckless. Not cruel. Not careless. He was divided. And a divided heart is more dangerous than an angry one.

“I need to go,” she said quietly.

“Kate.”

“I need to pray.”

It wasn’t dramatic. It was survival.

She ended the call before her voice could break. The room fell impossibly quiet. For a long moment she stood staring at her reflection in the dark glass.

Who am I now? Wife? Abandoned wife? Temporary wife?

She pressed her forehead against the cool window. “Lord,” she whispered, her voice quivering, “what just happened?”

No thunder answered. No sudden peace. Only the soft rustle of olive branches in the night breeze. And beneath the shock, beneath the confusion, beneath the humiliation—love. She still loved him.

That realization hurt more than the confession. Because love meant she could not simply detach. Love meant she would fight. But for what? A marriage? A man? A memory?

Outside, somewhere in the distance, a dog barked. Evidence that life continued. Inside the quiet room, Kate felt time split in two. There was before tonight and there was everything that would come after.

She climbed back onto the narrow bed but did not lie down. Instead, she drew her knees to her chest and stared into the darkness. Now she would discover whether covenant was as strong as she had always believed or whether even sacred promises could permanently fracture.

A tear slipped quietly down her cheek. Kate caught it with the back of her hand. Somewhere in her memory a verse surfaced, one she had read years ago and never forgotten.

You keep track of all my sorrows. You collect my tears in your bottle.

She looked at the faint shimmer of moisture on her skin. Maybe God just collected this one. Slowly she lowered her hand, letting the tear fall away. She knew it would not be the last.

CHAPTER 5
The Morning After

Monopoli, Italy

The sun rose as if nothing had happened.

Golden light spilled across the courtyard, warming the limestone walls of Villa Santoro. Somewhere beyond the low white walls, a rooster crowed. Dishes clinked downstairs in the kitchen.

Kate had not slept. She had spent most of the night praying and journaling, the way she always had when life threw her a curve ball. Her journal still lay open on the small bedroom desk, the page filled with large, uneven handwriting.

Oh Lord ... how could I have been so blindsided? How could Grant become so vulnerable, so easily deceived, that he would risk everything we've built together?

What am I supposed to do now? How am I supposed to respond?

Holy Spirit, I need to hear from You. Guide me. Show me how You want me to walk through this.

I am heartbroken. I am scared. I am angry. But I want to be surrendered to You so I can hear Your voice.

Please pursue Grant. Convict him of truth. Don't let him feel peace in something that is destroying our marriage.

Kate dressed and went downstairs before the others. She wore a simple sundress; her long hair pulled loosely back in a low pony. Without makeup, the swelling around her eyes was impossible to hide. Dark circles rested beneath them; evidence of a sleepless night filled with tears and prayer.

Marianne stepped into the kitchen wrapped in a soft cardigan over loose linen pants. "You're up early," she remarked. Then looking more closely at Kate's swollen and tired eyes, asked, "are you okay?"

Kate poured herself more coffee from the Moka pot. "Grant called close to midnight."

Claire stopped mid-step in the doorway. She was dressed in black workout leggings and a loose tank top, her short blond hair pulled into a small ponytail for her early morning walk.

Evelyn slowly set her mug down and approached Kate slowly resting her hand on her shoulder.

"He knows the time difference, right?" Claire asked cautiously.

Kate nodded.

"That's never good," Evelyn said quietly.

Kate stared down into her cup. "He's involved with someone."

The kitchen fell completely silent.

"He says he thinks he loves her," Kate added. "And he says he still loves me."

Claire closed her eyes briefly. "Oh, Grant …"

Marianne pulled out a chair beside Kate. "How are you feeling?"

The question cracked something open.

"I don't know," Kate admitted.

She watched the steam curl from her coffee. "I feel disoriented. Like someone moved the furniture in my house while I was asleep."

Evelyn spoke tenderly. "How are you processing all this?"

"I have no idea. I'm shocked. Heartbroken. Angry. Afraid."

Claire pulled out the chair across from her and sat down. "Can you forgive him?"

Kate's eyes flicked up. "I know the right answer. But at this very moment, I just don't know."

The tears that had been gathering all morning finally spilled down her cheeks. She wiped them away quickly.

"I don't know how to unknow something like this. I don't know how to erase the image of him loving someone else."

Marianne leaned forward. "What do you fear most?"

Kate inhaled sharply. "That he's already gone. That I've lost him forever."

She took a slow sip of her coffee and set the cup down with a sigh. "That the man I've known for over thirty-five years has quietly stepped into another life and I didn't see it happening."

Her composure trembled. "And I'm scared that even if he comes back, I won't ever relax again. I won't ever be able trust him. I'll always wonder who he's texting … why he's late … whether he's thinking of her when he's with me."

Her words began coming faster. "What if I wasn't enough? What if I've changed? What if I missed something? What if I've been naïve? What if this is the beginning of the end and I'm just the last one to know?"

She pressed her hand to her chest. “It physically hurts. My heart aches. And I can’t settle my body. I feel like I’ve had three cups of espresso and haven’t eaten in days.”

Marianne reached for her hand. “That’s trauma,” she said. “Your nervous system is trying to protect you.”

Claire spoke next, her voice quieter than usual. “I didn’t tell you this before,” she said slowly, “but when Mark cheated, it wasn’t the sex that destroyed me first.”

Kate looked up.

“It was the rewrite of history,” Claire continued. “Every memory felt contaminated. I replayed every dinner, every business trip, every ‘I love you’ and wondered which ones were lies.”

Evelyn watched her carefully.

“It took years,” Claire admitted. “Years before I could hear his phone buzz without my stomach dropping.”

Kate swallowed. “Did you ever trust him again?”

Claire hesitated. “Not the same way,” she said honestly. “Trust rebuilt over time, but differently. Slower. With guardrails.”

She exhaled slowly. “It worked for about ten years.” The room remained quiet. “Until it didn’t.”

Kate closed her eyes. “I don’t want guardrails,” she whispered. “I want the marriage I had.”

“You may not get that exact version,” Evelyn said carefully. “But you might get a truer one.”

Later that morning Claire insisted they take a walk. “Motion prevents spiraling,” she declared.

They wandered into a quiet lane where the homes were sun washed in soft whites and pale creams, their thick, textured walls warmed by years of light, with weathered blue and green doors tucked beneath simple stone arches.

“That house there,” Claire said casually, “belongs to my childhood friend Paolo’s mother.”

As if summoned, the iron gate opened. A tall man stepped out, carefully guiding an elderly woman down two shallow steps. The four women instinctively fell quiet.

Paolo was tall, at least six foot three, but it wasn’t just his height. It was how he carried it. Unhurried. Solid. As if he had never once needed to prove he belonged in his own skin. He wore pale linen slacks and a crisp white shirt with the sleeves rolled neatly at the forearms. His shoulders were broad in the natural way that comes from real work rather than gym workouts.

His face wasn’t pretty. It was classic. Angular jaw. Strong nose. Deep-set eyes shadowed slightly beneath heavy brows. His dark hair, gray at the temples, fell loosely across his forehead as he bent to steady his mother.

“*Piano, piano, Mamma*,” he murmured gently.

Slowly, slowly, Mamma.

When he straightened, he brushed back the hair that had fallen onto his forehead with the side of his hand.

Evelyn inhaled quietly. “Well.”

Claire smiled. “That’s Paolo!”

Kate noticed his eyes. Kind. Steady. Observant.

“Clairetta!” he called warmly when he recognized her.

They greeted each other easily.

"These are my friends," Claire explained.

He nodded politely. "Buongiorno. *Piacere di conoscervi*." Good day, a pleasure to meet you all.

Paolo offered each woman a small, respectful smile before turning back to Claire. "I'm sorry, Clairetta, but I have to rush. I'm taking my mother to a doctor's appointment."

After the car drove away, Evelyn leaned toward Claire. "Wow."

Claire laughed. "Yes. Paolo grew into a fine specimen."

Later that evening, Paolo appeared at the veranda carrying a small loaf of crusty bread tucked under one arm and a bottle of red wine in the other. The fading light caught him as he stepped into view, easy and unhurried, as if this were the most natural thing in the world.

"*Buonasera*," he said, offering a warm smile. *Piacere di conoscervi* … properly this time."

He lifted the bread slightly. "*Pane rustico*, from the bakery in town. And a local wine." A small pause, then with gentle apology, "*Mi dispiace* for this morning. We were running late for my mother's appointment. I did not want to rush away from you."

Claire waved it off immediately. "You're forgiven. Especially with offerings."

They laughed, and just like that, the moment settled.

He stayed only a few minutes, leaning lightly against the stone wall as they talked about Monopoli, about how long Claire had been away, about how the town had changed and how it hadn't. He pointed vaguely toward the road they had walked that morning, mentioning the best café for espresso, the bakery that still made bread the old way, the small market that opened early on Saturdays.

Conversation came easily. When he asked how long they were staying, Marianne and Evelyn answered together.

"Three months!"

Claire lifted her glass with a grin. "I'm staying indefinitely."

His eyebrows lifted slightly, impressed. Then his attention shifted to Kate. "And you?"

The question landed without pressure. Kate gave a small shrug, her fingers resting loosely around her glass. "I'm not sure yet."

He simply nodded as if that answer made perfect sense.

Not wanting to impose on the women's evening, Paolo said his goodbyes, and Claire walked him to the path.

"Your friend, Kate, yes?" he said quietly. "She seems to be carrying something?"

Claire let out a small breath. "She is."

A pause. "Her husband told her last night he's having an affair."

Paolo stilled. "Ah."

For a moment, he said nothing. His gaze drifted back toward the veranda, where Kate sat listening, her smile faint against the sound of the others' laughter.

"That is a hard thing to hear," he said finally. "It breaks something inside."

Claire nodded. "It does."

He exhaled slowly, as if weighing his words. "She holds herself together," he said, almost to himself. "But you can see … it has just happened."

"Yes."

Another quiet pause. "I'm glad she is not alone tonight," he said. "That matters."

Claire followed his glance back toward the veranda. "It does."

She watched him disappear down the path as the sky above Villa Santoro slowly deepened toward sunset. And Rosa called them to dinner.

CHAPTER 6
Facing Heartbreak

Monopoli, Italy

The Adriatic shimmered in the fading light, but no amount of beauty could soften the ache Kate carried within her.

Claire, Marianne, and Evelyn insisted Kate have a quiet moment to herself before dinner. The evening light just before sunset settled over Villa Santoro in a warm, golden wash, softening everything it touched. Kate sat quietly, turning the stem of her glass between her fingers, sipping the small pour of wine Claire had insisted on opening for each of them to taste.

As always, Rosa had taken command of the kitchen. She moved with confident ease, clearly in her element, waving the women away whenever they tried to help. Only when her dishes were ready did she allow them to carry the platters out to the veranda.

Then she fixed the three of them with a pointed look, a hint of a smirk tugging at her mouth. "*Le ragazze fanno i piatti dopo cena.*" A quick, dismissive wave of her hand followed. "The girls will do all the dishes after dinner."

Soon the long wooden table filled with bowls of fresh pasta, grilled branzino, olives, and crusty bread still warm from the bakery. The air carried the scent of garlic, olive oil, and the sea, wrapping around them in a kind of quiet abundance.

At first, conversation stayed light, drifting easily between stories and laughter as the women praised Rosa's cooking. Kate smiled along, grateful for their gentle attempts to pull her back into the conversation with humor, teasing, and the familiar rhythm of friendship that had carried them through so many seasons.

But before long, something inside her dimmed. Her fork moved slowly across her plate, more out of habit than hunger. She hadn't taken a bite in several minutes. The questions hadn't stopped since the night before. If anything, they had multiplied, circling back again, refusing to settle.

At last, she set her fork down. "I just can't stop the questions."

The others looked up.

"They don't stop," she said holding back a sob. "They just circle." She twisted her napkin. "Does he find her prettier? Smarter? More interesting?"

Her voice caught. "Am I just not fun anymore?"

No one answered immediately.

"What if she won't back down?" Kate continued. "What if she's decided she's not letting go?" She swallowed. "Has he … had sex with her?"

Marianne set her fork down. "Did you ask him?"

Kate blinked. "No."

"Why not?"

Kate stared into her wine glass. "I don't know if I want to hear the answer."

Evelyn leaned forward. "But your mind is answering it anyway."

Kate's shoulders sagged. "Is sex with her better than thirty-five years of comfortable bliss?" she whispered. "Does new always win over known?"

Claire reached across the table and squeezed her hand. "Comfortable bliss isn't small," she said emphatically. "It's earned."

But Kate's composure finally cracked. "I'm sixty-two years old," she sobbed suddenly, "and I feel like I'm competing with a ghost."

The women rose without discussion. Claire and Evelyn helped Kate upstairs while Marianne quietly gathered the glasses.

They eased Kate, still in her light cotton sundress onto the narrow twin bed.

"You are not being replaced," Claire whispered.

"You are not invisible," Evelyn added.

"You are not less," Marianne said.

But Kate's tears continued long after the door closed.

Morning came again. The women took an early walk to the beach they had enjoyed without a care in the world two short days earlier. How things had changed so quickly.

Kate stood staring at the Adriatic as waves rolled steadily against the stone.

"I can't stay," she said quietly. "I feel like I'm abandoning my post."

"Is that conviction … or panic?" Marianne asked.

Kate stared at the horizon. "I think it's obedience." She inhaled slowly. "I can't fight for my marriage from a distance."

Return to Reality

At the airport they each hugged Kate long and hard.

"If he hurts you again," Claire said fiercely, "I will personally fly over and handle it."

Kate laughed through tears.

"You are not foolish for fighting," Evelyn said. "You are brave."

Marianne held her last.

"Keep praying," Kate whispered.

Security called Kate forward. She turned once more. "Pray," she mouthed.

"Always," they mouthed back.

On the plane Kate closed her eyes. "Lord," she whispered. "Wake him up. Protect our family. Protect what you joined." Then quietly: "I am willing to fight. Just show me how."

The engines roared and Italy disappeared beneath the clouds. Across the ocean, her husband was living the life that had just shattered hers.

PART TWO

Season of Unraveling

CHAPTER 7
Home Alone

Austin, Texas—Grant

The confession had lifted the burden of secrecy, only to replace it with something far heavier.

Long after Grant's call to Kate had ended, he remained seated at the kitchen table, staring at the cell phone still trembling in his hand. His mouth felt dry, like cotton. He pushed back his chair and walked down the hall to the guest bathroom, splashing cold water onto his face. As he reached for the hand towel, he glanced at his reflection.

The man looking back at him felt unfamiliar. Older somehow. His shoulders slightly rounded, as if the weight of his confession had settled physically onto his frame. Had he just shattered thirty-five years of marriage with a midnight call? He had expected something—relief, maybe. But all he felt was fear and dread.

He stared at himself a moment longer, then looked away. When would Kate come home? And when she did, what would she see? Her husband of thirty-five years or a stranger who had betrayed her?

He ran a hand through his hair and exhaled slowly. "I didn't mean for it to happen," he had said. The words now felt thin and defensive. He leaned forward, bracing his palms against the counter, his gaze dropping to the smooth granite beneath his hands. Kate had chosen it fifteen years earlier, during the kitchen and bathroom remodel.

"We deserve something beautiful," she had said. "The kitchen is where our family will gather for years. And if we're doing this, we might as well do the guest bathroom too."

He could still hear the conviction in her voice. She had always believed in building something lasting. Grant swallowed. That had been one of the things he loved most about her and maybe one of the things that quietly undid him.

Grant had always known how to conduct himself with a manly strength. To provide. To support. To hold everything steady. He had learned it early.

In his childhood home, strength had a sound. His father's voice filled rooms before his body did, boots heavy on hardwood floors, laughter loud, opinions louder.

"Stand up straight. Don't mumble. Don't cry."

Grant was the younger son. Luke had come first and was bigger, faster, louder. The kind of boy coaches noticed. The kind of boy fathers bragged about.

"Luke scored again! Luke broke the school record!"

Grant clapped from the bleachers. He was good, too. Just not spectacular. He preferred books and music or conversations that lingered. He noticed things others missed, like the tension in a room or the sadness in his mother's eyes when his father dismissed her. He felt deeply. And he learned quickly that depth did not impress his father.

"Don't be so sensitive. You've got to toughen up."

So, he did. Or at least, he learned how to look like he had. By high school, he had built a quieter kind of strength. He had steady grades, disciplined habits, and a body trained more from obligation than passion. He lifted weights because that's what strong men did.

He lowered his voice. He swallowed tears. He became dependable. And dependable men rarely ask to be seen.

When he met Kate in his early twenties, she saw something different. She saw the part of him he had learned to hide.

"You're not like other guys," she told him once.

He wasn't sure whether it was praise or warning, but he was drawn to her certainty. Kate believed things deeply … about God, about people, about him. She spoke about faith as if God were personal and present, not distant and theoretical.

She never doubted Grant. She admired him. That admiration felt like oxygen. He married her because he knew she was the best thing that had ever happened to him. He married her with loyalty and intention. And for decades, he was faithful. But faithfulness was not the same as wholeness.

Grant worked hard. He provided, led his family, and prayed at the dinner table. He fixed what was broken, volunteered at church, and stayed late at the office when necessary. He became what everyone needed. Strong. Reliable. Solid.

But inside, something remained unexamined … a quiet ache, a subtle sense that he was always proving something. To his father. To his brother. To God. To himself. Even to Kate.

She respected and trusted him. She believed in him more than he believed in himself. Over time, that admiration began to feel like pressure. He could not falter. He could not confess weakness. He could not say, *I'm tired of holding everything together.*

Some evenings, Kate would come home energized from mentoring women at church, stories spilling from her lips about the lives she was helping guide. Grant listened. Proud of her. But occasionally, he realized the entire evening had passed without her asking how he was doing. Not intentionally. But still.

Their marriage had functioned beautifully for many years. But it no longer felt like it once had. She no longer reached for him with the same urgency, the same curiosity, the same need. Grant would never have said that out loud. He wouldn't have known how.

When his father died three years earlier, something shifted. At the funeral, relatives praised Luke's athletic career and visible leadership. Grant stood beside his mother. Dependable. Invisible.

"Your brother always had that fire," someone said. "But you… you're solid."

Solid.

The word followed him home. Solid men did not unravel. Solid men did not question their worth. Solid men did not admit loneliness. But loneliness had been creeping in for years.

Then came Lydia.

Since his father's passing, Grant had served as president and CEO of the Bennett Family Foundation, a regional philanthropic organization funding scholarships, small-business incubators, and community revitalization projects.

His brother had declined the role, choosing to focus on his professional sports franchise, leaving Grant to carry the family legacy alone. The endowment was substantial. The board discerning. Every funding decision bore his name and his father's. He jumped into the role, whether he felt ready for it or not.

He barely looked up when the receptionist buzzed.

"Mr. Bennett? Your ten thirty is here."

"Send her in."

The door opened and Grant looked up. Lydia Carter stood just inside the doorway. She was poised, not hesitant, in her early fifties and younger than he by nearly a decade. Her dark hair fell in a polished sweep at her shoulders. Tailored navy sheath dress. Structured. Professional. No flash. But it was the way she carried herself that caught him.

Lydia was confident in an unapologetic way.

She extended her hand. "Lydia Carter."

Her voice was low. Calm. No nervous chatter. No fabricated smile. Just complete composure.

Grant rose. "Grant Bennett."

Her grip was firm. Something flickered. Not attraction exactly. Recognition. She held his gaze a fraction longer than necessary, not inappropriate, just steady. As if she had already assessed the room and decided she belonged. During the interview she asked questions most candidates avoided.

"Do you want the foundation to remain regional," she asked, "or are you ready to expand influence nationally?"

Grant leaned back slightly. "Expansion has always been the goal."

"Then you're underleveraging your donor network."

He blinked. Most candidates tried to impress him. Lydia challenged him. After a pause she added quietly, "Do you ever get tired of carrying your father's name?"

The question landed deeper than she could have known. No one had ever asked him that. By the end of the interview, he made his decision.

"The position is Director of Strategic Advancement," he told her. "Long hours. Travel. You report directly to me."

Most candidates would have paused. Lydia didn't. "I wouldn't expect anything less."

In the months that followed, she delivered. New donor commitments. Strategic partnerships. Meetings Grant had chased unsuccessfully for years. She was effective. He learned she had been divorced just over a year. She mentioned it without drama. After meetings she lingered. They discussed strategy and leadership. He noticed that she looked at him as though he were compelling. Not dependable, smart, or reliable. Compelling.

At sixty-two Grant had begun to feel invisible in rooms he once commanded. Younger men rose in their lives and careers. Younger women drifted past without a glance. Kate noticed him the way a woman notices the familiar contours of her home—secure, known, unquestioned.

Lydia noticed him like a discovery. It had not felt like betrayal at first. It felt like oxygen after years of holding his breath.

The night he called Kate; he'd stood in the kitchen long after she hung up. He questioned the wisdom of his confession. Perhaps he could have figured this all out first before exposing his transgression. Did he really need to ruin Kate's much anticipated girl trip? Were his guilt and confusion more important than giving her that time without fear of what she'd face when she finally returned home?

The house felt hollow. He walked slowly into the bedroom. Kate's side of the bed remained untouched. A book rested on her nightstand. *Knowing God* by J.I. Packer. Of course. He picked it up and turned it over in his hands. Half the pages were underlined with Kate's careful handwriting filling the margins with small notes.

He sat on the edge of the bed. "I still love you," he had told her.

That was true. He loved her loyalty. Her steadiness. The life they built together. But love had begun to feel heavy. It was not burdensome, just weighty. Thirty-five years of shared memory meant every conversation carried decades of context.

With Lydia there was no weight. Only spark. He hated the comparison even as he made it. His phone buzzed on the nightstand. Lydia.

Are you okay? I've been thinking about you.

Grant stared at the message. He wondered why she was up so late. Did women really have that sixth sense that people talk about? He had no clue.

He did know that he still loved Kate. That had never stopped being true. When he imagined losing her, her laugh, her quiet prayers whispered beside him in the dark, his chest tightened. But when he imagined losing Lydia, something recoiled too. He felt split. One life anchored in covenant. One chasing possibility.

The first time Lydia had touched his arm, he should have stepped away. He hadn't. He had told himself he deserved to feel alive. Alive. The word sounded hollow now. He bowed his head.

"Lord," he muttered quietly, "what is happening to me?"

No thunder. No clarity. Just the slow awareness that something inside him had shifted months earlier. And he had not resisted it. He had fed it.

He opened Lydia's message again.

Are you okay?

He typed slowly.

I need space.

Space from whom? From Lydia? From Kate? From himself?

He pressed send.

Fear crept in then. Not fear of being caught. Fear of losing everything. And beneath that, a faint but persistent sense of shame.

At some point, Kate would walk through the front door and look at him with the same clear eyes that had trusted him for thirty-five years. And he had no idea what she would see.

He whispered into the empty room, "I never meant to hurt her."

But intention did not erase action. And somewhere beneath the hum of the air conditioner and the distant traffic outside, a harder truth pressed against his conscience.

He had not simply fallen.

He had chosen.

And whether he would choose differently now remained to be seen.

CHAPTER 8
Borrowed Ground

Austin, Texas—Lydia

Every time Grant's name appeared on her phone, a small part of Lydia wondered whether it would be the message that ended everything.

Her phone buzzed on the kitchen counter. She glanced down from the glass of Pinot Grigio she had just poured. Grant's name lit the screen.

I need space.

She stared at the message for several seconds. Space. The word tightened something in her chest.

Space from her?

Or space from the guilt that had finally caught up with him?

She hadn't been able to sleep tonight. She had sensed something was off. Now this message. She set the phone down without answering and leaned against the counter, staring out the window above the sink. Moonlight was reflecting off neighboring rooftops and casting a soft glow on the street below. She simply stood there, feeling the strange weight of waiting.

Lydia's marriage had not ended in a slammed door. It ended in apathy. There had been no explosive confession. No younger woman waiting in the wings with bright lipstick and reckless laughter. There had simply been distance. Years of it.

Years of living beside a man who came home every night and yet never quite arrived. Her husband, Tom, had been responsible. Steady and predictable. He paid the bills on time, fixed broken shelves, and attended activities and parties with her when she asked.

But slowly, in ways that were difficult to measure, he withdrew. He stopped asking how her day had gone. Stopped reaching for her in bed. Stopped noticing when she cut her hair. Eventually he even stopped arguing.

At first Lydia thought it was stress. Then she thought it was her. She read books about relationships and tried to be less intense. Understanding she was a "Type A" personality and what many called a "strong woman", she tried to be softer and more agreeable with Tom. She made daily effort to initiate meaningful conversations that felt increasingly one-sided. When she questioned his lack of interest in sharing his thoughts with her, he would reassure her saying,

"You're imagining things. We're fine."

They were not fine. They were functional. There is a difference. The physical intimacy faded gradually, so gradually she almost didn't notice it leaving. What had once been spontaneous became scheduled. Then postponed. Then avoided.

She did not cheat. But she fantasized. Not about another specific man at first, just about being desired. About being pursued. About someone leaning in instead of quietly pulling away.

She tried to pray during that season. But she'd never really felt very close to God and wondered if he even heard her … even cared about her marriage. Nothing dramatic happened. There was no revelation or heartfelt reconciliation. Just a slow erosion.

The day Tom finally admitted he "wasn't sure he loved her the same way anymore," it almost felt like relief. At least the truth had surfaced. There had been no other woman. Just emptiness. They divorced quietly. Civilly. Friends described it as mutual. But mutual endings still wound.

Thankful that they had never had children, she moved into a smaller townhouse, rebuilt her routines, and returned to work with renewed ambition. And somewhere inside, a quiet determination formed.

I will not feel invisible again.

When she met Grant Bennett at the foundation, she noticed immediately what had been missing from her life for years. He engaged with her, leaning forward when she spoke. He listened and asked her opinion. And he waited for the answer. It shouldn't have felt remarkable. But it did.

When he laughed at her dry humor during a late planning session, something in Lydia's chest loosened. She knew he was married. Of course she did. She had met Kate once, briefly at a donor reception Lydia herself had hosted. Grant had arrived with Kate on his arm, introducing her with quiet pride. Kate moved easily through the room that evening, greeting guests with calm warmth. She carried herself with effortless composure. Not flashy. Not the sort of woman who demanded attention. Yet people relaxed around her within minutes.

Lydia had watched her from across the room while refilling a guest's wine glass. Pretty, yes. But not dazzling. Capable. Self-possessed. The sort of woman one describes approvingly as a *good wife*. The phrase settled quietly in Lydia's mind. A good wife keeps life running smoothly. She remembers birthdays, manages schedules, stands beside her husband at events like this with grace and loyalty.

But a good wife, Lydia sometimes suspected, might not always notice the quieter things. The private doubts. The slow narrowing that can creep into a man's life as the years move forward. Whether that was true or not, Lydia found the thought comforting.

It made things easier to explain. She dismissed Kate that evening with a small inward shrug.

Lydia did not begin with intentional seduction. She began with authentic empathy. She just wanted to connect with this quality man, her new boss.

"You ever feel like life gets smaller after fifty?" she asked Grant once, half joking.

He didn't laugh. "Yes," he said quietly.

His "yes" felt like recognition. Their conversations grew longer after that. Less about budgets and planning meetings. More about life. Aging parents. The strange invisibility that can arrive with time. The quiet question of whether the best chapters have already been written.

And slowly, almost without meaning to, Lydia began to feel that she understood him in ways others did not. She listened to the pauses in his voice. Noticed the things he didn't say. Sometimes she found herself thinking that perhaps she saw parts of him even his wife had overlooked. The thought was subtle. Dangerous, but comforting.

There had been one moment early on when she recognized the boundary had been breached. They were sitting in the conference room after a long meeting. Everyone else had left. Grant had begun speaking about the pressure of leading the foundation, and about the quiet expectations attached to his father's name. For a moment Lydia felt the warning rise inside her.

This conversation is no longer professional. This is not your place.

She could have redirected the conversation. She could have stood up, gathered her papers, and wished him a good evening. Instead, she leaned forward.

"What does that kind of pressure feel like?" she asked gently.

The warning faded and something else began. She never intended to compare his marriage with her own life. But she did.

Grant described Kate with respect and admiration. He called her strong, independent, and capable. Those words lodged somewhere uncomfortable inside Lydia. Strong women, she thought, sometimes carry so much that they stop noticing when the man beside them begins to feel small. Whether that idea was fair or not hardly mattered. It explained things. And once something feels explained, it becomes easier to excuse.

She told herself she wasn't intruding on something whole, but something that had already begun to crack. After all, if his marriage were vibrant, he wouldn't be lingering. If it were airtight, he wouldn't be leaning toward her.

When he kissed her the first time, it felt less like sin and more like confirmation.

See? she thought. *This is what I was missing.* It felt so good to feel pursued. And when guilt tried to surface, she reasoned with it. *Surely God doesn't want people trapped in lifeless marriages,* she told herself.

Surely God understood loneliness. Surely, he cared about her joy. The thought comforted her. What she did not consider was whether she was listening to God or simply assigning her feelings to his voice to defend what she already wanted.

She glanced at her phone again. Grant's message still glowed on the screen.

I need space.

A memory surfaced suddenly. Tom standing in their kitchen years earlier, eyes tired, saying, "I don't think I can give you what you want."

She had hated that feeling. The slow realization that someone was stepping away from her life. She would not be dismissed again. And yet…beneath her resolve, a quieter truth whispered.

You knew he was married. You knew this would cost someone.

She pushed the thought away. Kate had thirty-five years. Lydia had no one. Surely there was room in the world for her happiness too. But as she lifted her wine glass, her hand trembled slightly. Because deep down beneath the justifications and wounded pride, she understood something she was not yet willing to say aloud. If he returned to his wife, it wouldn't just be rejection. It would mean she had been building on borrowed ground.

And the most frightening possibility of all was this: Lydia was beginning to wonder if the ground beneath her life had ever truly been solid at all.

CHAPTER 9
Homecoming

Austin, Texas—Kate

The house looked the same. That felt almost offensive.

The oak tree still arched over the driveway, its branches spreading wide enough to shade half the yard. The small wind chime beside the front door still stirred lazily in the warm Texas afternoon. Nothing in the quiet suburban street announced that her life had split in two.

Kate stepped out of the rideshare slowly, stiff from the overnight flight. Her auburn hair had been pulled into a loose knot that had begun to unravel during travel. Dark circles shadowed her eyes, and the exhaustion of sleepless nights rested visibly on her face. But her posture remained straight.

She took a deep breath and thought ... *thirty-five years.*

She had walked through this front door thousands of times, carrying groceries, carrying babies, carrying grief when her mother died, carrying celebration when their youngest graduated. Today she carried something heavier. Almost more than she could bear.

Her suitcase rolled behind her as she walked up the driveway. The front door opened before she reached it. Grant stood there. For a moment neither of them moved.

He looked older. Not dramatically in a way that anyone else might notice, but as if the air between them had aged him overnight. He wore faded jeans and the gray sweatshirt he often wore on weekends. The sleeves were pushed up halfway to his elbows. His hair looked slightly unkempt, as if he had run his hands through it too many times. A faint shadow of stubble darkened his jaw. He looked like he hadn't slept much either.

"Hi," he said quietly.

The word nearly undid her. "Hi."

They stood facing one another in the doorway, separated by three feet and decades of shared life. For a moment he looked as though he might reach for her. He didn't. Instead, he stepped forward and took the suitcase handle from her hand.

"I've got that." He moved aside. "Come in."

The familiar scent of their Austin home wrapped around her—coffee, wood polish, and the faint essential oil citrus cleaner she always used on the kitchen counters. Her suitcase wheels clicked across the hardwood floor. Normal sounds amid their abnormal lack of conversation. He closed the door behind her.

"You didn't have to come back so soon," he said. "We could have talked more once you'd had time to think."

Kate turned slowly to face him. "I absolutely did." Her voice was calm, controlled, and strong.

They moved into the living room almost instinctively, as if their bodies still remembered patterns their hearts no longer trusted. Kate sat on the edge of the sofa. Grant lowered himself into the armchair opposite her creating an awkward and unfamiliar distance. The framed photo of their three children at the Grand Canyon sat on the mantel behind him. Kate's eyes flicked to it briefly before returning to his face. She studied him carefully.

"Is it still happening?" she asked.

Grant exhaled slowly. "I told her I needed space."

That was not the same as no.

“Are you still in contact?”

A pause. “Yes.”

The honesty hurt more than denial would have. Kate nodded once. “Thank you for telling the truth.”

Grant looked up sharply. “I don’t want to lie to you.”

“You already did.”

The words were not cruel. Just factual. Grant leaned forward, elbows resting on his knees, rubbing his hands together as if trying to warm them.

“I never meant for this to go this far.”

“Grant,” she countered with an edge to her voice, “it went as far as you allowed it to.”

A hush settled between them. On the plane she had rehearsed anger—sharp accusations, questions meant to wound. But what she felt now was steadier and more useful than anger. Clarity of purpose.

“I am not here to beg you,” she said.

His shoulders stiffened.

“And I am not here to threaten you.”

She held his gaze. “I’m here to fight for our marriage.”

His eyes flickered.

“For us. You say you love me.”

"I do."

"You say you might love her."

He hesitated. "I think I do."

The truth of it settled painfully into her chest. "You have a divided heart," she said quietly.

He did not deny it.

Kate folded her hands in her lap so he wouldn't see them trembling. "Have you thought about Jesse?" she asked.

Grant blinked.

"Our son is raising a little boy," she continued. "He calls you for advice about being a husband and a father. He assumes what he saw in this house is solid."

Grant's jaw tightened.

"And Emma," she said. "She's planning her wedding. She asks me what makes a marriage last."

Her voice cracked. "What do I tell her if ours fractures?"

He looked away.

"And Nathan," she continued. "He still believes integrity is non-negotiable. He looks at you like you are the manly definition of steady ground."

Grant rubbed his forehead.

"I'm not saying this to shame you," Kate clarified. "I'm saying it because this isn't just about your feelings."

She leaned forward slightly. “It’s about the legacy we hand our children.”

Grant stared down at the floor. “I felt…” he began, then stopped.

“What?” she asked.

“Invisible.”

The word pierced her. Invisible. After thirty-five years. Kate swallowed. “I have never stopped seeing you.”

“I know.”

“Do you?”

He looked up then, and for a moment she saw the man she had married.

“I didn’t feel it,” he whispered. “Not for a long time.”

Kate nodded slowly. “That is different.” Then, more firmly: “You don’t dismantle a family because something feels good in the moment.”

She rose slowly and walked down the hallway toward their bedroom. Grant hesitated, then followed. At the doorway she paused and turned to face him.

“This room,” she began with a quivering voice, “has held thirty-five years of faithfulness.” Her hand rested lightly on the door frame. “It has held mistakes and forgiveness. It has held prayer.”

Grant stood behind her, silent.

“I am willing to work,” she continued. “I am willing to forgive. I am willing to rebuild.” She looked fully into his tired hazel eyes for a long moment and then continued. “But I will not share you.”

The words hung between them. "I can't share you, Grant. Not your heart, not your body. And until you know where you stand, I can't share this room with you either."

Grant flinched slightly.

"You need to choose," she clarified.

The word landed heavy

"I need time," he said.

Time. Kate closed her eyes briefly. "Time is what destroys marriages in situations like this," she retorted.

Grant stepped closer. "I don't want to lose you."

"Then don't."

It was that simple. And that impossible. They stood there inches apart, yet miles divided.

"I still love you," he said again.

"I know."

"And I don't want to hurt her either."

The words landed between them like a third person standing in the room. Kate closed her eyes for a moment before answering.

"This isn't about protecting *her* feelings," she cried. "It's about honoring your vow!"

Grant said nothing.

Kate understood that this was a spiritual battle for her marriage, for the covenant they had made before God all those years ago. She drew a slow breath and whispered a silent prayer for the Holy Spirit to give her the words that might still reach Grant's heart.

"Grant." She lifted her eyes and held his gaze. "For all their lives our children have watched us choose each other," she said steadily. "Through job changes. Through teenage rebellion. Through financial strain. Through exhaustion." Her voice trembled slightly.

"They believed in what we built." She lifted her chin. "And I am terrified of the day they look at us and see something broken that we chose not to mend."

Grant stared at her, his jaw clenching, his eyes glistening, and yet saying nothing.

"You could destroy more than our marriage," she said, her voice getting louder. "You could alter the way they understand covenant."

The room felt smaller.

"But I will not fight alone."

Kate stepped into the bedroom and set her suitcase beside the bed. This was her home. Her covenant ground. And she had not flown across an ocean to surrender it quietly. Not today.

CHAPTER 10
Alone Together

Austin, Texas

They had never been farther apart than they were right now … under the same roof.

Kate sat cross-legged on the bed, her journal open across her lap. The house was quiet in the late afternoon. A soft breeze slipped through the open window, lifting the corner of a page as if urging her to keep writing.

She had been home from Italy for less than twenty-four hours.

It felt strange to realize how much had changed in less than a week. Everything looked the same. The familiar photographs. The furniture. The faint scent of laundry soap drifting from the hallway.

Yet in less than a day, the house had taken on an entirely different feel. The tension that had settled over their marriage now lingered in every room. Everything had shifted. For the first time in their married life, Grant was sleeping in the guest room. He was still living here but somehow felt farther away than ever.

That morning, he had left for work at eight o'clock, just as he always did, coffee mug in hand.

Kate pressed her pen to the page again.

Lord, I don't know what to do.

The words came slowly at first.

I want to fight for our marriage. But I don't know how to reach him anymore.

She paused. The ink glistened faintly on the paper.

You know I'm not perfect. I know I've failed him in ways I don't even fully see yet.

Her chest tightened.

But thirty-five years... Lord, that must mean something.

She sat still as memories began to surface … not forced, but appearing methodically, one after another. She saw their first apartment. A tiny place with mismatched furniture and a kitchen barely big enough for two people to stand in at once. They had almost no money then. Grant was working long hours. She was juggling shifts and school. But she remembered how happy they had been.

One evening they had eaten peanut butter sandwiches at the kitchen counter because they were too tired to cook. Grant had looked at her and said with a grin, "You know we're rich, right?"

She had laughed. "How?"

He shrugged. "Because I get to come home to you."

Kate felt tears gather in her eyes as the memory replayed. Another scene followed. Their first house. Boxes stacked everywhere. Grant spinning her across the empty living room before they even owned a couch.

"You realize," he had said breathlessly, "we have no idea what we're doing."

Kate had laughed. "We'll figure it out."

They always had. Or at least, they had tried.

Her pen moved again across the page.

Lord, thank You for the life we've shared.

More memories rose. Their children being born. Grant standing beside her hospital bed, overwhelmed and protective. Late nights with crying babies. School plays. Family road trips that dissolved into laughter over wrong turns and fast-food dinners. And then another memory came. One she hadn't thought about in a long time.

Their twenty-fifth wedding anniversary. They had renewed their vows in a small ceremony in their backyard surrounded by family and close friends. Kate could still see Grant standing across from her that evening. His voice had been steady, but his eyes had been bright with emotion.

"I thought I knew what love was when we married," he had said. "But loving you for twenty-five years has taught me something deeper."

Kate felt the moment again as if it were happening now.

Grant had taken her hands. "I look forward to growing old with you," he had continued. "To discovering who we become in the years ahead."

He had smiled. "I wouldn't want to take that journey with anyone else."

Kate closed her eyes. The memory pricked painfully at her heart. For several moments she simply sat there. Then a quiet thought surfaced. Not loud. But unmistakable. Share these with him.

Kate blinked and wrote in her journal:

Lord? Is that thought from You?

The thought returned. *Share the memories.* She hesitated. Would that feel manipulative? Would it pressure him? But the prompting felt peaceful. Not demanding. Just clear.

Kate reached for her phone. Her thumbs hovered over the screen before she finally typed.

Would you be open to sharing a simple dinner tonight? I'd just like to talk for a little while.

She stared at the message before sending it. The three little dots appeared almost immediately. Grant's reply came seconds later.

Okay.

Kate exhaled slowly.

Dinner that evening was simple. A roast chicken. Steamed vegetables. Bread. No candles. No wine. Just the two of them sitting across from each other at the kitchen table. Grant looked tired. But not defensive. They ate in silence for a few minutes. Finally, Kate set her fork down.

"Grant?"

He looked up. "Yes?"

She hesitated. Then almost whispered, "Will you please indulge me for a little bit?"

He frowned slightly. "What do you mean?"

Kate held his gaze. "Would you allow me to take us on a brief journey back in time?"

Grant blinked. "What kind of journey?"

"Just memories."

He leaned back slightly. "Okay."

Kate felt a quiet steadiness settle inside her. "I was journaling earlier today," she began. "And I started remembering our early years."

Grant didn't interrupt.

"You remember our first apartment?"

A faint smile touched his face. "The one with the broken dishwasher?"

"Yes."

Kate laughed, remembering. "We couldn't afford to fix it for six months."

Grant shook his head. "I forgot about that."

"And the peanut butter sandwich dinners."

He chuckled. "Those were gourmet."

Kate's eyes warmed. "You told me we were rich because you got to come home to me."

Grant looked down at the table. "I said that?"

"You did."

Silence stretched for a moment. Uncomfortable, but thoughtful. Kate continued. "I remembered the day we moved into our first house."

Grant nodded slowly. "The spinning dance."

Kate smiled. "You remember."

"I remember everything about that day."

The conversation began to flow more easily. One memory led to another. Their first child. Their chaotic family vacations. The countless small moments that had stitched their life together.

Finally, Kate said quietly, "And our twenty-fifth anniversary."

Grant looked up. His expression softened. "You mean the vow renewal."

"Yes."

Kate studied his face. "You said something that night I've never forgotten."

Grant waited.

"You said loving me for twenty-five years had taught you something deeper about love."

His eyes flickered with emotion.

"And that you wanted to grow old with me."

Grant's jaw tightened slightly.

Kate's voice remained gentle. "I believed you."

She didn't accuse. She didn't plead. She simply let the words exist between them. Grant looked at her for a long moment. His expression had changed. Somewhere beneath the tension, something had softened.

"I meant it," he said.

Kate nodded. "I know."

The conversation faded after that. Not abruptly. Just naturally. They cleared the dishes together. Then Grant disappeared down the hallway toward the guest room. Kate remained in the kitchen for a moment, her hands resting on the counter. She had no idea what had shifted inside him. But she sensed something had.

Grant closed the guest room door behind him. The memories from dinner lingered in his mind. Kate laughing in their first apartment. Kate dancing in the empty living room. Kate standing across from him during their vow renewal.

He sat on the edge of the bed. His chest felt tight. For a moment something warm stirred inside him. Something familiar. Something that felt like home.

Then another voice crept in. Subtle, but sharp. *She's manipulating you*. Grant frowned. *You know what this is.* The voice pressed harder. *She's trying to make you feel guilty. Trying to pull you back. Trying to control the narrative.*

The warmth from dinner began to fade. Replacing it was something colder. Suspicion. Defensiveness. The thought: *You deserve to be happy.*

Grant rubbed his face. The memories that had softened him minutes earlier now felt distorted. Weaponized. Maybe she *was* manipulating him. Maybe the whole dinner had been strategic. He lay back on the bed, staring at the ceiling. The battle inside his mind intensified.

Upstairs, Kate returned to her bedroom. She opened her journal again and sat on the edge of the bed. Her heart felt both hopeful and uncertain. She began to write.

Lord, thank You for the time we had tonight.

Her pen paused.

I felt his heart soften for a moment.

She swallowed.

But I don't know what's happening inside him.

Kate closed her eyes briefly before writing again.

Please open Grant's mind. Open his heart. Protect our marriage from the lies of the enemy.

Her handwriting slowed.

I don't know how this story ends, Lord, but I trust You with the battle I cannot see.

Kate closed the journal and placed it on her nightstand. Then she turned off the light.

Down the hallway, Grant lay awake in the guest room, his mind caught between memory and deception. And neither of them yet understood how fierce the battle was yet to become.

CHAPTER 11
An Alternate Reality

Austin, Texas

Once, they had moved through life as naturally as breathing. Now even the simplest interactions felt rehearsed and uncertain.

As the week wore on, the house felt too large and too small. Too large when Grant went to work each day. Too small when he returned in the evening. He moved carefully around her, polite and distant, as if they were guests sharing space instead of spouses sharing history.

Since their short journey down memory lane, it felt like Grant was distancing himself as much as he could. Dinnertimes became awkward. Should they fend for themselves? Eat in their rooms? Sit across from one another pretending this was temporary?

One evening, when he'd gotten home long past their dinnertime, he stood at the kitchen counter reheating leftovers.

"You should eat something," he said without looking at her.

"I'm fine," she answered.

The words sounded composed, but they felt brittle. He nodded, accepting them too easily.

The next morning, they passed each other in the hallway. For a moment, they both paused, the old instinct to reach, to touch, to kiss goodbye hovering between them. He adjusted his watch instead. She folded her arms across her chest.

"Have a good day," he said.

“You too.”

They sounded like colleagues.

Each night, as Grant slept in the guestroom, Kate lay awake acutely aware of the silence, no longer hearing his slow, familiar breaths of deep sleep. She clutched the pillow from his side of the bed and held it to her chest like a child with a favorite teddy bear. Her tears fell silently until she had no more to shed. And then she drifted in and out of a fitful sleep, waking at every imagined sound.

One evening, Kate stood at the kitchen island rinsing a coffee mug while Grant unloaded the dishwasher. For a few minutes, neither spoke. She’d been ruminating all day on the fact that Grant had never addressed the elephant in the room … that Lydia apparently still worked for Grant … in his office.

She glanced over her shoulder and asked, “how is it working with Lydia now?”

Grant paused. “What do you mean?”

“You told me that you told her that you needed space. How are you handling that if she still works for the foundation?”

He slid a plate into the cabinet before answering. “I've sent her on a pretty extensive list of field assignments.”

Kate turned toward him. “Out of town?”

“Mostly. Site visits, partner evaluations, grant reviews. Things we've neglected for a while.”

She nodded slowly. “So, you're not seeing her at the office at all?”

“Nope.”

The word came easier than it should have. Immediately, another conversation surfaced in his mind. Eight days earlier, Lydia had sat across from him in the conference room. He had just told her that Kate was cutting her trip to Italy short and returning home.

"I don't think either of us should be in the office together right now," he had said quietly.

She had reluctantly agreed and after several uncomfortable minutes, they had settled on a plan. She would handle field projects, donor research, and work from home when she wasn't traveling.

His focused returned to the kitchen, where Kate watched him carefully. “So, she's gone for a while?”

“Probably months,” he said.

That part was mostly true. Several of the assignments would take months to complete. What he didn't say was that between trips, Lydia was still working remotely, attending occasional virtual meetings, and sending reports directly to him.

“Good,” Kate replied.

The single word landed heavily, and Grant forced a nod as he returned his attention to the dishes. He told himself the details didn't matter. Then, the familiar conviction stirred. He pushed it down. At least he was trying to create some distance from Lydia since Kate’s return. He wasn’t sure how long he could stay away from her. Only time would tell.

By the end of the first week, the quiet inside the house had begun to echo inside Kate’s chest. She walked past the kitchen table where they had once lingered over coffee. Past the living room where they had prayed with their children before prom nights and college departures. Everything looked intact but felt invisibly fractured.

Kate looked at her watch. Six o'clock. Grant would probably be home soon. She couldn't bear another awkward "Honey, I'm home, but I'm not home" moment. Without thinking, she grabbed her purse and headed to the garage.

She'd pulled out onto their street and was driving down the road before she realized she had no idea where she was going. All she knew was she could not be there when he walked through the door.

When she returned, she saw Grant's car in the driveway and the door to the guestroom shut, his lamplight dimly glowing under the door. She padded quietly down the long hall to her room and quietly shut herself in for the night.

Around 8:00 p.m., Grant knocked lightly before opening the master bedroom door, a formality that felt foreign between them.

"I'm heading out for a bit," he said, adjusting his keys in his hand. "Just a drive. I didn't want you to wonder if you heard my car leave."

Kate looked at him steadily. "A drive," she repeated flatly.

"Yes." He shifted. "I need some air. To think."

Her jaw tightened. "To think," she echoed, not as a question.

Silence stretched between them.

"Grant," she pleaded, "please don't insult me."

His brow furrowed. "What does *that* mean?"

"It means," she answered, her voice calm but firm, "if you're going to see her, just say that. Don't wrap it in something noble."

His expression hardened slightly. "You're assuming a lot."

"I'm not assuming," she said. "I know you."

"That's not fair," he replied. "I told you I needed space. You said you wouldn't compete. Now I can't even take a drive without being interrogated?"

Interrogated. The word landed like a punch. Kate felt something shift. Was she being gaslit by her own husband?

"I'm not interrogating you," she said. "I'm asking for honesty."

"You're reading into things," he said, exhaling sharply. "Not everything is about Lydia."

The way he said her name was controlled and defensive. It told her more than the words.

Kate swallowed. "Then go," she said curtly. "If you need to go, go. I can't handle half-truths. I won't live in that."

He stared at her, as if waiting for her to soften. She didn't.

"Just don't pretend it's something it isn't," she added.

His jaw tightened. For a moment, it looked like he might argue again. Instead, he gave a short nod. "Fine."

He turned and walked down the hallway. Kate felt the sharp, undeniable ache of a woman who realizes she is no longer arguing about facts but about reality itself.

CHAPTER 12
The "Drive"

Austin, Texas

Grant closed the front door behind him with more force than he intended.

The conversation with Kate still rang in his ears.

Please don't insult me.

The words had landed like an accusation. He stood on the front porch for a moment, keys dangling from his hand. For a split second he considered turning around and going back inside. But the tension in the house felt unbearable. So, he walked to the car and climbed in.

The engine hummed as he pulled away from the curb. He told himself he was just going for a drive. Just air. Just space. But Kate's voice followed him down the road.

If you're going to see her, just say that.

His grip tightened on the steering wheel. She thinks she knows everything. The thought flared hot and defensive. But another voice whispered beneath it. *Maybe she does.* Grant exhaled sharply.

He drove through the neighborhood without direction, passing familiar streets he barely noticed. The argument replayed in fragments. Kate's steady eyes. Her refusal to soften. Something about it made him feel exposed, judged, and cornered. He couldn't even breathe in that house anymore. The next thought slipped into his mind … *You deserve to be somewhere you're not constantly accused.*

Grant frowned. *I wasn't going to Lydia's. You don't have to explain yourself*, he thought. The inner voice pressed harder. *You just need comfort. Understanding. Someone who doesn't look at you like you're the enemy*. His jaw tightened.

The next turn came almost automatically. Before he realized it, he was driving toward Lydia's neighborhood. He noticed it too late to pretend otherwise.

Grant sighed heavily. "I'm not staying," he muttered aloud to himself.

Just talk. Just calm down. That's all. But deep down he knew the truth. The battle inside him had already begun.

Lydia opened the door almost immediately when he knocked. Her face brightened.

"Hey," she said seductively.

Then she studied him more closely. "What's wrong?"

Grant stepped inside without answering. The warm light of her kitchen filled the room. It felt familiar. Comforting. Too comforting.

"Bad night?" she asked.

Grant rubbed the back of his neck. "Something like that."

Lydia reached for a glass. "Wine?"

"No."

That surprised her. "Okay…"

She leaned against the counter, watching him. "You look like you just lost a fight."

Grant gave a humorless laugh. "Feels like I did."

"With Kate?"

He nodded. "She said if I was going to see you, I should just say it."

Lydia raised an eyebrow. "Well, she wasn't wrong."

Grant sighed. "I was seriously just planning to take a drive to clear my head." He ran his hand through his hair. "I feel like everything I do is interpreted as guilt."

Lydia stepped closer. "That's because she wants you to feel guilty."

The words slid into the tension he was already carrying.

"She keeps bringing things back to you," Lydia continued. "She won't let you breathe."

Grant didn't respond. Because something about that didn't feel entirely true anymore. But the exhaustion inside him was louder than clarity.

Lydia touched his arm lightly. "You're safe here. You can be yourself without judgement."

The phrase should have comforted him. Instead, it unsettled him. Safe. Safe from what? From pressure? From guilt? From truth?

Grant stepped back slightly. "I can't stay long," he said.

Her hand fell away. "Oh."

"I just needed a minute."

The disappointment flickered across her face. “You drove all the way over here for a minute?”

Grant looked down. “I’m trying to figure things out.”

Lydia studied him carefully now. “You mean you’re trying to figure out whether you’re leaving me.”

The bluntness startled him. “I didn’t say that.”

“You didn’t have to.”

She folded her arms. “What changed?”

Grant hesitated and then replied, “I’m not sure.”

That was the honest answer. The more time he spent inside this situation, the less certain everything felt. They sat at the kitchen table for a while. The conversation drifted.

“Your body is here, but your mind is somewhere else,” she said.

Grant stared at the table. “Yeah. You’re right.”

“Is it guilt,” she asked, tilting her head inquisitively.

The word landed hard. Grant didn’t answer. Because the answer was obvious. After less than two hours he stood up.

“I should go.”

Lydia blinked. “That’s it?”

“Yes.”

She tried to hide the sting in her voice without success. “Wow.”

Grant walked toward the door slowly. “I’m sorry.”

"For what?"

"For… everything."

The words sounded inadequate even as he said them.

Lydia's expression tightened. "Well," she said abruptly, "drive safe."

Grant nodded once and stepped outside. The cool night air hit his face, and he finally felt like he could breathe again. He arrived home just before ten. The house was dark. He removed his shoes and padded soundlessly down the hallway and slipped into the guest room.

He sat on the edge of the bed, elbows resting on his knees. The aloneness felt heavy and he suddenly felt exhausted. Not just physically. Spiritually. Like a man trying to swim against a current he couldn't see.

After a long moment he noticed the Bible he had put on the nightstand when he'd moved to the guest room. Truth was, he hadn't opened it for a long time before that. He flipped through the pages almost absentmindedly. The thin paper rustled under his fingers. Then the pages stopped.

Grant frowned slightly. He began reading.

Have mercy on me, O God, according to your unfailing love.

His chest tightened.

According to your great compassion blot out my transgressions.

He swallowed. The words pressed against something deep inside him.

Wash away all my iniquity and cleanse me from my sin.

Grant took a deep breath and slowly let it out. He knew this psalm. It was King David's confession after taking Bathsheba, another man's wife, and trying to conceal the consequences of his sin—her pregnancy. In a desperate attempt to cover his wrongdoing, David arranged for her husband, one of his most loyal soldiers, to be sent to the front lines of battle, where he was killed. The depth of David's failure made Grant's stomach tighten.

The realization hit him like a wave. David had destroyed lives. Yet he had cried out to God in deep anguish and repentance. Grant dropped the Bible onto his lap and covered his face with his hands.

"What is wrong with me?" he whispered hoarsely.

His voice cracked. "Why am I so weak?"

Tears burned behind his eyes. "Why are you letting this happen to me, God?"

The room was silent. But for the first time in months, Grant wasn't running from the conviction pressing on his heart. He sat there in the quiet. A man staring at the wreckage of his choices.

Little did he know the enemy would not be giving up just yet. A couple verses, one night of restraint, and a short prayer wasn't enough to send him away. It would take a whole lot more than that.

CHAPTER 13
Sisterhood

Austin, Texas and Across the Pond

There are few wounds that prayer and sisterhood cannot touch, and Kate needed both.

After the confrontation with Grant the night before, Kate realized how badly she needed to hear her friends' voices. Not texts. Not emojis. Real-time voices.

She needed Ev, Claire, and Marianne, the women who had known her through every life high and low. The women who had watched her marriage unfold in real time.

At 10:00 a.m. in Texas—5:00 p.m. in Italy—she texted the group.

Emergency Zoom summit needed!

Claire responded first. **Define emergency.**

Evelyn: **Do we need to crack open a bottle of vino for this?**

Marianne: **We just got back from the market. Anytime works.**

Kate smiled faintly despite herself. They would never let her fall alone. An hour later, she propped her laptop on the kitchen counter, the same counter where she and Grant had once prepared meals shoulder to shoulder, bumping hips, laughing about nothing.

She clicked "Join Meeting."

One by one, her friends appeared on their own devices. Marianne sat at the long wooden table outside Zia Rosa's villa on the courtyard, the Adriatic glinting faintly behind her. Claire joined from the kitchen, an open window behind her framing blue sky and terracotta rooftops. A half-finished glass of red wine sat beside her laptop. Evelyn appeared last, dramatically adjusting her camera angle as church bells rang faintly somewhere in the background.

"Well," Claire said immediately, "do we need bail money?"

Kate exhaled a breath that was half laugh, half exhaustion. "No felonies. Yet."

"Disappointing," Evelyn replied solemnly. "I had a speech prepared."

The humor steadied her. Then Kate told them everything. Not theatrically. Not weeping. Just plainly. "The problem is I don't even know what's true anymore," she finished with a deep sigh.

Three faces stared back at her.

"Last night he said he just needed a drive," Kate continued. "But when I asked him directly if he was going to see Lydia, he got defensive. Like I was accusing him of something unfair."

Claire tilted her head. "And was he?"

Kate shook her head slowly. "I don't know."

The admission felt heavier than anger. "He's so elusive with the truth right now. I can't tell when he's being honest and when he's hiding something."

Evelyn leaned closer to the screen. "That kind of ambiguity is exhausting."

"Yes," Kate agreed. "It is."

She hesitated. “I keep questioning myself. Am I being paranoid? Am I imagining things? Or am I just refusing to see what’s actually happening?”

Claire took a slow sip of wine. “If your instincts are this unsettled,” she said, “something isn’t right.”

“Kate,” Marianne chimed in, “Claire is right.”

Kate didn’t defend Grant. But she didn’t condemn him either. “He isn’t malicious,” she added. “He’s confused.”

Evelyn crossed her arms. “Confused men still cause devastation.”

A pregnant pause settled across the miles. Marianne studied Kate’s face carefully. “What do *you* want?” she asked gently.

Kate didn’t hesitate. “I want my marriage back.”

The simplicity of her answer stilled them all.

“I can survive alone,” she continued. “I’m not afraid of independence. But I don’t want independence. I want to grow old with my husband. I want our marriage to remain a legacy of hope for our children.”

Claire’s expression softened. “Speaking of children. Do they know?”

Kate swallowed. “No.” The word felt heavy. “And I’m praying they won’t ever need to. Once one of them knows, they’ll all know. And I don’t want them choosing sides or worrying before we know for sure what’s going to happen with our marriage.”

Marianne nodded slowly. “That’s wise.”

Jesse’s face flashed in Kate’s mind. His little boy climbing into Grant’s lap during their last visit to California. Emma’s wedding plans spread across her dining table in Dallas. Nathan's late-night theological debates from the East Coast.

"They believe in what we built." Kate hesitated. "And I'm not ready to shatter that belief."

Claire leaned in toward her computer screen. "And if he won't fight with you?"

Kate inhaled slowly. "Then I will know I fought clean."

Evelyn crossed her arms thoughtfully. "You always did like doing things the hard way."

"It's not about hard," Kate replied. "It's about honoring God and giving Grant a chance to make things right."

Marianne's eyes glistened. "You still love him."

"Yes. That's the hardest part." Kate paused and blinked back her tears. "I think the enemy is hell bent on devouring what we built," she whispered.

Claire exhaled sharply. "Spiritual warfare?"

"Yes."

Evelyn tilted her head. "That and midlife stupidity."

Kate managed a faint smile. "Both."

Marianne leaned forward. "Has he agreed to counseling?"

"He says he needs time."

"Time is what makes roots grow deeper," Marianne said kindly. "Especially unhealthy ones."

Claire nodded. "You need to ask him to speak to your pastor. Immediately."

"Not as punishment," Marianne added. "As protection."

"For both of you," Evelyn said. "He needs someone who isn't you speaking truth into this."

Claire lifted her glass slightly. "If he won't talk to a pastor, that tells you something."

The remark carried unexpected weight and Kate inhaled slowly. "I'll ask him."

They talked another hour about boundaries, about prayer, about not losing herself while she fought. When the call ended, the kitchen felt less hollow. But the house was still quiet.

The next day, Marianne called privately from the villa's terrace. "Tell me the truth," she said. "When he says he feels invisible… does it surprise you?"

The question pierced deeper than accusation. Kate stepped onto her back patio in Austin, wrapping a cardigan around her shoulders.

"I don't know," she admitted. "We've both been busy. Comfortable. Maybe too comfortable."

Marianne nodded slowly. "When John got sick," she said, "we had no illusions left. Everything became urgent. Honest."

Kate's throat tightened.

Marianne paused before continuing. "How long are you willing to wait for him to decide?"

Kate blinked. "I don't know."

“A month? Six months? A year?” Marianne pressed. “Because drift feels less urgent to the one drifting.”

The question brought resolve. “I will fight for my marriage for as long as it takes,” Kate said emphatically.

“Yes,” Marianne replied. “But you cannot drag a man across the finish line.”

She paused, waiting for Kate to reply. She didn’t.

“At some point,” Marianne continued, “your children will sense something. You need to decide how long you will protect them from all this.”

Kate exhaled slowly. “I’m trying to give him space.”

“Space for repentance,” Marianne corrected. “Not space for indecision.”

That distinction settled deep.

“Have you asked him to meet with Pastor Michael yet?”

“I’ve mentioned it, but he didn’t respond.”

“Keep asking,” Marianne said. “Like we already discussed, he really needs a godly man who knows the truth and will pray for him and hold him accountable. That is, if Grant tells him the whole truth and submits to that guidance.”

Kate sighed. “That’s two challenges in one! Telling the whole truth *and* accepting accountability.” She paused. “I’m not even sure I know the whole truth.”

Marianne exhaled dramatically. “You know we’re praying for you every day. Even when we don’t know what to pray, the Holy Spirit does.”

Kate smiled faintly. "All your prayers are keeping me sane, Mare. I spend hours crying out to God, but sometimes I don't even know what to ask. You should see my journal. I write so fast I can barely read it afterward."

"Good," Marianne said warmly. "Keep writing. God hears our spoken and unspoken prayers."

Later, Claire called via Zoom, standing in Zia Rosa's kitchen with flour on her hands and fire in her eyes. "I'm kneading dough and thinking about you," she said bluntly. "So, listen carefully."

Kate braced.

"When my ex cheated, I stayed in denial too long," Claire said. "I kept hoping remorse would appear like divine mail."

Kate swallowed.

"It doesn't work that way," Claire continued. "Remorse and repentance are chosen. Accountability is chosen." She leaned closer. "Has he cut off contact with her?"

"He told her that he needed space. But honestly, I have no idea."

Claire narrowed her eyes. "Has he scheduled a meeting with Pastor Michael?"

Kate hesitated. "Not that I am aware of."

Claire nodded knowingly. "Structure matters. If he wants to rebuild, he has to dismantle the other relationship completely." She paused. "And Kate, if you give him a year and he never ends it, what then?"

The question sucked the air from the room. "I don't know," Kate whispered.

“You need to know,” Claire replied firmly. “Hope without a boundary becomes self-betrayal.”

Kate felt the sting and the love behind it.

“You’re not being demanding,” Claire said. “You’re honoring your covenant. But covenant requires two people.”

Kate knew Evelyn would call before the day ended. And she did.

“Can I ask something?” Evelyn said.

“Of course.”

“How long do you wait before waiting becomes fear?”

Kate paused. All three women had asked some version of the same questions. “I don’t want to give up too soon.”

“I’m not asking about giving up,” Evelyn said gently. “I’m asking about self-respect.”

The words lingered. “If he repents and you rebuild, maybe the waiting was worth it,” Evelyn continued. “But if he doesn’t … you could lose years.”

Kate stared at the trees swaying in her backyard.

“There’s no guarantee either way,” Evelyn clarified.

“That’s not comforting at all,” Kate replied.

“No, but it’s honest. I’ve waited my whole life for certainty,” Evelyn admitted. “Sometimes I wonder if I confused patience with passivity.”

Kate nodded slowly.

"Marriage is terrifying," Evelyn said.

"Yes," Kate agreed. "And beautiful. And costly."

For a few moments, they sat in silence, separated by continents, bound by loyalty. She said her goodbye to Ev and as she set her phone down, she felt God's presence, steady and strong settle her. A peace that surpassed all understanding.

Upstairs, Grant wrestled with his divided heart. Downstairs, she felt anchored. Not by certainty. But by truth. By the love of God that did not require denial. And by women across the ocean who loved her enough to ask the hard questions.

Restoration was possible. But only if truth was invited fully into the light. Tomorrow, she would ask Grant to call their pastor. And that, she knew, would reveal more than any argument ever could.

CHAPTER 14
A Line in the Sand

Austin, Texas

Conviction had been knocking on Grant's door for days, but obedience was another matter entirely.

He stood at the kitchen sink rinsing a coffee mug that didn't need rinsing. The water ran longer than necessary. He knew the question was coming … again. Kate had been patient all week, but the patience felt temporary, like the quiet before something unavoidable.

Call Pastor Michael.

The thought had followed him for days. It had started the night he opened his Bible to Psalm 51. Since then, it returned at inconvenient moments—driving to work, standing in the shower, lying awake in the guest room staring at the ceiling.

Grant knew what he needed to do. He needed to meet with his longtime pastor. He needed to say the truth out loud. But every time the conviction surfaced, something else rose immediately behind it.

Not yet. You're not ready. Once you involve the pastor, everything becomes real.

Grant tightened his grip on the mug. The battle inside him had intensified all week, conviction pulling one direction, resistance pulling the other. And the strange thing was, he knew exactly which voice was right. He just didn't want to obey it yet.

Behind him, he heard Kate step into the kitchen. He closed his eyes briefly. *She's going to ask again.* When her voice came, it was calm. "Grant."

He didn't turn around immediately. "Yeah?"

"I need you to call Pastor Michael."

Something inside him tightened. Not because she was wrong. But because hearing it from her suddenly felt like shameful pressure. An ultimatum. The defensive part of him rose instantly to meet it and his earlier conviction to do the right thing recoiled. He set down the mug mid-rinse.

"Kate…"

"No," she said firmly. "Don't you dare dismiss this before you've even heard it."

He turned then, leaning back against the counter. "I don't want to drag the church into this."

"You already have," she replied.

His jaw tightened. "This isn't a public spectacle."

"I didn't say it was."

"I don't need someone lecturing me," he added.

"This isn't about lecture," she said steadily. "It's about truth."

He exhaled sharply. "I told you I need time."

"Time for what?" she asked.

He looked away. "To think."

"You've been 'thinking' since before I left for Italy." She emphasized the word with air quotes.

The honesty in her words disarmed him. He rubbed the back of his neck. "Why does it have to be Michael? Why not just … us?"

"Because we are not neutral anymore," she answered. "And because you need someone who will not be confounded by your confusion."

That stung. He straightened. "You don't trust me to work through this?"

She stepped closer. "I don't trust the version of you that is divided."

That hung between them. He shifted tactics. "This feels dramatic."

"No," she said calmly. "It feels protective."

He ran a hand through his hair. "Katie, I said I love you."

"And I believe you, but I don't trust you."

"I'm here, aren't I?"

"Physically," she replied.

His eyes flashed. "That's unfair."

She held his gaze. "What's unfair is asking me to wait indefinitely while you nurture feelings for another woman."

He didn't argue. She softened slightly but did not retreat.

"If you care even a little about our marriage," she said, "you will call Pastor Michael. Not because I demand control, but because you … *we* need accountability for our marriage to have any chance for survival."

He didn't respond. She inhaled slowly. "I am not asking you to promise me forever tonight. I am asking you to take one step toward truth."

He stared at her. "And if I'm not ready?"

She swallowed. This was the line in the sand she had to draw … this very day. "Then I will know where I stand."

The air shifted.

"You're giving me an ultimatum?"

"I am giving you a boundary."

The distinction mattered.

"If you refuse counsel," she continued, "you are choosing isolation. And isolation is where affairs grow more serious."

He flinched. She held steady. "I will not share my husband," she said again. "And I will not pretend we can fix this alone."

A long pause. Then finally, he replied. "I'll call him."

He certainly did not sound enthusiastic or even convicted. But he was compliant, for now. Grant picked up his cell phone and left a message for Michael while Kate looked on and listened.

"There. Done. Happy?" he asked with a tad more sarcasm than he'd intended to convey.

Kate's face visibly fell. She turned and walked to *her* master bedroom.

CHAPTER 15
Partial Confession

Austin, Texas

The most dangerous lies are sometimes wrapped in enough truth to sound convincing.

Pastor Michael had shepherded Austin Community Church for nearly twenty-five years. He was not flashy. Not charismatic in the stage-light sense. His sermons were steady, verse by verse, patient, careful. He believed Scripture meant what it said, and he believed it healed what it confronted. Some called him old school. He preferred faithful. He was not legalistic. He did not weaponize truth. But he did not dilute it either.

Over the past decade, he had watched too many Christian marriages dissolve insidiously, not because of abuse or abandonment, but because couples grew weary of fighting for something that required dying to self.

The paperwork often moved faster than repentance. Apologies replaced accountability. "Irreconcilable differences" became a rationalized description for what Michael called the "unexamined drift" of mature marriages. Each one grieved him. Not because he believed in preserving appearances, but because he believed covenant was sacred. He wanted his parishioners to take it as seriously as God did.

He did not speak of it often, but there had been a year early in his ministry when his own marriage had trembled. Not because of infidelity. Because of pride and his long hours and emotional absence disguised as ministry. The quiet arrogance that can settle into a man who believes he is shepherding everyone else while oblivious that he's neglecting the soul sitting across the dinner table.

His wife, Sara, had once looked at him in their small kitchen, exhaustion lining her face and said, "You preach covenant better than you practice it." The words had undone him.

They sought counsel. They wept and they rebuilt … not publicly nor dramatically but deliberately. That season marked him. It stripped him of the illusion that spiritual leadership insulated a marriage from decay. It taught him how easily drift begins and how fiercely it must be resisted before it hardens into something else.

So, when Grant called asking for a meeting, Michael felt a familiar weight settle in his chest. This was not a distant church member requesting an appointment. This was Grant Bennett.

They had served side by side in leadership for years. Grant had once been a deacon. He was steady, respected, and dependable. The kind of man younger husbands observed with admiration. They had sat in elder meetings together, prayed over budgets and building campaigns, navigated staff transitions and community crises.

Their wives had become friends and the four of them had shared many dinners, unhurried evenings around restaurant tables, laughter spilling too loud. They had attended each other's Christmas parties, graduation celebrations, and anniversary gatherings where other long-time friends filled the room. Their children had grown up in the same church hallways, memorizing the same verses, sitting under the same youth pastors.

This was not merely a counseling appointment. Grant had not given details in his voicemail message, only that he "needed to talk." But something in his tone alerted Michael. A heaviness? A hesitation that felt unfamiliar.

Michael had shepherded long enough to recognize when a man was standing at the edge of something he did not fully want to name. He did not know what Grant was bringing into the room. But he sensed it would not be small.

A quiet tightening settled in his chest, the kind he had learned not to ignore. Not anxiety. Not assumption. A warning. He bowed his head.

"Lord," he prayed simply, "help me hear and see clearly. May my words be Your words."

Detour

Grant had not seen or talked to Lydia since his "drive" when Kate's distrust had as much as propelled him into Lydia's arms for relief. In his now warped sense of rationalization, he figured he may as well follow through on the accusations since he was already declared guilty.

Now, here he sat in the church parking lot preparing himself to see Michael face to face. At least he could honestly tell him he'd not talked to or seen Lydia for seven days. He'd sent her on a business trip around the state and told her he needed a week to "sort things out". She'd assumed he was trying to permanently end things with Kate.

Grant rehearsed his words twice in the car before walking inside. Confession sounds brave in theory. In practice, it feels like stepping barefoot across glass.

Pastor Michael's office smelled faintly of old books and coffee. He closed the door and turned to face Grant, his eyes holding contact until Grant looked away.

"What's going on?" he asked.

Grant sat down slowly. "I've crossed a line."

It sounded smaller than it was. Michael waited.

Grant exhaled. "With another woman."

There it was.

Michael's face didn't change. Not shock. Not judgment. Just gravity.

"How far?" he questioned.

Grant hesitated. "Kissing," he said.

The lie came easily. Too easily.

Michael held his gaze a fraction longer than necessary. Not confrontational. Not accusing. Just measuring.

"And what does Kate know?" he asked.

Grant shifted in his chair. "She knows there's … something. That I've been emotionally involved."

"Does she know about the physical line?"

Another pause. "No."

Michael nodded once. "You understand," he said carefully, "that partial truth is still deception."

The truth landed clear and firm, Grant's jaw tightened. "I'm trying to handle this without destroying her."

Michael's eyes did not leave his. "Sin does the destroying," he said. "Truth does the exposing."

Silence.

"So, bottom line, Grant. Is it over?" Michael's eyes were piercing as he asked.

Grant looked at his shoes. "I told her I needed space."

"That's not what I asked."

Grant looked up for a brief second and then back at the floor.

"Grant," Michael continued carefully, "are you trying to save your marriage, or are you trying to keep your options open?"

The question lodged in Grant's chest. "I love my wife," he answered immediately.

"And the other woman?"

Grant swallowed. "I care about her."

Michael nodded slowly. "Then you're divided."

That word again. Grant stared more intently at the carpet, memorizing its pattern.

Michael leaned forward slightly. "I've stood in that place before," he said. "Not with another woman but with a divided heart. And I can tell you from experience, division never heals on its own. It hardens."

Grant looked up, surprised. "I didn't plan this," he said. "It just … grew."

"Sin rarely announces itself," Michael replied. "It normalizes itself."

Grant flinched at the word sin. He preferred words like mistake. Confusion. Drift.

"You need to cut it off completely," Michael said.

Grant didn't respond.

"Completely," Michael repeated, looking him directly in the eye. Then he added, "And you need accountability."

Grant stiffened slightly.

Michael continued. "Not just advice. Structure. If you are serious about fighting for your marriage, you don't fight alone."

Grant's silence deepened.

"I'm offering myself," Michael said plainly. "You call me when you feel the pull. You meet with me weekly. You give me access to the truth, not the edited version."

Grant's eyes flickered.

"And you tell Kate everything," Michael added. "She cannot heal what she does not fully know."

That landed harder.

Michael softened his tone. "I am not here to shame you. I am here to help you protect what you will regret losing."

Grant swallowed. "I will end it," he said.

But even as he said it, his mind drifted elsewhere. To Lydia's laugh. To the way she leaned toward him. To the lightness he felt in her presence.

Michael watched him carefully. "Ending it begins with cutting off access," he said. "No meetings. No texts. No 'closure conversations.' Total severing."

Grant nodded. "I will."

After leaving the church office, he sat in his car longer than necessary. He had confessed. Sort of. He had not said everything.

He had not said that the line had been crossed weeks ago. That the kissing had not been isolated. That the sexual boundary had already fallen. He told himself the details didn't matter. He was trying to end it. Wasn't that enough?

His phone buzzed.

Lydia: **Can we talk?**

He closed his eyes. He should ignore it. He knew that.

Instead, he typed: **Where?**

CHAPTER 16
Slip Sliding Away

Austin, Texas

It had been over a week since Grant had been in contact with Lydia.

Seven days of total silence. Seven days of restraint. Seven days of convincing himself that space was progress. Not seeing her each day had helped, but not enough. She had stayed in his thoughts. Her smile. Her attractive figure. Her touch.

He wasn't sure why he had responded to her text so quickly after leaving Pastor Michael's office. He should have ignored it. Why had she texted at that exact moment when he was feeling so worthless? He told himself he answered because he needed closure. They needed closure.

It was only 4:00 in the afternoon. He could be back home before 6:30 p.m. and Kate would not even question his whereabouts. He reminded himself that he needed to end it cleanly with Lydia. He'd promised Michael.

He needed to prove to himself that he was capable of control. That was the story he carried with him as he pulled into the parking lot of her townhouse. He sat in the car a long while before cutting the engine and opening his door.

Lydia opened her front door before he had taken a step away from his car. She had been watching for him. That detail unsettled him and drew him in at the same time.

As he approached her, waiting in the doorway she smiled cautiously.

"You look tired," she said tenderly.

"I am."

He stepped inside. The air smelled faintly of something warm, vanilla, maybe. Familiar. Intentional.

"I've missed you so much, Grant."

Still standing in the entryway, she edged closer and took both his hands in hers. Not urgent or desperate, but steady and intentional. His shoulders dropped without permission.

"Come," she said, guiding him toward the living room. "Sit down. Let's talk."

He sat on the edge of the couch. She sat beside him, not touching at first. That restraint made the space between them louder. For a few minutes they spoke about neutral things. Work, a board decision, a mutual acquaintance. It was an ordinary conversation. Then she turned toward him fully.

"Did you tell your pastor about us?"

"Yes."

"How much?"

He hesitated. "That I crossed a line. That I was emotionally involved."

"And physically?" she pressed.

"I told him we kissed."

The word hung in the air.

Lydia studied him. "And?"

"He told me to tell Kate everything if I want our marriage to have a chance."

The word "chance" unsettled Lydia. "Do you want it to have a chance," she probed.

He looked at his shows but did not answer.

She inhaled slowly. "What are you doing, Grant? What do *you* want?"

Grant looked down at his hands. "I don't know."

There it was again. That pull between two realities. Two identities. Two versions of himself.

She moved closer, just enough that their knees brushed. "You don't have to decide tonight," she assured him. Relief flooded him at the suggestion. No ultimatum. No confrontation. Just suspension. That was the problem. He didn't want to decide. He wanted the pressure to stop. He wanted the ache to quiet.

She reached for his face then, her fingers brushing his jaw as if reacquainting herself with something she had nearly lost.

"Do you love her?" she asked.

"Yes." The answer came quickly.

"And me?"

He met her eyes. "I care about you."

Not equal. Not commitment. But enough for now. Quietness stretched between them, charged and fragile.

She leaned forward first. The kiss was not urgent. It was familiar. And that familiarity undid him. He should have pulled away. He thought about Pastor Michael's office. About the word *sin*. About Kate standing in their bedroom doorway, saying, *I will not share you.*

For half a second, clarity flared. Then it faded.

He kissed her back. At first it felt like comfort. Then it became confirmation. She drew him closer, and he did not resist. He told himself it was the last time. That he was already too far in. That ending something didn't require immediate coldness. That one more evening wouldn't change the trajectory.

Rationalization is quiet. It sounds reasonable. It whispers instead of shouts.

Later, as he lay awake beside her, staring at a ceiling he did not recognize, clarity pierced through the haze. The townhouse was silent except for her breathing. This was no longer drift. It was repetition. He had just confirmed the fracture. Not accident. Choice.

He rolled onto his side carefully, creating a sliver of space between them. His phone lay on the nightstand. Kate's name sat at the top of his recent calls. His chest tightened. He had told her they had only kissed. He had told Michael the same. Now the lie had multiplied. And with it, the cost.

He whispered into the darkness: "What am I doing?" But the more honest question pressed harder: *Who am I becoming?*

CHAPTER 17
A Woman Knows

Austin, Texas

Kate felt anxious all afternoon, knowing Grant was meeting with Michael.

Would he tell their pastor the whole truth? Perhaps even more than he'd told her? She imagined various scenarios. In one, Grant broke down and wept in Michael's office, conviction cracking him open, humility driving him straight home to her. In another, he remained measured and controlled, a man confessing a temporary misstep already resolved.

Which would it be? Or something even more dangerous? Her mind circled back to the question she had asked him days earlier.

"Have you slept with her?"

He had held her gaze and said, "No."

But something in his eyes had flickered. Not anger or defiance, but avoidance. Thirty-five years teaches you the difference.

She pressed her palms together. Her imagination tormented her. Laughter. Touch. Familiarity. With another woman.

"Lord," she whispered, "guard my mind."

Still, her spirit felt unsettled. Not hysterical, but intuitive. She poured a small glass of white wine, the one she and Grant had shared on countless evenings on the deck and stared at the clock. Five thirty p.m. If the meeting ended on time, he would be home by six.

By seven, unease crept in. By eight, her chest felt tight. She considered calling. She didn't.

Instead, she went upstairs, opened her laptop, and turned on an old sitcom, something harmless and familiar. She didn't laugh. She drifted in and out of shallow sleep.

Then suddenly she jolted upright. Her room was totally dark. She reached for her phone. It was 9:02 p.m. The house was still. Had she missed him coming in? No. She would have heard. Downstairs, headlights cut briefly across the wall. Her stomach dropped.

Grant sat in his car for a full minute before turning off the engine. The house looked the same, warm and welcoming with a well-lit porch. It had always felt so comforting. Now, it taunted him.

He ran through the version of the evening he had constructed in his head. Michael had been firm. Lydia had been soft. He felt split down the middle. He touched his mouth unconsciously and stepped out of the car.

When he opened the front door, the house smelled like lemon cleaner and something faintly floral like Kate's lotion. He closed the door as quietly as he could hoping Kate was already in her room.

She was not. She was sitting at the kitchen table in her nightgown. Lights low. Hands folded. She did not stand. She did not greet him. She had already decided that she would not speak first.

He set his keys down too carefully. "Hey," he drew out the word softly with a hint of surprise as his eyes adjusted to the darkened room.

She looked up. "You met with Michael?"

"Yes."

"How did it go?"

"Good."

The word sounded hollow even to him.

She studied him. "Have you seen her again?"

The question landed without drama. A pause. "Yes."

The honesty stunned her. "And?"

He exhaled. "Kate..."

"Just answer."

He swallowed. "I care about her."

There it was again. Something inside her tilted. She stood and took one step toward him, looking directly into his eyes. "Did you … sleep with her?" she asked, her voice caught mid-question.

He met her gaze. The image of Lydia's townhouse ceiling flashed in his mind.

"No." The lie came smoother this time.

Her stomach tightened. Something in the set of his jaw did not align with the word. "You're sure?" she pressed.

"Yes."

Silence stretched between them. "Then why do I feel like I'm standing on sand?" she asked.

His shoulders stiffened. "Because you don't trust me."

The deflection surprised even him.

"I'm trying to," she said.

"You're interrogating me."

Her chin lifted slightly. "I'm asking direct questions."

There it was. Not yelling. Just an edge she had rarely shown him, a shift in her demeanor he had never seen directed at him until his confession.

"You're assuming the worst," he replied.

She studied him carefully. "Are you saying I shouldn't?"

He dragged a hand through his hair. "I'm saying this didn't happen in a vacuum."

The sentence dropped like a stone.

Her breath stalled. "What does *that* mean?"

He hesitated and then leaned into the rationalization he'd been building since leaving Lydia's driveway. "We've drifted," he said. "You've been busy. Independent. You don't need me the way you used to."

The words struck deeper than any confession.

"I didn't realize needing you was a requirement for faithfulness," she said sarcastically.

"That's not what I meant."

"Then what did you mean?"

He struggled. "I felt secondary in my own home."

Secondary. Thirty-five years. Children. Grief. Intimacy. Shared beds. Shared prayers. Secondary?

Her composure cracked. "I have stood beside you through everything," she said, her voice trembling. "Through layoffs. Through your father's decline. Through every leadership crisis. I have prayed for you. Defended you. Loved you."

"I know."

"Do you?"

He broke eye contact. And in that moment, something inside her gave way. Not rage. Collapse. She sank back into the kitchen chair.

"I thought we were safe," she whispered.

The tears came steadily. She could no longer hold them back and did not even try. "I thought we were safe," she repeated, as if to herself.

Her voice sounded younger, like a child discovering something disturbing for the first time. Grant stood frozen. He had expected anger. He had prepared for anger. He had not prepared for this.

She wiped her cheeks. "I feel like a little girl whose parents are divorcing," she said. "Like the ground shifted without warning."

He stepped toward he and then stopped. He didn't know if he had the right.

"I don't want independence," she whispered. "I want you."

Guilt surged in Grant's chest and beneath it, fear. *If she is this hurt, then I am the villain.* He did not want to be the villain. So, his mind reached again for shared responsibility.

"We both contributed," he said.

His words hit her like shattering glass.

She looked up slowly. "Contributed?"

He heard it. The distortion. But it was too late.

She stood. "I will own anything I did wrong," she raised her voice slightly. "But I will *not* own your betrayal."

Her strength returned—steady and controlled. She turned, but at the doorway, paused. "Please," she said, "don't rewrite our history to make this easier for yourself."

Down the hall, her door closed with a bang, and he could hear the door locking. Grant remained in the kitchen. The walls of his family home felt like they were closing in on him. He had given in to Lydia's touch because he wanted a moment of relief. Instead, his guilt had deepened.

Now, the truth formed without euphemism: He was not drifting from his wife. He was dismantling his life, piece by piece.

CHAPTER 18
The Lies He Believes

Austin, Texas

Kate did not sleep.

She lay still in the dark, staring at the ceiling, replaying every word from the night before.

We both contributed.

The sentence pulsed like a bruise. By dawn, something inside her had shifted into a sense of resolve.

When she heard Grant moving in the kitchen, she rose, tied her robe tightly, and walked downstairs. He stood at the counter, coffee untouched, staring at nothing. He looked up when she entered, and they held each other's gaze longer than usual.

"I need the truth," she said.

No accusation. No raised voice.

"I told you the truth."

She shook her head slowly. "No. You told me a version that protects you."

He stiffened. "You think I'm lying?"

"I think you are minimizing."

The silence was torture, each waiting for the other to speak first.

"Grant," she continued, her voice steady, "I may have been blindsided by this affair, but I am not foolish. You are not this emotionally entangled with another woman without crossing physical lines."

Her words were delivered without drama, but the heat rose in his chest.

"You don't know that."

"I know you," she looked intently into his eyes. "Thirty-five years. I know when something doesn't align."

He looked away. "That's insulting."

"No," she snapped. "It's intuitive."

His jaw tightened. "You're assuming the worst."

"I am asking you to stop editing."

He felt cornered. He was trapped between confession and exposure. His mind raced, building a defense. *She doesn't trust me. She's already decided I'm guilty. Why confess if I'm condemned anyway?*

"Maybe you just need someone to blame," he retorted.

The accusation startled even him.

Kate blinked and her eyes widened. "Blame?"

"You've been distant for years," he continued, the rationalization rising. "Independent. You don't need me. This didn't happen in isolation."

She stood very still. "Are you saying I drove you to another woman?"

"I'm saying we both drifted." The lie began to feel easier—shared responsibility was much lighter than full ownership.

A floorboard creaked as the house adjusted to morning. Something else shifted inside him, a kind of palpable spiritual tremor. He had prayed the night before. Kneeling beside the bed in the guest room, he had whispered into the darkness: "God, which one?"

The audacity of it barely registered at the time—choosing between women as if covenant were optional, as if vows were negotiable, as if God were a consultant in desire. He had waited for thunder. For conviction. For clarity. Instead, there had been silence. And in that silence, his own voice grew louder. *You deserve to be happy. You deserve to feel seen. This isn't all your fault.* By morning, those thoughts felt reasonable.

Kate's voice pulled him back. "Grant," she said insistently, "I need full disclosure. If there is more, say it now. Don't let me build forgiveness on half-truth."

Her eyes were clear. Steady. He could end it right there. Confess fully and potentially begin rebuilding. Instead, something darker rose in him, pride mixed with fear. If he confessed now, he would be the bad guy … the sinner … the marriage wrecker. If he held his ground, maybe she would soften. Maybe she would doubt herself.

"I told you everything," he said.

The lie landed cleanly. Kate's face didn't contort. It simply changed like a door closing silently. "I see," she said.

The calm unsettled him. "I can't live with constant interrogation," he continued, pressing forward. "I can't breathe under constant suspicion."

She held his gaze. "You are not suffocating. You are feeling conviction. Stop running from it. The enemy is feeding you lies. He wants to destroy us."

As she spoke, Grant felt his heart locking down, shutting Kate out. He had convinced himself, or allowed himself to be convinced, that they shared responsibility for their marital crisis. To believe otherwise would force him to take it all. He needed to be strong, like his father had taught him. Kate needed to admit her failures too.

"I think we need space," he said too quickly, as if the words had been waiting.

She inhaled slowly. "You mean separation."

"For now."

"For how long?"

"I don't know."

He grabbed his keys from the counter, momentum carrying him now.

"Where will you go?" she asked.

"I need time."

"Where?"

He didn't answer. Because answering would mean naming her. He walked past her toward the hallway. At the door, he paused as if waiting for her to stop him. She didn't.

"Grant," she said, "running will not make this less true."

He didn't turn around. The door closed, and their home now housed only one lonely occupant.

Two Days Later

Grant had been gone forty-eight hours. He texted occasionally.

I need space. Don't worry. I'm thinking.

Thinking where? Kate had not asked again. She wasn't sure she wanted the answer.

Later that morning, Claire called from the terrace at Villa Santoro. "Where is he staying?" she asked bluntly.

"He didn't say."

"You didn't ask?"

"I did. He deflected."

Claire exhaled sharply into the phone. "Kate."

"What?"

"You both have iPhones."

Kate blinked. "So?"

"Find My. The app."

The words hung in the air.

"That's for lost devices, right?" Kate asked.

"Yes, but it's also for shared locations."

Kate felt a flicker of recognition. Two years earlier, their youngest son, Nathan, had insisted on setting up family location sharing.

"For safety," he'd said. "If someone gets in an accident, you'll know."

She had rolled her eyes at the time.

"Can you really see exactly where someone is?" she asked now.

"If he hasn't turned it off," Claire said calmly.

"Claire, that feels…"

"Like what? Spying?"

Kate hesitated. "I don't want to become that woman."

Claire's voice softened. "You're not stalking him. You're grounding yourself in truth."

That distinction settled something in her.

Kate looked down at her phone. Her hands trembled slightly as she opened the app. *Find My.* She tapped "People."

Grant's name appeared. Active.

Her breath stalled as she pressed it, and a map expanded slowly. A small blue circle pulsed over downtown Austin. His office. Relief flooded her.

"There," she sighed. "He's at work."

"Check again later," Claire encouraged her.

CHAPTER 19
Running into the Fire

Austin, Texas

The affair had taught Lydia to measure Grant's feelings by his presence, his touch, and his choices, and lately all three seemed to be pointing in her direction.

After Monday night, Lydia no longer felt uncertain about her relationship with Grant. He had left his pastor's office and driven to her townhouse after Kate had demanded he meet Michael. He did not arrive accidentally or in confusion and was not resisting temptation.

They had been sexually intimate again. Men repairing marriages do not return to other women's beds. Whatever language he used with his wife, his body had chosen Lydia. And she was finished pretending that didn't mean something.

Yes, he had gone home later that same night. Lydia understood that he needed to confront Kate with the truth of his feelings, but she was confident that he was moving toward closure. She sensed he would be leaving Kate permanently sooner than later.

Still following up on multiple donor opportunities for the foundation, Lydia had not been in the office for almost two weeks, so she had not seen Grant during work hours. On Tuesday evening, she texted him as she concluded her last meeting of the day.

Dinner? Somewhere quiet?

He responded within minutes.

Okay.

They met in a small town twenty minutes outside Austin, far enough to feel removed, close enough to feel intentional. Grant looked exhausted.

"You look worn out," she said as they sat down.

"I am."

"From what?"

He exhaled slowly. "From the fallout."

She waited.

He stared at the table for a moment before speaking again. "I told Kate we need to separate for a while."

Lydia felt her pulse shift, but her expression remained steady. "You did?"

"Yes."

"How did she take that?"

"She thinks I'm running."

"Are you?"

"She wouldn't stop interrogating me," he continued, frustration creeping in. "Every answer wasn't enough. Every word was dissected."

The framing was subtle. He was the exhausted one. Kate, the relentless one.

"And you needed space," Lydia added.

"Yes."

"How much space?"

He hesitated and then added, almost defensively, "I packed a small suitcase. It's in my trunk."

The sentence landed between them, heavier than he intended. He had not planned to say it. But once spoken, it clarified something: he was prepared.

Lydia absorbed that slowly and clarified. "You came here tonight with your suitcase in your car:"

He shifted. "I didn't know where I'd land."

The honesty was rawer than he meant it to be. For a few seconds, neither of them spoke. She could feel the moment pivoting. He had not come to dinner undecided. He had come mid-transition.

"You don't have to go back there tonight," she said finally.

He looked up.

"My townhouse," she clarified. "You know I have a guest room."

She delivered it calmly with no urgency or seduction. Just an option. "You said you needed space. I'm offering you space."

He stared at her.

"You don't have to share my bed," she added. "Stay in the guest room. Clear your head."

The offer sounded generous and reasonable. He imagined driving home and the weight of confrontation waiting inside. Then he imagined Lydia's townhouse. Soft lighting. No interrogation and no moral inventory.

"I don't want to complicate things more," he replied.

"It's already complicated," she replied. "You're living between two realities." She leaned slightly closer. "You don't need to keep proving your remorse to me."

The words struck more deeply than he expected because that was exactly what he had been doing. He was trying to demonstrate enough sorrow to separate himself from the man who had caused so much damage.

"You need a few days to decompress," she continued. "You don't have to decide everything this week."

The pressure was subtle, but real. He ran a hand over his face. "My suitcase is in the trunk," he said again, almost to himself. Then, after a beat, "Okay."

Lydia did not smile, but something inside her settled.

That Night

Lydia moved carefully without any outward celebration or show of triumph. She poured wine, turned on low lamps, and asked nothing about Pastor Michael or Kate. Instead, she asked about the foundation, about his father's expectations, about the weight of leadership. And she let him talk. She could feel him beginning to unwind.

"I don't want to be the villain," he admitted.

"You're not," she answered immediately.

The affirmation slid into the space his conscience had left open.

Later, she stood in the doorway of the guest room. "You'll be okay in here?"

He nodded.

She lingered just long enough. “You don’t have to carry everything alone,” she whispered.

He reached for her before he fully decided to. The line blurred quickly. The wine had lowered his boundaries, and her familiar touch, combined with the ache of being understood, drew him in. He told himself it was comfort. He told himself he was already too far in for restraint to matter. He told himself the separation had begun anyway.

The guest room went unused.

Much later, he lay beside her, staring into darkness that did not belong to him. Guilt returned, heavier now as reality settled in. He had asked for a separation and packed his things without further discussion. Then he had chosen Lydia, not time alone to seek clarity.

Outside, the street was quiet. Inside, Lydia lay close against him, already imagining something steadier than secrecy. She did not feel conflicted. She felt certain, not because she had won, but because he had moved.

He hadn’t just said he needed space. He had needed her. In the dim light, she allowed herself a small, dangerous thought: *He’s already halfway gone. All he needs now is permission to finish.*

She traced her fingers lightly along his shoulder. “Rest,” she whispered.

He closed his eyes in exhaustion and slept for three hours.

CHAPTER 20
Find My Husband

Austin, Texas

There is a strange mercy in certainty, even when certainty hurts.

It was Tuesday evening and once again and Kate wished the time difference between Texas and Italy did not exist.

At 8:42 p.m., she closed the Find My app and set her phone face down on the kitchen table. By 9:00, she had reopened it. The blue dot had not moved. At 10:00, it was still there.

Geography does not argue. It simply confirms.

Two years earlier, before any of this had surfaced, Grant had hosted a small donor reception at Lydia's townhouse. It was the one and only time Kate had met her. That memory had surfaced again the night Grant called with his midnight confession while she was in Monopoli.

She remembered the tight row of brick townhomes. The iron gate at the entrance. The small balcony above the front door. And the street name. She and Grant had laughed at who would ever name a place *Bumblebee Court*?

Now the blinking blue dot pulsed directly over that same street. It was not moving. It was absolutely steady.

"He's there," she whispered into the empty kitchen.

She did not call or text her friends. It was only 5:00 a.m. in Puglia. Instead, she sat in the quiet house, listening to the hum of the refrigerator and the low ticking of the hallway clock.

Thirty-five years of marriage and she now knew exactly where her husband was sleeping. Not hypothetically. Not emotionally. Precisely. She went upstairs around midnight but did not undress. She lay on top of the covers, staring into the dark. By 5:00 a.m., she gave up. She reached for her phone and typed into the group text:

Emergency. I need you. Please Zoom as soon as you can.

It would be nearly noon in Italy. Claire responded immediately.

Setting up our laptops now.

Kate exhaled slowly.

Zoom Meeting

The screen flickered to life and Claire appeared first, sunlight flooding the whitewashed walls behind her. Marianne leaned into the frame beside her. Evelyn entered last on her own laptop, adjusting her glasses, scanning Kate's face immediately.

"What happened?" Claire asked, skipping humor entirely.

Kate swallowed. "I know where he is."

The women's eyebrows rose and mouths gaped open in sync across Kate's screen. It would have been funny given different circumstances.

"How?" Marianne questioned.

Kate explained the Find My app, the blinking dot, the exact street. The townhouse she had once stood inside with a paper plate and polite laughter. She spoke evenly. Too evenly.

"He's still there," she finished.

Claire closed her eyes briefly. "Are you sure?"

"Yes."

"Did you confront him?"

"No."

"Why?"

Kate hesitated. "Because confirmation changes something," she said. "And I wanted to sit with it before I spoke. And I needed to talk to you."

Evelyn's voice sharpened slightly. "Clearly, he's moved from what he keeps calling drift to decision."

Kate nodded. "I thought he needed space," she said. "But space doesn't have an address."

The sentence lingered.

Claire stood abruptly and stepped out of frame before returning. "Pack a bag."

Kate blinked. "What?"

"Get on a plane. Come back here." Claire leaned toward the screen. "You need distance from him. And you need us. Not a phone. Not text messages. Us."

Kate shook her head slightly. "I can't just leave."

"Yes, you can."

"Claire …" Kate began to respond before Claire interrupted her abruptly.

"Listen to me," she said firmly. "You are sitting in a house that now feels contaminated by betrayal. You are alone. He is not. That imbalance matters."

Marianne nodded slowly. "You will find more clarity with distance."

"And safety in sisterhood," Evelyn added.

Kate stared at the screen. "You want me to run away?"

"No," Claire said immediately. "I want you to reposition."

The word landed carefully.

"You do not chase a man who has already chosen," Claire continued. "You step back and let him feel the weight of that choice."

Tears gathered in Kate's eyes. "This is my home."

"And it will still be there," Claire said more gently. "But right now, you need steady ground. Come to Puglia. Sit at Zia Rosa's table. Walk by the sea. Let your nervous system breathe."

Marianne spoke carefully. "Before you book anything, meet with Pastor Michael."

Kate looked up. "Why?"

"So, you know in your spirit you're not reacting," Marianne replied. "Let him speak into it. Let him confirm that this is wisdom and not avoidance."

Evelyn nodded. "If you leave without counsel, you'll question yourself the entire flight."

Claire exhaled but didn't argue. "Fine. See Michael. But don't let that turn into weeks of analysis."

Marianne leaned in with a gentle smile. "This isn't running. It's retreating with intention."

Kate closed her eyes briefly. "I don't want to abandon the battlefield."

"You're not," Marianne said. "You're regrouping."

Claire added, "And if Michael tells you to stay, you stay. But if he confirms space is healthy, you board that plane without guilt."

Looking into each of her friends' kind eyes, though an ocean away, Kate felt steadier and supported. She wiped a stray tear away with the back of her hand and blew her nose in a tissue.

"You are *not* abandoning him," Marianne said.

"And you are *not* foolish," Evelyn added.

"And you are *not* powerless," Claire finished.

Kate nodded slowly. "I'll call Michael this morning. And then I'll decide." But somewhere deep inside, she already knew the decision was forming.

The Zoom call ended. The house was quiet again. She was once again alone, while across the city, her husband had been going to sleep and waking up in another woman's bed.

Kate opened her laptop and typed: *Flights to Bari.* Her hand trembled slightly. This time, the distance from Grant would be intentional. But before she could leave, she needed to follow her friends' advice.

CHAPTER 21
Permission to Breathe

Austin, Texas

The church office felt different when you entered it wounded.

Kate had walked these halls for decades. She planned retreats, mentored younger women, organized prayer teams, and hosted bridal and baby showers in the fellowship hall. Today, she entered as someone undone.

Pastor Michael stood when she stepped into his office. His expression shifted immediately.

"Kate."

She closed the door behind her and remained standing for a moment, steadying herself. She was emotionally unable to offer her usual warm greeting when seeing Michael for the first time in over two weeks and blurted out before even taking a seat,

"You didn't get the whole story from Grant."

Michael didn't defend him. He simply gestured for her to sit. "Tell me what you know."

"I think he told you they'd only kissed. It took him forever to admit that to me."

Michael nodded once. "Yes."

"Well, that was a lie. It's gone much further." She paused and took a deep breath willing herself to continue. "Now, he's staying at her townhouse. He said he needed space. He didn't say where. I confirmed it."

Michael absorbed that without visible reaction. "Do you know how long the physical relationship has been happening?" he asked carefully.

"No," she said honestly. "But I know this: You don't entangle your heart like that overnight."

She swallowed. "When I was in Italy, something in him had already shifted. He was divided before he ever confessed."

Michael nodded slightly.

"And since I've been home, he's been rewriting the narrative. Suggesting drift. Shared responsibility." She exhaled slowly. "He is not just confused. He is defending himself."

Michael's jaw tightened subtly.

"He minimized everything," she said. "From the beginning."

That was the wound. Not only betrayal, but more deception layered on top of it.

Michael leaned back slowly. "Yes, he told me there was only kissing. It felt somewhat contained."

Kate nodded once. "I had hoped it was contained, too." She folded her hands in her lap. "I don't know the full timeline. But I know that his heart was already compromised. And he gaslit me from the moment I got home and started asking specific questions."

Gaslit. The word sat heavy but accurate. Michael did not correct it. "And he is actually living with her now?" he asked.

"Yes."

Michael took a deep breath and sighed audibly. "I am so sorry."

She nodded. “I need to ask you something important.”

“Ask.”

“Do I have biblical grounds to step away?”

The room quieted. Michael did not answer quickly. “Yes,” he said. “Sexual unfaithfulness is explicitly addressed in Scripture.”

She nodded. “I know that.”

He studied her. “But that’s not what you’re asking.”

“No.” Her voice trembled slightly. “I don’t want permission, but I do want clarity on what it means for me stay committed.”

Michael leaned forward. “Restoration first requires repentance from Grant.”

“I know.”

“And repentance cannot be forced.”

“I know that too.”

“What are you considering?” he asked.

“Leaving town.”

His brow lifted slightly.

“Not leaving the marriage,” she clarified. “Leaving the proximity.”

She explained the villa, the women, the time difference, the impossibility of sitting in the same city while her husband slept in another woman’s bed.

"I cannot hover here," she cried. "Waiting, monitoring, and checking his location on my app."

Michael's expression softened. "You discovered his location?"

"Yes."

He nodded slowly. "Kate, you are a wise, godly woman."

That nearly undid her. "But I feel foolish," she admitted.

"You trusted your husband. That is not foolishness. That is covenant."

She swallowed hard. "If I leave the country for a season," she asked, "am I running?"

Michael shook his head. "No, not in this instance." He paused. "You are creating space for truth to surface."

She exhaled slowly. "I don't want to abandon the battlefield."

"You are not abandoning it," he said. "You are stepping out of the fog."

That resonated.

"Let him feel your absence," Michael continued. "Not as punishment. As consequence."

She nodded.

"Faithfulness does not mean proximity," he added. "You are free to pursue peace while he wrestles with conviction."

She looked down at her hands. "I cannot sit in that house and pretend this is temporary. He is not drifting anymore. He is choosing."

“Yes,” Michael said.

The honesty steadied her. “And if distance finalizes it?” she asked.

“Then you will know you did not coerce repentance. You invited it.”

Tears gathered and pooled in her eyes. “I feel like I’m standing in the doorway of something I never imagined.”

“You are,” he replied gently.

She wiped her cheeks. “I don’t know if leaving will wake him up.”

“It may not,” he answered honestly.

“And if it doesn’t?”

“Then you will know you honored both God and youself.”

A peaceful quiet settled in the office.

“I would like to pray for you both,” Michael tilted his head like it was a question.

She nodded.

He came around the desk, not as authority, but as a shepherd, and placed a steady hand lightly on her shoulder.

“Father, You are not surprised by this moment. You see covenant. You see fracture. You see what is hidden and what is hardened.

“Lord, I lift up Grant to you, not in condemnation, but in truth. Where his heart is divided, bring clarity. Where pride has built defense, bring humility. Where deception feels easier than confession, bring holy discomfort.

"Holy Spirit, do what no spouse, no pastor, no consequence can do. Bring conviction that pierces deeper than shame, not the kind that drives him further into hiding, but the kind that calls him home.

"And guard Kate's heart. Keep bitterness from rooting. Keep self-blame from distorting. Remind her that betrayal is not proof of her failure. Anchor her identity in you, not in Grant's choices.

"Restore what can be restored. Redeem what can be redeemed. But above all, let truth prevail.

"And if restoration comes, let it come through genuine repentance, not fear, not convenience, not loneliness, but surrender. Amen."

The room felt still. Sacred. Michael stepped back. Kate opened her eyes slowly.

"God never overrides a person's free will," he said.

She nodded. "I know."

"Conviction can come. Consequences can surface. The Spirit can press. But only Grant can choose whether he faces truth fully, sees his sin without minimizing it, repents authentically, and surrenders."

Wrapping her arms tightly around herself and rocking forward and back, Kate swallowed down her tears and looked intently at Michael trying to absorb his wisdom.

"That choice may not happen quickly."

She exhaled. "And it may not happen at all," she cried.

"That is possible," he answered honestly. "Repentance is voluntary. If restoration comes it will be because he chose it, not because you managed it."

A faint, weary smile touched her lips. "I've been trying to out-pray his will."

Michael's expression softened. "You cannot out-pray free will."

That truth landed firmly.

"But you can entrust him to God," he added. "And entrusting is not the same as controlling."

She inhaled deeply. "I will leave space for God to work."

Michael nodded. "And while God works on him, He will sustain you."

She stood slowly. The weight had not lifted, but it had shifted. For the first time since the blinking blue dot appeared on her screen, Kate felt something more than just the pain of abandonment. She felt God's perfect love and protection delivered through the wisdom and compassion of her pastor.

Now, she could return to Puglia to wait on God as she entrusted Grant into His perfect care.

PART THREE

Season of Surrender

CHAPTER 22
Arrivederci

Austin, Texas

Grant was in the kitchen when Kate told him.

He had returned mid-afternoon to gather mail and more of his clothes. A stack of unopened envelopes sat on the counter. He had just noticed her wedding ring resting in a small ramekin by the sink when he heard the patio door open.

Wiping a stray hair away with the back of her hand, Kate entered the kitchen. She had been watering her potted plants, trying to distract herself from the weight of what she needed to tell Grant.

"Oh, you're here," she said, surprise in her voice.

She noticed immediately that he looked weary and unsettled. She resisted the urge to interpret her observation.

"I'm glad you came by. I was going to call you," she said calmly.

He glanced up, confused. "Really? Why?"

"I'll be leaving Austin for a while."

His brow furrowed. "What? What do you mean you're leaving? To where?"

"I'm going back to Puglia."

Her words settled heavily between them.

"For how long?"

"At least three months."

His face shifted. "Three months?"

"Yes."

She held his gaze. "I've already told the hospital I won't be available for per diem shifts for the foreseeable future."

He stared at her. "That's extreme."

"No," she said. "Living with another woman is extreme."

He flinched. How did she know? Had someone seen them? Had she followed him? Or was it simply instinct? He chose not to ask.

"I need distance," she continued. "Not to punish you. To survive this."

He ran a hand along his jaw rubbing the scruff of his unusually unshaved face. "So, you're just leaving?"

"I'm stepping away."

"Or running away?"

The words hung between them.

"Running? Really?" she quipped.

"Yes. You're leaving the country while I'm trying to figure things out."

She looked at him. Really looked at him. "You left our marriage before I booked a flight." She held his gaze until he looked away. "I'm not closing the door," she continued steadily. "I'm closing access."

His brow furrowed. “What does that even mean?”

“It means no contact for three months. Unless there is a genuine family emergency.”

His posture stiffened. “That’s unreasonable.”

“It’s necessary.”

Her voice did not rise. “I cannot heal while you are auditioning two lives,” she said, holding his gaze.

The sentence hit. He shifted defensively. “You’re the one choosing to escape.”

She shook her head slowly. “No. I’m refusing to hover.”

He didn’t fully understand the distinction, but he felt its weight. If she left, if she truly detached, he would no longer have her presence to steady him or to absorb part of the blame.

“I’ll pray,” she continued. “I’ll seek peace. But I will not monitor you or your conscience.”

He swallowed. “What if I need you? For the children or our grandchild?”

“You didn’t need me these past weeks,” she muttered. “And our children are grown. They’re self-sufficient.”

The truth was not loud, but it was harsh. He grasped for leverage. “What do you think Michael would say about you leaving like this?” he asked quickly.

The question hung in the air.

Kate’s lips curved just slightly. Not in warmth. “Funny you should ask.”

Something shifted in his stomach.

"I met with him yesterday," she said evenly.

His expression changed. "You what?"

"Yes."

"And?"

"And I told him the truth."

He felt the ground tilt. "What truth?"

"All of what I know," she clarified. "Including that you told him the two of you had 'only kissed.'"

He stared at her blankly and didn't blink.

"I also told him that when a man is this emotionally and physically entangled, it rarely ends with kissing."

Her words were precise. "I don't know exactly when it crossed that line," she continued. "Whether it began while I was in Italy or before. But I do know this—you've been gaslighting me from the moment I returned home."

He opened his mouth and closed it again.

"I will let you clarify details with Michael during your next accountability session."

The word *accountability* felt like exposure. Heat crawled up his neck.

"You had no right—" he began.

“I had every right,” she barked back “You forfeited secrecy when you forfeited fidelity.”

The room went still. For a moment, something flickered in him—anger, yes—but beneath it, shame. He had minimized and now the minimization was seen.

He paced once across the kitchen. “I told you I’d cut it off.”

“You told me many things.”

That one landed.

“I can meet with Michael again,” he said quickly. “I will. I’ll call him. I’ll … um … we’ll talk.”

The promise sounded rushed. Desperate. “I mean it,” he added. “I’ll reconnect with him today. I don’t want this to spiral.”

Spiral. As if it were happening to him.

Kate watched him carefully. “I hope you do,” she retorted. “But I will not stay here waiting to see if you follow through.”

Her tone softened slightly. “I am not divorcing you.”

Relief flickered in his eyes.

“But I am not living in limbo.”

The relief vanished.

“If you want this marriage,” she continued, “you will have to choose it. Fully and without conditions. Without rewriting history to make your conscience cleaner.”

He felt exposed again. “I never said I was leaving you. I just asked for time apart.”

"You packed a suitcase and are staying at Lydia's."

The words dropped like a verdict. He froze. She had known. Of course she had.

He felt cornered. "I just needed space."

"You have it. Three months."

The boundary stood between them like a line drawn in sand. She moved toward the door. "I am not punishing you," she said. "I am protecting what's left of me."

She paused. "If you choose repentance, it will not be because I hovered. It will be because you saw clearly."

He stepped forward instinctively. "Katie …"

She looked at him one last time. "Don't call me that. I love you, but I will not be a doormat."

The words were steady. Unweaponized. Unmanipulated. "And that is why I am leaving."

She turned and walked down the hall to her bedroom and disappeared behind the door. Grant stood in the kitchen alone and realized this house, their home, did not feel like something he was escaping. It felt like something he was losing.

Now, it was not the guilt clawing at his heart. It was fear. Somewhere deep inside, a quieter, more dangerous realization surfaced: He might not be able to control how this would end.

CHAPTER 23
Full Court Press

Austin, Texas—Bumblebee Court

Lydia received the news with visible relief.

“She’s leaving?” she repeated, searching his face.

“For three months,” Grant said.

“For three months?” she echoed again, slower this time.

“Yes.”

She leaned back against her kitchen counter, arms folding loosely, not defensive, but contemplative. “That tells you something.”

He frowned. “What? What exactly do you think it tells me?”

“She’s choosing distance instead of fighting.”

He bristled. “She fought. She abandoned her long-planned girl trip and came back to fight.”

Lydia shook her head side to side in disagreement. “And now she’s leaving the country and running to her girlfriends.”

He remembered telling Kate that her plan sounded extreme. The word he’d wanted to use was abandonment, but he realized how that would sound to her given the circumstances.

“I think she just wants some sense of control in all this, so she’s set a boundary,” he muttered.

“She set a timeline,” Lydia corrected. “That’s different.”

He didn't respond.

Lydia moved closer, her tone gentler now. She placed both her open hands directly on his chest. "Grant, sometimes when someone steps away like that, it's because they already know it's over."

He didn't want that to be true. But it felt easier than admitting the alternative, that Kate was giving him sacred space to see clearly and decide without pressure from her. He knew her well and imagined she was asking God to be the One exerting all the pressure.

"You can't live suspended forever," Lydia continued. "She made a move." Then, more carefully she added, "If she really believed this marriage could be restored, would she disappear?"

The suggestion slipped in before he could filter it. *Disappear.* Hadn't Kate grown more independent over the years? More self-contained? Strong enough not to need him?

"She said she's not divorcing me," he said weakly.

"But she's leaving," Lydia replied.

Silence settled over the townhouse. Grant stared at the hardwood floor.

"She met with Michael," he said finally.

Lydia's eyes sharpened. "She did?"

"She told him I minimized things."

"Did you?" Lydia asked.

He hesitated. "I didn't tell him everything."

Lydia exhaled slowly, almost sympathetically. "So, she went to your pastor behind your back."

He stiffened. "I can't fault her for that. He's her pastor as well."

"Maybe," Lydia conceded. "But that's not unity, Grant. That's escalation."

Escalation. Another reframing. He hadn't thought of it that way. "She told me to reconnect with him," he added.

"And will you?"

"I said I would."

"Do you want to?"

He hesitated too long. Lydia nodded, as if she already understood. "Grant, you don't need more pressure right now."

Pressure. That word fit.

"I don't feel convicted," he admitted. "I feel cornered."

She stepped closer. "That matters. If God were convicting you," she continued, "wouldn't it bring clarity instead of confusion?"

The sentence was simple, but it shifted the ground. He wondered if his lack of conviction was a sign that Kate had truly been culpable in the deterioration of their marriage. She had told him he was shifting the blame, but was he? His thoughts were interrupted by Lydia's voice softly confirming and comforting him.

"You're not running from truth," she said. "You're running from constant interrogation."

The word *interrogation* settled. It was a lot more comfortable than *sin*.

"You told her you needed space," Lydia reminded him. "That was honest. You need time to breathe and think."

"Yes."

"It means you're choosing peace, rather than conflict." she added.

Peace. He had not felt peace. He had felt relief. Which felt similar.

"And Grant, you deserve to be seen," she continued. "Not managed."

He thought of Kate's steady questions, her calm precision, her spiritual language. Had it felt like management? Maybe. Judgement? Probably.

"She said she's closing access," he muttered.

Lydia's lips tightened slightly. "That sounds punitive."

"She says it is supposed to be protective."

"For her," Lydia replied.

The emphasis was subtle.

"And what about you?" she asked.

He looked up.

"What protects you?"

No one had asked him that yet. Everyone else had asked what he had done, the sins he'd committed, the things he'd broken. No one had asked what *he* had needed.

"You told me you felt invisible," she said. "You told me you felt secondary in your own home."

The words brought him validation. The guilt drew back like a slow tide.

“If she really wanted to repair this,” Lydia continued, “would she leave the country for three months?”

Each time Lydia said it, it sounded truer.

“She said she’s protecting herself,” she continued. “Well, I’m protecting myself too. I told you I won’t stay someone’s second choice.”

The pressure was no longer hidden. It was measured. “I’m not asking you to sign divorce papers,” she clarified. “I’m asking you to live where you are wanted.”

Wanted. He hadn’t realized how much he craved that feeling. That need. It had become almost insatiable.

“Stay,” she implored him. “Stay here. Let the noise settle. Let her distance clarify things for you, too.”

Clarify. It sounded spiritual enough to soothe him.

He exhaled slowly. “I know she thinks I’ve single handedly dismantled our marriage.”

Lydia stepped closer and placed her hand over his. “Maybe it was dismantled long ago,” she whispered.

There it was, the final reframe. Not betrayal, but rather the discovery of the fracture. Exposure that both Kate and Grant had contributed to the drift.

Grant did not notice how craftily his narrative was being edited. He only felt the relief of alignment. No interrogation. No accountability session. No tears. Just warmth and understanding … and wine poured generously into two glasses.

“Come sit,” Lydia patted the seat beside her on the leather couch.

And as he lowered himself beside her, something inside him shifted again. Not toward truth. Toward comfort.

The enemy rarely shouts. He reframes. And Grant, weary and untethered, began to believe the reframing was clarity.

CHAPTER 24
What to Tell the Children?

Austin, Texas

The children didn't know. But they felt something.

For several weeks, the Grant family conversations had been separated, one parent at a time. Jesse would call his dad about work and investments, and when Kate wasn't there to share in the conversation, he'd text his mom about the baby. Emma would call Kate to talk wedding details, but since Grant was rarely around when she asked to speak with him, she'd send her father quick updates about venues and guest counts. Nathan checked in sporadically, usually late at night, usually with whichever parent answered first.

No more spontaneous three-way calls. No more casual *"Put Mom on"* or *"Let me say hi to Dad."* It hadn't been intentional. It had just happened. And none of them had pressed.

They had also accepted Kate's earlier explanation without question when she'd cut her first Italy trip short. "A little female issue I need to deal with," she had said lightly. And that had been that. It was a female issue, after all. Just not the one they imagined.

Two nights before her second departure, Kate called Grant.

"I think the kids are starting to sense something," she said.

"I know," he replied.

"I don't want to expose this yet," she continued, "not while they're scattered across the country."

Jesse was in California with a toddler and deadlines. Emma in Dallas, working full-time while planning a wedding. Nathan was buried in grad school pressures on the East Coast. They were grown, but they were not braced for hearing their parents' marriage was on shaky ground.

Grant leaned back against Lydia's kitchen counter. "I agree," he said quickly.

"I won't lie," Kate clarified. "But I'm not announcing a separation."

"For now," he said.

"Yes, for now."

They were strangely aligned in that moment, co-managing information the way they once managed teenage curfews.

"I'll send a group text," Kate said. "Preemptive."

"Good," he answered.

He meant it. The fewer conversations requiring explanation, the better.

The night before her flight back to Puglia, Kate sat at the kitchen table alone and opened the family thread.

Jesse + Rachel
Emma
Nathan
Mom & Dad

She stared at the blinking cursor. Then she typed:

I have a little surprise. The girls in Puglia have been urging me to come back and stay longer. They have a room waiting at

Villa Santoro, and I finally said yes. I'm heading back for about three months.

She paused. Then added:

It feels like something I need right now.

She pressed send and the responses came quickly.

Jesse:
Three months?! Mom, that's incredible.

Rachel:
Yes!! Italian summer round two!

Emma:
I love this for you, Mom!

Nathan:
Does this mean unlimited pasta?

Kate smiled despite the ache in her chest. Then she swallowed hard as she read the next message.

Jesse:
Dad going too?

There it was.

She answered carefully:

Dad's got a packed schedule this quarter and a few major projects he can't step away from. So, it'll just be me this time.

A beat passed. Then:

Emma:
Classic Dad.

Nathan:
He better visit.

Jesse:
Mom deserves this. She's been nonstop for years.

The tone was light and affectionate. She felt relieved that they seemed unaware of any trouble brewing. Kate exhaled slowly. For now, they were excited for her. For now, the narrative held.

Later that evening, Grant scrolled back through the thread from Lydia's couch. Three months. It sounded adventurous in text form—restorative and intentional. He felt something close to gratitude for the space she was creating. It would give him space to breathe, or so he thought.

Only Kate, Michael, and Lydia knew the full extent of their fracture. The truth was contained, for now. Grant had been "exposed" to Michael and Kate more than he had intended. But not to the children. Not yet. He leaned back, exhaling slowly. This could still be managed.

Lydia entered the room with two glasses of wine. "They're excited?" she asked.

"Yes."

"And suspicious?"

"No."

She nodded. "Then maybe this is the space you both need."

He wanted to believe that.

Across the country, three adult children went to bed believing their mother was embarking on an extended Italian adventure.

In Austin, two lives were dangerously diverging. And for now, the silence felt merciful. But silence has a shelf life. Eventually, someone would ask a question that required more than a well-phrased answer.

CHAPTER 25
Open Hands

Somewhere over the Atlantic

The jet hummed steadily and Kate's thoughts kept pace.

She had always liked this part of flying; the long, suspended stretch when the ground was no longer visible and the destination still felt distant. A place between worlds. And now, it was also a place between the past and the future.

The cabin lights were dimmed and most passengers around her slept, but Kate had pulled the small leather journal from her carry-on and opened it on the tray table. The open blank page waited for her thoughts and for a moment she simply stared at it.

The broken pieces of her thirty-five years of marriage compelled her to this flight. It was not the romantic return to their original meeting place she had imagined sharing with Grant in retirement. Instead, it was a personal retreat seeking God and peace. She took a slow breath and began writing.

Lord,

I don't know what the next three months will hold.

The pen paused. She stared out the window at the faint outline of clouds below.

I have tried to imagine every possible outcome. Grant waking up in deep conviction. Grant hardening further. Our marriage restored. Our marriage ending.

She stopped again. For weeks she had lived inside those possibilities—analyzing, replaying conversations, trying to read meaning into every word Grant spoke. But that was finished. At least for now.

She wrote again.

Tonight, I release the need to predict what is happening back home. You are there. I am not.

The words steadied her.

I choose to seek You first. Your love. Your truth. Your presence.

A tear slipped down her cheek, but she did not wipe it away.

If our marriage is to survive, it will not be because I hovered or managed the outcome. It will be because Grant responds to the Holy Spirit's promptings of conviction and comes to a place full repentance that can lead to redemption.

She underlined the word redemption. Not partial confession. Not regret. Redemption.

I pray for his heart tonight. Break through the lies he is believing. Expose whatever darkness has taken root. Call him home, not to me first, but to You.

The plane shifted slightly in a pocket of air. Kate waited for the movement to settle before continuing.

But Lord ...

Her pen slowed. This part required courage.

Prepare me for whatever may come. If restoration, let our covenant become stronger than it was before. Like a bone that heals thicker at the fracture. Let our family not merely survive this but grow deeper, humbler, more honest.

She inhaled deeply. Then she wrote the words that felt hardest.

And if Grant chooses another path...

She stopped again. Not to erase the sentence. But to let it exist.

Then teach me how to live fully in the life You still have for me.

Her mind drifted briefly to the women waiting in Puglia. Claire divorced but vibrant, her laughter filling every room. Marianne, widowed, grief transformed into quiet wisdom. Evelyn, never married, but somehow the most adventurous spirit of them all.

Each of them living rich lives in their sixties. Each of them faithful. Each of them deeply loved by God. None of them defined by the absence of a husband. Kate had always assumed she would grow old beside Grant. But maybe the deeper truth was this: No matter what may come, she would grow old in God's hands. She resumed writing.

Please Lord, help me to trust that my life is not over if this marriage ends. Help me believe that joy is still possible in every circumstance.

The cabin remained quiet. A flight attendant passed silently down the aisle. Kate rested her pen for a moment, then finished the page.

For the next three months, I choose hope. I choose joy. I choose to look for Your goodness everywhere. And I choose to leave Grant in Your hands. Amen.

She closed the journal slowly. The words did not erase the pain. But they had shifted something inside her. For weeks she had felt like a woman abandoned on uncertain ground. Now she felt something else. Not certainty. But steadiness.

Several hours later the captain's voice came booming over the intercom. "We've begun our descent into Bari."

Kate lifted the shade beside her seat. The Adriatic appeared below—endless blue stretching toward the horizon. A familiar coastline curved into view. Something in her chest loosened. Adventure stirred alongside grief. She gathered her things and slipped the journal back into her bag.

Three months. Maybe longer. She didn't know what waited ahead. But as the plane touched down and the wheels met Italian soil, Kate felt a surprising rush of anticipation. Puglia held friendship, sea air, long dinners, and quiet mornings with God. And perhaps something even deeper. Healing.

She stepped into the aisle with a small smile forming. Whatever the next chapter held—reconciliation or reinvention—she was ready to live it fully.

As Kate stepped out of the airport terminal to locate her Uber driver, she embraced a new hope that nudged her forward as she lifted her face to absorb the Italian sunlight.

CHAPTER 26
La Dolce Vita

Monopoli, Italy

When Kate entered Villa Santoro for the second time, she physically felt her body and mind decompress.

Here, she would rediscover how to smile and then laugh again.

Italians have a way of celebrating life with passion. No matter what challenge life may bring, there is always room to enjoy good food and wine and embrace deep friendships. It is the way of *la dolce vita*—the sweet life.

The villa seemed to welcome her back as if nothing in the world had shifted. Sunlight poured through the tall windows, pooling across the stone floors. The scent of espresso drifted from the kitchen. Somewhere outside, the church bells rang in the distance, their sound soft and familiar.

Claire appeared first, wiping her hands on a kitchen towel. "Well, look who decided to come home," she said dramatically.

Kate barely had time to set down her bags before Claire wrapped her in a hug that nearly knocked the air out of her.

"Careful," Marianne called from the doorway. "She just got off a plane. Let her breathe before you squeeze the life out of her."

Claire stepped back but kept her hands on Kate's shoulders, studying her face. "You look tired."

"I am."

"You also look ten pounds lighter," Evelyn added thoughtfully from across the room. "Stress diet."

Kate laughed. "That is not a diet plan I recommend."

Rosa shuffled in from the back patio holding a small basket of figs. "Ah," she said warmly. "Now the house is balanced again."

Kate kissed her on both cheeks. "You picked those this morning?"

"Of course," Rosa said proudly. "And if you are very lucky, I might let you help me make jam tomorrow."

Claire leaned toward Kate and whispered loudly, "That means we will be standing in the kitchen for six hours while Rosa tells us we are doing everything wrong."

Rosa pointed a fig at her. "You are doing everything wrong."

Everyone laughed. The sound surprised Kate. It seemed so long since laughter had come so easily.

That afternoon they walked into town together, the narrow streets of Monopoli alive with the soft hum of early evening. Laundry fluttered from balconies overhead. Scooters zipped past like determined insects. Old men sat in plastic chairs outside the café arguing passionately about football.

Claire pointed toward a small bakery ahead. "That place," she announced, "has ruined every American pastry for me."

Kate looked skeptical. "That's a bold statement."

"You'll see."

As they neared the bakery, Claire stopped so abruptly in front of the entrance that Marianne nearly walked into her.

"Oh yes," Claire whispered reverently, one hand pressed to her chest. "They have *both* my favorites."

Inside, the bakery smelled like butter, sugar, espresso, and warm pastry dough—the kind of smell that felt almost impossible to recreate outside of Italy. Glass cases stretched along the narrow shop, crowded with pastries dusted in powdered sugar and lined up like jewels beneath the morning light.

An older woman behind the counter greeted Claire with rapid Italian that sounded half welcome and half interrogation. Claire answered confidently enough to impress the others, pointing dramatically through the glass.

"*Due pasticciotti ... no, aspetta ... due di ciascuno.*" She turned toward the women with widening eyes. "We're getting two of every kind."

"Every kind?" Evelyn repeated.

"Yes, this is not the moment for restraint."

The woman behind the counter slid golden *pasticciotti* onto small paper trays—oval pastries with glossy tops and delicate crusts the color of toasted butter. Some were filled with traditional custard, others with pistachio cream, ricotta, chocolate, and dark Amarena cherries that bled slightly into the pastry.

"They look too pretty to eat," Marianne murmured.

"No," Claire corrected. "They look exactly right to eat."

Then came the *sporcamuss*. Warm squares of flaky puff pastry were split and overflowing with pale pastry cream, powdered sugar cascading over the tops so heavily it looked like fresh snow. Even lifting one caused sugar to drift onto the counter.

"What does *sporcamuss* mean?" Kate asked.

Claire grinned wickedly. "Literally? 'Dirty your mouth.'"

Evelyn narrowed her eyes. "That feels threatening."

The first bite of *pasticciotto* silenced the table. Kate closed her eyes almost immediately as warm vanilla custard spilled softly against the crisp pastry shell, the faint brightness of lemon lifting the richness just enough to keep it from feeling heavy.

"Oh, my word," she whispered.

Marianne made a small sound of approval she normally reserved for meaningful spiritual insight.

Claire pointed triumphantly. "SEE?"

Even Evelyn looked briefly emotional. "This," she declared carefully after another bite, "is what happens when people respect butter."

Laughter rippled through the café.

The *sporcamuss* proved even less dignified. The moment Kate bit into one, powdered sugar scattered down the front of her blouse while warm pastry cream slipped onto her fingers.

Claire nearly choked laughing. "No one survives these gracefully."

Marianne dabbed at her mouth, laughing too hard to maintain composure, while Evelyn finally gave up entirely and leaned over her plate to catch the avalanche of sugar falling from the pastry.

"Oh, these are dangerous," Evelyn muttered. "I would absolutely ruin my life living here."

Outside, morning light spilled across the harbor, church bells echoing faintly through the narrow streets while the women sat around the tiny café table passing pastries back and forth, powdered sugar on their fingers, espresso growing cold beside them. And for a little while, Kate forgot to think about Grant at all.

“That’s illegal,” Marianne declared. “There should be regulations against pastries that good.”

Evelyn laughed. “I’m fairly certain Italians would consider that an attack on their national identity.”

They stepped back out into the golden light and Kate took a few steps toward the stone wall of the harbor and looked out across the Adriatic. As she inhaled the fresh, salty air, she observed the fishing boats rocking gently in the water, their ropes creaking against the dock. She felt the tightness in her chest loosen and her shoulder relax.

“You’re breathing again,” Marianne observed.

Kate turned toward her. “Is it that obvious?”

Marianne nodded. “You were barely holding yourself together when we left you at the airport.”

“And now?”

“I can see you’re letting the air back in. You’re allowing your soul to embrace the joy of the moment.”

Later that evening, Kate, Claire, Marianne, Evelyn, and Zia Rosa approached Claire’s favorite *trattoria*, a small family owned restaurant in Monopoli. The scent of garlic, wood smoke, and simmering tomatoes drifted out into the narrow stone street before they even reached the door.

The owner, a round-faced man named Antonio, spotted Rosa immediately and threw his arms wide. "*Zia Rosa!*" he called, hurrying outside to kiss both her cheeks before greeting the others as if they were longtime friends rather than recent arrivals.

Inside, the trattoria glowed with warm light reflecting off honey-colored stone walls lined with old family photographs, baskets of wine bottles, and shelves crowded with olive oil tins and ceramic plates. Tables sat close together beneath exposed wooden beams, and the room hummed with conversation, laughter, and the occasional clatter of dishes from the kitchen.

Before anyone opened a menu, Antonio appeared with a bottle of local Primitivo and several small plates "from the kitchen" that everyone knew would somehow still appear on the bill. Claire made sure everyone had their wine in hand before raising her glass and declaring:

“To Kate!”

“To survival,” Evelyn added.

“To friendship,” Marianne said.

Rosa lifted her glass last. “To life,” she declared simply.

They clinked glasses. The wine was crisp and cool. At the table beside them a large Italian family was celebrating something loudly, a birthday perhaps, or anniversary. Children ran between chairs while grandparents gestured animatedly over plates of pasta.

Claire leaned toward Kate. “This,” she whispered, gesturing around them, “is what Italians do best.”

“What?”

“They refuse to postpone joy.”

Course after course arrived at an unhurried pace—fresh burrata, warm focaccia, handmade orecchiette, grilled fish, and vegetables harvested that morning from a nearby farm. Nobody seemed concerned about the time; meals here were less about eating and more about lingering together. By the time tiny cups of espresso and a platter of pastries appeared, the women felt less like customers and more like family gathered around a table that had been waiting for them all along.

Kate watched the scene. No one here seemed worried about tomorrow. Or next year. Or whether life had gone exactly as planned. They were simply eating, laughing, living.

"Americans schedule happiness," Marianne added. "Italians practice it."

Kate smiled slowly. "Well then," she said, lifting her glass again. "I suppose I'm here for practice."

Claire grinned. "Oh, we will train you properly. These girlfriends have been getting very high marks in embodying Italian joy!"

Evelyn pointed her fork at Kate. "Rule number one: no checking your phone every five minutes."

"Rule number two," Marianne added, "you must learn to argue passionately about olive oil."

Claire leaned back in her chair. "And rule number three—very important—you must nap whenever possible."

Kate laughed again. A deep laugh this time. No restraint, just hearty and real.

As the sun lowered into the sea, casting the harbor in amber light, the women sauntered home in in relaxed conversation. And Kate realized something she had not expected. Her heart was not only surviving, but it was also learning how to find join in the little things and live again.

CHAPTER 27
Bread and Blue Sky

Monopoli, Italy

Mornings unfolded slowly at Villa Santoro.

Today, the four women lingered around the kitchen table long after breakfast, lazily sipping *cappuccini* while morning light streamed through the open windows. Outside, the olive trees shifted gently in the breeze, and somewhere deeper in the house Zia Rosa could be heard arguing with a radio announcer as if he could personally hear her objections.

Marianne stirred milk into her coffee. "Okay," she announced, "I need Zia Rosa or someone to explain a few words I hear Italians use incessantly. It's the *same* four words repeated over and over, but I have no idea what they mean"

Kate smiled. "I've noticed that too." She tilted her head and tried to recall one. "*Allora!* All the time, *allora.* Zia Rosa says it to herself as she works in the kitchen and all through the day."

"Exactly!" Claire pointed triumphantly. "I know those words. They are like fillers. I've heard them all my life but never understood what they mean or when to use them."

Evelyn nodded in agreement, "Every conversation sounds like: *Allora... ecco... quindi... dai!*'

"I swear," Claire continued, "Italians can have a fifteen-minute conversation using only hand gestures and the word *allora.*"

At that moment Zia Rosa entered carrying a bowl of figs from the garden and immediately narrowed her eyes suspiciously.

“You are making fun of Italians again.”

“We are trying to understand Italians,” Claire corrected.

“Impossible,” Rosa replied calmly.

The women laughed.

Kate leaned forward. “Actually, Rosa… what does *allora* mean? Everyone says it constantly.”

Rosa set the figs onto the table and sat down with them. “Ahhh.” She smiled knowingly. “*Allora* is everything.”

“That is not helpful,” Evelyn said.

Rosa ignored her. “It can mean ‘so…’ or ‘well then…’ or ‘okay…’ or sometimes nothing at all.” She lifted one shoulder. “Usually, Italians say it when thinking what to say next.”

Claire nodded. “So basically, like I said, Italian filler words.”

Rosa pointed at her. “*Esattamente*!”

The women burst into laughter.

“And *ecco?*” Marianne asked.

“*Ecco* means…” Rosa paused gesturing dramatically with both hands. “How do I explain? Like…” She grabbed a loaf of bread from the counter and held it up and extended it to Marianne. “*Ecco!* Here!”

The women stared blankly. Claire blinked. “That explained absolutely nothing.”

Rosa sighed. “It means, ‘here it is’ or ‘there you are’ or ‘see?’ Italians use it for everything. If the plumber arrives? *Ecco.* If your husband finally apologizes after being stupid for six months? *Ecco.*"

"Useful word," Kate murmured dryly.

Rosa smirked knowingly but wisely chose not to comment.

"And *quindi?*" Evelyn asked.

"*Quindi* means 'therefore' or 'so.' Italians use it when trying to sound logical even when they are absolutely not being logical."

"That feels universal," Marianne said.

Claire pointed toward the doorway dramatically. "And *dai!* Everybody says *dai!*"

At this, Rosa laughed outright. "Ahhh, *dai.* Very important word."

"What does it mean?"

"It depends."

"Of course it does," Claire muttered.

Rosa grinned. "It can mean 'come on,' 'hurry up,' 'you're kidding,' 'stop it,' 'please,' or sometimes simply emotional frustration."

She threw both hands into the air. "Like this—*Dai, Claire! Stop talking nonsense!*"

"Well, that's a relief," Evelyn replied. "I thought y'all were telling us to die … spelled D-I-E, not D-A-I! I was thinking Italians must be easily offended!"

The women laughed in unison again as Paolo appeared in the doorway carrying a crate of tomatoes from the market. He paused, looking between the laughing women and his grinning aunt.

"What is happening here?"

Claire pointed at him dramatically. "We're learning that Italian is not actually a language. It's emotional theater."

Paolo considered this seriously for a moment. "Yes," he said finally. "That is correct."

Zia Rosa laughed at that and replied, "Paolo, these women are in serious need of Italian lessons!" She pushed herself back from the table, and sighed "*Allora! È ora di preparare il dolce per stasera.*" Okay! It is time to prepare the dessert for tonight.

New Rituals and Routines

The Saturday market in Monopoli had its own rhythm. It began early before the sun fully committed to the sky when trucks backed into the piazza and men unfolded metal tables like instruments in a well-rehearsed orchestra. Crates of citrus thumped onto cobblestones. Buckets of flowers appeared beside piles of tomatoes so red they almost looked painted.

Someone was always playing music on a radio. Someone was always arguing about olives. And someone was always frying something that smelled too good to ignore.

After many weeks in Italy, the women had adopted the market as their Saturday ritual. Claire loved it most. She said it was the only place in Italy where you could hear five languages before reaching the second stall.

This week, Zia Rosa insisted on coming with them. "I have watched you choose tomatoes like you are selecting jewelry," she announced, tying her scarf at the back of her neck. "Today, I teach you how to choose like women who plan to eat."

Claire laughed. "We *are* women who plan to eat."

Rosa gave her a look. "No. You are women who plan to *shop*. There is a difference."

They wound through the narrow streets into the market square, already alive with voices and color. Crates of tomatoes spilled over in deep reds and sun-warmed golds. Bunches of basil perfumed the air. Vendors called out greetings as Rosa passed, each one addressed by name, each exchange layered with familiarity.

She moved slowly, pausing at a stall piled high with tomatoes. The women instinctively reached forward, but Rosa stopped them immediately with a sharp little click of her tongue.

"No, no," she warned sternly. "In Italy, you do not manhandle all the produce like Americans in a supermarket."

Evelyn pulled her hand back. "Noted."

Rosa nodded toward the vendor first, offering a few respectful words in Italian and a small lift of her brows—asking permission before touching anything. Only after he smiled and gestured his approval did she carefully pick up a single tomato.

"You ask," she explained. "Always. These are his work. His pride."

She turned the tomato over in her hand, pressing it lightly with her thumb. "Too hard," she said, setting it back carefully.

She selected another with even more tenderness, almost as if she were handling something alive. A gentle squeeze. Then a satisfied nod. "This one understands the sun."

Evelyn blinked. "The tomato understands the sun?"

Rosa shrugged. "Of course. Everything here understands the sun. That is why we do not rush."

Claire grinned. "In America, we refrigerate everything."

Rosa stopped mid-reach and turned slowly. "You put tomatoes in the refrigerator?"

Claire hesitated. "Sometimes…"

Rosa placed a hand over her heart. "*Madonna mia.* And you wonder why your food has no joy."

The women burst into laughter.

As they moved from stall to stall, Rosa filled their baskets with quiet authority—eggplant, zucchini, bread still warm from the bakery. She handed items to each of them as if assigning roles.

"Marianne, you cook this slowly. Not like you are chasing something."

"Evelyn, more olive oil. Always more than you think."

Claire raised a brow. "What about me?"

Rosa didn't miss a beat. "You talk less and watch more."

Claire laughed out loud. "That might be the hardest assignment of all."

Kate walked beside Rosa, carrying a basket that had grown heavier with each stop. She watched the older woman greet people, pause, listen, choose—never hurried, never distracted.

"You make this look easy," Kate said.

Rosa glanced at her. "It is easy."

Kate smiled. "It doesn't feel easy."

Rosa adjusted the scarf at her neck. "Because you are still thinking too much."

Kate let out a soft breath. "That sounds about right."

They stopped near a stall of cheeses, and Rosa leaned slightly closer, lowering her voice. "In America," she said, "you like to solve everything quickly, yes?"

Kate nodded. "We do."

"You have a problem, you fix it. You have a question, you answer it. You have pain, you remove it." Rosa shook her head. "Here, we sit with things."

Kate looked at her. "Even when they hurt?"

"Especially when they hurt."

The words settled deeper than Rosa's tone suggested.

Rosa picked up a small round of cheese and handed it to Kate. "You see this? It takes time. You cannot hurry it, or it becomes something else. Not better. Just wrong."

Kate turned the cheese in her hand, understanding more than Rosa had said.

Rosa studied her for a moment. "Your heart is like that now," she added gently. "If you rush, you change what it is becoming."

Kate swallowed. "And if I wait?"

Rosa smiled faintly. "Then you taste something good at the end."

They continued walking, the market noise swelling around them again. Claire was bargaining loudly over lemons. Evelyn was insisting she had been cheated on olives. Marianne was laughing at both of them.

Kate lingered half a step behind Rosa. “You see everything, don’t you?” she asked.

Rosa shrugged. “I am old. It is my job.”

Kate smiled. “Do you think I’m doing the right thing?”

Rosa didn’t answer immediately. She stopped at a stall of fresh bread, broke off a small piece, and handed it to Kate.

“Eat,” she said.

Kate took a bite, still warm, simple and perfect.

Rosa watched her. “When you taste something good,” she said, “you do not question it so much. You receive it.”

Kate nodded slowly.

“And when something is not ready,” Rosa continued, “you do not force it to be ready.”

Claire called out from across the square, “Zia Rosa! We need your expertise over here immediately!”

Rosa sighed dramatically. “These women would starve without me.”

Kate laughed.

As Rosa moved toward Claire, she paused just long enough to glance back at Kate. “Your life,” she said, tapping her fingers lightly against her own chest, "is not a grocery list you check off. It is a meal you prepare slowly."

Kate stood there for a moment, the sounds of the market rising and falling around her. Voices were calling out prices, laughter weaving through the narrow aisles, and the clatter of crates shifting from one stall to another. Something in her softened. It felt like permission to slow down and just breathe. To trust that not everything needed to be decided in a single day. Perhaps this season would take longer than she expected, longer than a summer, maybe even a year. She would have to learn the rhythm of this place and let it reshape her. She exhaled, steadying herself, then moved to catch up with the others.

At the fish stand, Claire and Evelyn were already deep in discussion with the vendor, while Marianne examined a row of gleaming silver fish laid neatly over crushed ice. Kate arrived just in time to hear Zia Rosa's firm voice cutting clearly through the noise.

"No, no," Rosa said, lifting a branzino with practiced ease. "You do not ask for it without the head. The head tells you everything."

Evelyn blinked. "Everything?"

"Of course," Rosa replied, tapping the fish lightly. "The eyes must be clear. Bright. Not tired." She glanced at the women. "If the eyes are tired, the fish has already told you goodbye."

Claire laughed. "That feels like life advice."

Rosa gave a small shrug. "It is life advice. In Italy, we do not separate these things."

She handed the fish back to the vendor, then added with a knowing look, "And if you remove the head, you remove the truth. It is easier, yes, but you no longer know what you are working with."

Kate felt the words land deeper than Rosa likely intended.

As they completed their purchase, a voice called out behind them. “Clairetta!”

Claire turned immediately, her face lighting with recognition. “Well, look who finally showed up.”

Kate didn’t need to turn to know. But she did anyway. Paolo stepped through the crowd with the easy familiarity of someone who belonged to the morning. A long loaf of bread was tucked under his arm, a paper bag in his other hand, linen shirt sleeves rolled casually to his forearms.

Claire grinned. “You’re late.”

“I am on time,” Paolo said mildly. “You are early.”

Marianne leaned toward Ev. “He says that every time.”

“And he’s always wrong,” Ev whispered back.

Paolo smiled at them both, then his gaze moved across the group. Marianne. Ev. Claire. And finally, Kate. The recognition in his expression was immediate. Not surprised, just a quiet and gentle awareness of her presence.

During their first dinner together weeks earlier, Claire had briefly explained Kate’s situation—the fracture in her marriage and the painful season she was walking through. Paolo knew only the outline of the story, nothing more. Later that same evening Claire had told Kate that Paolo already knew. It had removed the awkwardness of explanations between them. Some things did not need repeating.

“Kate,” he said.

His tone carried the quiet warmth of someone greeting an old friend rather than a returning guest.

"Hi, Paolo."

Claire crossed her arms with satisfaction. "Look at that. Our market is whole again."

Paolo tilted his head slightly. "You left," he said to Kate.

"For a little while."

"And now you return."

"Yes."

He nodded once, as if the explanation was sufficient. Then he lifted the bread under his arm.

"My mother will accuse me of neglect if I do not deliver this soon."

"Do you still cook for her a couple times a week like you used to?" Claire asked.

"I cook *with* her," Paolo corrected. "She supervises."

Marianne clasped her hands together. "That's adorable."

"It is survival," he said dryly.

"Yes, this wise son understands the ways of la mamma," Zia Rosa chimed in.

The women laughed. Claire gestured toward the café at the corner of the piazza.

"We're headed for espresso. It's been a couple hours." She laughed with a shoulder shrug.

Paolo glanced toward the café door. "Then I will escort you," he said.

"Escort?" Ev repeated. "Listen to him."

"Very official," Marianne added.

They walked together through the crowd, weaving between stalls and baskets. Vendors called out greetings to Paolo as they passed.

"Ciao, Paolo!"

"Buongiorno!"

He lifted a hand in greeting without slowing.

"Your celebrity status grows," Claire said.

Paolo laughed. "It is only because I have lived here my whole life," he said. "I'll give you a few months and they will greet you the same way."

Inside the café the air smelled of coffee and sugar. They slipped into their usual small table by the window. Paolo ordered in Italian. The barista nodded, already preparing five tiny cups and one extra.

For a few minutes the talk stayed light. Paolo asked Marianne about her progress with Italian. She lifted her chin proudly. "I can order confidently now."

Paolo tilted his head. "Confidently… or correctly?"

Claire nearly choked on her espresso.

"Both," Marianne insisted.

Ev leaned forward eagerly. "Okay, but listen, last week we discovered something important."

Paolo waited.

"The *taralli,*" she said.

Recognition flickered across his face. "Ah," he said slowly. "Dangerous territory."

Marianne pointed at him. "Exactly! No one warned us."

Kate looked between them. "What am I missing?"

Ev lifted a small paper bag and shook it. Tiny rings of baked dough rattled inside. "These," she said. "They look innocent."

Paolo nodded gravely. "They are not innocent."

Claire laughed. "We bought one bag the first week."

"Then two," Marianne added.

Ev sighed. "Then we discovered they come in flavors."

"Fennel," Claire said.

"Olive oil," Marianne added.

"Chili," Ev finished.

Paolo's smile deepened. "You have begun the descent."

Kate raised an eyebrow. "The descent?"

"Yes," he said solemnly. "Soon you will buy them by the kilo and pretend it is for guests."

Marianne pointed at him again. "You're judging us, but I saw you buy two bags just now."

Paolo lifted the paper sack in his hand. “These are for my mother.”

“It is not polite to lie, Paolo.” Zia Rosa shook one finger at him and grinned.

He shrugged lightly. “Mamma taught me everything I know about excuses.”

Even Kate laughed at that—softly at first, then freely. For a moment she noticed something she hadn’t expected. How easy it felt to laugh again. Not because anything had been solved. Just because, for a little while, she had forgotten the weight she had been carrying.

Paolo lifted his espresso cup. “That,” he said, “is called culture.”

Claire clapped her hands suddenly. “Okay,” she announced. “Enough philosophy for a café.”

Marianne leaned forward eagerly. “We’re doing this properly tonight.”

Ev nodded. “Dinner.”

Claire pointed at Paolo. “You’re coming.”

Paolo blinked. “Tonight?”

“Yes,” Marianne said. “You need a full update on our Italian adventures.”

“Don’t worry, Paolo,” Rosa chimed in. “I will be supervising all the cooking.”

Paolo looked from one determined face to another. Then he sighed with mock resignation. “All right,” he said. “But only if I may bring something.”

“Bread?” Marianne guessed.

“Always bread,” he replied.

“And occasionally wine,” Claire added.

“Only when supervised,” Paolo answered.

Claire leaned back, satisfied. “Perfect.”

Paolo stood, leaving a few coins beside his empty cup. He picked up the paper bag and tucked the loaf beneath his arm again.

“I will see you tonight,” he said.

Then he stepped back into the brightness of the piazza and disappeared into the market crowd, bread under one arm and the blue Italian sky stretching wide above the rooftops.

Kate watched the doorway for a moment before turning back to the table.

Ev grinned. “You know,” she said, “it’s refreshing to spend time with a man who likes markets, bread, and conversation as much as we do.”

Claire laughed. “Paolo has been hanging out with women his whole life.”

Marianne nodded thoughtfully. “It shows. It’s so rare to find a quality man who cooks and isn’t scared away by women talking at once. It’s a rare skill.”

Kate smiled and nodded in agreement. There was something unexpectedly easy about Paolo’s presence. He moved through conversation with joyfulness and calm, never seeming rushed or self-conscious. She could tell he fully embraced the simple pleasures of good company. After the heaviness of the past week, that felt like a gift.

Zia Rosa pushed back from the table and pointed toward the market square. "Allora," she said with a wink, "We'd better finish our shopping. Paolo will be the only man at dinner. We must feed him properly."

Marianne brightened immediately. "Pasta."

"Osso buco?" Ev questioned hopefully.

"*Dolce,* lots of *dolce*," Claire added with a grin.

Kate sighed and smiled. This Italian lifestyle—*la dolce vita*—was exactly what she needed to rediscover joy in the moment despite the uncertainty of her future. It delighted her to realize she was looking forward to cooking and gathering to break bread, drink wine, and eat unrestricted amounts of homemade pasta with both new and old friends.

CHAPTER 28
The Long Table

Monopoli, Italy

The beauty of a long table is not found in what is served upon it, but in the people gathered around it.

Late that afternoon, in preparation for their special dinner guest, Rosa had reluctantly relinquished her *cucina* to the four younger women. She supervised from a distance nodding approval, clucking out a few instructions, and chuffing with indignation when they did something too American to meet her standards.

Slowly, they developed a kind of rhythmic "cooking dance" around one another. Each of them discovered, almost without noticing, a kind of inner *nonna* they hadn't known they carried. Inspired by Rosa, they began to cook by instinct—tasting, adjusting, arguing lightly over salt and timing.

Eventually, Rosa, still perched in her usual chair with quiet authority gave a small nod of approval. That, more than anything, felt like a victory.

Paolo arrived just before sunset. Kate knew because Claire announced it like a town crier.

"He's here," Claire declared, peering through the shutters. "And he brought bread again. Italy refuses to be subtle."

Evelyn stood, smoothing the front of her blouse, her posture straightening instinctively. Marianne continued setting plates along the long courtyard table simple white ceramic warmed by the afternoon sun. A linen cloth drifted lightly in the breeze, anchored at the corners with small bowls of olives.

Paolo stepped through the courtyard gate, looking more handsome than ever, if that was even possible. He carried a paper-wrapped bundle and a dark glass bottle that caught the last amber light of evening.

"*Buonasera*," he said warmly. "Good evening."

"*Buonasera*," Marianne replied with practiced ease.

Claire lifted her chin. "At least she knows one Italian word."

Paolo smiled. "Only one is necessary if it is the correct one."

Claire paused thoughtfully. "Pizza?"

He laughed.

"Then we are fluent," Evelyn said dryly.

Kate felt herself grinning, an easy, unforced softness that surprised her.

Paolo placed the bundle on the table and unfolded the paper. Warm focaccia, olive oil glistening across its golden surface, rosemary fragrant in the cooling air. Beside it, he set a round of cheese and a small basket of figs so ripe they had begun to split.

"And this," he said, lifting the bottle slightly, "is not famous wine. But it is honest."

Claire nodded approvingly. "That's my favorite kind."

They sat, and the meal began the way Italian meals always seemed to begin—slowly, almost ceremonially, as if time itself had decided to sit down with them. The sky softened from gold to rose as plates passed from hand to hand. Pasta with fresh tomatoes so sweet they tasted like summer. Small wedges of cheese that carried the quiet memory of pasture and sun.

Claire set down a shallow platter of *pollo al forno*, roasted simply with garlic, lemon, and rosemary, the skin crisped just enough to crack beneath the knife. Marianne followed with a pan of slow-simmered beef, tender slices cooked down with onions and a splash of red wine until the sauce clung to everything it touched.

As the dishes settled, Paolo paused, his hand resting lightly on the table. "May I?" he asked.

The women grew quiet as he bowed his head. His prayer was simple, thanking God for the food, for friendship, and for the gift of people finding one another far from home.

When he finished, Claire lifted her chin and eyes upward. "Well," she said, "that just made the pasta taste holier."

Paolo did not dominate the table, but somehow the conversation orbited him naturally. He asked questions that invited stories.

"How long have you been friends?" he asked.

"Since the early nineties," Marianne said.

Claire snorted. "We survived shoulder pads together. That's covenant."

Kate nearly choked on her wine.

Paolo blinked. "Shoulder pads?"

Evelyn leaned in solemnly. "It was an era of aggressive silhouettes."

Paolo pressed a hand to his heart. "I honor your suffering."

Laughter spilled across the table.

Later, he turned to Evelyn. "And what has Italy taught you so far?"

She didn't hesitate. "That Italians eat constantly and remain suspiciously thin."

Paolo shrugged. "This is because we walk everywhere and argue loudly."

Marianne nodded thoughtfully. "I believe that arguing burns calories."

Claire pointed her fork at him. "And the bread. Explain the bread."

Paolo looked genuinely puzzled. "The bread needs explanation?"

"You show up with it every time," Claire said.

He smiled faintly. "In my family, you never arrive at someone's table empty-handed."

Kate watched the way he said it, not as a performance, but as a quiet rule he lived by.

The conversation drifted to stories from their younger years, mispronounced Italian words, Claire's failed attempt to negotiate for lemons using what Paolo later described as "very aggressive hand gestures."

Kate laughed. Really laughed. The sound startled her. She hadn't heard herself express joy this fully in months. Across the table, Paolo glanced up at the sound of her laughter before returning to his espresso, the corner of his mouth lifting slightly as if the moment had pleased him more than he expected.

Later, as plates emptied and the air cooled, Marianne carried out espresso cups and a small plate of *pasticciotti*. The courtyard lantern flickered to life above them. For a moment, the conversation softened.

Paolo leaned back in his chair, looking out at the darkening sky. "You know," he said, "Italians believe something Americans do not."

Claire leaned forward immediately. "Tell us."

"That life should expand in the evening."

"How so?" Marianne asked.

"In the morning, we work. In the afternoon, we worry." He gestured toward the table. "But in the evening, we remember we are alive."

The women fell quiet. It wasn't a speech. Just a truth, offered across breadcrumbs and empty plates. Kate felt the words settle somewhere deep inside her. Alive.

Paolo turned slightly toward her. "And you, Kate … are you rediscovering Puglia?"

She took a breath. "Yes. It's bringing a much-needed calm to my life. The slower pace you talk about … the beauty, the food. But mostly the people."

Paolo nodded thoughtfully. "That is what keeps many of us here. The sea is beautiful, and the food is good, but it is the people who make a place feel like home."

The word *home* settled between them.

Claire broke the moment with a grin. "Careful, Paolo. If you keep saying profound things, we'll make you come to dinner every night and maybe one night even cook for us."

He lifted his hands in surrender. "My mother would approve."

Marianne smiled. "So, she welcomes men in the kitchen?"

He shrugged lightly. "She says a man should know how to feed the people he loves."

Evelyn leaned back. "I'm writing that down."

The lantern light flickered across the table as the night deepened. More Stories. More memories shared. More laughter.

At one point, Paolo described restoring old stone houses across Puglia. "Old buildings teach patience," he said. "You cannot rush them. If you try, they collapse."

Near the end of the evening, he rose slowly, brushing crumbs from his hands. "*Domani*, eh...tomorrow" he corrected himself, "if you want, I can show you a small village nearby. A place that remembers how to live slowly."

Claire's eyes lit. "Yes."

Evelyn pretended indifference. "We will evaluate your proposal."

Marianne smiled warmly. "We'd love that."

Paolo nodded once. "*Buonanotte*."

"*Buonanotte*," they replied.

When he walked down the stone path toward the gate, the courtyard grew quiet again. Marianne leaned in closer and whispered. "He's charming."

Kate lifted an eyebrow. "You say that like it's illegal."

"It might be," Claire whispered. "In Texas."

Kate laughed.

The table was scattered with crumbs and empty cups. The cicadas' chirping filled the night air. For a while, none of them moved, just breathing in the satisfaction of the evening. It had been a simple meal of classic Italian dishes. But more than the food, it was the stories, the shared laughter, the deep friendship that steadied her, not healing everything, not solving anything, but holding her in place.

Unexpected joy had pulled up a chair at the table and this time; she didn't feel the need to push it away.

CHAPTER 29
Piano, Piano

Monopoli, Italy

“Are you ready for our field trip with Paolo, ladies?” Claire called up the stairs.

“You are exactly like herding cats,” she announced as one woman emerged from her room and another immediately turned around to retrieve something she had forgotten.

The vehicle that rolled up the gravel drive was not the dusty white work van the women had expected from a man who spent his days restoring centuries-old homes. Instead, Paolo drove a dark blue Alfa Romeo Stelvio, well cared for but not flashy. Like its owner, it was quietly handsome—practical, dependable, and distinctly Italian.

Claire peered out the window and frowned dramatically. "Well, that's disappointing."

Marianne laughed. "What's disappointing?"

"I was expecting a rusty work truck. Maybe one held together with duct tape and a prayer."

The women laughed as Paolo stepped out of the SUV.

"What?" Claire called. "You restore old houses. You're supposed to drive something with peeling paint and tools falling out the back."

Paolo glanced at the Alfa Romeo and laughed. "My work van is much uglier. Trust me."

"Now that's the Paolo I was expecting," Claire said.

Shaking his head, he opened the rear hatch for their bags. "Buongiorno, ladies. Is everyone ready?"

Within minutes, all five of them were settled inside, the scent of leather and a faint trace of espresso lingering in the cabin as Paolo steered them toward their destination.

As they wound up the narrow hill toward the small village, the faint scent of the sea drifted through the open car windows. Paolo drove carefully along the ribbon of road that curled through olive groves and low stone walls. The road seemed barely wider than the car itself.

“This road is technically two-way,” he said calmly.

Claire leaned forward from the back seat. “Technically?”

“Yes,” Paolo replied. “In practice, it becomes something more like a negotiation.”

Just then another small car appeared around a bend ahead of them.

Evelyn gasped. “There’s no room!”

Paolo slowed, smiling faintly. “This is what we call the Italian car dance.”

The other driver stopped. Paolo eased the car backward a few feet toward a slightly wider patch of road. The drivers exchanged a wave of understanding and a few quiet hand gestures before the other car slipped past.

Marianne laughed. “That was choreography.”

Paolo shrugged. “In Italy, we learn patience early.”

As they continued climbing, the road narrowed even further before finally opening onto a small cluster of white buildings stacked against the hillside like sugar cubes in the sun.

“This is called *un paese*,” Paolo explained. “A village.”

Marianne repeated it carefully. “Un pah-eh-zeh.”

“Perfetto,” Paolo said. “This *paese* is called Locorotondo.”

After parking near the edge of town, the women stepped out and collectively paused. Locorotondo looked as if someone had painted it with sunlight. Whitewashed homes curved around the hilltop in a perfect circle, their balconies overflowing with red geraniums and pink bougainvillea. Narrow stone lanes wound between arched doorways and flower-filled courtyards. Every corner seemed more picturesque than the last.

"It doesn't even look real," Marianne said, reaching for her phone.

"It looks like a wedding cake," Evelyn added.

Paolo laughed. "The name helps explain that."

"What does it mean?" Kate asked.

"'Luogo Rotondo,'" he said slowly. "Round place."

Claire turned in a circle, taking in the village. "It really is round."

Paolo nodded. "The old town was built in a circle on top of the hill. From above, it almost looks like someone drew it with a compass."

"It is one of my favorite places in Puglia," Paolo said. "People come here because it is beautiful. But I like it because of the name."

Kate glanced at him. "The round place?"

He smiled. "Yes. Life is rarely a straight line. Sometimes we think we are moving away from something, only to discover God is bringing us back to where we need to be."

For a moment, no one spoke. A warm breeze stirred the flowers spilling from the balconies.

Kate looked out across the valley and wondered if perhaps healing was a little like that too—not a straight path, but a journey that slowly brought a person home again.

Claire looked around. “It feels like stepping into a story.”

“In some ways, it is,” Paolo said. “Families have lived here for generations.”

They walked through narrow streets lined with potted basil and blue shutters. The afternoon sun painted everything gold. Somewhere, a radio played a slow Italian song that sounded like a memory. The village seemed to move at half the speed of the outside world.

They wandered past a pottery shop where bowls and pitchers filled the window, painted in deep blues and soft yellows that mirrored the sea and the sun.

Marianne stopped immediately. “Oh, my goodness.”

Inside, shelves were lined with handmade plates, cups, and vases. An elderly man worked at a small wheel, shaping a bowl, while a woman arranged finished pieces along a wooden table.

Claire lifted a ceramic dish painted with lemons. “Imagine serving pasta in this.”

“You will buy half the store,” Evelyn predicted.

“Only the meaningful pieces,” Claire said solemnly.

Paolo leaned against the doorway, watching them. “In Italy, we believe beautiful things should also be useful.”

Marianne nodded approvingly. “I like that philosophy.”

A few doors down they found a tiny jewelry shop tucked between a bakery and a linen store. The window shimmered with delicate silver chains and bracelets threaded with Murano glass beads.

Kate paused. A slender bracelet caught the light. It was sterling silver with three small beads: soft blue, pale green, and garnet red.

Paolo noticed her hesitation and asked, “You like it?”

“It reminds me of the water.”

“And the sky,” Marianne added.

“And the wine,” Claire said.

Evelyn leaned closer. “Definitely the wine.”

Kate smiled and ventured into the shop to make her first purchase since arriving in Puglia. The shop clerk wrapped the bracelet in tissue while Paolo translated a few Italian phrases between them.

When Kate stepped outside again, she slipped the bracelet onto her wrist. The glass beads caught the afternoon sun. Something about it felt like a small promise to herself. A reminder.

Paolo noticed the quiet satisfaction in her expression and smiled to himself. It was a small thing, he thought, to see someone reclaim a piece of joy.

"Murano glass has a long memory," he said. "Every color, every swirl, every tiny imperfection tells the story of the fire that shaped it."

He nodded toward the bracelet. "Perhaps that is why Italians love it so much. It reminds us that beautiful things are rarely made easily."

Kate glanced down. “I think I’ll remember this day every time I wear it.”

They walked slowly, savoring every sight and sound of Locorotondo. Soon they were standing beside the little Church of San Rocco. Its modest stone doorway could easily be missed, yet candles flickered inside before a small altar where generations of villagers had come to pray. Its doors were open, as if inviting them into the quiet shade inside.

“This is one of the many little churches where my mother used to bring me when I was stubborn,” Paolo said with a faint smile.

Claire’s eyes widened. “I remember Zia Rosa telling me about that when I visited. She quoted your mother: ‘One day that boy will be a kind man of God or a priest, if I drag him into that church every time he talks back.’”

The women laughed. Paolo shook his head, amused. “My mother has always believed the solution to most problems is prayer.”

“And bread,” Marianne added.

“And bread,” Paolo agreed.

Kate noticed the way Paolo’s expression softened as he glanced inside. It wasn’t showy. Just familiar. The kind of quiet reverence that comes from years of walking through the same doorway.

Claire folded her arms thoughtfully. “Your mother clearly succeeded.”

Paolo looked mildly confused. “In what way?”

"In raising a good man."

He shrugged slightly, uncomfortable with praise. "My mother prayed more than she instructed. That is usually more effective."

Kate had noticed it over the past few days—the way faith seemed to move quietly through his life. Not announced or performed, just naturally practiced. Paolo spoke of God the way some people spoke of family, as if conversation with the Lord had always been part of the rhythm of his days.

Claire smiled warmly. "Nice to see a grown man of your stature still places such high value on his faith."

Paolo's expression softened. "In my experience, the older we become, the more we realize how much we need it."

For a moment, no one spoke.

Then Evelyn broke the quiet with a grin. "Well, if stubborn boys turn into this, perhaps all mothers should try the church method."

Paolo laughed again, the sound echoing across the small piazza. The little church behind them stood quietly, as if it had been listening to them the whole time. Later they wandered through a small open market where a woman pressed slices of peach into Kate's palm.

"*Assaggia*," the woman urged. "Taste."

Kate smiled. "Grazie."

Paolo nodded approvingly. "Good. Always say thank you here. *Grazie* opens doors."

Evelyn bought a scarf she absolutely did not need. "It's for my future mysterious life," she declared.

Claire bought olive oil. "This is what heaven tastes like," she announced, holding up a bottle.

Later they sat at a café overlooking a small square. Children ran in circles. Old men played cards. A dog slept beneath a chair as if the sun belonged to him.

Paolo ordered with easy confidence. "*Un cappuccino, due caffè, una spremuta d'arancia*," he said—one cappuccino, two coffees, one orange juice and then glanced at Kate. "And for you?"

Kate hesitated. "Coffee."

Paolo smiled. "*Un caffè per la bella signora.*"

Kate understood enough to feel warmth rise in her cheeks.

"You are blushing," he observed lightly.

"I'm … warm," she corrected.

He laughed.

The afternoon ended at a stunning viewpoint, Belvedere di Locorotondo. The overlook seemed to reveal all of Puglia at once. Vineyards stitched together the hillsides below, while ancient olive trees spread across the landscape like a silver-green tapestry. White trulli and stone farmhouses dotted the countryside, their sunlit roofs gleaming against the deep green valley. The view felt less like looking at a place and more like looking at a painting.

As the women ooh'd and aah'd over the view, Kate took a few steps away from everyone to breathe in the beauty of Puglia. The afternoon breeze lifted her hair from her shoulders, and she closed her eyes for a few seconds.

Paolo slowly approached Kate and stood beside her, leaving respectful space. “I think people forget,” he said, “that life continues after heartbreak.”

Kate opened her eyes and turned her head toward the sound of his voice but didn’t answer immediately.

“Sometimes healing comes slowly, but it always comes if you allow it,” he continued.

“That sounds easy in Italian,” Claire called from behind them. “Does it come with subtitles?”

Paolo smiled. “In Italian we say, *Piano, piano.* Slowly, slowly.”

Kate looked down at the bracelet on her wrist. The Murano glass beads caught the sunlight.

She repeated the phrase. “*piano, piano.*” Slowly. Slowly.

She knew healing would take time, with or without Grant. When impatience rose in her heart, impatience with Grant, impatience with God, she would glance down at the small bracelet and whisper the words again.

Piano, piano, and trust that God was still writing the story.

Chapter 30
Italian Lessons

Monopoli, Italy

Days turned into weeks, and Kate was falling in love …

With Italy.

She had always been drawn to the language and the culture. But this visit was different. She didn't feel like a tourist or an observer. She felt as if she were slowly absorbing and melding into the intentional rhythm of *la dolce vita.*

The mornings unfolded gradually. The afternoons lingered. Even the evenings seemed to breathe more slowly than the ones she had left behind in Texas. It fed her soul. She felt closer to God than she had in years.

Sometimes it happened in the simplest ways—standing on the terrace as the sky melted into gold and rose over the Adriatic. Other times it was the echo of church bells drifting across the rooftops in the late afternoon. Each time it happened, she felt as though God were carefully caressing her heart. Not correcting or scolding. Just reminding her that He was still there and that she was not forgotten.

Paolo became part of their rhythm the way sunlight did, naturally, without asking permission. At Claire's request, Paolo began coming three evenings a week to help Ev, Marianne, and Kate improve their Italian so they could venture out more confidently on their own.

What the women didn't realize was how much he welcomed the change. Since Sofia's death, Paolo's life had grown quiet in ways he had never expected. He still cooked dinner once or twice a week with his elderly mother and joined her for church on Sunday mornings, but most of his days were spent alone or working to restore old stone houses across the region. Work. Home. Church. Repeat.

People in town knew him and greeted him warmly when he passed through the market or stopped for coffee. Yet during those early months of grief, he had declined so many invitations to dinners, celebrations, even simple evenings with friends that eventually the invitations had stopped coming. The quiet had settled around him like dust.

And though he had learned to live within his solitude, the sudden energy of four American women attempting Italian with heroic confidence had become a welcome disruption.

At first the lessons were serious. At least they began that way. Paolo would sit at the long wooden table with a small notebook, writing words carefully in neat columns.

“Pronunciation matters,” he would say patiently.

“Then we may already be in trouble,” Claire replied.

The first week was full of mistakes. Marianne once asked a vegetable vendor for six husbands instead of six onions. Ev confidently told a café owner she was “very pregnant” when she meant to say she was “very full.” Claire spent two full minutes thanking a man’s dog instead of the man himself.

Paolo tried to correct them with dignity. Eventually he gave up and laughed with them. By the third week, things had improved. They practiced ordering food. Paolo would play the part of an unimpressed waiter.

“What would you like?” he would ask in Italian.

Ev straightened confidently. “*Vorrei un bicchiere di vino rosso.*”

Paolo nodded approvingly. "Very good."

Claire leaned forward. "I will have the same thing but larger."

Paolo raised one eyebrow. "In Italy we do not order wine like gasoline."

The courtyard erupted with laughter.

Kate found herself enjoying the lessons more than she expected. Language had a way of opening small doors. Each new word felt like discovering a hidden key to the culture she loved. And Paolo had a way of making the lessons feel less like studying and more like living.

Sometimes he brought small handwritten lists of phrases. Other times he simply asked them questions in Italian and waited patiently for them to puzzle through the answers. Progress came slowly. But it came.

Claire, of course, could not let at least one of their sessions pass undocumented. One afternoon, at some point between verb conjugations and Paolo patiently correcting their pronunciation, she pulled out her phone and began snapping photos. Paolo standing at the head of the long table like a very handsome professor. Marianne leaning forward in concentration. Evelyn squinting skeptically at her notes. And Kate mid-laugh over a mispronounced phrase.

Within minutes, Claire was tapping furiously, uploading a small series of photos to Facebook and tagging everyone with theatrical efficiency. *Italian lessons at Villa Santoro. We came for the scenery, stayed for the teacher,* she captioned it. "There," she announced, setting her phone down with satisfaction. "Now it's official. We're cultured."

A few weeks later, Paolo sat at the long wooden table attempting another Italian lesson while the women dutifully repeated phrases from their notebooks.

"*Vorrei un cappuccino, per favore,*" Marianne said carefully.

"Very good," Paolo replied.

Claire sat up straighter. "*Vorrei due cappuccini, per favore.*"

Paolo laughed. "Of course you would."

"Always order for the future," Claire said wisely.

Kate managed a reasonably accurate sentence about finding the post office, while Evelyn continued waging war against Italian verb conjugations.

Just then, Zia Rosa appeared in the doorway carrying a basket of laundry. She paused. Listened. Then slowly shook her head. "Madonna mia."

The women immediately started laughing.

"What?" Claire asked.

Rosa looked at Paolo and spoke rapidly in Italian. "*Hai molta pazienza. Più di un santo.*"

Paolo chuckled.

"What did she say?" Marianne asked.

Paolo grinned. "She says I have a great deal of patience. More than a saint."

The women laughed as Rosa pointed toward Evelyn. "*Quella non sta imparando l'italiano. Sta inventando una nuova lingua.*"

To Rosa's surprise, Evelyn burst out laughing. "You said I'm not learning Italian. I'm inventing a new language."

Rosa froze. Then narrowed her eyes. "You understood that?"

"A little."

The older woman turned dramatically toward Paolo. "*Sono nei guai adesso.*"

Kate smiled. "That means you're in trouble now."

Now Rosa looked genuinely alarmed. The women erupted.

Paolo leaned back in his chair, thoroughly enjoying himself.

Rosa pointed a finger at the group. "Three weeks ago, you knew nothing."

"Not true," Claire said. "We knew *ciao.*"

Rosa rolled her eyes. "Americans learn three words and suddenly think they are Italian." She stared at them for a moment, then slowly smiled. "Well," she admitted, "perhaps there is hope for you after all."

"That's the nicest thing you've said all week," Evelyn replied.

"Don't get used to it," Rosa said, turning toward the kitchen.

As she disappeared through the doorway, they heard her call back over her shoulder. "*E ricordatevi... le ragazze fanno i piatti dopo cena!*" The girls do the dishes after dinner.

The women groaned. Paolo laughed. Some lessons, apparently, everyone understood perfectly.

One evening Marianne successfully ordered dinner for the entire table in Italian. Paolo placed his hand dramatically over his heart.

"I am witnessing a miracle."

Claire lifted her glass. "To linguistic survival."

The women began setting an extra place at the table without ever discussing it. It simply appeared. A sixth plate. A sixth glass. Just in case Paolo would stay for dinner after their lesson was finished.

At some point the lessons had stopped feeling like lessons. And Kate found herself anticipating them. At first, she had been cautious about the friendship forming with Paolo. Now she felt something gentler. Peaceful. There was no urgency in it. No pressure. Just the quiet unfolding of companionship.

One evening Paolo arrived carrying a pot instead of bread. "My mother's lentil soup," he announced as he set it on the table.

The rich, earthy aroma drifted through the courtyard. "This is what we eat when life is heavy," he said.

Marianne grinned. "Then we should eat it often."

Claire tasted it and closed her eyes briefly. "This soup is therapy."

Evelyn leaned back in her chair and asked Paolo about his work. "What are you restoring these days?" she asked.

He wiped his hands on a cloth before answering. "An old stone farmhouse outside Bari," he explained. "The roof has collapsed, and half the walls have shifted. My job is to repair what time has worn."

Kate watched his hands as he spoke. Steady. Careful. Capable.

Paolo brushed a crumb of bread from the table. "Most people assume a building is lost when they see the cracks," he said. "But cracks are not the same as collapse. Sometimes the foundation is still strong beneath everything. When that is true, restoration is possible."

He shrugged lightly. "It simply requires humility from the one doing the rebuilding."

"And when a building cannot be restored?" Marianne asked.

Paolo grew quiet. "Then you honor what it was," he said. "You do not pretend it never mattered."

Kate felt her throat tighten.

Later, when the others drifted inside to clear dishes and argue about dessert, Paolo remained in the courtyard with Kate. The night air was warm and soft. Cicadas hummed beyond the olive trees. Paolo did not rush the silence. He let it breathe.

"You are thinking," he said eventually.

"I do that," she replied.

He smiled slightly. "I know."

Kate looked toward the dark outline of the grove. "I miss my husband," she admitted.

Paolo's expression didn't harden. It didn't judge. For a moment he looked away into the dark, as if steadying his own thoughts.

"Your marriage still deserves honor," he said quietly. "Even when it is wounded."

Then he looked back at her. "It is possible," he said gently, "to miss someone and still be wounded by them."

Kate swallowed. "You are kind," she said.

"I am honest," he corrected softly. "Kindness without truth is artificial comfort."

The words felt like a handrail. Kate's eyes stung. "I don't want to do this separation wrong," she whispered. "I don't want to numb myself with attention."

He looked at her steadily. "Then do not numb," he said. "Be awake."

She exhaled shakily. "You make it sound simple."

"It is not simple," he said. "But it can be pure."

Pure. Not perfect. Pure.

He stood slowly. "I should go," he said, "before staying would become complicated."

The honesty startled her. He did not wait for her response. He simply bowed his head slightly in a quiet gesture of respect.

"*Buonanotte,*" he said.

"*Buonanotte*," she whispered.

When he left, Kate remained in the courtyard beneath the widening sky. The stars stretched above the trees like quiet witnesses. She pressed her hand lightly against her chest. The feelings inside her were not rushing forward. They were arriving like the tide.

Slow. Steady. Persistent. Undeniable.

And yet she sensed something else too—something steadier beneath it all. As if, after many weeks of drifting, her feet were finally touching solid ground again.

CHAPTER 31
Unexpected Tenderness

Monopoli, Italy

The feelings we resist most are often the ones that reveal we are finally alive again.

Paolo turned the key in his front door and stepped inside, setting the empty casserole dish on the kitchen counter. The faint scent of garlic and lemon still clung to it. His mother had insisted, again, on sending leftovers home with him.

"You eat like a man who forgets he must feed himself," she had said, waving him toward the door.

Paolo smiled faintly at the memory. Cooking for her once or twice a week had become their rhythm since Sofia died three years earlier. His mother pretended she needed the help. He knew better. Grief rarely announces itself loudly in Italian families. It settles quietly into routine.

He rinsed the dish and placed it beside the sink. Normally he would make tea and sit for a few minutes before bed. Tonight, his thoughts refused to settle. They kept returning to the same person. Claire's friend, Kate. Paolo frowned slightly and leaned against the counter.

For three years after Sofia's death, he had not allowed himself to look at another woman with personal interest. Not once. Friends had tried to introduce him to widows. Neighbors had mentioned kind women from church. His mother had suggested a schoolteacher from the next village who "had a good heart."

Paolo had declined every time. Not because the women lacked kindness or appeal, but because something inside him had remained closed. His love for Sofia had not disappeared when she died. It had simply changed shape. And until recently, he had been content to let it remain that way.

He walked to the window and looked out across the dark hills. Kate had not done anything improper. If anything, she had been careful. Respectful. Almost cautious around him. Yet he found himself noticing her in ways he hadn't expected—her quiet strength, the gentleness she carried even while speaking about the turmoil in her marriage. And her eyes.

There was sorrow there. Not bitterness. Not anger. It was the kind of deep sorrow that comes from loving someone faithfully and being wounded by it.

Paolo rested his forearms on the windowsill. What unsettled him most was not her beauty, though she was beautiful in a way that had nothing to do with youth. It was her loyalty. Even while speaking carefully about the pain in her marriage, she never spoke of her husband with contempt.

She still loved him.

Paolo had seen that clearly. That kind of devotion was rare. And he respected it more than he could explain.

He exhaled slowly.

Part of the pull he felt toward her began to make sense. They both knew what it meant to carry a broken heart. For three years, Paolo had believed that losing Sofia was the deepest kind of grief a person could experience. Death was final. Absolute.

But tonight, a different thought came to him. Kate's loss was different. And in some ways … even more cruel.

When death takes a spouse, the love between them is not erased. It remains intact. The memories stay honorable. The bond is not diminished.

But betrayal … betrayal carries a different wound.

If Grant did not ultimately choose her, Kate would not only grieve the loss of her marriage but also carry the weight of being rejected.

The realization tightened something in his chest. Paolo straightened slowly. That kind of pain could cut far deeper than death. Because it left questions behind. Questions about worth, about identity, about whether love had ever truly been returned.

He rubbed a hand across the back of his neck. No wonder her eyes carried that quiet sadness. No wonder she guarded her heart so carefully.

He walked to the small table where Sofia's photograph still stood. Her smile looked the same as it always had—bright, uncomplicated.

"You would like her," he said. The thought surprised him as he spoke it.

Kate and Sofia were very different women. But they shared something essential—a quiet steadiness, a strength that did not need attention to prove itself. They were the kind of women who knew how to endure suffering without letting it poison their hearts.

Paolo set the photograph back down carefully, then stepped outside onto the small stone patio. The night air had cooled. Above him, the sky stretched wide and clear. He folded his arms.

"Lord," he whispered. It had been a long time since he had prayed about something like this. "I do not want to dishonor Kate."

The breeze moved gently through the olive trees. "I do not want to complicate her life while she is already walking through something painful."

He paused. "And I do not want to dishonor the love I had for Sofia."

The words hung in the night air. After a moment, he added, "But I also see her pain." He looked up at the stars. "If You have placed me in her path for a reason, help me to be kind."

He exhaled slowly. "Help me be careful."

Then one more thought surfaced—one he hadn't realized was already in his heart. "And help me remind her, if she ever needs it, that being betrayed does not mean she was unworthy of love."

The night remained quiet. But as Paolo stood beneath the stars, one thing became clear. Whatever this unexpected tenderness was, it would require careful guarding. Not because it was wrong. But because wounded hearts were sacred things. And sacred things deserved protection.

CHAPTER 32
Uninvited Emotions

Monopoli, Italy

The heart has an inconvenient habit of feeling things the mind has not yet approved.

Most evenings after dinner, the women lingered around the long wooden table, talking until the night air cooled and someone eventually suggested sleep.

Tonight, Kate slipped away early. She carried her journal out to the terrace behind the villa, where trees cast soft shadows across the moonlit hills. A candle flickered on the table beside her. For several minutes, she simply sat. The countryside had a way of slowing everything down. Even her thoughts seemed to move more slowly here.

But one thought had followed her all evening. Paolo.

Kate sighed and leaned back in her chair. She had not intended to think about him at all. When she first arrived in Italy, he had simply been Claire's friend—a kind local man who helped them with language and occasionally joined their dinners or walks. Yet over the past few days, something had shifted.

Not in his behavior. Paolo had been consistently respectful. Careful, even. But something inside her had changed.

Kate stared at the candle flame. "I'm too old for this nonsense," she muttered under her breath.

She picked up her journal and opened it, though the pen remained still in her hand. The truth was uncomfortable. She liked talking with him—more than she expected. He listened. Really listened. Not with the distracted politeness she had grown used to in a long marriage where conversations had gradually become routine. Paolo paid attention.

And something about the way he spoke—slow, thoughtful, never trying to impress—made her feel seen. The realization unsettled her, because she could finally admit that feeling had been missing long before Grant's confession. And the deeper truth, the one she did not want to name even to herself, was this: it felt good. Not thrilling. Not romantic. Just steady. Comfortable. Like being understood without having to explain everything.

Kate closed the journal and rubbed her temples lightly. "Lord," she sighed, "I need to say something out loud. I think I'm beginning to feel drawn to him."

The words sounded unfamiliar in the stillness. Kate shook her head slowly. "This is ridiculous. I'm sixty-two years old."

But age had never made the human heart simple. What unsettled her even more was that the feeling didn't seem shallow. It wasn't about romance or excitement. It was something quieter, a sense of ease and understanding between two people who had both known deep losses.

Kate stared out across the hills. "I didn't come to Italy looking for another man," she said. The thought almost made her laugh. "I came here to hear You, not myself."

The candle flame flickered, and slowly another truth surfaced. What she felt toward Paolo wasn't only attraction. It was gratitude. Gratitude for his kindness in a season where so much of her life had collapsed. He had never asked intrusive questions, never encouraged bitterness toward Grant, never crossed a line. If anything, he seemed to guard the boundaries between them more carefully than she did.

Kate exhaled slowly. "That should make this easier," she murmured. "But it doesn't."

Because kindness had a way of softening defenses, and softened defenses could become dangerous. She picked up her pen and finally began to write.

Lord, I don't want to dishonor my marriage.

Her pen paused. Even writing the words hurt, because she no longer knew what her marriage would become. Grant had already taken steps toward separation, maybe even divorce. Yet the covenant still existed, and Kate was not willing to treat it lightly.

She continued writing.

If this friendship with Paolo is something You have allowed to encourage me in a painful season, I'm grateful. But if my heart is beginning to wander somewhere it shouldn't, please convict me quickly.

Kate closed her eyes. "Guard my heart," she whispered.

The prayer felt heavier than she expected, because a quiet voice inside her asked a question she wasn't ready to answer.

What if Grant never comes back? Kate pushed the thought away immediately. "That's not tonight's question," she said.

Tonight's question was simpler. Faithfulness. What did faithfulness look like right now?

Kate blew out the candle and stood. The terrace fell into darkness, lit only by the soft silver of the moon. As she walked back toward the villa, one decision settled clearly in her mind. She would not allow Grant's rejection to make her careless.

Whatever friendship grew between her and Paolo, it would remain honest, guarded, and surrendered to God. Because some seasons of life required patience more than answers. And until God made the future clearer, Kate intended to walk this one with integrity.

The next evening, the women's conversation began lightly, as most of their evenings did, but it didn't stay that way. Paolo was absent and Rosa had retired early.

The four of them were still lingering around the long table, the last of the dishes pushed aside, a second bottle of wine open between them. The lantern light softened everything.

Claire was the one who said it. "Okay," she began, pointing her glass toward Kate, "we've all been thinking it. So, I'm just going to say it."

Kate smiled cautiously. "That's always a dangerous sentence."

Claire didn't back down. "What is going on with you and Paolo?"

Evelyn let out a small laugh. "Finally."

Marianne didn't laugh. She just watched Kate carefully.

Kate looked down at her glass, turning it slowly between her fingers. For a moment, she said nothing. Then she exhaled. "I don't even know how to answer that," she admitted.

"Try," Claire pushed.

Kate hesitated, then looked up. "I like him." The truth landed quietly, but clearly. No one reacted dramatically. No teasing. No surprise. Just stillness.

Evelyn leaned forward slightly. "Like? You *like* him?"

Kate nodded once. "Yes."

Marianne replied. "Well, that doesn't make you a bad person."

"I know," Kate said. "But it complicates everything."

Claire tilted her head. "In what way?"

Kate looked out past them, toward the dark beyond the courtyard wall. "I've been asking myself a question I don't like very much," she said.

"What question?" Evelyn asked.

Kate swallowed. "What would happen if Grant divorced me?"

The table went quiet.

"And if he does," she continued slowly, "what would it look like if I didn't hold back anymore?"

Claire's voice softened. "You mean with Paolo?"

Kate nodded. The words came more easily now, though her voice remained steady. "I've imagined it," she said. "Not constantly. But enough to know I'm not immune to the idea."

No one interrupted.

"I think about what it would feel like to be with someone who listens," she continued. "Someone who notices things. Someone who is kind in a way that doesn't feel complicated."

Her hands tightened slightly around her glass. "And that scares me."

"Why?" Evelyn asked.

"Because it would be easy," Kate said. "Too easy."

She looked at them, her expression honest. "I could justify it. I could tell myself my marriage is already broken. That I didn't cause this. That I deserve something good after everything that's happened."

Claire nodded slowly. "Those would all be very believable arguments."

"They are," Kate said. "That's the problem."

Marianne leaned in slightly. "But what does your heart say when you're not trying to justify anything?"

Kate didn't answer right away. Finally, she spoke. "It says I'm not free yet."

The words settled heavily.

"It says my marriage still exists, even if it's wounded. Even if Grant is the one walking away." She paused. "And I don't want to be the person who abandons it just because it became difficult."

Evelyn sat back, studying her. "So, you're choosing restraint."

Kate nodded. "I'm choosing faithfulness," she said. "Even when no one would blame me for choosing something else."

Claire reached across the table and squeezed her hand. "That's not weakness, you know."

"I don't feel weak," Kate said. "I feel obedient."

Marianne gave a small, knowing smile. "That's usually where the right decisions get made."

A silence settled over the table. Not uncomfortable. Just honest.

Then Evelyn lifted her glass slightly. "Well," she said, "for what it's worth … if Paolo ever does become part of your future someday, I think we would all be very supportive."

Claire shot her a look. "Ev."

"What?" Evelyn said lightly. "I said *someday.*"

Kate smiled, but it was a soft, thoughtful smile. "Maybe," she said. "But not now."

Claire nodded. "Not now."

Kate glanced toward the doorway, where the faint sound of the night drifted in. "For now," she said, "I want to be able to look back on this season and know I didn't cross a line just because it was available."

Marianne raised her glass. "To that kind of clarity."

They all lifted theirs. And for a moment, the weight of everything Kate was holding felt just a little lighter.

CHAPTER 33
Empty House

Austin, Texas

Grant moved back into their house the same afternoon Kate left for Italy.

He told himself it was the right thing to do. It was their home with thirty-five years of life lived within those walls: birthdays, Christmas mornings, late-night conversations at the kitchen table. Walking away from it would have felt like admitting something final. So, he came back.

He even said a quiet prayer when he unlocked the front door.

Lord, help me do the right thing.

He noticed that about himself lately—the small prayers, the attempts to consider God's will. It reassured him he hadn't abandoned his conscience completely. He was trying and that mattered.

The house greeted him with the faint scent of lemon polish and something softer that had always belonged to Kate—lavender, maybe. Nothing had moved. Her books still rested on the end table beside the couch. A favorite soft lap blanket lay across the armchair. Even the small ceramic bowl on the narrow table by the door still held the spare house key and a few coins.

Grant walked slowly through the rooms. He told himself he was honoring the life they had built. Staying here proved something. He wasn't the kind of man who simply walked away.

He set his suitcase down in the bedroom they had shared for decades. For a moment, he hesitated. Then he placed his clothes in the dresser like he had done a thousand times before—a man returning to his life.

Later that evening, he called the church office.

"Pastor's schedule is pretty full this week," the secretary explained kindly. "But he could see you Thursday afternoon."

"Thursday works," Grant said.

It felt good to say it. Responsible. Accountable. He entered the appointment in his calendar. By Tuesday, he had already convinced himself he might need to move it. A foundation board meeting had come up unexpectedly. And really, these conversations with pastors required time and focus. It wouldn't be fair to rush something that important.

So, he called back. "Something came up," he said. "Could we reschedule for next week?"

The secretary sounded understanding. Grant hung up, feeling oddly relieved. He had made the effort. That counted.

The house felt too quiet most evenings. At first he tried filling the silence with television. Later, he started working longer hours. But eventually he found himself driving across town more often than he'd expected …to Lydia's townhouse.

He never invited her to his house. Not once. That would cross a line he wasn't willing to cross. His house was different. Sacred, almost. Kate's photographs still lined the hallway. Their daughter's childhood drawings were framed beside the staircase. The dining table still bore the faint scratches from decades of family meals. Bringing Lydia here would feel wrong.

Grant took a strange comfort in that boundary. It allowed him to believe he still respected something. So, he went to Lydia instead.

Her townhouse was warm and carefully arranged with soft lighting, candles that smelled faintly of vanilla, and music playing low in the background.

Lydia greeted him at the door as if she had been waiting all evening. “You look stressed,” she said gently.

“It’s been a week.”

“You say that every time.”

“Because it’s true.”

She smiled and stepped aside so he could enter. Dinner appeared easily—pasta, bread, a bottle of wine already open. Lydia listened when he talked about work. She asked questions that made him feel interesting again.

“You carry so much,” she said, touching his hand across the table.

“It’s part of the job.”

“No,” she said. “It’s part of who you are.”

Grant didn’t argue. The attention felt comforting. With Lydia, there were no decades of shared history pressing against every conversation. No memories asking whether he had changed. Just the present moment and Lydia looking at him as though he were still the man he remembered being.

Later, she moved closer on the couch, her head resting lightly against his shoulder. Grant hesitated. He had told himself he didn’t want things to cross the sexual line again. Physical closeness complicated things. It wasn’t good for him, and it wasn’t fair to her.

Lydia seemed to sense his hesitation and moved through it anyway. “You worry too much,” she murmured. “We’re adults.”

Grant stared at the dark window across the room. "We should be careful," he muttered.

"Careful of what?"

He didn't answer immediately. Careful of God. Careful of Kate. Careful of the life he wasn't quite ready to dismantle.

Lydia lifted her head slightly, studying his face. "You deserve happiness," she said.

Grant had heard the sentence before. It landed every time.

"You've spent your whole life being responsible," she continued. "You can choose something for yourself now." Her hand found his again, warm and certain.

Grant told himself she was probably right. Thirty-five years of marriage. Decades of providing, leading, carrying responsibility. Was it wrong to want something that felt good for once?

Lydia kissed him softly—not urgent, but intentional. He didn't pull away. But part of him remained oddly distant, as if he were watching his own life unfold from across the room.

Later, when he drove home, the house offered no warmth. only a quiet that felt unfamiliar. He stood in the entryway, listening to it. The contrast from Lydia's townhouse pressed against his conscience more than he wanted to admit. It was as if the years of family and shared love had dissolved into something distant—real, but no longer reachable.

Grant loosened his tie and walked slowly into the kitchen. The refrigerator hummed. Moonlight stretched across the floor through the window. He poured himself a glass of water and leaned against the counter. He was trying. He ran through his validations again: He had moved back into the house. He had called the pastor. He was keeping certain lines intact.

That meant something. Didn't it?

But even as he stood there convincing himself, another realization crept through the cracks of his reasoning. The attention Lydia gave him soothed him in the moment. But it did not quiet his conscience.

Somewhere beneath the structure of excuses he had carefully built, Grant knew a truth he wasn't ready to face. He wasn't at peace. He was simply distracted.

CHAPTER 34
Who's the Italian Guy?

Austin, Texas

The call came casually one evening.

Grant had returned from Lydia's townhouse an hour earlier and was standing on the back deck, wrestling with his conflicting emotions. He sipped a glass of white wine and stared into the starlit sky when his phone buzzed. It was his daughter.

"Hey, Dad."

"Hey, sweetheart," he said, forcing a normal tone.

They exchanged the usual updates—work, schedules, the weather that seemed to change every five minutes in Texas. Then she said it.

"Mom seems… different."

Grant paused. "Different how?"

"Peaceful," she said thoughtfully. "Lighter."

The word cut deeper than he expected. Lighter. He leaned against the kitchen counter. "Well, that's good, isn't it?"

"I think so," she said. "We did a Zoom call with her and her friends earlier tonight. I love those women. They're such a hoot."

Grant smiled faintly. "Yes. Your mom is blessed to have such good friends."

"They really are having the time of their lives over there. They were all talking at once about their Italian lessons. You must have seen Claire's Facebook post. She tagged Mom."

Grant frowned slightly. "Italian lessons?" He paused, searching for something neutral. "Gosh, honey, I rarely log onto Facebook. That's your mom's thing. I'll take a look."

"Yeah," she said. "Apparently some local guy has been helping them practice. His name is Paolo."

The name meant nothing to Grant.

"I guess he's a childhood friend of Claire's or something," she continued. "He actually walked into the courtyard while we were still on the Zoom call."

Something tightened in Grant's chest. "Oh?"

"Dad," she said with a laugh, "the women were practically giggling."

Grant forced a light chuckle. "That sounds like your mom's friends."

"No, I mean it," she said. "This guy looks like he stepped out of an Italian movie. Tall, dark hair, gray at the temples. Very charming. Even through Zoom you could tell."

Grant stared at the dark window above the sink. "Is that right?"

"Yeah. Mom seems really happy."

Happy. The word lingered.

"Haven't you been talking to her most days?" she asked casually.

Grant hesitated just long enough to notice it. "Most days. Time zones make it tricky."

"True," she said. "I'm just glad she seems to be having a great time. I think she needed this. She's always going a hundred miles an hour when she's in Texas."

They talked a few more minutes before hanging up, but Grant barely heard the rest. Images had already begun forming in his mind. Kate laughing in the sunlight, a man leaning slightly closer than necessary, her attention drawn somewhere else.

He pushed away from the counter. This was ridiculous. Kate was in Italy with her friends. Nothing more. And yet…

He was so charming.

Grant walked into the living room. The television murmured, but the space felt hollow. He pictured Kate again, only now she was laughing at something Paolo said, leaning toward someone who listened to her. The thought unsettled him.

For months, he had told himself she had grown distant. Independent and self-sufficient. He had convinced himself she didn't need him anymore. But what if that had never been true? What if she had simply stopped asking?

The idea landed heavily. He sat down slowly on the couch. If she had been the one to stray … if she had slept with another man, would he have been able to extend grace?

No. He would have demanded loyalty. Repentance. He would have expected her to fight for the marriage. And yet he had expected her allegiance without offering his own. The hypocrisy struck hard.

His imagination turned again to Paolo's hand brushing Kate's arm, Kate smiling, leaning toward someone who saw her the way he once had. Jealousy rose. Not rage. Panic.

What if she moves on? What if someone else sees what I stopped seeing?

Across town, Lydia was probably still awake, thinking about their evening together. But suddenly her attention felt different. Not comforting. Her constant reassurance that he deserved happiness had begun to feel like pressure. Even manipulation. Had he mistaken intensity for connection?

By contrast, Kate's absence now felt enormous. The house was too quiet. Too empty. He realized how few days he had ever spent here without her. He looked around slowly and noticed all Kate's touches in the décor, in the organization, and in the comfort of their home. Then it hit him with terrifying clarity; he wasn't gaining freedom … he was losing her.

The realization stole the air from his lungs. He leaned back, staring at the ceiling. For a long moment, he said nothing. Then he whispered into the empty room,

"What have I done?"

CHAPTER 35
Paper & Poison

Austin, Texas

Grant could not get the image of Paolo out of his mind.

He had studied the Facebook photos more times than he was willing to admit. There was nothing inappropriate in them. Kate wasn't even sitting close to him. Still, the images sharpened over the following days growing more detailed, more intrusive.

Grant imagined Paolo arriving at the courtyard, confident, effortless. Italian men had a reputation—bold, expressive, and attentive when they admired a woman.

Ahh, belladonna.

The imagined scene twisted something deep in his chest. He pictured Kate laughing, brushing her hair back, while Paolo watched her with open admiration. Maybe the lessons had become something more. A walk through the village. Espresso at a quiet café.

Grant's jaw tightened.

He told himself he was angry because Kate had given up. She left the country. Set boundaries. Enforced them.

What kind of wife does that? The answer came quietly.

A wife protecting what you were destroying.

He pushed the thought away. Instead, he gathered what little information he had—his daughter's story, the photos—and assembled it into something darker. Something useful.

By the time he reached Lydia's townhouse that evening, the story had hardened into something that felt like truth.

"She's spending all her time with this guy," he said, pacing. "He's teaching them Italian. Showing them around. Apparently, he's always there."

Lydia listened carefully. "And your daughter saw him?"

"Yes. On the Zoom call."

"And he was… charming?"

Grant exhaled sharply. "Of course he was."

Lydia's expression softened. "That must feel humiliating."

The word landed. Grant stopped pacing.

"I'm not saying anything inappropriate is happening," she continued. "But she left the country, Grant. Surrounded herself with friends … and this man. She's forcing your hand."

"What do you mean?" he asked.

"She's shaping a narrative," Lydia said. "She becomes the wounded wife finding peace in Italy. And you're the husband who betrayed her."

Grant's jaw tightened.

"She gets to be the saint," Lydia added sarcastically.

Kate had never said that. But lately, he heard it anyway—in her calm voice, her boundaries, her silence. Especially the silence. It echoed through the house. Through the kitchen. Through his empty bed.

Silence leaves room for imagination. And Grant's imagination had grown dangerous. A thought slipped in—quiet, convincing. *She thinks she's better than you.*

Grant inhaled sharply. At least Lydia wanted him. At least she didn't withdraw. Didn't go silent. At least she accepted him … or demanded him? He didn't examine the difference. He only felt relief.

Days passed. He reached for his phone repeatedly but never called. He knew the rule. Her rule. Three months. No contact.

Thirty-five years replaced by quiet. Quiet leaves space for suspicion. One afternoon, something in him snapped.

"I'm done being punished," he muttered.

Lydia lifted her chin. "Then stop letting her control the narrative."

"How?"

"Take some kind of action," she said. "Stop waiting."

The idea landed with force. He drove to a lawyer's office the next morning. The waiting room smelled faintly of coffee and printer toner. Grant flipped through his paperwork but had no idea what he read. The entire moment feeling surreal.

"Legal separation is often a first step," the lawyer explained. "It provides clarity while protecting both parties."

Grant nodded. A first step. Reasonable. Responsible. His hands were steady as he signed the documents. But beneath that calm, something else moved.

This wasn't just legal. It was leverage.

He told himself he was creating clarity. But the truth sat just beneath the surface. He wanted to force Kate to respond. To break the silence and force her to respond.

That evening, he sat at his desk staring at the email draft.

Family Matter—Please Respond

He told himself it counted as an emergency. Not because anything had happened, but because it would force communication. He typed carefully using a respectful tone. Legal language softened with concern.

When he finished, he read it once more. Then he hit send.

The message disappeared instantly and something twisted inside him.

Not relief.

Fear.

Grant leaned back, staring at the dark window. He had drawn a line. And lines, once drawn, have a way of becoming permanent. Somewhere beneath the jealousy, the anger, and the justifications, a quieter voice spoke.

The silence Kate had chosen was meant to save their marriage.

And he had just used it as a weapon.

Paper and poison.

CHAPTER 36
Family Matter

Monopoli, Italy

The email arrived on a quiet Tuesday morning.

Kate sat in the courtyard with Ev, sunlight warming the wooden table between them. Two small cups of espresso rested on white saucers, the last ribbons of steam fading into the air. Beyond the low stone wall, the hillside stretched pale and still, the hum of the city rising and falling in the distance.

Marianne was inside on a video call with her grandchildren. Claire had gone to the market, declaring she needed "therapeutic produce and possibly cheese."

The morning felt gentle. Almost sacred.

Kate picked up her phone absentmindedly, expecting nothing more than a message from one of the women or perhaps a photo of Claire triumphantly holding a basket of tomatoes.

Instead, her stomach dropped.

Subject: Family Matter—Please Respond

Her pulse quickened instantly. Family matter. Her mind raced through the possibilities—one of the children in crisis … an accident, a hospital, a diagnosis. Her breath caught as she opened the email, bracing for impact.

Please God, let everyone be safe.

The message loaded. Legal terminology. Measured paragraphs. Formal phrasing.

Kate blinked, confused, and read again, slower this time. Temporary arrangements. Asset considerations. Legal separation. The meaning assembled itself piece by piece until there was no mistaking it. Her breathing grew uneven. Her hands trembled.

Across the table, Ev leaned forward. "What is it?"

Kate didn't answer. She kept reading. Each sentence landed heavier than the one before. Grant had consulted an attorney and was proposing legal separation. He believed this was the appropriate "next step."

Next step.

Kate lowered the phone and stared past Evelyn toward the sun-washed stone wall. Nothing around her had changed. The sunlight still warm, the courtyard still quiet, but something inside her had shifted sharply, as if a fault line had opened without warning.

"This isn't about the kids," she said faintly.

Ev's voice tightened. "What do you mean?"

"He's filing."

"For divorce?"

"A legal separation."

The words tasted metallic. Kate looked back down at the screen as emotion rose in waves—shock, disbelief, then something hotter. Why this? Why now?

He had broken the no-contact boundary. He had written "Family Matter." And this was what he sent? Her grip tightened around the phone.

You frightened me. How dare you, make me think one of our children was hurt.

Anger surfaced, hot, pure, and explosive. After thirty-five years, this is how you choose to speak? She wanted to scream at the top of her lungs. If Grant were here, she'd love to throw something at him. But he wasn't. He had attacked from a distance.

She read the email again, noticing the tone more clearly now. It was careful, legal, and controlled. As if the dismantling of their life could be handled like a business transaction.

"This is manipulation," she said quietly.

Ev reached across the table and took her hand. "What do you need?"

Kate shook her head. "I don't even know." Shock still hummed through her, but beneath it something deeper was rising. Grief. "He's taking the first step toward divorce," she added with a sigh.

"You don't have to respond right away," Ev offered. "Take some time to pray and think."

Kate nodded, but the courtyard suddenly felt too contained. "I need air."

She stood and walked past the stone archway toward the narrow path that led away from the villa. Gravel shifted beneath her shoes, the sound too loud against the quiet as her thoughts tumbled through fear, anger, sadness, and confusion.

A marriage built over decades, reduced to a legal email.

She didn't hear Paolo approach. She sensed him.

"*Che succede*?" he asked softly. What happened?

She turned, struggling to steady her voice. "My husband sent an email. He's asking for a legal separation."

Paolo's expression shifted immediately, not in curiosity or opportunity, but sorrow. "I am sorry," he said.

Kate lifted the phone slightly. "He wrote 'Family Matter.' I thought something had happened to one of our children."

The words broke her composure. Tears spilled before she could stop them.

"That must have been frightening," Paolo said quietly.

"It was. And then … this."

They walked slowly along the path, the heat of the morning warming the stone walls, the distant toll of a church bell marking the hour.

"I asked him for three months of quiet," Kate said. "Three months to pray. Three months without pressure so we could both hear God clearly. I thought silence might give us a chance to heal."

Paolo nodded. "Silence often reveals truth."

"And now?"

"Now he has forced the conversation before the silence could do its work."

The clarity of it settled in her chest. "I feel angry," she admitted. "And heartbroken. And confused. All at once."

"That is normal."

She wiped her cheeks. "Am I overreacting? Did I force his hand by leaving? I don't know how to respond."

Paolo met her gaze. “Of course you feel uncertain. This is your marriage.”

“What should I do?”

He shook his head. “I cannot be the one to advise you, Kate. It would be too easy to benefit from another man’s failure. That would not honor God.

His restraint steadied her.

“You still love him,” Paolo said.

Kate closed her eyes briefly. “Yes.”

“Then that love deserves respect.”

They stood quietly for a moment, the distant bell fading.

“So, what do I do—just for today?” she asked.

“You breathe,” he said.

A faint, tired smile touched her lips. “And then?”

“And then you keep walking with God. One step at a time.”

Kate nodded.

As they turned back toward the villa, a painful realization settled fully into place. The three months she had asked for were meant to protect her marriage. Grant had used them to pressure it.

Each step felt heavy as she slowly returned to the courtyard she’d come to cherish. The familiar sounds drifted toward her. Claire’s laughter from the kitchen, Marianne debating with Evelyn about whether basil belonged in everything. Life was continuing. But inside Kate, something had shifted.

She sat down once again at the long table, her journal still beside the untouched espresso. For a long moment she stared at the blank page, the shock moving through her once again like a quiet tremor.

Years of marriage reduced to this moment and the devastating reality that Grant had obviously chosen ...

Lydia.

Her first instinct was to respond—to explain, to defend the covenant they had built. But another realization settled in, quieter and steadier. Grant had not written to understand. He had written to force his position.

Kate closed her eyes and placed her hands flat against the table.

"Lord," she whispered.

No words followed. Only tears.

CHAPTER 37
Wise Counsel

Monopoli, Italy

The email from Grant still lingered in Kate's mind like a wound she kept revisiting.

She waited several days before reaching out to Pastor Michael. From the moment she began to come down from the initial shock of Grant's email, she knew she needed her pastor's wisdom and guidance. But she needed to quiet the storm inside her first.

She still couldn't shake the memory of those few terrible seconds, believing something had happened to one of their children. Instead … separation papers. Even now, her chest tightened when she thought about it.

That morning, she opened her laptop and sent a short message asking if Michael had time for a quick Zoom conversation. He responded within the hour.

When his face appeared on the screen, emotion rose unexpectedly. He looked the same as always—steady, thoughtful, the kind of presence that had guided their family through so many seasons.

"Kate," he said warmly. "How are you?"

She exhaled slowly. "Honestly?"

"Yes, of course."

"I'm confused and heartbroken."

Michael didn't interrupt.

Kate gathered her thoughts. “As you know, I asked Grant for three months of no contact when I left for Italy—not as punishment. I needed space to hear God clearly without the constant confusion.”

Michael nodded. “That makes sense.”

“I told him the only reason to break that silence would be a true family emergency.” Her voice tightened slightly. “But then he sent an email with the subject line ‘Family Matters.’”

Michael’s brow furrowed.

“For a moment, I thought something terrible had happened,” she continued. “But it hadn’t. He sent me his filing for a legal separation.”

The words still felt strange to say out loud.

Michael leaned back slightly, absorbing it. “And how did you respond?”

“I didn’t.”

He raised an eyebrow just slightly.

“I didn’t want to react emotionally,” she explained. “And I didn’t want to be pulled into communication just because he labeled it an emergency.”

Michael nodded slowly. “That’s wise.”

“I’ve been praying,” she said. “A lot.” She paused. “But I’m not sensing clearly what God wants me to do.”

Michael waited.

"I'm trying to honor the boundary I set," she continued, "but now Grant has taken a legal step toward divorce." Her voice cracked. "I honestly thought the distance might soften his heart."

Silence settled between them.

"But instead," she added, "it feels like he's moving farther away."

Michael's expression softened. "That must feel devastating."

"It does."

She hesitated. "So now I don't know what my next step should be."

Michael leaned forward slightly. "What options are you considering?"

Kate voiced the options she'd considered as questions. "Do I sign the documents? Do I call him? Do I respond to the email? Do I keep fighting for my marriage when everything he's done since the affair has been to move further away?"

Her eyes lifted to the screen. "All I've been able to do so far is keep the silence. No matter how much I pray, nothing else feels right."

Michael sat quietly for a moment before answering. "Let me start with something important," he said gently. "Your silence was not unkind."

Kate blinked. "It wasn't?"

"No," he said firmly. "You created a boundary so you could hear God without constant emotional pressure. That's not manipulation. That's wisdom."

A small wave of relief moved through her.

"But legal action does change the landscape," he continued.

She nodded. "That's what I was afraid of."

"However," he added, "legal separation papers do not mean the marriage is over. Sometimes people file because they feel out of control. Sometimes it's an attempt to force a reaction."

Kate's shoulders lowered slightly. "That's exactly what it feels like."

"Which means your response still needs to come from prayer, not pressure."

Kate folded her hands. "So, what do you think I should do?"

Michael answered carefully. "First, do not rush to sign anything. Legal signatures can move processes forward that you may not want to advance."

"That makes sense."

"Second, I would not break the no-contact boundary casually."

Kate looked surprised. "You wouldn't?"

"Not unless you sense the Lord clearly prompting it."

She exhaled slowly. "That's what my spirit has been telling me."

Michael smiled. "Then pay attention to that."

"But what if he thinks I'm ignoring him?"

Michael tilted his head. "Kate, you are not responsible for managing Grant's emotions right now."

The sentence landed with quiet clarity.

"You are responsible for walking in integrity before God."

Kate nodded slowly.

"Sometimes silence reveals things words cannot," he added.

She considered that. "I don't want to seem vindictive."

"You're not," he said calmly.

Kate leaned back slightly. "So, you're saying … wait?"

"I'm saying keep praying," he replied. "God is not confused about what is happening in your marriage."

Her eyes filled unexpectedly. "That's comforting."

Michael's voice softened. "I also believe something else."

"What?"

"I believe your prayers matter more than you can currently see."

Kate wiped a tear. "I hope so."

"Stay steady. Stay humble. Stay prayerful," he said. "Let's see what God does before you take any legal steps that cannot easily be reversed."

Kate nodded.

Then Michael added thoughtfully, "If Grant ever actually shows up for an accountability meeting, how would you feel about me sharing some of what we discussed today?"

She blinked. "You mean explaining why I haven't responded?"

"Yes. It would allow you to maintain your boundary while still giving him some understanding."

Kate exhaled slowly. "That hadn't even occurred to me."

She thought for a moment, then nodded. "Yes. I'd be comfortable with that. You can share anything we discussed."

"I'll handle it carefully," he said.

He paused, then added, "Sometimes the first real step toward repentance is simply a man deciding to walk through the right door."

Kate let that settle. "I hope he finds that door."

"I'm praying for you every day."

"Thank you, Michael. We need those prayers."

The call ended.

Kate closed her laptop slowly. Outside, the late afternoon light softened across the stone walls. She opened her journal, her pen hovering for a moment before she began to write.

Lord, I still don't know how this story ends.

She paused.

But I trust that You do.

For now, that was enough.

The Long Pause

The Docusign request still sat unopened in her inbox. She had read it once. That had been enough. Now the laptop remained closed on the small desk beside her bed.

Outside, the day unfolded slowly, the way days did in Monopoli. Morning light stretched across the villa courtyard. Claire moved through the kitchen humming as coffee brewed. Marianne watered the pots of basil and lavender along the terrace. Ev argued with a translation app over the correct pronunciation of a bakery order.

Life continued.

Kate stepped onto the terrace with a cup of coffee and sat in the quiet warmth of the morning. The Adriatic shimmered faintly in the distance beyond the rooftops. Somewhere nearby, a scooter buzzed through a narrow street. One of dozens that would pass before the day was done.

She found herself wondering about the unseen lives around her. What burdens did that driver carry today? Or was it simply an ordinary morning? She longed for ordinary. But nothing inside her life felt ordinary anymore.

Her thoughts returned to Grant—to their home in Texas, to the man she had loved for more than three decades. She thought about the night of his confession. About the words he had spoken. And about the separation papers now waiting quietly in her inbox, like a door she had not chosen to open.

Her fingers tightened slightly around the mug. "Lord," she whispered, "what do I do now?"

No answer came—at least not the kind she had hoped for. No clear instruction. No sudden clarity. Only the same quiet steadiness she had sensed during her conversation with Pastor Michael.

Keep praying. And wait.

Kate exhaled slowly. Waiting had never come easily to her. It was far easier to act—to fix things, to talk, to resolve, to move forward. Silence felt like standing still while everything else continued without her.

But something deeper in her spirit recognized the difference between fear and peace. This was not fear. This was restraint. So, she waited.

She prayed as she walked through the narrow streets of Monopoli with her friends. She prayed when the church bells marked the afternoon hours. She prayed as evening light settled over the water and turned the horizon gold.

And slowly, almost without noticing, the noise inside her began to quiet. What had once felt like emptiness began to feel protected. As if God Himself were guarding the space she had chosen not to fill.

Days passed. The email remained unanswered. And somewhere across the ocean, the silence she had chosen began to echo in ways she could not yet see.

CHAPTER 38
Rumors

Monopoli, Italy

In Italy, gossip was treated much like fresh bread—best shared while still warm.

One Saturday morning, the women followed Zia Rosa through the outdoor market just as the town was fully waking up. Vendors called out prices over crates of tomatoes and peaches while the scent of fresh bread and strong espresso drifted through the narrow streets.

As they rounded the corner near the café beside the piazza fountain, Claire suddenly slowed.

"Oh no," she muttered.

"What?" Marianne asked.

Claire nodded her head toward a small cluster of older women seated beneath a striped awning. "The council has convened."

Kate laughed as she recognized Teresa, Maria, and Nenita already gathered around a café table cluttered with espresso cups, half-eaten pastries, and enough opinions to govern a small nation.

Seated directly beside them was an elegant older woman Kate had not yet met but remembered seeing the first time she met Paolo. She wore a stylish navy dress with pearl earrings and perfectly styled silver hair, her posture straight despite her age. Unlike the others, whose voices bounced freely through the piazza, this woman carried herself with quiet dignity.

"That," Claire whispered, "is Paolo's mother. Signora Adriana Moretti."

At the mention of Paolo's name, Kate instantly wished she were invisible. Too late. Nenita spotted them first.

"Ahh! *Le Americane*!" she announced loudly, waving them over as if summoning distant relatives.

Zia Rosa sighed dramatically beneath her breath. "Madonna, give me patience."

The women approached cautiously while the older ladies openly inspected them from head to toe. Maria leaned toward Adriana without lowering her voice nearly enough.

"The red-haired one is definitely in love with your Paolo."

Kate nearly choked as Claire burst out laughing.

"See?" she whispered. "This is exactly what I warned you about."

"That is not true," Zia Rosa snapped in Italian, swatting the air with her hand. "And even if it were, it would still be none of your business."

Teresa lifted one shoulder innocently. "We are only observing."

"You are never only observing," Rosa shot back.

Meanwhile Nenita was studying Evelyn with suspicious concentration. "That one," she announced, pointing openly, "is either a famous tennis player or secretly CIA."

Evelyn blinked. "What did she say?"

Claire grinned wickedly. "She thinks you're an international spy."

"Honestly," Marianne said thoughtfully, "that's kind of flattering."

Adriana finally smiled. "You must forgive them," she said in careful English. "They have very small lives and very large imaginations."

"We heard that!" Maria protested.

"You were supposed to," Adriana replied calmly.

The table erupted into overlapping Italian complaints.

Zia Rosa folded her arms. "And another thing," she scolded. "You are all making up ridiculous stories about these women."

Nenita looked genuinely offended. "No, we are not."

"You told Father Lorenzo that Claire came to Italy searching for a retired Sicilian count with a vineyard."

Teresa gasped dramatically. "Well… she *is* divorced."

Claire laughed so hard she had to grab Kate's arm to steady herself.

"And" Rosa continued relentlessly, "Maria told the fishmonger that Marianne was writing a scandalous American book about the town."

Maria shrugged unapologetically. "She carries a notebook everywhere."

"I'm trying to remember my new Italian vocabulary," Marianne protested.

"Whatever you say," Maria replied.

Then Nenita lowered her voice conspiratorially and glanced directly at Kate. "But the Paolo situation…" she whispered.

"There is no Paolo situation," Rosa barked immediately.

Adriana lifted one elegant eyebrow. "Not yet," she murmured quietly into her espresso.

Kate felt heat rush straight into her face while the others burst into helpless laughter. And then, she joined in realizing she had become the most gossip worthy story of the day. Only in Italy.

The women laughed all the way back toward Villa Santoro while Claire continued protesting her innocence and the *nonne* shouted unsolicited relationship advice from across the piazza.

That evening, the villa had settled into its familiar rhythm. Dinner dishes had been washed. The kitchen was finally quiet. Zia Rosa had retired for the night after issuing one final round of instructions no one intended to follow.

The four women gathered in the living room, curled into overstuffed sofas and chairs with small glasses of chilled limoncello in their hands.

Marianne was scrolling through the hundreds of photos on her phone she had taken that week while Evelyn sat next to her offering a running commentary on each one.

Kate found herself smiling more than talking. Around her, laughter drifted easily through the room as her friends recounted their favorite adventures in Puglia. For the first time in weeks, she wasn't replaying every conversation with Grant. She wasn't analyzing every mistake or imagining every possible outcome.

The questions still existed. The pain still existed. But neither felt quite as heavy tonight. She leaned back into the cushions and listened to the familiar sounds around her and a quiet peace settled over her.

Not because anything had been resolved. Not because she suddenly knew what the future held. But because, for the first time since Grant's confession, she felt no need to figure everything out tonight.

God knew. And for now, that was enough.

Nearly six thousand miles away, Grant sat alone in a silent house wondering if he had already lost her.

CHAPTER 39
The Sound of Silence

Austin, Texas

Grant expected a response the same day.

Silence had never been Kate's weapon. And yet now, it was the only answer he was receiving. She had always been responsible that way—someone who believed important conversations shouldn't linger unresolved. Even during their hardest seasons, she rarely let a day end without at least acknowledging what had been said.

So, when his phone stayed quiet that first day and night, he told himself it was the time difference. Italy was asleep. She would see the email and respond.

The next day passed. Still nothing.

Every day that passed found Grant checking his phone more often than he realized. At first it was casual, a glance between meetings, a quick look while waiting for the office coffee machine to finish its slow drip. Day after day … no response.

And day after day, he reopened his email to her and reread what he had sent. The language was measured. Calm and professional. He had even told the lawyer he wanted the tone respectful. This wasn't meant to be cruel. It was meant to bring clarity.

He had written *Family Matter* in the subject line because it was a family matter. It was about their marriage, their future … their lives.

Grant leaned back in his office chair and stared at the screen wondering when Kate would respond. She had to.

The silence stretched on for days and now the quiet began to feel different. Not accidental, but intentional.

Many times, throughout each day Grant started to call Kate, then stopped himself before pressing the final digit of her number. She had asked for three months. No contact unless it was truly urgent. At the time, it had sounded reasonable. Now it felt like a wall.

Tonight, he tossed his phone onto the coffee table and ran a hand through his hair. "This is ridiculous," he muttered.

Across town, Lydia was probably expecting him later that evening. She had texted earlier—something about a new recipe and a bottle of wine she wanted him to try. He should have felt relieved. Instead, he felt unsettled.

The house, their home, no longer felt like the place that had anchored him for decades. Grant moved slowly through the living room and down the hallway. Everything was in its place.

Except Kate.

He had told himself the separation papers were a step toward clarity—a way to force an honest conversation. But the silence that followed felt like something else. Like stepping into an empty room and realizing no one intended to follow.

Grant picked up his phone again. Still nothing. No email. No text. Not even a short acknowledgment.

Received. We'll talk.

The quiet had a way of amplifying thoughts he didn't want to hear.

What if she doesn't respond?

The idea landed harder than he expected.

Of course she would respond. Kate didn't avoid difficult conversations. That had frustrated him for years. She asked questions when he didn't have answers. She pushed for clarity when he would have preferred to wait.

"Let's never let the sun go down on our anger," she used to say early in their marriage, quoting Scripture with quiet conviction.

But what if this time she didn't want resolution? Grant leaned against the kitchen counter. What if she's done? The thought tightened something deep in his chest. He had imagined this playing out differently. Kate would be angry. Maybe even furious. She would demand explanation. They would argue.

But silence? Silence gave him nothing to push against. Nothing to defend. Nothing to control.

Grant rubbed his face with both hands. "What am I doing?" he muttered.

The silence didn't answer. It simply remained. And something deeper began to settle in his chest.

Not fear of losing the argument.

Fear of losing her.

Grant sat down slowly on his couch while Across town, Lydia was waiting … warm, interested, certain. But the things that had once drawn him to her felt different now. What had seemed comforting began to feel like pressure. Like expectation. Like something he was no longer sure he still wanted.

Kate's absence, by contrast, felt enormous.

He leaned back and stared at the ceiling. The house hummed quietly around him. "The sound of silence," he murmured.

Silence, he was beginning to realize, was not empty. It was loud. And it was forcing him to look at things he had carefully avoided for months. Things he no longer knew how to ignore.

CHAPTER 39
Friendship Can Be Holy

Monopoli, Italy

Two weeks had passed since Grant's email.

The days continued with their familiar rhythm—market mornings, slow walks through narrow streets, and evenings gathered around the courtyard table, but something inside Kate had shifted.

The legal language of the separation still echoed in her mind. She had written pages in her journal. She had prayed until words ran out and silence took their place. She had listened as her friends offered comfort, wisdom, and the occasional blunt truth.

Still, the question remained. What now?

That evening, dinner stretched long and warm. Ev told an animated story about accidentally ordering five pounds of lemons instead of five lemons, convinced she understood the vendor's question. Claire teased her mercilessly. Marianne laughed so hard she nearly spilled her wine. Paolo stayed mostly quiet through it all, listening the way he always did.

When the plates were cleared and the others drifted inside to finish the dishes, Kate lingered in the courtyard, stacking the last of the empty glasses. Lantern light glowed softly against the stone walls.

"You do not have to do all of that," Paolo said as he came up behind her.

She glanced over her shoulder. "It gives me something to do."

He stepped forward and set one of the glasses down beside her.

For a moment, neither of them spoke. Finally, he looked at her. “It has been two weeks.”

Kate understood immediately. “Yes.”

Paolo rested his hand lightly on the edge of the table. “How are you processing Grant’s request for separation?”

She exhaled slowly. “I wish I had a simple answer.”

He waited.

“Some moments I feel peaceful,” she said. “Like maybe God is holding things in ways I can’t see yet.”

“And other moments?” he asked.

“Other moments, I feel angry.”

A small, rueful smile crossed her face. “I still so angry that he wrote ‘family matter’ in the subject line.”

Paolo’s expression tightened. “That was not fair.”

“No,” she said quietly. “It wasn’t.”

She paused. “And sometimes … I’m just sad.”

Her voice softened. “Thirty-five years is a long time to share a life with someone.”

Paolo nodded slowly. “Yes.”

Kate rested her hands on the back of a chair, her gaze lowering for a moment. “I keep asking God the same question.”

Paolo glanced toward her. “What question?”

She hesitated. “What does faithfulness look like right now?”

The words lingered between them. A faint breeze brushed across the courtyard, lifting a strand of her hair. She tucked it behind her ear.

“Sometimes I wonder,” she continued quietly, “if even having a friendship with you could be considered being unfaithful to Grant.”

Paolo didn’t react defensively. He simply considered her words. “That’s a serious question,” he said.

“I mean it,” she replied. “My marriage may be wounded, but it isn’t over. And I don’t want to cross a line just because I’m angry or lonely.”

Paolo nodded. “That kind of caution is not weakness. It’s reverence.”

Kate looked up at him. “So, what do you think?”

He chose his words carefully. “I think faithfulness right now looks like protecting what is sacred … even when it costs you something.”

The truth of it settled in her chest.

“And if that means we shouldn’t be friends?” she asked.

Paolo met her eyes calmly. “Then we would accept that.”

The answer surprised her. “You wouldn’t argue?”

He shook his head. “No.” A faint smile touched his face. “Because the goal is not to become important in your life. The goal is to help you remain faithful to the life you already have.”

Something inside her loosened. “Thank you,” she said quietly.

Paolo glanced toward the villa behind them. "Friendship can be holy," he said gently, "but only when it protects what God has already joined."

CHAPTER 40
A Widower's Heart

Monopoli, Italy

Three days passed, and Paolo did not appear for a single dinner.

On the fourth day, he called Claire to say he would be out of town on a project for several more days and would miss their usual Italian lesson.

Kate found herself breathing a little easier each day. The sharp edges of Grant's request for legal separation no longer cut quite so deeply. In its place, a quiet sense of peace had begun to return—fragile, but real. She knew she was following God's prompting by maintaining the three months of silence she had asked for.

Each morning, she brought her marriage to God in prayer and journaling. And each morning, she left it there. Then she tried to live the day in front of her.

One evening, after dinner, the four women set out for a walk. Evelyn had declared, "We need to burn today's carbs so we can eat more tomorrow, girls!" And so they complied.

Their conversation flowed easily; new Italian words, a shoe store Claire insisted required a second visit, and whether Marianne had finally chosen which ceramics to ship home.

The warmth of the day still lingered as they rounded the bend near the small stone house at the edge of the property. Just then, the gate opened and Paolo stepped out.

Claire spotted him first. "Another gourmet dinner for your mamma, Paolo?"

He laughed, placing a hand over his heart. "Ah, *buonasera*, ladies. Yes, tonight she insisted I cook early. Pasta with lemon and herbs. Apparently, she has a very important film to watch."

Evelyn gestured down the road. "Then you've earned a walk. Join us."

Marianne added quickly, "It's been nearly a week. Come along."

Paolo hesitated only a moment before falling into step beside them. Within minutes, the conversation divided into smaller streams. Claire and Marianne launched into a lively debate about the best cannoli in the region, while Evelyn argued passionately for a pastry shop two villages away. Their voices drifted ahead, animated and cheerful.

Kate walked more slowly behind them.

Paolo noticed and allowed the others to move ahead and fell into step beside her. "You are quiet tonight," he whispered.

Kate smiled faintly. "I'm enjoying listening."

They walked in companionable silence as the last light faded behind the hills. Then, surprising herself, Kate asked, "Tell me about your wife, Paolo."

He slowed, studying her for a moment, then nodded and continued walking. "As you know, her name was Sofia."

He spoke her name with care, as if it carried weight. "She was the bravest person I have ever known."

Kate listened quietly.

"She had a way of making ordinary days feel like gifts," he continued. "She noticed everything—the first olive blossoms, the way the church bells sounded different after rain … even when my mother pretended not to cry."

Kate smiled. "She sounds remarkable."

"She was."

He took a breath. "Sofia was ill for the last two years of her life. We were married for over thirty years. Just the two of us. We had hoped for children which never came, but we were content."

Kate didn't interrupt.

"It began as something small," he said. "A cough. Shortness of breath she tried to ignore." He gave a faint smile. "She did not like being the one who needed care."

"They told us it was a progressive lung condition. One that does not rush but does not stop."

He looked down briefly. "At first, we believed we had time."

They walked slowly.

"For a while, life still felt normal. Slower walks. More rest. You begin to notice everything—the way someone breathes, the moments they pretend they are stronger than they feel."

Kate felt the quiet weight of his words.

"As the illness progressed, her world became smaller. Rooms instead of streets. Windows instead of open air."

His voice softened. "And I learned what it meant to simply be present."

He continued quietly. "I sat with her when breathing became work. I learned the sound of the oxygen machine in the night." He exhaled. "You do not sleep the same when the person beside you is fighting for every breath."

Kate's chest tightened.

"But she never became bitter," Paolo said. "Not once. Even near the end, she would take my hand and say, 'Paolo, we are still here. This is still our life.'"

A faint smile touched his face. "She believed heaven was near. That we were only saying a temporary goodbye." He paused. "She thought it would be harder for me than for her."

Kate turned toward him. "Your love story is beautiful."

"Yes," he said. "And she taught me that love is not only what you feel when things are easy. It is what remains when everything becomes difficult."

The air stilled around them.

"When she died, it was quiet," he added. "Just… the absence of breath."

Kate swallowed.

"For a long time, I believed that was the deepest loss a person could know. Because death ends the story cleanly."

He looked at her. "But what you are walking through is different."

He didn't finish the thought. He didn't need to. They walked in silence for several steps. Ahead, Claire's laughter drifted back toward them.

Kate glanced at him. "Do you tire of people encouraging you to move on?"

A faint smile appeared. "In Italy, they say it more politely. But yes, they think it."

"And what do you think?"

Paolo considered carefully. "I think love does not disappear when someone dies. It changes shape."

Kate nodded. "That makes sense."

There was a pause. Then he spoke again, more slowly this time. "You have made me think about something I did not expect."

Kate turned to look at him as they continued walking.

"For a long time, my heart felt closed," he said. "Not broken. Just finished." He exhaled quietly. "And now, I find myself noticing that it is not as closed as I believed."

Kate's breath caught slightly.

"That surprises me," he continued. "And I will be honest. It unsettles me."

He met her eyes briefly, then looked away. "Because the person who has awakened that awareness is not truly available."

The words settled between them. Kate said nothing.

"And perhaps," he added quietly, "there is a kind of safety in that."

She understood. A connection that could not be pursued was a connection that could not be lost.

"I feel a great respect for you," he said. "And a fondness I did not intend."

Kate's voice was soft. "I feel it too."

The honesty hung between them—clear, unguarded.

"And that is why we must be careful," Paolo said.

"Yes," she whispered.

"Neither of us wants to cause harm," he continued. "Not to each other. Not to your marriage. Not to what God has already joined."

Kate nodded slowly.

"So, we name it," he said. "And we guard it."

They walked a few more steps in silence. Then Paolo spoke again, returning to steadiness. "That kind of caution is not weakness. It is reverence."

They walked the rest of the road in thoughtful silence. By the time they reached the villa, the sky had deepened into a wide field of stars. Kate paused and sat on the low stone wall near the gate. He sat beside her, leaving a respectful distance.

After a moment, he asked quietly, "May I pray for you?"

Kate nodded.

He bowed his head. "Lord, protect Kate's heart."

Kate closed her eyes.

"Protect her marriage." The words settled deeply. "And protect us from becoming something we should not."

Kate swallowed.

"Give her wisdom," he continued. "And give her peace while she waits for Your answer."

When he finished, the silence felt full.

Kate opened her eyes. "That may be the kindest prayer anyone has prayed for me in a long time."

They reached the villa gate and paused, neither of them quite ready to step fully back into the light. The laughter of the others drifted faintly from inside—familiar, grounding, unchanged.

Paolo inclined his head slightly. "*Buona notte*, Kate."

"Good night," she answered.

He turned first, walking down the narrow path past his mother's house toward his own, his figure gradually dissolving into shadow. Kate remained where she was for a moment longer. The night air pressed softly against her skin, still warm from the day. Somewhere in the distance, a church bell marked the late hour—slow, deliberate, unhurried.

She wrapped her arms lightly around herself. Something had shifted. Not in a way she could define. Not something she could act on. But something real. And something that required care.

Kate lifted her gaze to the sky, the stars scattered wide above her, steady and unmoved by the complexities of human hearts.

"Lord…" she whispered, though no full prayer followed. Not yet. She turned and stepped inside the villa, closing the door quietly behind her.

Across the hills, Paolo walked the familiar path home in silence. The gravel shifted beneath his steps. The scent of citrus and dry earth lingered in the night air. He had walked this path countless times, but tonight it felt different—heavier, more deliberate.

He did not rush. There was nothing to outrun. And nothing he could ignore. By the time he reached his door, one truth had settled clearly within him:

This was not something to be explained. It was something to be surrendered.

And in two separate rooms, under the same wide sky, both would come to the same quiet place before morning—the place where desire gives way to obedience, and where the heart must choose not what it wants, but what is right.

CHAPTER 41
Not My Will, But Yours

Monopoli, Italy

Two hearts, in two separate places, carried the same unspoken weight.

Paolo knew his thoughts about Kate were going to keep him up tonight without Divine intervention. His beautifully restored ancient house grew still around him, the familiar creaks settling into the walls. He stepped outside onto the small terrace behind the house, the night air starting to feel cool against his skin. The scent of citrus drifted faintly through the darkness, and above him the sky stretched wide, scattered with stars.

For a long moment, he stood looking into the night sky. Then he exhaled.

"*Signore...*" Father God.

The word came soft and familiar. A son calling out to his father.

"Ho bisogno del tuo aiuto." I need Your help.

He rested his hands on the stone ledge, grounding himself. "You know my heart."

A pause. "And You know that I have tried to guard it."

The truth pressed against him.

"I did not expect this," he said quietly. "I believed that part of my life was finished. Not broken ... just complete."

His voice softened. "I had made peace with that. And now, I feel something waking again."

He let the words rest in the open air.

"I respect her," he said. "More than I can easily explain. Her strength. Her restraint. The way she seeks You even when everything around her is uncertain."

He lifted his gaze. "And that is what makes this difficult. Because she is not free."

The words came clearly now. "And I will not take what belongs to another man, not even in my heart."

His hands pressed more firmly against the stone.

"I have seen what love looks like when it is faithful," he said, his voice softening at the memory. "I lived it with Sofia. I will not dishonor that by choosing something less now."

The breeze moved gently around him.

"So, I am asking you … if this affection is not from you, please take it. And if it is something you are allowing, then teach me how to carry it without crossing a line."

He closed his eyes briefly. "Give me discipline. Give me clarity. And give me the strength to step back if that is what love requires."

Silence answered him. "Help me protect her," he said quietly. "And help me protect my own heart."

He remained there a moment longer, then turned and stepped back inside, closing the door quietly behind him.

At the villa, Kate stood at the open window of her bedroom. Moonlight spilled across the tiled floor, casting pale shadows against the walls. The air moved quietly through the curtains, carrying the faint scent of jasmine and the distant hush of the sea.

She rested her hands on the windowsill and looked out into the night. "Lord…" The word felt both small and necessary. "I don't understand what You're doing."

Her voice steadied as she continued. "I thought coming here would bring clarity. I thought this time would make things simpler."

A breath.

"But everything feels more complicated." She closed her eyes briefly. "My marriage feels like it's slipping away," she said. "And I don't know how to stop it."

Her fingers tightened against the stone. "I asked for space to hear you. I thought silence would help." A pause. "But now everything is moving and I'm not."

The stillness offered no explanation. "And then there's Paolo." His name barely left her lips. "I didn't expect that," she whispered. "I didn't come here looking for anything. But something in me feels awake when I'm around him and that frightens me."

She drew in a slow breath. "Because it would be so easy to justify it."

Her eyes opened again. "So easy to say my marriage is already broken. That I didn't cause this. That I deserve something good. Maybe those things are even true."

Her voice steadied. "But that doesn't make them right."

The distinction settled deeply.

"I don't want a life built on what I can justify," she said. "I want a life that honors You." She placed her hand over her heart. "So, I'm asking you, Lord, please guard this beautiful friendship."

A tear slipped quietly down her cheek. "Guard my heart from anything that would pull me away from Your will."

She inhaled slowly. "If my marriage can still be restored, help me to protect it."

The words felt fragile. "And if it cannot ..." She hesitated, then continued. "Then help me walk through that with integrity."

Her hand pressed lightly against her chest. "Not with bitterness, or escape, or compromise. But with you."

The room felt still.

"And back to Paolo. If this is not from you, take it away." A tear followed the first. "And if it is something you've allowed for just for this season..." She swallowed. "Then teach me how to carry it without crossing a line."

The words echoed across the distance between them, unheard yet somehow shared.

"I don't want to close my heart," she whispered. "But I don't want to open it in the wrong direction either." She lifted her gaze to the sky beyond the window. "So, I'm choosing this..."

A breath.

"Not my will ... but Yours."

The words settled into the night.

A quiet, steady peace moved through her, not because she knew what would happen next, but because she had placed it where it belonged.

In His hands.

Miles apart, under the same sky, two hearts had asked for the same thing.

Not their will…but His.

CHAPTER 42
Comparison Game

Austin, Texas

Affairs thrive in isolation; reality enters when comparisons begin.

Grant did not go to Lydia's townhouse that night. He told himself it was because he was tired. Because work had been heavy. Because the silence from Kate had unsettled him. But the truth was simpler.

He didn't want the contrast. So, he stayed home.

The house felt different now, less like something he was holding together and more like a quiet witness to everything he had broken. Kate's presence and her absence seemed magnified in every room.

Her grocery lists still tucked into the kitchen drawer. Her favorite blanket folded at the foot of the bed. Her reading glasses resting in the small ceramic tray she had brought home from Santa Fe. The house felt like a museum of a life he had damaged. And the longer the silence stretched, the harder it became to ignore.

Lydia noticed the shift immediately the next time he saw her. They sat in her living room, music playing low in the background. She had poured wine, something expensive she had picked up earlier that day.

Grant hadn't touched his glass.

"You're quiet tonight," she said.

"I'm thinking."

"About Kate?"

He didn't answer. Which was answer enough.

Lydia shifted closer, tucking her legs beneath her as she studied him. "You look exhausted."

Grant rubbed his jaw.

"This whole situation is wearing you down," she continued.

Still, he said nothing.

"You've been carrying that marriage by yourself for a long time."

Grant glanced at her. "How?"

"The distance. The silence. The martyr routine in Italy."

He frowned slightly. "She set boundaries."

Lydia hesitated just long enough to soften the edge. "I'm not judging her," she said. "But leaving the country for three months … that's a pretty strong statement."

Grant didn't respond.

Lydia lowered her gaze, turning the wine glass slowly in her hand. "You know," she said quietly, "I never imagined my life ending up like this."

He looked at her.

"I never planned to be the woman someone leaves his wife for."

The words lingered in the space between them.

"Life just… happened," she added.

Grant said nothing.

She set the glass down and reached for his hand. "All I know is that when you're here, you seem lighter. Less burdened."

Her fingers tightened slightly around his. "You deserve peace too, Grant."

The words were familiar. They had once comforted him. Now they sounded rehearsed.

"She left the country," Lydia added. "She won't talk. And somehow you end up being the one who's wrong."

Grant looked down. "I never said she told anyone that."

Lydia paused. "Well… it feels that way."

Did it? Grant wasn't so sure anymore.

The comparisons had begun quietly. At first, he resisted them. But the mind has a way of noticing what the heart tries to avoid. Kate had never chased him. Never clung. Never needed constant reassurance. Lydia did.

Lydia leaned closer, her hand resting lightly against his chest. "You deserve someone who wants you."

Once, that would have stirred something in him. Now it made him feel cornered.

"You're thinking again," she said.

"Yes."

"About her."

Grant stood and moved toward the kitchen. The place suddenly felt too warm. He stepped out onto the balcony, letting the night air settle around him.

The thoughts kept coming.

Kate had never tried to control the narrative, not even when she discovered the affair. She hadn't screamed. Hadn't begged. Hadn't competed.

She had simply drawn a line. A quiet, dignified line.

And when he pushed further, she stepped away, across an ocean, to protect what remained of her heart and her covenant with God.

The memory unsettled him. Because now, looking at it clearly, her restraint didn't look like weakness. It looked like strength.

Lydia appeared behind him. "You disappeared."

"I needed air."

She stepped closer from behind, wrapping her arms around him and resting her head on his back.

"Come back to the couch."

Her voice was soft. Inviting. He used to find it irresistible. Now it felt heavy and possessive. As if her comfort came with an expectation.

"You're slipping away from me," she said quietly.

Grant turned and looked at her—really looked. For the first time in months, something became unmistakably clear. Lydia had never encouraged him to repair his marriage. Never suggested counseling. Never asked whether reconciliation was still possible.

She had never asked what God might want. She had only offered escape. Escape from guilt. Escape from responsibility. Escape from consequences. And he had taken it. Willingly.

For a moment, Grant felt a surge of resentment. Why hadn't she challenged him? Why hadn't she pushed him back toward Kate? Why hadn't she asked the questions that now seemed so obvious?

The answer came almost immediately. Of course she hadn't. Lydia wasn't the one who had stood before God and vowed faithfulness to Kate. Lydia wasn't the one who claimed Christ as the foundation of his life. Lydia wasn't the one who knew better.

He was. The conviction landed heavily.

It was ridiculous for him to expect Lydia to provide a restraint she never claimed to possess. He had started to quietly blame her for not helping him stop something he should have stopped himself.

The fault was not hers. It was his. He was the married one. He was the one who understood where this path would lead long before either of them admitted what was happening. And yet instead of leading, he had followed. Instead of protecting, he had participated.

If he had truly cared about Lydia, he would have established boundaries the moment he recognized the attraction. He would have protected her from becoming attached to a man who belonged to someone else.

And if he had truly loved Kate the way he claimed he did, he would have guarded his own heart long before another woman had the opportunity to occupy it.

The weight of it pressed down on him.

For months he had thought of himself as a man caught between two women. Now he saw the truth. He had been unfair to both. Kate had suffered because of his selfishness. Lydia had suffered because of his weakness. And the man most responsible for both was staring back at him in the mirror.

Later that night, Grant sat alone at his kitchen table. The quiet felt different now. Not punishing. Revealing.

As he lay in bed unable to sleep, he found himself thinking about Kate in ways he hadn't allowed for months. Her patience. Her steadiness. Her quiet, unwavering faith. He remembered mornings when he had come downstairs early and found her sitting at the table, her Bible open, coffee growing cold beside her. Not asking for anything dramatic. Just seeking wisdom.

What man wouldn't want a woman like that as his wife? The thought surprised him. For years, he had misread her. Her strength as indifference. Her independence as distance. Her quiet confidence as disinterest.

Now those same qualities looked different. They looked rare. Valuable. Another thought surfaced. *Paolo.*

The name had hovered at the edge of his mind since his daughter mentioned it. Some Italian man helping them learn the language. Grant pictured him. Tall. Confident. Effortless charm. The kind of man who knew how to make a woman feel seen. The image tightened something in his chest.

But then another thought followed. What if Paolo wasn't a threat? What if he simply saw Kate clearly? Her kindness. Her integrity. Her faith.

The very things Grant had slowly stopped noticing. The realization unsettled him even more. Because if another man could see those things, how long before someone else valued them?

Grant buried his face in his hands. "God, what have I done?"

The words came out before he could stop them. Not a casual prayer. A real one. And with it came clarity. He had blamed circumstances. Blamed loneliness. Blamed Kate. Blamed confusion. But the truth was simpler. He had opened the door.

Welcomed the attention. Enjoyed the flattery. And convinced himself it meant something more.

"I've made the biggest mistake of my life," he whispered.

The words settled into the quiet. Not dramatic. Just true.

His phone sat on the kitchen counter. Pastor Michael's number was still there. Grant had canceled three appointments already. Work. Travel. Scheduling conflicts. Each time telling himself he would reschedule. Soon. Soon had never come. Until now.

He picked up the phone. His hands trembled slightly as he dialed. The call rang twice.

"Hello?"

Grant swallowed. "Pastor … it's Grant."

A pause. Then Michael's steady voice: "Grant. I've been praying for you."

The words nearly undid him.

"I need to see you."

"When?"

Grant exhaled slowly. "As soon as possible."

Another pause. "I can make time tomorrow."

Grant closed his eyes. He felt something shift inside him. Not relief. Not yet. But the first fragile step toward truth.

"Thank you," he said quietly.

And deep down, he knew tomorrow would change everything.

PART FOUR

Season of Redemption

CHAPTER 43
A Shepherd's Warning

Austin, Texas

Godly conviction never truly disappears but waits patiently until a man runs out of places to hide.

Grant sat in his car with the engine off, staring at the church office building across the parking lot. The familiar brick structure he had walked into hundreds of times over the years felt different today. Today, it felt like judgment. Not the loud, condemning kind, but the quieter whisper of conviction that comes when a man finally runs out of explanations and sees things clearly for what they truly are.

Resting his hands on the steering wheel, Grant closed his eyes. He had rehearsed versions of this conversation all morning. Edited and carefully worded versions. But sitting here now, none of them felt honest. For months he had managed the truth the way a lawyer manages evidence—revealing only what supported his case. He was quite sure Michael had seen through it the first time and knew he wouldn't get away with it again.

Inside that office was a man who knew Kate and knew his marriage. A man who had celebrated and prayed over it many times in the years he'd been their pastor and friend. Michael would not be fooled by half-confessions or carefully softened language.

Opening the car door, Grant noticed the morning air felt cooler than he expected. Each step across the parking lot seemed louder than the last. When he reached the building, he paused with his hand on the door.

One thought pressed into his mind with uncomfortable clarity. If I walk in there, everything changes. For a moment he considered turning around and driving away. He could reschedule again. But the thought that followed was heavier. Running had not helped him these past months.

Grant opened the church office door and stepped inside. It smelled faintly of coffee, old paper, and the leather binding of Bibles handled for decades. Nothing about the room had changed. The same shelves. The same reception desk and lamp in the corner casting a steady pool of light.

Michael's assistant, Susie was not there, so Grant stood in the quiet of the room for a moment steadying himself. He had been here countless times before. But not like this, not stripped of his self-protection. Not this close to saying the truth without rearranging it first.

Before he could knock on Michael's private office, the pastor swung open the door.

"You made it," he said.

Grant let out something that was almost a laugh. "Barely."

Michael nodded toward the chair across from his desk. "Sit."

Grant sat as Michael closed the door behind him and moved to sit behind his desk. For several seconds neither of them spoke. Michael simply waited with the kind of patience Grant had once admired and now resented because it left him alone with himself.

Finally Michael said, "Your request to meet me sounded urgent."

Grant stared at his hands. "It is."

Michael folded his own across the desk. "Then start where it's hardest."

Grant swallowed and said the thing that sat heaviest on his chest. "I lied to you."

Michael didn't move.

Grant looked up briefly, then away. "The first time I came in here, I lied."

A long pause. Michael nodded once, not in approval, just acknowledgment. "What did you lie about?"

Grant's throat tightened. "How far things had gone with Lydia."

The name sounded uglier in this room than it ever had elsewhere.

Michael's expression remained steady, but something in his eyes sharpened. "How far *have* they gone?"

Grant's first instinct was still to soften it, still to edit and protect one last corner of himself. The memory of the deafening silence from Kate returned to him with pain and conviction. In the moment, he realized he was simply too tired to keep managing his own image.

"We've been sleeping together," he said quietly. "And I moved in with her for a while before Kate went back to Italy. Kate told me she sought your counsel before she decided to go, so I'm guessing you already know all this."

Michael inhaled slowly through his nose. "When did the sexual intimacy begin?"

Grant rubbed his forehead. "Months ago."

"Before Kate went back to Italy?"

"Yes, even before she went the first time." The answer barely made it out.

Michael leaned back slightly in his chair absorbing Grant's confession. "And when you first came to me," he said carefully, "you told me it had only been kissing."

Grant nodded. "Yes."

Michael was quiet for a moment. Then asked, "Why?"

The question nearly broke him. Not because he didn't know. Because he did. "Because I wanted relief without full exposure," Grant admitted. "I wanted to feel like I was doing something right without actually surrendering anything."

There it was. Michael didn't pounce on it or shame him. But neither did he soften the truth. "That's called managing sin," he said. "Not confessing it."

Grant closed his eyes. "I know."

"No," Michael said quietly. "I think you're just now beginning to know."

The words stung because they were true. Grant looked down at the carpet. "I've made a mess of everything."

Michael did not argue. "Yes."

Grant laughed once under his breath, a hollow, disbelieving sound. "You don't waste words."

"You don't need anything but the truth, Grant."

Silence returned. It pressed against Grant's ribs until he finally said, "I don't even understand myself anymore."

"Then let me help," Michael responded, leaning forward.

Grant lifted his eyes.

"What you are calling confusion," Michael said, "is not confusion."

Grant frowned.

"It's compromise," Michael continued. "Layered compromise. Repeated compromise. Protected compromise."

The words landed one by one.

"You did not wake up one morning and find yourself in adultery by accident. You let smaller lies prepare the ground. You excused what should have been confronted. You called it drift when it was desire. You called it care when it was hunger. You called it confusion when it was disobedience. Let's be honest and call it what it really is ...sin."

Grant felt each sentence like a tightening band around his chest. He wanted to protest and say it wasn't that simple. That marriages were complicated. Midlife was complicated. Loneliness was complicated. But the protest died before it formed because Michael was not wrong.

Michael watched him carefully. "You are not the first man to confuse feeling seen with being loved," he said quietly. "And you are not the first man to mistake relief for peace."

Grant stared at him. That line found him precisely because relief was exactly what Lydia had offered him. Relief from his insecurities. Relief from tension. Relief from the ache of feeling unneeded. But not peace. Never peace.

Michael continued. "You've spent months rewriting what happened so you could bear it. You told yourself Kate was distant, independent, and hard to reach. Maybe all of that contains fragments of truth. But none of it changes what you chose."

Grant's jaw tightened. "I know that."

"Do you?" Michael asked sternly. "Because according to Kate, every time you two talked about this, you seemed to believe there was shared blame."

Grant looked away.

Michael's tone was calm. "There may have been weakness in your marriage. There may have been neglect. There may have been years of assumptions, comfort, and emotional drift. Those things matter."

Grant looked back at him, almost relieved.

Then Michael finished. "But they do not explain away adultery."

The relief vanished.

"Do you understand me?"

Nodding once, Grant replied, "Yes."

"Say it."

Grant swallowed. "My marriage may have had cracks," he said slowly, "but I chose betrayal."

Michael held his gaze. "Again."

"My marriage may have had cracks," Grant repeated, voice lower now, "but I chose betrayal."

Something in him recoiled from the nakedness of that sentence. And something else—quieter, deeper—recognized it as truth.

Michael leaned back. "That's where repentance starts."

Grant's shoulders sagged. He suddenly felt older to himself. Not in the mirror sense. In the soul sense.

“What do I do?”

Michael did not answer immediately. “When did you last see Lydia?”

Grant hesitated. “Last night, before I went home and called you,” he admitted.

Michael’s eyes did not leave his face. “Even though I made it clear the first time we met, if there was any hope for your marriage, you had to cut it off.” It was a statement of fact, not a question.

“Yes.”

“Did you even attempt a breakup?

“Not really.”

Michael sighed. “And why not?”

Grant laughed bitterly. “Take your pick. Shame. Anger. Self-pity. Feeling cornered. Kate confronted me and I …”

“And you wanted to be comforted by the very person helping destroy your marriage,” Michael finished.

Grant went still. “Yes.”

Michael nodded once. “That is how bondage works.”

The word hit harder than Grant expected. Bondage. Not romance. Not connection. Not helplessness. Bondage.

“You are not dealing with a love triangle,” Michael said. “You are dealing with sin, addiction to emotional relief, and a heart that has practiced self-deception.”

Grant stared at him. There it was again. No theatrics. No raised voice. Just truth.

Michael folded his hands. "So, here is my warning."

Grant felt his spine straighten.

"If you do not cut this off completely—fully, cleanly, immediately—you will lose more than your marriage."

Grant's face tightened and Michael continued.

"You will lose your integrity. Your spiritual authority. Your peace. Your clarity. Your children's trust when this comes fully into the light. And if you keep nurturing this double life, you will reach a point where repentance no longer feels desirable to you."

That sentence chilled Grant. "Can that happen?"

Michael did not soften. "Yes."

Grant's mouth went dry.

"Sin lies," Michael said. "At first it lies about pleasure. Then it lies about control. Then it lies about consequence. And if you let it run long enough, it will lie to you about God Himself."

Grant felt the room narrow and asked, "Do you mean spiritual warfare? Is this all a spiritual battle and not my own moral failure?"

Michael looked at Grant intently and said, "Don't go trying to shift all blame to Satan, Grant. You can be sure you're in a spiritual battle, but it was your free will and poor choices that gave him permission to ransack your life."

Grant knew this to be true. He was just beginning to see with his former "godly eyes" how deceived he'd allowed himself to become. He now remembered how weeks ago he'd had the audacity to ask God which woman he should choose. As if covenant were optional. As if God might bless what He had forbidden. As if desire could rewrite Scripture.

Michael saw something change in Grant's face. "What?"

Grant looked down again. "I prayed something," he admitted. "And even saying it now sounds sick."

"Say it anyway."

Grant forced the words out. "I asked God which woman I should choose."

The silence afterward was absolute. Michael did not look angry. He looked grieved. And somehow that was worse.

"Grant," he said quietly, "you have been grieving the Holy Spirit for so long that your instincts are no longer trustworthy."

The sentence landed with devastating precision.

"You are trying to hear God through a conscience you have been steadily numbing."

Grant covered his face with one hand. "What is wrong with me?"

Michael let the question sit. Then said, "Nothing that confession and true repentance cannot confront. But you must stop calling darkness unclear."

Grant dropped his hand. Tears burned unexpectedly behind his eyes. "I don't know if Kate will ever forgive me."

Michael nodded. "She may not."

The honesty hit like cold water.

"But whether she forgives you is not your first assignment."

Grant stared at him. "What is?"

"Obedience."

The word sat between them.

"You end the affair."

Grant inhaled shakily.

"You confess the truth to your wife—fully. And submit yourself to accountability." And then, softer but somehow heavier: "And you stop asking whether this costs too much."

Grant looked at the floor.

Michael's voice gentled. "Let me tell you what I think is happening."

Grant didn't move.

"I think God is answering Kate's prayers. I think He is tearing the lies away one layer at a time. I think the discomfort you're feeling is mercy. Severe mercy, maybe. But mercy."

Grant's chest tightened. "Because?"

"Because if God intended to leave you alone in this, you wouldn't feel this torn. You would feel justified."

That rang true in the deepest part of him. He had felt justified. For a while. Now he felt sick.

Michael stood and walked around the desk, not looming—just near enough to make avoidance impossible. "Here is the shepherd's warning, Grant."

Grant looked up.

"If you keep going the way you are going, you will become someone you do not recognize. And by the time you are done, the devastation will reach far beyond you. Obviously to Kate and your children. But also, the people in our church who love and trust you. It will contaminate your relationship with God. Sin does not stay contained just because you prefer it private."

Grant nodded once, tears now threatening openly.

"So, choose today."

The words were firm.

"Not tomorrow. Not after one more conversation. Not after one more night of relief. Today."

Grant's voice nearly failed him. "What if I can't?"

Michael's face softened, but not his answer. "You can."

Michael paused and watched Grant's eyes and expression to ensure he was hearing him clearly. "You may not want to. You may fear what obedience will cost. But do not call unwillingness inability."

That stripped the last of Grant's defenses. His eyes filled. For the first time in months, he was not trying to protect the version of himself he preferred. He was simply a man sitting in the wreckage of what he had chosen. And he could finally see it.

Then, like a man surfacing after being underwater too long, he let out a long, unsteady breath. "I've made the biggest mistake of my life."

Michael did not contradict him. "Yes," he said.

"What do I say to Lydia?" he whispered.

Michael answered immediately. “The truth. No blame. No ambiguity. No comfort you have no right to offer.”

Grant nodded slowly. “And then?”

“And then you spend lots of time with God,” Michael said. “Stay in the safety of your home. Not because home feels easy. Because it is the place where truth now waits for you.”

Grant wiped his eyes with the back of his hand and asked, “Any other advice, Pastor?”

“Yes, Grant. You commit and follow through with meeting with me once a week for accountability. Will you do that?”

Grant nodded, tears slipping freely now. The room grew quiet again. For months he had blamed confusion, loneliness, midlife uncertainty. But sitting there now, he could finally see the battle for what it was. Not between Kate and Lydia. Between truth and deception. Between repentance and pride. Between obedience and the slow erosion of his soul.

And now he knew with full clarity and conviction which side he needed to choose.

CHAPTER 44
The Amputation

Austin, Texas

Grant had always imagined repentance would feel clean, like relief, like finally breathing again.

Instead, it felt like loss. Pastor Michael had called it obedience. Grant was beginning to understand it felt more like he was cutting off his own limb.

He sat in his car outside Lydia's townhouse, his hands resting on the steering wheel. The street looked the same as it had every other evening he had arrived here. The same quiet row of houses. The same porch light glowing beside her door.

What was not the same was the anticipation that once pulsed through him when he pulled into her driveway. Tonight, it was completely gone. All he felt was dread and grief.

Pastor Michael had used a word that lingered in Grant's mind.

Amputation.

"You cannot heal while the infection remains," the pastor had said quietly. "Sometimes obedience requires removing something that once felt like life."

Grant hadn't argued. Because deep down he knew it was true.

He stepped out of the car and walked slowly to the door. For a moment he stood there. Then he knocked. Lydia opened it quickly. She smiled at first. But the smile faded when she saw his face.

"What's wrong?"

Grant stepped inside. The familiar scent the candles she liked to burn, and her favorite expensive perfume he had given her as an extravagant gift filled the air. So many memories lived inside this space now. And every one of them felt heavier than they had before.

They moved to the kitchen table. Lydia sat across from him.

"You're scaring me," she said.

Grant folded his hands together. "I need to talk to you."

Her eyes narrowed slightly. "About Kate?"

"Yes."

Silence settled between them.

"I met with my pastor yesterday," Grant continued.

"And?"

"And I told him everything."

Lydia leaned back in her chair. "Everything?"

"Yes."

A quiet tension entered the room.

"And what did he say?" she asked carefully.

Grant took a breath. "He told me the truth."

"And what's that?"

Grant met her eyes. "That what we've been doing is more than just wrong, it is sinful and without excuse."

The words hung there. Wrong. Sinful.

Lydia's expression hardened. "So now you're letting your pastor decide your life?"

"No," Grant said quietly. "I'm letting God correct my life."

Her jaw tightened. "After all this time?"

"Yes."

The honesty hurt. But it also felt clean.

"I can't live divided anymore," Grant said.

Lydia stared at him. "So, you're choosing her."

Grant nodded his head slowly. "Yes, I'm choosing obedience."

A short, bitter laugh escaped her. "Don't dress cowardice up as spirituality."

The words stung. But Grant didn't defend himself. "I care about you," he said quietly.

Her eyes flashed. "Not enough."

The truth landed between them.

Grant nodded. "You're right."

That surprised her.

"You're right," he repeated. "Because if I truly cared about you, I never would have invited you into this."

Her expression faltered slightly.

Grant looked down at the table. "I sinned against my wife," he said quietly. "But I also sinned against you."

Lydia blinked. "What?"

"I invited you into a relationship that could never be blessed."

The words felt heavy but honest. "I let you believe we were building something real. But it was built on betrayal."

Lydia looked away. Her voice softened slightly. "I never wanted to be the other woman."

Grant felt something twist in his chest.

"But here I am," she continued quietly. "Exactly that."

She gave a small, humorless laugh. "I guess every woman thinks she's the exception until she realizes she's the pattern."

For a moment neither of them spoke. Finally, Lydia looked back at him. "What if she doesn't reconcile?"

The question hung there.

Grant exhaled slowly. "I've been grieving the Holy Spirit long enough," he said. His voice was steady now. "I've been living for myself long enough."

He paused. "Whether Kate forgives me or not, this relationship can't continue or ever resume."

Lydia studied him carefully. "You're serious."

"Yes."

"Even if it means losing both of us?"

Grant nodded. “Yes.”

The honesty seemed to take the air out of the room.

Anger flashed across Lydia’s face. “So that’s it? You just walk away?”

Grant shook his head. “No.”

“Then what?”

He met her eyes. “I need to ask for your forgiveness.”

She blinked. “For what?”

“For inviting you into my sin.”

The words felt raw. “I knew better. And I ignored it.”

He swallowed. “You deserved honesty. Not half-truths and secrecy.”

Lydia’s eyes glistened slightly, though she fought it.

“You made me feel like I mattered.”

“You do matter,” Grant said quietly. “But not like this.”

Silence stretched between them.

Lydia sat very still, absorbing what he had said. Then she lifted her chin slightly. Grant could tell she was fighting hard to maintain her composure.

She took a deep breath and reset her expression, her lips tightening and her eyes hardening. “So, how do we handle our work relationship?”

She paused, her gaze sharpening. “Am I supposed to tuck my tail between my legs and just disappear?”

Grant met her gaze, steadier now than he had been before.

“Professionally,” he said, “your position is secure. That doesn't change. But I think it would be best for both of us if you reported directly to one of the senior executives instead of me. We can make that transition quickly and cleanly. And if working remotely would make this easier, I'll support that as well.”

He paused, softening just enough to acknowledge what this cost her.

“I understand if you decide this isn’t something you want to stay in. If you choose to leave, I’ll make sure you have a strong recommendation—honest, detailed, and reflective of the work you’ve done.”

He held her eyes a moment longer. “You won’t be disadvantaged by this, Lydia. Not professionally. Think about it and let me know.”

Lydia’s expression shifted and she asked almost timidly, “What happens now?”

Grant exhaled. “Now I repent.”

She scoffed lightly. “That sounds dramatic.”

“Maybe,” he said. “But it’s true.”

He looked down at the table. “And I pray that God does the same work in your heart that He’s beginning in mine.”

Her eyes narrowed. “You want to convert me now?”

Grant shook his head. "No, I want God to heal both of us." He hesitated and then said something unexpected. "Would you let me pray for you?"

Lydia stared at him. For a long moment she didn't answer. Finally, she leaned back in her chair. "This is the strangest breakup I've ever had."

Grant gave a faint, tired smile. "I imagine it is."

She looked at the table. Then nodded slightly. "Fine."

They sat across from each other. No touching. Just two people facing the wreckage they had created together.

Grant bowed his head. "Lord," he said quietly. His voice trembled slightly. "I confess the sin that brought us here." The words felt heavy. "And I ask Your forgiveness."

Lydia sat silently.

Grant continued. "Forgive me for betraying my wife. And forgive me for drawing Lydia into something that dishonored her."

The room was still.

"God, you love her too." He swallowed. "Bring her the same clarity you're bringing me. Protect her heart. And lead her into truth."

When he finished, the silence lingered. Lydia didn't speak immediately. Finally, she looked up at him. "You really believe all that."

"Yes."

She studied his face. There was no ambiguity there. No double meaning and no emotional escape route. Just resolve.

“Well,” she said quietly. “I guess this is goodbye.”

Grant nodded. “Yes.”

He stood slowly. Lydia didn’t move. He walked to the door, then paused.

“I truly am sorry,” he said.

She nodded faintly. “You should be.”

Her comment found its mark and landed hard.

Grant stepped outside. The night air felt colder than before. The withdrawal hit immediately. Her attention. Her affirmation. The rush of being desired.

Repentance felt less like freedom and more like detox. But for the first time in months, the direction of his life was finally clear. And clarity, even painful clarity, was a gift.

CHAPTER 45
The Convicting Psalm

Austin, Texas

God's truth is patient. It waits quietly at the door of the heart until we finally stop running from it.

Grant arrived early for the accountability meeting. Pastor Michael's office door was still closed when he walked down the quiet hallway of the church building. Morning sunlight filtered through the high windows, casting long rectangles of light across the carpet.

Grant sat in one of the chairs outside the office. Waiting. His mind drifted, uninvited, back to the night he had told Kate he was "just going for a drive," only to end up at Lydia's townhouse and in her bed.

He remembered coming home late. The house quiet. Too quiet. And then the strange, sudden pull toward the Bible sitting on the guestroom bedside table. He had picked it up. Opened it without thinking. Somewhere near the middle. Psalm 51. He had read only a few verses, but the words had landed with an uncomfortable clarity—sharp, undeniable and then he had closed it and tried to push King David's confession out of his mind.

The office door opened. "Come in, Grant."

Grant stood and stepped inside. The room felt calm in a way his life had not been the last time he sat here. Michael didn't sit immediately. Instead, he walked to the small table near the window and placed a Bible on it. "Let's start here today."

Grant sat across from him and Michael opened the Bible slowly. "Psalm 51."

Grant felt his stomach tighten.

Michael glanced up. "You recognize it."

Grant nodded. "Yes. I read part of it recently."

He paused, then continued more deliberately. "I told Kate I was going for a drive, and I believed it at first. I told myself I just needed to clear my head."

Michael remained still, giving him space.

"But I didn't turn around," Grant said quietly. "I went to Lydia's. Again."

The word hung there. Michael didn't interrupt.

"That night," Grant went on, "I was angry. I felt like Kate was judging me and trying to control me." He shook his head slightly. A brief pause. "I almost turned around," he added.

Michael's voice was gentle. "Almost?"

Grant nodded. "But I didn't."

Silence settled between them.

"When I got home," Grant continued, "there was the Bible I had put on the bedside table, like some kind of performance. Like I was trying to prove something."

He let out a quiet breath. "I felt compelled to open it." He glanced toward the Bible on the table. "And I landed on Psalm 51."

His voice lowered. "I read the first few verses." He swallowed. "And then I closed it."

Michael didn't react outwardly. "What made you close it?" he asked.

Grant looked down at his hands. "Because if I kept reading…" he said slowly, "I knew I wouldn't be able to pretend anymore."

The room fell quiet. Michael slid the Bible toward him. "Read it now."

Grant hesitated. Then he began.

"Have mercy on me, O God, according to Your unfailing love, according to Your great compassion blot out my transgressions."

His voice grew quieter as he continued. *"Wash away all my iniquity and cleanse me from my sin."*

Grant stopped reading. He stared at the page.

"That word," Michael said quietly. "Sin."

Grant nodded. "I spent months trying to call it something else."

"What did you call it?"

Grant gave a hollow laugh. "Confusion."

Michael nodded. "Anything else?"

"Loneliness. Midlife crisis."

Grant rubbed his face. "Spiritual warfare."

Michael's expression remained calm. "Was any of that the truth?"

Grant shook his head slowly. "No."

"What was the truth?"

Grant swallowed. "I chose it."

Michael leaned back slightly. "David chose it too."

Grant looked down at the page again. "David destroyed lives," he said quietly.

"Yes. And yet he still cried out to God."

Grant's voice dropped. "I read it that night." He paused. "And then I just continued deepening my entanglement with Lydia anyway."

Michael let the silence sit. Finally, he spoke. "Do you know the difference between conviction and repentance?"

Grant shook his head. "Conviction is when God shows you the truth."

Michael pointed toward the open Bible. "Repentance is when you stop arguing with it."

Grant closed his eyes briefly. "I felt conviction that night."

"Yes," Michael said. "But you did not yet want repentance."

Grant nodded slowly. "That's exactly what it felt like."

Michael leaned forward. "And yet here you are."

Grant looked up. "I'm tired," he said quietly. "Tired of lying. Tired of pretending this is complicated."

Michael nodded. "Sin always tries to make itself complicated."

Grant glanced down again at the Psalm. One line seemed to press into him harder than the others.

Create in me a clean heart, O God. Renew a right spirit within me.

Grant swallowed. "Will God actually help me clean my heart and renew my spirit?" he asked quietly.

Michael's voice was steady. "Yes."

Grant looked at him. "Even after all this?"

Michael didn't hesitate. "David committed adultery. Arranged a murder. Lied to protect himself." He tapped the page. "And God still restored him."

Grant stared at the words again. Then he whispered something almost to himself. "I closed the Psalm that night."

Michael nodded. "But you opened it today."

Grant felt something inside his chest loosen slightly. Not relief. Not yet. But something close to hope.

Michael folded his hands on the desk. "Grant, repentance is not a moment."

Grant looked up.

"It is a path," Michael added. He nodded toward the open Bible. "And this Psalm is the beginning of that path."

Grant looked down at the page again. And across the ocean, Kate was still praying for the man she had married and asking God to reach the part of Grant's heart that had been hidden even from himself.

CHAPTER 46
While She Waits

Monopoli, Italy

Silence stretches time in strange ways.

Days passed at Villa Santoro that felt both peaceful and unfinished, like a song that had paused before the final verse. Kate had not heard from Grant since the email he sent two weeks after she'd returned to Monopoli.

Summer had settled over Puglia in full bloom. Bougainvillea spilled over white stone walls. The Adriatic shimmered endlessly beneath the sun. Church bells drifted across the town each afternoon like a reminder that time continued whether hearts were ready or not.

Kate continued to maintain her commitment to three months of no contact. She was thankful Grant had not broken the silence again and yet she continually wondered if he was still pursuing Lydia … and even divorce.

Pastor Michael had encouraged patience. "Stay steady. Stay humble. Stay prayerful."

So, she waited. Not passively. Not anxiously. But deliberately.

Piano, piano.

Slowly, slowly.

The phrase had become a quiet companion in her thoughts.

Life had moved into a comfortable rhythm she cherished. Many days she walked the narrow streets of Monopoli alone praying and pondering about her future. Other times, Claire joined her and they practiced Italian phrases with shopkeepers who had begun to recognize them.

Some afternoons she sat on the terrace at Villa Santoro with Zia Rosa, learning how to shape fresh pasta while the older woman corrected her technique with affectionate authority. Sometimes, Rosa would offer beautiful nuggets of advice for living a life of contentment, saying things like "Life is not measured by what you lack, but by what you learn to hold close. I never had a husband, but God gave me a table always full of love."

Evenings almost always were around the long table beneath lantern light with simple meals and always fresh bread, olive oil, and stories drifting across the courtyard.

Wondering about Grant's decision remained in the background of it all. Not loud. Just present. Her friends rarely mentioned him now, but Kate could see the concern in their eyes from time to time. They all understood what the waiting meant.

Grant might be changing … or he might be moving farther away. Kate simply did not know. And learning to live inside that uncertainty had become its own quiet discipline.

By early July, plans at the villa began to shift again. Ev and Marianne's return flights were approaching in about two weeks.

"I refuse to admit it's time to leave," Ev declared one afternoon while beginning dinner prep, knowing her days cooking in this beloved *cucina* were winding down.

"You're welcome to stay longer," Claire replied dryly.

Marianne laughed from the doorway. "Some of us have jobs."

"And neither of us have Visa's," Ev added.

"Allora," Claire grinned. "That can easily be remedied."

Kate watched them with quiet gratitude and wondered silently just how long she would be staying at Villa Santoro. The villa felt much more like home than the one she left behind in Austin.

Meanwhile, Claire had begun conspiring with Zia Rosa about something entirely different—the future of the villa. What started as casual conversation had quickly turned into something more intentional. They spoke about it constantly now. Opening a few of the upstairs rooms to travelers. Not tourists rushing through, but people who wanted to stay. To experience. To linger.

"Not a hotel," Claire emphasized one afternoon as she was sketching ideas on a scrap of paper at the kitchen table. "Villa Santoro is a place for people come to *live* for a while."

"*Una casa con anima*," Zia Rosa nodded as she kneaded dough. A house with a soul.

Claire's ideas grew more detailed by the day. Small cooking evenings hosted by local chefs who still made everything by hand. Long-table dinners under the courtyard lights where guests didn't just eat—they connected. Morning espresso on the terrace with Italian lessons woven naturally into conversation. Seasonal stays built around harvests, festivals, and quiet rhythms instead of packed itineraries.

"People don't need more places to go," Claire said one evening. "They need places that make them feel something."

She talked about restoring the upstairs rooms … white linens, open shutters, the scent of citrus and sea air drifting in. Simple. No pretense. Authentic.

"And no rushing," she added. "If someone stays here, they agree to slow down."

Ev raised an eyebrow. "So, you're creating an anti-American experience?"

Claire smiled. "Exactly."

They laughed, but Claire didn't.

Zia Rosa watched her carefully, something knowing in her expression. This wasn't just an idea anymore. It was becoming a calling.

"You realize you're planning a boutique hotel," Ev told her one evening.

Claire shrugged. "Someone has to keep the place interesting."

"But not a hotel," Marianne added quietly.

Claire shook her head. "No, something better."

Zia Rosa smiled in quiet agreement.

Kate watched the exchange, a small sense of wonder settling in her chest. Claire wasn't just imagining a future for the villa, she was stepping into one. Bringing life back into a house that had been waiting for voices again. And somehow, without announcing it, Villa Santoro was already beginning to change.

Paolo had returned to being part of their weekly rhythm. Not intruding. Simply present. He had resumed their Italian lessons three evenings a week. As always, he brought fresh flowers, bread, figs, or a new wine he'd discovered and wanted to share.

The lessons often turned into conversation. And the conversations often became something deeper. His relationship with Kate was relaxed, but careful. Only the two of them knew how challenging it was to guard their hearts from cultivating romantic feelings. They knew that unguarded hearts would lead them down a premature path. Neither wanted to hurt or be hurt.

Paolo rarely spoke much about himself. It wasn't secrecy so much as reserve and a genuine interest in asking and listening over talking about himself. But over time, pieces of his life surfaced.

Recently, he mentioned a small, abandoned farmhouse he had quietly purchased in a nearby village. "It is nothing right now," he said with a faint smile. "Just stone and weeds. But I will restore it slowly. Not for clients. For myself."

He described the place with thoughtful patience. Thick stone walls. A narrow balcony overlooking a valley of olive trees. A small courtyard where herbs and tomatoes would someday grow.

"And outside," he added, "there will be a long wooden table."

Kate smiled. "For guests?"

"For family," he said.

That was when he mentioned something she had not heard before. "My sister and her husband live not far from there," he said. "They have three children who believe they are already adults."

Kate smiled at the image.

"And my brother in Bari has two little ones who climb everything. My mother says they inherited that from me."

The way he spoke about them carried quiet affection. "When the house is finished," he continued, "I imagine them all there sometimes. My mother at the end of the table giving instructions. The children running in and out of the garden. Too much bread. Too much noise."

He shrugged lightly, almost embarrassed by the picture he had painted. "But that is how a house should feel."

Kate listened, picturing it. Warm evening light. Voices drifting across the hillside. A long wooden table surrounded by laughter. For one fleeting moment she saw herself there. Not as a visitor, but at the table as if she belonged there. The image startled her. She imagined reaching for bread, listening to his nieces argue, his mother laughing from the head of the table. And then just as quickly the picture dissolved.

Paolo noticed the change in her expression. "You are quiet," he observed.

Kate blinked, pulling herself back to the present moment. "Just thinking," she said.

But the truth was something she wasn't quite ready to say aloud. Because somewhere between the stories of stone houses and children climbing trees, she had realized something that unsettled her. Paolo wasn't just kind. He was the type of man who quietly built a life worth stepping into. And that thought frightened her more than she expected.

One evening, Paolo joined Kate for a walk. The other women had insisted they could handle the dinner dishes without her. They walked beyond the villa along the narrow road. The sun had begun its slow descent toward the sea.

"You are quiet tonight," Paolo observed.

Kate smiled faintly. "I'm thinking too much."

"About your husband?"

"Yes."

"And about us?"

She hesitated. Then nodded.

Paolo stepped a little closer. Not enough to crowd her. Just enough to be present. "I do not want to be your distraction," he said.

"You're not," she replied quickly.

"Then what am I?"

Kate searched for honesty. "Peace. Comfort. Kindness," she whispered. "And possibility." She exhaled slowly. "And that scares me."

He studied her, not rushing to respond. The quiet between them deepened, not uncomfortable—just undeniable.

"For weeks," he said carefully, "we have both been pretending we do not feel what is already there."

Kate's breath caught slightly. "Yes."

His hand lifted slowly, brushing a strand of hair from her face. The gesture was deliberate, giving her space and time to step back. She didn't.

The air between them shifted. He leaned in and kissed her. Soft. Brief. But unmistakably alive.

Warmth stirred in her chest and a memory of what it felt like to be seen and desired not as someone's wife or someone waiting, but simply as a woman. For a suspended moment, the world narrowed to breath and heartbeat. Then reality returned.

Kate stepped back. "I am still married," she whispered, tears rising.

Paolo's expression tightened. "Yes."

She pressed her fingers lightly to her lips. "I'm sorry."

"I don't regret kissing you," he said quietly. "But I will not let passion outrun integrity."

The steadiness in his voice calmed her.

"I don't know what my future is," she said, her voice breaking. "I don't know if my husband is fighting for our marriage or already moving toward divorce."

She wiped at her tears. "It would be so much easier to know. At least then I could stop waiting."

Paolo stepped forward and drew her into a gentle embrace. She rested there for a moment, letting herself be held. It had been so long since she'd felt a strong, loving embrace. She was tempted to allow herself to melt into him. Then she pulled back.

"You are stronger than you realize," he said softly.

"I don't feel strong."

"Strength is not loud."

A small smile touched his mouth. "In Italy we say…"

"Piano, piano," she finished.

He nodded. "But it's not about time," he said quietly. "It's about restraint … choosing not to rush what matters."

She felt that. Deeply.

They walked back toward the villa. Not touching. But aware now that something deeper had taken root and would have to be handled with even more care.

That night, long after the house had gone quiet, Kate sat alone on the terrace. The bracelet she had purchased weeks ago rested lightly on her wrist. She admired the delicate sterling silver threaded with the Murano glass beads that had caught her attention in the shop and now reflected the lantern's light. She turned it between her fingers.

Piano, piano.

Perhaps healing was not meant to arrive in one dramatic moment but served a deeper purpose by arriving slowly. Through prayer. Through patience. Through choosing integrity even when the heart longed for certainty.

Kate looked out across the darkened olive grove. Somewhere beyond the hills the sea moved quietly beneath the moon. She did not yet know where her story with Grant would lead. But she knew one thing.

God was still writing it. And while she waited, she would guard her heart and take everything … slowly.

Piano. Piano.

CHAPTER 47
Girl Talk

Monopoli, Italy

There is a beautiful kind of grace that unfolds when women gather around a table and tell each other the truth.

The four friends lingered at the long wooden table, which still held the remnants of dinner … olive oil pooling in shallow dishes, torn pieces of bread, empty glasses that had once held wine. No one reached for plates. No one stood. They simply sat in a comfortable contentment that deep friendships afford.

From the kitchen, they could hear Zia Rosa singing as she worked on a special *dolce,* she had planned for tomorrow, when Paolo would join them again for dinner.

Earlier, she had announced with delight, *"Questo dolce farà danzare il tuo palato dalla gioia."* This dessert will make your palate dance with joy.

Ev leaned back, stretching her legs beneath the table. "All right," she said, glancing around. "We've been talking about everyone except ourselves for weeks now."

Claire smiled faintly. "That's not entirely true."

Ev raised an eyebrow. "We've talked about Kate. We've talked about Grant. We've talked about Paolo. We've heard a few of your ideas about Villa Santoro, Claire. Oh … and of course we've discussed Rosa's rules for life." She gestured toward the kitchen. "But we haven't really talked about the three of us."

"She's right," Marianne replied nodding.

Kate looked up from her cup of tea. "I'd love to talk about the three of you instead of me and all my drama for a change."

Claire reached for the olive oil, dipping a piece of bread as if buying herself time. "What exactly are you proposing?"

Ev's expression softened. "Let's stop pretending we're just here for a vacation," she said. "We didn't fly across the ocean in our sixties just to eat pasta and admire the scenery."

"We're here because something in each of us needed something," Claire added.

Ev nodded. "And I think it's time we say what that is."

The table grew still. Not tense. Just honest.

Marianne was the first to speak. She didn't rush. "My marriage was good," she said quietly. "Solid. We didn't have a dramatic story. We had a steady one."

Her fingers rested lightly against the edge of her empty wine glass. "Gary was my person," she continued. "For decades, he was the one person I told everything to. The one who knew what I was thinking before I said it. The one I planned everything with—even small things, like what we'd have for dinner or where we'd go on a Saturday morning."

A small smile touched her lips. "We built a life that worked." The smile softened into something more reflective. "And then … one day, he wasn't there anymore."

No one interrupted. "The hardest part wasn't just losing him," she said. "It was losing the shared life—the constant conversation, the quiet companionship. You don't realize how much of yourself exists in relation to another person until they're gone."

Kate felt that deeply.

Marianne continued, her voice steady. "The children were grown. Busy with their own lives—which is exactly what we had hoped for them. But suddenly, I was making decisions alone. Eating meals alone. Processing thoughts alone."

She paused. "That first year was disorienting."

Ev nodded.

"I didn't know who I was without being part of a 'we,'" Marianne said. "And I didn't like how quiet everything felt."

A longer pause. "But over time, something shifted."

She lifted her eyes. "I didn't replace him. And I didn't try to. But I began to discover that my life still had purpose beyond being someone's wife."

Kate watched her closely.

"My work became more meaningful," Marianne continued. "As a social worker, I had always helped people, but now I understood loss differently. I could sit with people in their grief without trying to fix it."

Kate nodded in understanding.

"And at church, I started mentoring younger women. Not because I had all the answers, but because I had walked through something hard and survived it."

Her voice softened. "And slowly, I found contentment again."

Her words were settled. "But I also know this," she added, her tone shifting slightly. "God is not finished with me."

The words carried quiet conviction. "I didn't come here just to rest. I came here because I sense there's still something ahead for me.

Something meaningful. A way to finish this season of my life with intention."

Ev leaned forward slightly. "A legacy."

Marianne nodded. "Yes. Not something grand. But something that lasts. Something that matters to someone else long after I'm gone. Being here, at Villa Santoro, embracing this slower rhythm … it's given me space to breathe and think. I feel like I'm seeking God more earnestly and hearing Him more clearly."

Silence settled again. Kate broke it. "Marianne, do you have any desire to remarry one day?"

Ev and Claire exchanged quick glances, eyebrows lifting in interest.

Marianne smiled coyly. "That's a question I would have answered with a firm no before this trip," she said. "But I've watched how organically you and Paolo have connected, Kate. I'm not saying you'll end up together. I'm just saying that I think God could place a godly man in my path one day if I'm open to it."

"You never know, my friend," Claire said, leaning across the table to touch her hand. "Maybe on your next trip to Puglia, he'll be waiting."

Marianne laughed quietly.

"That confession calls for a toast," Claire declared, pushing back her chair. "I'm going to grab the limoncello. Don't share anything meaningful without me."

"I love this conversation," Kate said, smiling. "Who's next?"

Claire returned moments later with a small tray—four *bicchierini* and a chilled bottle of bright yellow limoncello.

"What did I miss?"

Ev leaned back, folding her arms loosely. "Nothing yet."

She took a breath. "I suppose I'm the outlier."

The others turned toward her.

"I've been single a long time," she said. "Not because I couldn't have married, but because I never felt compelled to."

Claire raised an eyebrow. "That sounds very you."

Ev smiled faintly. "I've had a good life. Full. Independent. I've made my own decisions, kept my own schedule, answered to no one but God and occasionally my principal."

A small pause. "And I've been content. Mostly."

Kate believed her.

"But contentment isn't the same as fully embracing all God's possibilities," Ev continued.

"I think I became so comfortable on my own that I stopped considering what it might look like to share my life with someone."

Marianne nodded.

"I'm not hoping for some dramatic romance," Ev added dryly. "At this point, that would require more energy than I'm prepared to give."

Claire laughed.

"But…" Ev said, glancing down briefly, then back up, "I would welcome companionship. The right kind. Someone steady.

Someone who doesn't need me to become someone else but also doesn't let me stay exactly the same."

"That sounds like growth," Kate said.

"Or a miracle," Ev replied.

They all laughed understandingly.

"I'm also aware," Ev added, lifting a finger, "that I am very set in my ways. I like my mornings quiet. I like my space. I don't negotiate well before coffee."

"Noted," Claire said.

"So, if God brings someone into my life at this stage," Ev said, "he's going to have to be very special and very flexible."

The humor softened the truth.

"But I'm open," she said finally. "Open in a way I haven't been before."

She lifted her glass. "To possibilities and potential."

"To possibilities and potential," the others echoed.

Claire grew quiet. That alone caught everyone's attention. She set her glass down slowly.

"I usually make a joke right about now," she said. "Something about my divorce being my most expensive real estate transaction."

Ev smiled. "You do."

"It's easier that way."

The humor faded.

"My divorce …" she began, her voice softer, "wasn't clean or mutual or empowering the way people like to describe it after the fact. It was painful and disruptive. And for a long time, I didn't know who I was without that life."

No one spoke.

"So, I did what I knew how to do," she said. "I worked." She inhaled deeply and sighed. "Harder than ever. Bigger deals. Longer hours. Constant motion. I told myself I was rebuilding." She paused. "But I wasn't rebuilding. I was numbing."

"I stayed so busy I didn't have to feel how deeply I'd been hurt. And for a while, it worked. At least on the outside."

She gave a small, knowing smile. "I looked successful. Independent. Thriving."

Ev nodded. "That's what we saw."

"I know." A longer pause. "But eventually, I burned out. Quietly. The kind where you wake up one day and realize you have nothing left to give to the life you built."

Her fingers stilled. "And in that space, I started to hear something I had been avoiding."

Marianne leaned in.

"That God wasn't asking me to work harder," Claire said. "He was asking me to step away."

The words settled.

"I didn't understand it at first. Why walk away from something that made sense on paper?" She looked around the courtyard. "But when this trip started taking shape, something in me recognized it."

"A door?" Kate asked.

Claire nodded. "I didn't say it out loud then. But even before we left, I sensed this might not just be a visit."

Ev leaned forward. "You thought about staying?"

"Yes." She took a long breath. "And once I sold my business, I knew I wasn't supposed to rush back into that life." She glanced toward the villa. "And then there's this place."

Zia Rosa appeared briefly in the doorway, listening.

"The more time I spend here, the more it feels like something is waiting," Claire said. "Not just a house. Something unfinished. Something meant to gather people."

Smiling faintly, Zia Rosa slipped back inside.

"I don't think I came here to escape," Claire said. "I think I came here to step into what's next."

The words settled. "I don't know all the details yet. But I do know this … I'm not going back."

Ev raised an eyebrow. "That's big."

"It is," Claire said. "But it doesn't feel reckless." She looked at them. "It feels … directed … by God."

All eyes turned to Kate. She hadn't spoken. Not yet.

"Y'all know that I didn't come here looking for a new life," she said finally. "I came here because the life I had was falling apart."

The words lingered in a pregnant pause.

"But something unexpected happened," she continued. "I've started to remember parts of myself I had set aside." Her voice softened. "And now I want to rebuild with honesty and with courage."

The table fell quiet. Four women. Different stories. Same turning point.

Ev lifted her glass. "Well," she said, "this is either the beginning of something remarkable, or we've all lost our minds at the same time."

Claire smiled. "Possibly both."

Marianne raised her glass. "To not disappearing quietly."

Kate lifted hers last. "To becoming who God meant us to be."

They clinked glasses.

From the kitchen doorway, Zia Rosa had heard more than the women realized. She had not meant to listen. But life, she had learned, did not always ask permission before revealing something sacred.

She stood still for a moment, a dish towel draped over her shoulder, watching the four women at the table, their heads bent together, their voices softer now, their laughter threaded with something deeper than it had been when they first arrived.

Donne coraggiose, she thought. Brave women. Not because their lives had been easy. Because they were still willing to grow.

She moved quietly back to the counter, her hands returning to their familiar rhythm as she prepared the *dolce* for tomorrow evening.

Sugar, eggs, lemon zest—the simple things that, when handled with care, became something beautiful.

"*La vita è così*," she murmured to herself. "*Piano, piano*." Life is like this. Slowly, slowly. She paused, glancing once more toward the courtyard.

"They think they are starting over," she said out loud to herself, a hint of a smile touching her lips. "But they are not starting over." She turned back to her work. "They are finally becoming."

CHAPTER 48
The Doctor

Monopoli, Italy

There are moments when God lovingly turns the mirror around, not to condemn us, but to remind us how desperately we all need His grace.

Kate tossed and turned in bed for what felt like hours. Paolo's kiss had stirred something inside her—something warm and alive. But it had also unsettled her spirit in ways she hadn't expected.

Eventually she drifted into sleep while whispering a prayer for clarity. But few short hours later, the moonlight spilling through the open window pulled her awake again. At first, she thought she had been dreaming. Then she realized it wasn't a dream. It was a memory.

A memory she had not thought about in more than twenty years.

"Oh no," she whispered into the quiet room.

The details of this sudden recollection returned with startling clarity. The smell of hospital disinfectant. The steady hum of the night shift. And Dr. Matthew Reeves.

He had been brilliant. Charming. Single. And attentive. He noticed her. At first it had seemed harmless. Two colleagues sharing coffee between deliveries in the hospital break room.

"You deserve more appreciation than you get," he had told her once, leaning against the counter while the coffee machine sputtered. The compliment warmed her more than it should have.

Grant had been traveling often then. Those were the early years of his career, before children, before life settled into its long rhythms. She had been lonely. Grant had been busy. She had energy and ideas and dreams about the future. Grant often came home exhausted.

Matthew listened. He asked questions about her work. About the families she helped him deliver babies for. About the life she imagined someday.

He laughed easily. Sometimes when he laughed, his hand would brush her elbow lightly. It felt harmless. Until it didn't.

One night after a long shift he suggested they grab a drink.

"Just one," she had promised herself.

She remembered the bar now—the dim lights, the quiet hum of conversation, the strange comfort of being seen by someone who seemed interested in every word she said.

It was nearly two in the morning when she pulled into the driveway.

Grant stirred as she slipped into bed. "Everything okay?" he asked sleepily.

"Emergency C-section," she replied.

The lie came too easily.

That realization had haunted her later. For nearly a year she drifted emotionally. They'd never even kissed, but her heart had wandered into dangerous territory.

She avoided intimacy with Grant, claiming exhaustion after long shifts. Headaches. Stress.

In truth, it was guilt.

She imagined things she never should have imagined. What it might feel like to start over. What life might be like with someone who seemed to notice her in ways Grant had not during those busy years.

Nothing happened. But it might have if Matthew's sister had not died suddenly. If he had not relocated across the country within weeks. If life had not intervened and closed the door she had been slowly approaching.

Kate sat up in bed, her heart pounding. "But by the grace of God…" she whispered.

The truth settled over her with quiet clarity. The seed had been there. She had been capable. Maybe not in action. But certainly in her heart.

She slipped quietly out of bed and crossed the room to the small desk near the window. Switching on the lamp, she opened her journal and began to write.

Lord,

I had buried this memory so deeply that I have not thought about it in decades.

I remember asking Your forgiveness back then. I remember thanking You for the mercy that removed Matthew from my life before I crossed a line that might have destroyed my marriage.

At the time, I never sensed You wanted me to tell Grant. Our marriage was still young. Perhaps he would not have understood the difference between temptation and action.

I don't know.

But I believe You brought this memory back to me tonight for a reason.

All this waiting ... all this praying ... I realize something. I don't think I've truly forgiven Grant yet. I think I've been waiting to see what he decides. Waiting to see whether he chooses our marriage or continues walking away. But forgiveness cannot depend on his decision or the outcome of our marriage.

You forgave me long before I deserved it. So, Lord, teach me how to forgive Grant the same way.

Not conditionally. Not cautiously. But completely. Even before I know what our future holds.

Amen.

Kate closed the journal and sat quietly for a moment.

Two Scriptures surfaced in her mind almost immediately; words she had read many times but felt differently tonight. She whispered them softly into the quietness of the night.

"*If we confess our sins, He is faithful and just to forgive us our sins and to cleanse us from all unrighteousness*."

And then another.

"Be kind and compassionate to one another, forgiving each other, just as in Christ God forgave you."

The words settled over her heart like warm water over a wound. Not excusing what Grant had done. But reminding her that grace was never meant to flow in only one direction.

When she finally returned to bed, the turmoil inside her had softened. Paolo's kiss still lingered in her thoughts. Grant's betrayal still ached. But beneath both of those emotions something steadier had begun to grow … a quiet understanding that forgiveness often must begin long before reconciliation ever became possible.

Kate lay back against the pillow and stared at the moonlight spreading across the ceiling. The persistent tightness in her chest loosened and she realized something quietly profound.

Grant's repentance was no longer something she could control. Neither was his decision. For months she had been waiting for his answer. Tonight, she finally released the outcome.

"Lord," she whispered into the darkness, "I give You, my marriage."

The words surprised her with their simplicity. Whether Grant returned. Whether he walked away. Whether their future held reconciliation or loss. God would still be faithful.

Kate closed her eyes and somewhere in the quiet spaces of her heart, forgiveness took root before she even knew what the next chapter of her story would bring.

CHAPTER 49
Repentance

Austin, Texas

Grant had always believed repentance would feel dramatic.

There would be tears. Relief. A sense of spiritual clarity. Perhaps even a rush of peace. Instead, it felt like silence.

Two months had passed since he ended it with Lydia. Sixty-three days, if he counted precisely. He did count precisely. Once his business associate informed him she had decided to resign from the foundation and seek other employment, he had deleted her phone number and blocked her email.

He now had told Pastor Michael every detail he had once withheld. He regularly sat in rooms with other men who did not look shocked by his confession because they had fallen in quieter ways themselves.

Two months clean. It sounded clinical. Detox. That was closer to the truth.

The first week, he reached for his phone constantly—not to call her, but to check if she had tried to reach him. There was something humiliating about admitting that part. He wanted to be wanted even as he was choosing obedience. Withdrawal did not feel spiritual. It felt raw.

Lydia had been affirmation on demand. She had admired him. Needed him. Framed his dissatisfaction as depth. His restlessness as suppressed greatness. When he removed her from his life, the silence revealed something he hadn't wanted to see. The affair had not filled a void, it had masked one.

Now there was no masking. Just the void.

He sat alone at the kitchen table, staring at a cup of coffee gone cold. He had chosen legal separation in anger. That fact still lodged like gravel in his throat. He had called it clarity. But now he could honestly admit that it had been leveraging.

He had wanted Kate to respond. To break her boundary and come back pleading. Instead, she had stayed in Italy.

He exhaled slowly and rubbed his hand over two days of stubble. Obedience felt smaller than he expected. Less heroic. It was simply doing the next right thing when no one was watching.

Pastor Michael had told him, "Repentance is not what you feel. It's what you refuse."

So, he refused. He refused self-pity when it rose. He refused the narrative that Kate had been distant first. He refused to romanticize what he had with Lydia and to minimize the months of lying. He refused to rehearse explanations that softened his guilt.

It left him with a cleaner sentence. I betrayed my wife. No qualifiers.

The first time he said it in men's group without context, he felt exposed. No one gasped. One man across the circle simply nodded. "That's where change starts," he said quietly.

Grant had gone home that night and stared at his reflection in the bathroom mirror for a long time. He did not recognize the man who had needed admiration more than integrity. He did not recognize the man who had felt invisible and solved it with attention.

He stood and walked to the patio window. The evening light had begun to fade. He had always liked dusk. It was forgiving. Edges softened. There was nothing soft about this season.

Two months clean. A lifetime to go.

He had not contacted Lydia even once. He had not tried to contact Kate. He had honored her boundary. Pastor Michael had insisted on that.

"You don't pursue restoration while still craving emotional relief," Michael had said.

So, he waited. Waiting was harder than chasing.

He had started individual counseling. The therapist had not let him stay at the surface.

"You said you felt invisible," she had said in their second session. "When did you begin believing your visibility depended on admiration?"

He had not known how to answer that. He thought of his early career. Of leadership roles. Of rooms where his opinions mattered. He thought of aging and of being needed less. Of becoming dependable instead of compelling.

He thought of Kate—strong, capable, self-sufficient. He had twisted her strength into evidence that he was unnecessary. That had been easier than admitting he feared irrelevance.

The therapist had leaned forward gently. "Feeling insecure is human," she said. "Choosing betrayal to soothe it is dangerous."

There was no cruelty in her voice. Just clarity.

He closed his eyes now and let that truth sit again. He had not been seduced. He had pursued and volunteered his attention. The realization no longer sparked defensiveness. It sparked grief.

He missed his wife. Not the version of her that admired him. The version that challenged him. That prayed out loud when she didn't know what to do. That knew his worst traits and stayed anyway.

He remembered the night she said, "Please don't rewrite our history to make this easier for yourself."

He had been rewriting. Calling it "drift" instead of sin. Calling it loneliness instead of entitlement. Calling it confusion instead of choice. The words had been sandbags against shame. Now he let himself stand in the shame. Not to drown in it. To learn from it.

His phone buzzed on the table. He froze. For a second, old reflex surfaced. What if it is Lydia from another number? He walked slowly to the table and picked it up.

It was a calendar reminder for therapy. He almost laughed. The adrenaline spike had revealed something important. The craving wasn't fully dead. It was just managed.

Repentance wasn't a single decision. It was daily refusal. He sat back down and opened his laptop. There was a document he had been working on.

He titled it plainly: Confession.

He had rewritten it three times. The first version had explanations woven through it. The second had apologies but too much self-reference. The third was shorter. Cleaner.

Kate,

I sinned against you.

I chose attention over integrity. I chose secrecy over covenant. I chose my ego over your safety.

You did not cause my betrayal.

I did.

I do not expect forgiveness on my timeline.

I am seeking to become a man who honors God and honors you no matter how I feel in the moment.

Whether or not you return to this marriage, I will not return to that version of myself.

Grant

He stared at the screen for a long time. He did not send it. Pastor Michael had told him not to use words as leverage.

"Live it first," he had said. "Let fruit grow before you offer it."

So, he saved the document. Closed the laptop. And sat in the quiet.

Two months clean. No Lydia. No narratives. No grand gestures. Just the slow dismantling of pride.

He did not know whether Kate would take him back. That uncertainty no longer fueled panic. It fueled prayer.

He bowed his head. "God," he said quietly, "strip from me anything that made betrayal possible."

There was no thunder or surge of emotion. For the first time since the affair began, he was not trying to manage the outcome. He was trying to change the man in the mirror.

Somewhere across the ocean, his wife was breathing without him. He had no idea whether they would ever sit at their table together again. But if they did, she would not be sitting beside the man who had spent months chasing admiration. She would be sitting beside a man beginning to understand that covenant is not sustained by being desired. It is sustained by being faithful.

Two months clean from Lydia. That was the phrase Michael had used. *Clean.* An interesting choice of words.

Grant had hoped the separation would feel simple once it was over, but instead it came with loss, grief, guilt, and shame. The word *clean* did not feel light or easy. It felt costly. Like something being stripped away. A purging of body, soul, and spirit.

CHAPTER 50
Pastor's Report

Monopoli, Italy

The morning the text message arrived, the light was unusually soft.

Puglia had a way of diffusing sunlight so that even sharp things seemed gentler. Somewhere far beyond the low stone wall, a neighbor was hanging laundry—white sheets lifting and falling like surrender.

Kate's three months of silence from Grant was only twelve days away from completion. She pondered how and when to reestablish communication. A text? A phone call? Zoom? She wasn't feeling ready to return to Texas. There were far too many unknowns.

As she sat at the long wooden table in the courtyard; hands wrapped around an espresso cup, her phone vibrated once. A message. From Pastor Michael:

Grant is two months clean from his break with Lydia. No contact. Weekly counseling. Men's group. He's asking if he should go to Italy.

Kate read it twice. Two months clean. The phrase landed differently than she expected. Not triumphant, nor urgent, but a sober reality. Marianne walked out into the morning sunshine and eyed Kate setting down her phone.

"News?"

Kate nodded once. "He's been broken up with Lydia for two months. No contact whatsoever with her."

Marianne studied her face. "According to whom?"

"That was a text from Pastor Michael. Grant's asking if he should come here to Italy."

Marianne sat down slowly. "What do you feel?" she asked gently.

Kate didn't answer immediately. She watched a thin line of ants moving along the stone wall—determined, orderly, purposeful.

"I feel steady," she said finally.

That surprised her. Two months ago, she would have felt a surge. Hope colliding with fear. Anger rising to meet it. Now there was something quieter beneath it. Discernment.

"He ended it?" Marianne asked carefully.

"Yes, and he's doing the work."

"Repentance needs to be observable," Marianne murmured.

Kate smiled faintly. "That sounds like something Michael would say."

"It's something I've learned," Marianne replied softly. "Grief teaches you to watch behavior, not words."

Kate inhaled slowly. Two months. Sixty days of no Lydia. Almost ninety days of silence on her end. She had not broken the boundary. There had been nights she wanted to. Moments when loneliness crept in quietly and begged her to reach out.

Since her memory about Matthew, the Holy Spirit had leveled something in her. She was no longer standing on higher ground. She was standing on shared humanity.

The backfire of a scooter in the distance brought her back to the moment.

"Do you want him to come?" Marianne asked.

Kate closed her eyes briefly. "Yes."

The word rose immediately. But want and wise were not always the same.

"I don't want him to come to convince me," she said slowly. "I want him to come because he's already convinced."

Marianne nodded. "That's different."

"Yes."

Kate stood and walked toward the edge of the courtyard, resting her palms against the warm stone. Italy had changed her. Not in dramatic, external ways, but in nervous-system ways. Her breathing was slower here. Her thoughts less frantic. She had stopped gripping for outcomes. That had been the true healing.

Paolo's voice drifted in from the small side gate. "*Posso entrare*?" May I come in?

She turned. "Yes."

He stepped into the courtyard carrying bread… again, as if it were an extension of his character. "*Buongiorno*," he said, eyes warm but measured.

"*Buongiorno*."

He set the basket down and noticed immediately that something was different. "You have something heavy on your mind," he observed.

Kate smiled faintly. "Is it that obvious?"

"Yes," he said simply.

Marianne stood. "I'm going to give you two some space," she said, already moving toward the villa door.

Kate shot her a look, but Marianne only winked. Paolo remained where he was, not crowding her.

"News?" he asked tentatively.

"Yes."

She walked back to the table and picked up her phone. "My pastor texted me this morning. Grant broke up with Lydia two months ago. No contact. Consistent counseling and accountability. He wants to talk … to see me in person."

Paolo nodded slowly. "That is not small."

"No," she agreed.

"He asks to come here?"

"Yes."

Paolo absorbed that quietly. The breeze lifted his shirt slightly at the sleeves. "And what do you feel?" he asked.

She appreciated that he didn't ask what she would do. "I feel protective of the peace I've found," she said honestly. "And also, aware that our chance for restoration cannot happen across an ocean."

He nodded. "Sometimes, it is easier to heal when the wound is far away."

"Yes."

"But eventually," he said, "you must test whether the wound has closed."

She studied his face. There was no jealousy there. No tightening. Just truth.

"I don't want to lose what being here has done in me," she said quietly.

"What has it done?" he asked.

"It has removed my superiority," she admitted. "And my panic. I no longer need to be right. I need to be obedient."

Paolo's expression shifted slightly, respect deepening. "You are stronger now," he said.

"I am humbler now," she corrected.

He smiled. "That is stronger."

Silence settled between them—not awkward, but comfortable and safe.

"I will not stand between you and your marriage," he said.

She met his eyes. "I know."

"And if he comes," he continued, "I will step back. No more visits or lessons even with the others if he is here."

The words cost him something. She could see it.

She felt a flicker of grief at the thought. "Paolo…" she began.

He lifted a hand and gently placed his finger to her lips. "No promises," he said. "No future declarations. Just honesty."

She nodded. "I don't want to use you to test my healing," she said.

“You are not,” he replied. “You have been awake from the beginning.”

She inhaled deeply. “If he comes,” she said slowly, “it will not be for romance. It will be for reckoning.”

Paolo nodded. “That is good.”

She studied him. “And if the reckoning leads to reconciliation?”

He held her gaze. “Then I will bless it.”

The simplicity of that nearly undid her. Not because she loved Paolo, but because he represented something rare. A man who did not grasp. A man who did not maneuver for his benefit. A man who did not try to control.

She swallowed. “And if it doesn’t?”

He did not answer immediately. “Then we will walk *piano, piano*,” he said. Slowly, slowly.

The words settled like a benediction.

Claire’s laughter echoed faintly from down the road. Life moving. Choices coming. Kate picked up her phone again. She typed a quick message to Pastor Michael.

Tell him he may come. But not to persuade. Only to be truthful.

She hesitated, then added:

He cannot stay here. He must arrange lodging nearby.

Boundaries were not punishment. They were clarity. She pressed send. The message left her hands without tremor.

Paolo watched her quietly. “It is decided?” he asked.

“It is permitted,” she corrected.

He smiled faintly. “Good.”

She looked out at the beautiful landscape of Monopoli once again and said a silent prayer for wisdom and God’s will.

Two months clean for Grant. Three months of learning to breathe and see clearly for her. Restoration was no longer about reclaiming what they had been. It was about discerning whether something new could be built from what had been broken.

She turned back to Paolo. “Stay for coffee?” she asked.

He nodded. “Yes.”

They sat at the long table again, bread between them, sunlight soft on stone. Nothing urgent. Nothing hidden.

Soon, across the ocean, a man who had dismantled his pride would be packing a suitcase, not to win back his wife, but to face her. And in that difference, hope began to form.

CHAPTER 51
Cautious Approach

Austin, Texas

Grant imagined his arrival in Italy.

He would arrive. She would see him across a sunlit courtyard. There would be tears. Words. A cinematic reconciliation framed by olive trees and late-afternoon gold. But he knew it would be far less cinematic than his romantic daydream. It would be painful, perhaps even heartbreaking.

Pastor Michael sat across from him in the quiet office where so much of his life of deception had unraveled.

"You have two months clean," Michael said. "That's a beginning."

Grant nodded. He no longer inflated small milestones. Two months did not undo his betrayal. It simply proved his capacity.

"She's open to you coming," Michael continued. "But you understand the difference between pursuit and pressure?"

"Yes."

"Say it."

Grant inhaled slowly. "Pursuit is offering repair. Pressure is demanding outcome."

Michael nodded once. "And if she decides she cannot reconcile?"

Grant felt the familiar tightening in his chest. "I accept that," he said.

Michael held his gaze longer than usual. “Say it again.”

Grant swallowed. “I accept that.”

The words tasted like surrender.

For the first time since this began, he was not strategizing how to win her back. He was preparing to stand in front of her without defense.

Michael leaned forward. “You go to Italy to own what you did. Not to explain it. Not to minimize it. Not to wrap it in loneliness. You own it.”

“I will.”

“And you stay somewhere else.”

“Yes.”

“No late-night emotional talks. No ambushes. No grand gestures.”

Grant almost smiled. “I don’t feel very grand.”

“That’s good,” Michael said quietly.

Silence settled between them.

“Grant,” Michael added, “you are not going to Italy to resurrect the old marriage.”

Grant nodded slowly.

“I know.”

“You are going to see if something new can be built.”

The word *new* unsettled him. He had clung to nostalgia at first. Thirty-five years. Shared history. The children. The house. History had not protected them. Integrity might.

He stood. “I’m afraid,” he admitted.

Michael’s expression softened. “That’s appropriate.”

The Humble Approach

The airport felt anonymous. He had traveled many times for work. Always with purpose. Meetings. Deadlines. Deliverables. This time, he carried no presentation. Just confession.

He sat at the gate staring at the runway lights blinking against the dusk. What if she’s moved on? The thought rose uninvited. He had heard and thought about Paolo, the local friend of Claire’s who taught the women Italian and joined them for meals. Jealousy had flared like a fire in his gut for a while. Now it felt quieter. He had forfeited the right to outrage. If someone else had seen her while he was looking elsewhere, that was not betrayal. That was a space he had left unguarded.

He closed his eyes briefly. “God,” he whispered, “strip from me the need to win.”

He didn’t want to arrive defensive. He didn’t want to arrive needy. He wanted to arrive clean.

He did not sleep. He replayed moments he had once minimized. The first lie. The second. The way he had told Lydia she “understood him better.” The way he had blamed drift. The way he had filed legal for separation to force a reaction. That memory made his stomach turn. Control dressed as clarity. He had called it decisiveness. It had been fear.

At thirty thousand feet above the Atlantic, the illusion of control felt absurd. He had almost destroyed the one relationship that had seen every version of him.

The cabin lights dimmed. Passengers around him slept. Grant stared into the dark.

If she says no… He forced himself to finish the thought. If she says no, I remain obedient.

That was new. Earlier in the process, rejection would have sent him spiraling. Now, it would grieve him but not undo him.

The plane descended over the Adriatic just after dawn. He saw it first as a thin band of silver-blue beyond the clouds. Italy.

The wheels hit the runway with a muted thud. His heart pounded harder than he expected. He walked through customs in a daze, the language around him unfamiliar but musical.

"Buongiorno." "Grazie." "Prego."

He caught fragments but understood next to nothing.

The air outside the airport was warmer than he anticipated. Softer. He paused near the taxi stand, adjusting the strap of the bag on his shoulder. He had booked a small room in a guesthouse two villages away from where Kate was staying. Not too close. Not presumptuous.

He climbed into the taxi and gave the address. As the car wound through narrow roads lined with olive trees and pale stone walls, his chest tightened.

She is here. Breathing this air. Walking these streets. Healing without me. The thought was both painful and clarifying. He had assumed she would wither without him. Instead, according to Michael, she had grown.

The taxi slowed as they approached a small square. He paid, stepped out, and stood still. The village was quiet in the morning light. A woman swept her doorway. A café owner arranged chairs. Life continued. He was not the center of it. That realization steadied him.

He checked into the guesthouse. The room was simple. White walls. Iron bedframe. Small window overlooking a courtyard. He set his bag down and sat on the edge of the bed.

For a moment, he considered texting her. *I'm here.* He didn't. She had told Michael he could come. Not that she would receive him immediately. He would wait.

He bowed his head. "God," he said quietly, "I am not here to reclaim something. I am here to own what I broke."

The words felt heavy. But true.

Outside the window, church bells rang in the distance. He closed his eyes. Months ago, the sound of bells had marked fracture. Now, they marked arrival. Not into romance. Into reckoning.

He stood and walked to the window. The courtyard below filled slowly with morning light. Somewhere nearby, she was beginning her day. He did not know what she would decide. Would she forgive him? And if she did, would it turn into reconciliation? He only knew this: He had come not to persuade her. But to face her.

For the first time, fear did not feel like weakness. It felt like humility.

He exhaled slowly. Italy was not cinematic. It was quiet. And quiet, he was learning, was where truth held its ground.

CHAPTER 52
The Reunion

Monopoli, Italy

Grant saw her before she saw him.

She was standing near the long wooden table in the courtyard, one hand resting lightly on the back of a chair, her head tilted as Claire spoke animatedly about something involving "improperly priced peaches." Sunlight filtered through olive branches, scattering soft shadows across the stone.

Kate looked different. Not younger. Not styled. Steadier. There was less tension in her posture. Less vigilance in her eyes. She wasn't bracing for impact anymore. She was breathing.

His chest tightened as he stepped through the small iron gate quietly. It creaked. She turned. Time did not slow. It sharpened. For a moment, neither of them moved.

Claire noticed first. "Well," she muttered under her breath, glancing at Marianne and Evelyn. "That would be the husband."

Marianne's hand found Claire's wrist in silent caution. Kate did not rush forward. She did not retreat. She simply stood.

Grant walked toward her, stopping a respectful distance away, far enough that she could feel safe, close enough that avoidance would have felt absurd.

"Hi," he said quietly.

Her expression didn't flicker. "Hi."

The women lingered for half a second, assessing.

Then Marianne spoke first. “We’ll be inside.”

Claire paused just long enough to make eye contact with Grant. It wasn’t hostile. It was protective. Then they disappeared into the villa.

Italy hummed quietly around them—distant voices, the rustle of leaves, the faint clink of dishes from a nearby courtyard.

Grant swallowed. “You look well,” he said.

She studied him. “You look thinner.”

“I am.”

Neither comment was accusation. They were observations.

“I’m staying two villages over,” he added quickly. “A guesthouse.”

Her chin lifted slightly. “Good.”

The word wasn’t sharp.

He nodded. “I didn’t come to surprise you,” he said. “Michael told me when it was appropriate.”

“I know.”

Another silence. He had rehearsed this. But rehearsed words felt hollow now. So, he abandoned them.

“I betrayed you,” he said plainly.

The confession seemed to echo between them. No qualifiers. No loneliness narrative. No invisibility explanation. Just truth.

Kate’s jaw tightened—not in anger, but in steadiness. “Yes,” she said.

He nodded once. “I ended it. Completely. Two months ago.”

“I know.”

“I’ve told Michael everything. And I’ve been consistent with weekly accountability and counseling. Plus, I joined a men’s group at church. Full transparency. I broke it off with her 66 days ago.”

She didn’t respond immediately. She watched his face. Looking for something. Not remorse. Not desperation, but consistency.

“Why did you file for a legal separation?” she asked quietly.

The question was surgical. He did not flinch.

“Control,” he said.

Her eyes sharpened slightly.

“I wanted to force you to react,” he continued. “I told myself I was creating clarity. I was trying to regain leverage.”

The honesty cost him. He didn’t soften it. “I’m sorry.”

She inhaled slowly. “That almost hurt more than the confession,” she said.

“I know.”

He did know.

“You don’t get to destabilize a marriage and then rush its ending,” she continued calmly.

“You’re right.”

He did not defend. He did not explain.

The wind shifted, lifting a wisp of hair from her shoulder. She tucked it behind her ear without breaking eye contact.

"Answer three questions," she said.

"Okay."

"Have you ended it completely?"

"Yes."

"Are you willing to live in truth even if I don't return?"

His throat tightened. "Yes."

"Are you doing the work to become a man who won't repeat this?"

"Yes."

She held his gaze longer than was comfortable. "What does that mean?" she asked.

He exhaled slowly. "It means I've stopped blaming drift. I've stopped calling insecurity depth. I've stopped pretending admiration equals connection." He paused. "It means I'm learning that faithfulness isn't sustained by being desired."

Something flickered in her eyes. "And?" she pressed.

"And I am not entitled to your timeline."

That was the line. It landed.

Her shoulders shifted—not softening but releasing something small.

He saw it. "I don't want the old marriage back," he said carefully.

Her eyes narrowed slightly. "Good," she replied.

The word surprised him.

"The old marriage was solid," she continued. "But it wasn't examined. It wasn't humble."

He nodded slowly.

"I don't want nostalgia," she said. "I want integrity."

He felt something in his chest loosen. "So do I."

Silence returned, but different now. Less guarded. Not warm. Not cold. Measured.

"I'm not ready to leave Italy just yet. You can stay as long as you want or your work allows," she said finally. "But not here at La Villa Santoro."

"I understand."

"And no late-night conversations or emotional shortcuts. If we talk, we talk intentionally."

"Yes."

She studied him again. "And if I decide I cannot do this?"

He inhaled slowly. "I will not punish you for it."

The words hung there. She believed him. Not because of tone. Because there was no fight in him. Just gravity.

From the path beyond the courtyard, footsteps approached. Grant turned slightly. A man stood near the gate—linen shirt, woven basket under one arm.

Paolo.

He stopped immediately when he saw them. His expression registered understanding in seconds. Kate didn't move toward either man. She remained exactly where she was.

"*Buongiorno*," Paolo said politely.

Grant straightened.

Kate replied quietly, "Good morning."

Paolo's eyes met Grant's—not competitive, not hostile. Assessing. Grant felt it. This man knew her here. In her healing. That realization humbled him further.

"I can return later," Paolo said to Kate. "I just picked up some fresh fish for Claire for tonight." He held up a bundle wrapped in butcher paper.

She shook her head slightly. "No. It's fine."

Paolo stepped inside the gate slowly, placing the package on the table.

He turned to Grant. "I am Paolo."

Grant extended his hand. "Grant."

The handshake was firm but restrained.

"I have heard of you," Paolo said evenly.

Grant nodded once. "I'm sure."

There was no sarcasm in it.

Paolo's gaze remained steady. "I respect marriage," he said quietly.

Grant felt the sentence like a weight. "I am learning to," he replied.

Paolo held his eyes for a moment longer, measuring the sincerity. Then he inclined his head slightly. "I will give this to Claire and be on my way."

He stepped into the open door of the kitchen and they could hear a few whispered words from Claire and him before he reentered the courtyard. Nodding at them both, he walked back through the gate leaving Kate and Grant alone once more.

Grant watched him go. Then he turned back to Kate.

"I'm not here to compete," he said quietly.

"You don't get to," she replied.

A small pause. "Then what are you here for?" she asked.

He swallowed. "To own what I broke. And to see if you believe I can become different."

The words didn't soar. They settled.

Kate looked around the courtyard—the table, the sunlight filtering through olive branches. This place had steadied her. She would not let it become a battlefield.

"We can meet again tomorrow," she said. "In the afternoon."

Hope flickered in him, but he didn't grab it. "Thank you."

She nodded once. "I think this is all I can process for today."

Grant stepped backward slowly. “I’m here for as long as needed and work will allow,” he said, “unless you ask me to leave.”

She didn’t answer that.

He turned and walked toward the gate. As he stepped into the narrow stone path beyond, he felt the tremor in his hands for the first time. Not just fear of losing her. Fear of not being worthy of her.

Behind him, Kate remained in the courtyard, standing in the center of her peace. She knew the months of silence had prepared them both to pursue their future with purpose, not panic. She could sense God shaping them as they each faced and embraced truth. And she knew from God’s word that only real, solid truth can set you free.

CHAPTER 53
Letting Go

Monopoli, Italy

The women did not wait long after Grant left.

Claire emerged first, carrying three wine glasses even though it was barely after noon. “Well,” she said, setting them down with theatrical restraint, “that was … civil.”

Evelyn followed behind her, arms folded. “He looked different.”

Marianne said nothing at first. She simply studied Kate’s face. Kate remained standing in the courtyard, her hands resting lightly on the back of the chair she had not moved from.

“I’m not shaken,” she said quietly, as if answering a question they hadn’t yet asked.

Claire tilted her head. “That’s what concerns me.”

Kate almost smiled. “No,” she clarified. “I’m not numb. I’m … clear.”

Marianne stepped closer. “Clear about what?”

Kate inhaled slowly. “He’s definitely changed.”

Silence settled across the courtyard.

Evelyn raised an eyebrow slightly. “Or he’s learned how to sound changed.”

Kate shook her head. “No. That wasn’t a performance.” She turned, leaning back against the warm stone wall. “He didn’t

defend himself. He didn't blame drift. He didn't rush me."
She paused. "That's new."

Claire handed her a glass. "And what do you feel?" she asked.

Kate didn't hesitate. "Grief."

The word surprised them.

"For what?" Marianne asked.

"For the man he could have been all along."

The silence deepened.

Claire nodded slowly. "That makes sense."

Marianne watched her carefully. "And what else is swirling in your mind and heart?"

Kate closed her eyes briefly. "I care for and trust Paolo."

The honesty felt fragile in the open air. The women waited.

"I trust him more than I trust Grant," she continued quietly.
"That's the truth."

No one flinched.

"He is steady," Kate said. "He does not rewrite. He does not grasp. He does not pressure. He does not perform. He honors God and my marriage."

Claire exhaled slowly. "And that feels safer?"

"Yes."

The word carried weight. Safer.

“I don’t have to brace myself with him,” Kate added.

Evelyn studied her carefully. “And are you falling in love with him?”

Kate’s breath caught slightly. “Yes.”

The admission came quietly. Not dramatic. More like the tide acknowledging its rise.

“I don’t want to,” she whispered.

Marianne reached for her hand. “But you are.”

Kate nodded. “Yes.”

Claire leaned against the table. “And if Grant hadn’t come?”

Kate hesitated. “I don’t know,” she said honestly. “That’s what scares me.”

Silence stretched across the courtyard. Marianne squeezed her hand. “You don’t need to decide anything today.”

Paolo came at dusk. Not with bread this time. With distance. He stopped just inside the gate.

“You wish to walk?” he asked.

Kate nodded, sensing this might be their last walk for a long while. Perhaps forever. They took the narrow path that curved beyond the villa toward the olive grove. The air had cooled, and the light was turning honey-gold across the trees. For several minutes, neither spoke.

Finally, Kate broke the quiet. “He has changed.”

Paolo nodded once.

She studied him. “You were not threatened.”

“No.”

“Why?”

He looked out toward the olive trees as they walked. “Because you are not mine to possess,” he said calmly, “and I am not in a competition. I found a deep and meaningful connection with you as a friend first, as a woman second.”

The words settled deeply.

“And if Grant and I don’t reconcile?” she asked.

He turned toward her. “Then I will trust God to show us His will and His way.

Kate swallowed. “I trust you,” she said.

His gaze did not waver. “I know.”

“You feel safe,” she continued. “Safer than Grant.”

Paolo inhaled slowly. “That is understandable.”

“It’s more than understandable,” she said. “It’s real.”

She stopped walking. He did too.

“I don’t need to protect myself with you,” she admitted. “I don’t feel watched. Or evaluated. Or compared.”

His eyes softened. “You are not competing for oxygen here,” he said.

Her chest tightened. "With Grant, even before the affair, there was something performative. Strong marriage. Faithful marriage. Successful marriage."

"And with me?"

She exhaled slowly. "With you, I am just a woman walking."

He stepped slightly closer, but not touching. "You have deep feelings," he said quietly.

"Yes."

"And you are afraid of them."

"Yes."

He nodded. "I will never move faster than your integrity."

Her throat tightened. "You deserve certainty," she said.

"I deserve truth," he corrected.

Tears rose in her eyes. "It would be easier," she whispered, "to choose the safer man."

He held her gaze. "Safer is not always truer."

Kate looked down. "I don't know what God is doing."

Paolo's voice remained gentle. "Then ask Him."

She closed her eyes. Right there on the narrow path between olive trees, and whispered,

"Lord ... not my will. Not my comfort. Not my fear. Your will."

The prayer felt simple. And terrifying. When she opened her eyes, Paolo stood steady in front of her.

"Kate," he said softly, "I promised God that if Grant came here, I would step away from Villa Santoro. I do not want you to feel abandoned. But I cannot stand in the way of you restoring your marriage if his repentance is real and if God is preparing your heart for reconciliation."

Kate exhaled slowly. "So, I won't be seeing you for a while?"

He nodded. His head bowed slightly, and a single tear slipped down his cheek before he brushed it away.

They resumed walking. No handholding. No declarations. Just two people aware that their affection would not be allowed to express itself. As they approached the villa, Kate felt the ache of uncertainty settle beside the peace of surrender.

She loved her husband, but she also was beginning to love and trust another man. She was no longer trying to control which one would win. She was asking God to decide and waiting.

As Paolo turned toward the village road, the ache in his chest surprised him. Not because he was losing something certain. But because he had discovered he could love again.

For years after Sofia's death, that possibility had felt closed. Kate had not reopened his heart intentionally. But somehow, she had.

And even if their friendship became nothing more than a three-month memory, he knew he would always be grateful that she had reminded him that a deep romantic connection might still exist beyond his grief.

CHAPTER 54
Trust Has No Timeline

Monopoli, Italy

Trust cannot be negotiated, explained, or rushed. It must be earned one faithful day at a time.

The villa had grown noticeably quieter over the past few days. Paolo had kept his promise to step away, and Kate felt the absence of his steady presence more than she expected.

Marianne and Ev boarded their flight back to Texas soon after. They left reassured that Kate was no longer walking through the storm alone and that Claire was more than enough "girl power" to support her if Grant did anything "weird," as Ev had put it.

Kate suspected that God knew she was ready for fewer distractions. She was grateful Clare remained close by, always ready with the glass of wine and time to listen, but also wise enough to recognize when Kate needed silence instead of conversation. That kind of friendship was rare.

Taking in a deep, slow breath Kate walked toward the village square, anticipating her second face-to-face conversation with Grant. She wasn't exactly nervous. More unsettled. Too many unknowns still lingered.

The café sat at the edge of the square, where old men played cards in the morning and children chased pigeons in the afternoon. It wasn't romantic. It was ordinary. She had intentionally chosen neutral ground. Not the villa. Not his guesthouse. Nothing too scenic or romantic.

Grant was already seated when she arrived. He stood immediately, not out of habit, but awareness. She noticed that. And for a brief, disorienting moment, she noticed something else too—how familiar and quietly handsome he still looked when he wasn't trying to impress anyone.

"You look rested," he said.

She almost smiled. "Italy forces you to slow down."

He nodded and gestured for her to sit. A waiter approached, speaking quickly in Italian.

"Due caffè. Grazie," Kate replied without hesitation.

Grant watched her. "You sound at home."

"I'm learning."

The coffee arrived—small, strong, unapologetic. Grant lifted the tiny cup and examined it.

"This is it?"

Kate raised an eyebrow. "It's espresso."

He frowned at the size. "In Texas, this would be considered a sip."

She laughed. "That's because Texans drink coffee like it's survival rations."

A small smile broke across his face.

The square hummed around them with children laughing, cups clinking, a church bell marking the hour without urgency.

Grant leaned back slightly. "I understand something now."

She studied him. "What?"

"This pace," he said. "No one's rushing. No one's performing. It's just … life."

She nodded. "Yes. That's exactly it."

He glanced around the square. "It soothes you."

"Yes."

He swallowed. "I didn't realize how fast we were living."

"Fast isn't always wrong," she said evenly.

"No," he agreed. "But I was chasing something."

"Yes."

The honesty no longer startled her.

"Here," he continued quietly, "no one seems desperate to be admired."

The sentence hung there, heavy with meaning. Kate didn't rescue him.

"You wanted admiration," she said calmly.

"Yes."

"And I wanted stability," she added. "Maybe too much."

He nodded slowly. Silence settled again—not uncomfortable, just deliberate.

"I don't expect this to move quickly," he said.

"Good."

"I know two months clean isn't all that impressive."

"It's not," she replied evenly.

He didn't flinch. "It's a start."

"Yes."

He wrapped his fingers around the espresso cup. "How long?"

"For what?"

"For trust."

She didn't hesitate. "It's impossible to know. It depends on you. But my instinct says it could take more than a year."

He nodded.

She held his gaze. "You don't rebuild trust because you stopped doing the wrong thing."

"I know."

"You rebuild trust because you live differently long enough that the change becomes your character."

"Yes."

"And that takes time."

"Yes."

A small flock of white seagulls wheeled overhead, their cries echoing though the square, oblivious to the couple tentatively testing possibilities in the café below.

"Let's talk practically," he said.

She nodded.

"If we move toward reconciliation," he said carefully, "what would that look like?"

She appreciated the *if*.

"Slow," she said immediately.

He nodded.

"Very slow."

He waited.

"I'm not sure if we would live in the house together right away."

"Okay."

"And even when you did, you would stay in the guest room for a while."

He nodded again. "And if I couldn't tolerate that?" he asked.

"Then we wouldn't be able to move forward."

The words were steady. Not punishing. Just clear.

He inhaled slowly. "What about two homes? For how long?"

"As long as needed."

She glanced out at the square. "I don't want a performative reconciliation. I don't want to announce healing before it's real."

"I don't either."

She turned back to him. "And I don't know yet if I can do this."

The vulnerability came without tears.

He nodded. “That’s fair.”

“Don’t say that lightly.”

“I’m not.”

She held his gaze. “I still love you.”

The words hovered. He didn’t rush toward them.

“I love you,” he replied.

“But love isn’t enough,” she said.

“No.”

They both knew that now.

She exhaled slowly. “I’m guessing you know there’s someone here I care about deeply.”

He didn’t look surprised. “I know.”

That startled her. “You met him,” she said. “At the villa.”

“Paolo.”

She nodded.

Grant lowered his eyes briefly, then looked back at her. “He seems like a good man.”

“He is.”

Silence again. “Claire said he’s been giving you space,” Grant added.

"Yes, he is keeping his promise," she confirmed.

Grant nodded. "I respect that."

She studied him. "Does it anger you?"

"No." He exhaled. "It humbles me."

The answer came without hesitation. "If you had met someone first," he continued, "I would have been devastated."

"I know."

"And I don't have the right to outrage."

The sentence cost him. She saw it.

"He's a widower," she said. "He understands loss. He moves slowly. He doesn't grasp."

Grant absorbed that. "And you feel safe with him."

"Yes."

The word landed without apology.

He nodded once. "I want you to feel safe … to be safe."

She looked at him, her voice softening. "This is why I don't know."

"Because he's easier," he said.

"Yes, but more than easier. There's no betrayal I would have to learn to live with."

Silence again. "But easy isn't the same as covenant," he said.

She held his gaze. “No. It’s not.”

“And covenant,” he said quietly, “is something I almost destroyed.”

They sat there, two people no longer pretending that strength alone was enough. Trust was the currency now. And trust could not be rushed.

He finished his espresso. “If we move forward, I will earn trust without demanding access.”

She nodded. “And I will do my best to discern without punishing.”

The words surprised her even as she said them. They felt balanced.

The church bell rang again. An old woman laughed loudly at a nearby table. Life continued—unhurried, indifferent to their reckoning.

“I don’t know how this ends,” she said.

“Neither do I.”

He didn’t try to predict it. Didn’t promise permanence. Didn’t reach for her hand. They stood at the same time, facing each other in the middle of the square. Not reconciled but not severed. Something in between.

“Italy suits you,” he said.

She almost smiled. “It slows me down.”

“Maybe we needed that.”

“Maybe.”

He stepped back first. “I’ll see you tomorrow?”

"Yes."

No embrace. No lingering touch. Just measured space.

As she walked back toward the villa, the rhythm of the village steady around her, she felt the weight of both men in her chest. One was history and heartbreak. The other was promise and possibility. She was nowhere near a decision.

By the time the villa came into view, the late afternoon air felt as quiet as it had that morning. Kate settled into the reality that Grant being clean and accountable for two months was not near enough to establish trust. Trust must be built one day at a time. Time after time. And time, she was learning in Italy, moved like stone.

Piano, piano.

Slowly, slowly.

And only shaped by patience.

CHAPTER 55
Forgiveness is Not a Feeling

Monopoli, Italy

"Forgiveness isn't saying what happened was acceptable," Kate recalled Pastor Michael telling her. "It's surrendering your right to become its prisoner."

As she prepared for her next meeting with Grant, Kate tried to keep her expectations grounded. Though she felt more hopeful than she had in months, she also knew the risk. If reconciliation failed, the disappointment could cut even deeper than before.

She didn't choose a café for this meeting. She chose movement.

A narrow stone path traced the edge of the old city, where ancient walls dropped toward the Adriatic and the air carried the scent of salt and sun-warmed limestone. Late-afternoon light stretched across the water, softening the sharp edges of the world.

Kate walked at an unhurried pace knowing Grant would find her along this stretch of shoreline. He had insisted on coming to her this time. That mattered.

A fisherman stood near the edge of the shore, mending a net with patient hands. A young couple leaned against the wall a few yards away, speaking in low, animated voices. Somewhere behind her, a scooter echoed briefly through the maze of streets, then disappeared. Ordinary life. Uninterrupted.

As she rested her hands lightly against the warm stone ledge, the late afternoon sun reflected off the soft linen of her dress—a pale, sea-washed blue that moved easily in the breeze. The fabric skimmed her frame without effort, simple and unstructured, the kind of piece she never would have chosen at home but now felt entirely natural in. She wore a pair of tan leather sandals dusted lightly with the chalk of the old city streets, and her favorite bracelet of Murano glass beads catching the light each time she moved her hand. Her auburn hair was pulled loosely back, though a few strands had already escaped, lifted by the wind coming off the Adriatic.

Grant came into view along the narrow path, his pace measured, more deliberate than she remembered. He wore faded blue jeans and a cream-colored button-down shirt; sleeves rolled just below his elbows, the fabric stirred by the same breeze that moved through the air between them. His hair, once carefully kept, now shifted more freely, slightly longer at the edges, as if routine had given way to something less controlled. There was a quietness about him, not just in his movement, but in the way he held himself as though he had set something down he had been carrying for a long time.

He stopped a few feet behind her, giving her space before speaking.

"I wasn't sure if you'd still be here," he said.

"I said I would be."

Her voice was calm. Not distant.

He stepped closer, but not beside her. For a moment, neither of them spoke. The water below shifted in a quiet rhythm against the rocks.

"Well, I'm glad you are," he said.

She didn't answer right away. Instead, she turned slightly enough to face him, but not enough to close the distance.

"Not being certain of me is something you will need to get used to," she said, not sharp, just clear. "I'm not playing games. But I am allowing myself all the time and space I need to hear God and be certain you are a transformed man."

He accepted it with a small nod. "Fair."

A breeze moved between them, lifting a strand of her hair across her face. She brushed it back absently.

"You came to me this time," she said.

"Yes."

"Why?"

He didn't answer immediately. Because this mattered.

"Because I've spent a long time expecting you to meet me where I was," he said. "And I'm starting to understand that wasn't where you needed me to be."

She studied him carefully. That was new. Not just the words, but the awareness behind them.

"You're learning," she said.

"I'm trying to."

She turned her gaze back to the water. "Trying isn't the same as changing."

"I know."

Silence settled again, but this time it felt less like distance and more like space being respected.

A gull swept low across the water and disappeared toward the harbor.

Grant stepped forward just enough to rest his hands lightly on the stone wall beside hers, not touching, but close enough to acknowledge proximity.

"I've been thinking about forgiveness," he said.

Kate didn't look at him. "Have you."

"Yes."

A pause. "I used to think it was something you gave when you were ready," he continued. "Like a decision that ended something."

"And now?"

He exhaled. "Now I think it's something we're called to practice repeatedly. Even when we don't feel it."

She turned fully toward him then, and he met her gaze. For a moment, neither of them spoke. Then Kate gestured toward a small stone bench set back on a patch of grass just off the path.

"Let's sit over there."

Grant followed her. Once she settled, he took the far end of the bench, angled toward her but leaving space.

Kate drew in a slow breath of sea air, then began. "There are two things I need to say to you today."

Grant straightened slightly. "All right."

She held his gaze. "I've been thinking a lot about forgiveness, too. Until now, I understood it mostly from a biblical perspective—something I received as a free gift from Jesus because I'm a fallen human being. Or something I was supposed to offer when someone hurt me, to prove I was a mature Christian who didn't hold a grudge."

She paused, eyes drifting briefly toward the horizon. "I don't think I ever really understood the power of forgiveness or God's expectation of me until I lived through your betrayal of our marriage."

Her voice steadied. "I had never experienced hurt at that level. At first, I was so broken and angry I couldn't even think about forgiving you."

Grant didn't look away. His eyes filled, and he nodded once.

"I need you to know," she continued, "that God and I have wrestled with what forgiving you means. And I have finally surrendered."

She paused. "I have chosen to forgive you."

Something shifted in his face—not relief, not triumph. Something quiet and cautious.

Kate continued before he could speak. "I'm not saying that because I trust you again."

He stayed still.

"And I'm not saying it because I've forgotten what happened. I haven't."

She held his gaze. "I'm saying it because during these months of silence, God has made something very clear to me. Forgiveness is not a feeling. It's not pretending betrayal hurt less than it did. It's not calling evil good. And it's not skipping grief."

Grant's eyes didn't leave hers.

"It is a decision," she said quietly. "A decision not to hold your sin against you. A decision to release my right to punish you. A decision to leave justice in God's hands instead of carrying it in my own body like poison."

His jaw tightened slightly.

She continued. "Forgiveness does not mean trust is restored. It does not mean consequences disappear. And it does not mean reconciliation happens automatically. But it does mean this: if your repentance is real and if it remains solid, I am willing to move toward reconciliation."

She let that land. "Not quickly. Not cheaply. But honestly."

Grant lowered his eyes. When he looked up again, they were wet. "I don't know what to say to that."

"You don't need to say anything yet."

He nodded once.

Kate leaned forward, elbows resting on her knees, hands clasped. She took a long breath, then sat back again, her eyes fixed on the horizon.

"I have something else I need to tell you, she said. "And it's even harder."

That got his full attention. She looked down briefly, then back up.

"A few nights ago, a memory came back. After I'd prayed, when I was trying to sleep."

Grant didn't move.

"It was from early in our marriage. Something I buried. Something I haven't thought about in years."

She held his gaze. “There was a doctor at St. David’s. Matthew Reeves.”

His expression shifted, subtle, but unmistakable.

“We drank coffee between shifts. We talked too much. I let his attention matter more than it should have. One night I had drinks with him and came home after two in the morning.”

Grant stared at her. “I remember that night,” he said quietly. “You said there was an emergency surgery.”

“Yes, I lied.”

His jaw tightened.

“I never slept with him,” she said carefully. “Nothing physical happened. But that’s not the same as innocence.”

She didn’t look away. “For months, maybe close to a year, my heart drifted. I pulled away from you. I fantasized. I entertained an emotional disloyalty that never became physical, but it was still sin. It still damaged something.”

Grant leaned back slowly, exhaling. “I remember that year.”

“I know.”

“I thought …” He stopped.

“What?”

He swallowed. “I thought you didn’t want me anymore.”

Her throat tightened. “I know.”

An uncomfortable silence lingered as Kate gathered her thoughts.

"At the time," she said, "I asked God to forgive me. And I believe He did. Then Matthew's sister died suddenly, and he relocated. The whole thing ended before it could become something worse. I took that as mercy and I closed the door."

Grant looked down at his hands. "And you never told me."

"No."

"Why?"

She answered honestly. "Because I minimized it. Because nothing physical had happened. Because I told myself it would only wound you unnecessarily. And because I wanted to move on and pretend my heart had never gone somewhere dangerous."

He gave a short, humorless exhale. "That sounds familiar."

"Yes," she said quietly. "It does."

He looked at her again. "So why tell me now?"

"Because God didn't bring it back so I could protect myself with it. He brought it back so I could see something clearly. She paused. "That I am not forgiving you from some superior moral position."

His expression shifted. "I am not your innocent opposite," she said. "I didn't do what you did. But I now understand with far more humility that I was capable of betrayal in my heart too."

He said nothing.

"And I need to ask your forgiveness for that season. For the lie. For the distance. For turning away from you while you slept beside me all those years ago. And, for acting as if you were the only one who had ever drifted these last months"

Grant rubbed his hand slowly across his mouth. For a long moment, he didn't respond.

Finally, he said, "That hurts."

"I know."

"I'm not saying that to punish you."

"I know."

He looked at her with something like sorrow and recognition. "It's strange," he said quietly. "I only feel a fraction of what I put you through. But even that..."

He shook his head.

"It disorients you," Kate said.

"Yes."

She nodded. "That's what I needed you to understand."

Another silence. Then Grant leaned forward, elbows on his knees, eyes lowered before lifting them again.

"I do forgive you," he said.

The words came simply. Without performance.

"But I also understand now, in a way I didn't before." His voice roughened. "What it feels like to be physically beside someone who is somewhere else in their heart."

Tears pressed behind Kate's eyes. "I'm sorry," she whispered.

"I believe you."

The simplicity of that nearly undid her. He drew in a breath.

"And Kate … thank you for telling me the truth. Not because it makes us equal, it doesn't, but because it means we're finally standing in the same light."

In the same light. No hero. No villain. No wounded saint and fallen husband. Just two people who now understood more than they ever wanted to.

Kate shifted slightly, turning more fully toward him. "Forgiveness is not a feeling," she said again, almost to herself.

Grant nodded. "No. It's a decision you keep making."

She looked at him. "Yes."

He hesitated. "What happens now?"

Kate let the question breathe. "Now," she said, "we tell the truth. We move slowly. We watch for fruit, not promises. And we let trust rebuild at the pace trust requires."

He nodded. "Piano, piano."

His use of the phrase surprised her, and she gave the faintest smile.

"Yes, slowly, slowly."

For the first time, he smiled too. Small. Unsteady. Real.

Neither of them reached out. Neither tried to close the distance with sentiment. But something had changed. Not because the wound was gone. Not because trust had returned. But because grace had entered the conversation without erasing truth. And that, Kate thought, might be the beginning of something holy.

CHAPTER 56
Testing Ground

Monopoli, Italy

Trust returned in whispers, not declarations, yet somehow the heart recognized its voice.

The days following Kate's conversation with Grant on the seashore settled into a rhythm neither of them had expected. They met nearly every day during Grant's final week in Italy. Sometimes for coffee in the same small café overlooking the square. Sometimes for slow walks along the harbor where fishing boats rocked with the tide. Once they sat for nearly an hour on the same stone bench where Kate had shared her confession, saying very little at all. It was the holy place where forgiveness had begun its spiritual redemption plan.

Kate noticed the changes in him more each time they met. Not dramatic or rehearsed humility. But consistency. Grant answered every question she asked without defensiveness. When she spoke about the pain of the past months, he did not soften it or try to explain it away. He simply listened.

One afternoon as they walked along the seawall, Kate said quietly, "I'm not testing you."

Grant glanced at her.

"It probably feels like it though," she said, looking deeply into his eyes. "I'm observing you."

He nodded thoughtfully. "That seems fair."

They walked several more steps before he added, "I'm observing myself too."

That answer stayed with her longer than she expected. They talked about many things that had nothing to do with the affair. Italian food. The slower pace of life. Memories from their early years of marriage. Those memories were like water in the desert to her parched soul. There was something miraculously healing about lingering over each decade and recounting their countless experiences as a couple.

Once, sitting outside a café as the evening light softened the stone buildings around them, Kate studied him across the table.

"You've changed something," she said.

Grant looked up. "I hope so."

"No," she said slowly. "I mean something deeper than behavior."

He waited.

"You're less certain of yourself."

A faint smile touched his face. "That's accurate."

She nodded. "It makes you easier to be around."

He laughed quietly. "Humility as a personality improvement."

"Apparently."

For a moment the tension between them softened. Not romance. But something human. Something familiar.

Reality arrived sooner than either of them wanted. Grant could not remain in Italy indefinitely. His work responsibilities in Texas were waiting. They sat together one morning at the café near the harbor.

"I need to return in a few days," he said gently.

Kate had known it was coming. Still, the words settled heavily between them.

"I thought so," she said.

Grant watched the water for a moment. "What happens next?"

Kate took her time answering. She had spent many nights praying about that question. "I'm not ready to leave Italy yet," she said finally.

He nodded slowly. "Okay, I understand … I think."

"I think I need a couple more weeks here."

"With Claire?"

"Yes."

Grant leaned back slightly in his chair. "And… Paolo?"

The question came out carefully. Almost cautiously. Kate studied him. He hadn't asked accusingly. He was simply trying to understand the reality he had created.

"I don't know," she said honestly.

Grant nodded once. "That's fair."

"You were trying to ask if I would see him again," she asked.

Grant gave a small, rueful smile. "I suppose I was."

"And?" she asked.

He exhaled slowly. "I don't get to control that."

The humility in his voice softened something in her chest.

"Paolo has already stepped away more than he needed to," she said quietly.

Grant nodded. "That sounds like the kind of man he is."

She studied him. "Does it bother you?"

He met her eyes. "Of course it does."

The honesty lingered between them. Then he added, "But not as much as the man I used to be bothers me."

"If everything continues the way it has these past weeks," Kate said slowly, "I'm willing to come home."

Grant didn't celebrate. He simply asked, "What would that look like?"

"Counseling continues."

"Yes."

"Your accountability with Pastor Michael continues."

"Yes."

"And when we return to the house…" She paused. "…you stay in the guest room."

His answer came without hesitation. "Of course."

She studied him carefully. "You're not negotiating."

"No."

"Why?"

He held her gaze. “Because rebuilding trust isn’t something I get to bargain over.”

The answer settled quietly between them. For the first time in many months, Kate felt something she had not allowed herself to feel. Hope.

Grant left Italy two days later. Kate walked with him to the small taxi waiting near the harbor. Neither of them rushed the moment.

“I’ll keep meeting with Pastor Michael,” he said.

“I know.”

“And counseling.”

“I know.”

He hesitated before asking, “Will you come home?”

Kate answered honestly. “I think so.”

That was enough for now. Grant nodded once, then stepped into the taxi. Kate stood on the sidewalk as the car disappeared down the narrow street. For a moment she simply watched the empty road. The future still felt uncertain. But the fear no longer felt overwhelming.

The Slow Road Home

The two weeks that followed passed slowly. Claire kept the villa lively with her usual blend of humor, strong opinions, and generous glasses of wine. But she also gave Kate space when she needed it.

Kate walked often through the streets of Monopoli. She prayed. She wrote in her journal. And she paid attention to what her heart was doing. The anger she had once carried toward Grant had softened, but caution remained and bitterness no longer dominated her thoughts.

Healing, she realized, had begun quietly. Long before she had noticed it. And something else had begun to settle in her heart as well. For weeks she had been measuring her future against two men. One she had loved for thirty-five years and one whose quiet presence had reminded her she was still capable of being seen.

Paolo had never pursued her. He had never tried to step into the void Grant had created. Yet something about his steady kindness had awakened a part of her she thought was gone forever. For the first time since the betrayal, she remembered she was still a woman who could be admired. Still a woman who could be chosen. That realization had surprised her more than anything.

But another truth had followed closely behind it. Her future did not depend on whether one man returned to her, or another might someday want her. Her life still had purpose. Her identity had never belonged to a husband or to a marriage.

Slowly, quietly, something deeper had settled in her spirit. No human love, however faithful, had ever been meant to carry the weight of her soul. Only Christ could do that. Paolo had reminded her she was still desirable. But Jesus had reminded her she was already complete. That realization brought a peace she had not felt in many months.

The afternoon before her flight back to Texas, Kate walked toward the olive grove outside the village. Paolo was waiting near the edge of the trees. The sunlight filtered through the leaves, turning them silver in the late afternoon light. For a moment neither of them spoke.

Paolo studied her. “You are leaving tomorrow.”

"Yes."

"And your husband?"

"He's already back in Texas."

Paolo nodded slowly. "And you?"

"I think our path forward is together."

He received the words calmly. There was no bitterness in his face. Only understanding.

"That is where your covenant lives," he said.

"Yes."

A soft silence settled between them. Kate looked down briefly before meeting his eyes again.

"You helped me remember what it feels like to be seen."

Paolo's expression warmed. "That was always there in you."

"Maybe," she said. "But I had forgotten."

He nodded. "I'm glad it was me who reminded you."

Emotion caught in her throat. "If our lives had crossed in a different season…" she began.

Paolo smiled sadly. "But they did not."

"No."

"And that is all right," he said.

She nodded. "Yes. It is."

Paolo opened his arms briefly. Kate stepped forward and embraced him. When they separated, he smiled tenderly.

"*Piano, piano*," he said.

She smiled back.

"*Piano, piano*."

Later that evening, Claire stood in the courtyard of Villa Santoro watching Kate finish packing her suitcase.

"You're really going back," she said.

Kate laughed guardedly. "It appears so."

Claire leaned against the stone wall. "I knew it."

"You knew what?"

"That God wasn't done with your marriage."

Kate smiled faintly. "I hope you're right."

Claire folded her arms. "Oh, I'm right."

Kate raised an eyebrow. "That sounds confident."

Claire grinned. "Because I've been praying about this for months."

Kate zipped her suitcase. "Well then, I suppose I'm grateful for your persistence."

Claire stepped closer. "This story isn't over, you know."

Kate looked around the courtyard. "I know."

Claire gestured toward the long wooden table beneath the string lights. "And when it's finished—when that husband of yours finally earns his redemption properly—you two are coming back here."

Kate smiled. "For what?"

"A month."

Kate laughed. "A month?"

"Yes. Girlfriends' month. Except this time your husband can join us."

Kate shook her head, still smiling. "That sounds dangerous."

Claire waved dismissively. "Please. By then he'll know how to behave."

Kate hugged her tightly. "I'll come back," she promised.

Claire squeezed her once more before stepping back. "And when you do," she said confidently, "this whole redemption story will be something beautiful."

Kate picked up her suitcase. "I hope you're right."

Claire smiled. "Oh, I know I am."

As Kate stepped through the iron gate of La Villa Santoro one last time, she paused and looked back at the courtyard glowing softly in the evening light. So much had changed in her in this place. Not all wounds were healed yet. But the path forward no longer felt impossible.

For the first time since the storm began, Kate understood something she had not fully grasped before. Redemption doesn't arrive all at once. It begins the moment two people decide they are willing to walk back toward each other—even if the road is still long.

CHAPTER 57
Slow Redemption

Austin, Texas

Grant was relieved that Kate had not required that he find another place to live.

They were walking the slow road toward trust and hopefully full restoration. However, he had no intention to push the envelope and had already moved all his things into the guest room. That mattered to Kate. He didn't pause at the doorway of their master bedroom. He didn't linger. He didn't suggest proximity as proof of progress. He closed the guest room door quietly and gave her space.

Some nights, Kate lay awake in the dark, aware that trust does not return with luggage. It returns with consistency. The first months were not romantic. They were disciplined. Counseling continued. Accountability remained. His phone passwords stayed open and their calendars were shared. Their phones kept both their locations visible. Grant continued to offer transparency without resentment. That mattered too.

Sometimes he would say, "I know you didn't ask, but here's where I was today."

She noticed he no longer flinched at the discomfort of being examined. He did not call it punishment. He called it rebuilding. There were moments that surprised her.

Once, at church, a woman from the congregation lingered too long in conversation with him. She was younger, polished, and complimentary of him. Kate felt the old tightening in her chest. The familiar flicker of fear. She watched from a distance.

Grant stepped back physically, small but clear, placing space between himself and the woman. He redirected the conversation to logistics. Then he introduced Kate intentionally. Not defensively, but deliberately.

On the drive home he said quietly, "I saw it."

She didn't pretend ignorance. "I know."

"And I felt the old ego rise for half a second," he admitted.

Her stomach tightened.

"But I also felt disgust at it," he continued. "That's new."

That was new. Trust did not leap forward. But it breathed.

Kate's humility deepened in ways she had not anticipated. There were nights she woke from dreams of Paolo walking through olive trees, sunlight on his shoulders. The memory of safety and ease. She would lie there in the dark beside a closed guest room door and whisper, "Lord, guard my mind."

Sometimes the enemy did not accuse Grant. Sometimes he whispered to her:

You chose harder. You chose risk. You chose the man who broke you.

The thoughts came quietly. Spiritual warfare rarely shouts. It suggests.

One evening she confessed it aloud. "I still think of him sometimes."

Grant didn't collapse. He nodded slowly. "I think you always will."

Her eyes filled. "Does that hurt?"

"Yes," he answered honestly. "But not the way you think."

"How?"

"It humbles me."

The word stunned her.

"I understand now what it costs to leave something that felt alive," he said quietly. "Even if it wasn't right."

She saw the symmetry. He had left Lydia. She had left Paolo. Neither departure had been clean of ache. And that shared pain began to knit something fragile between them.

There were setbacks. Once she searched his email history without telling him. When he discovered it—not by accusation, but by digital trail—he didn't bristle.

"I wish you'd asked me," he said cautiously.

"I didn't want to need to."

"I understand."

No defensiveness. Just acknowledgment.

Another time, he grew impatient during counseling.

"I've said I'm sorry," he muttered.

Kate felt something collapse inside her. *There it is.* But later that night he knocked softly on the master bedroom door.

"I'm not tired of apologizing," he said quietly. "I'm tired of knowing I caused this."

That mattered more to her than always responding perfectly in every situation.

Around month seven, she invited him into the bedroom. Not as restoration. As proximity. He stood still at the doorway.

"Are you sure?"

"No," she admitted.

Honesty was their new currency. They slept side by side that night without touching. It felt sacred.

Grant became aware in quiet ways that Paolo had not been imaginary. He could see it in the way Italy lingered in her. The way she paused over food. The way she stepped outside at dusk. The way she said *slowly* like it meant something holy.

He understood that saying goodbye to that man had cost her. And instead of resenting it, he let it sober him. God was not just restoring a marriage. He was dismantling pride in both of them.

At month nine something shifted. They laughed more freely. Not cautiously. Not as therapy. Naturally. It startled them both. He reached for her hand in the kitchen. She didn't brace. It was small. But it felt enormous.

Still, Kate's doubts crept in at night. *What if this is temporary? What if he performs change long enough to relax? What if I grow complacent again?*

She would sit in the living room alone and pray, "Lord, don't let fear rewrite what You are rebuilding."

And slowly—so slowly it was almost imperceptible—peace grew louder than suspicion. Grant was not dramatic in his repentance. He was consistent. He did not preach about lessons learned. He lived differently.

When old insecurities surfaced, he named them instead of feeding them. When ego rose, he confessed it. When she wept unexpectedly months later at a memory of the affair, he did not defend himself. He sat beside her and let the grief pass through them both.

A year from the day she returned from Italy, they sat on the back patio. The same place where they had once toasted growing old together. The air was warm. Ordinary.

Grant looked at her carefully. “I don’t feel clean because time passed,” he said. “I feel clean because I don’t want anything hidden in me anymore.”

She studied his face. There was no performance. Just steadiness.

“I don’t feel naïve anymore,” she replied.

“And that might be our greatest protection.”

He nodded.

They had lost innocence. But they had gained clarity.

She reached for his hand first this time. That mattered most. They had not rushed forgiveness. They had practiced it. They had not demanded trust. They had earned fragments of it daily. And somehow—imperfectly, painfully, humbly—they had made it.

Not because they were strong. Because they surrendered. And surrender, they now knew, is where redemption begins.

CHAPTER 58
Restoring Legacy

Austin, Texas

Not every healing happened privately.

The first Christmas after Italy, they gathered the children and finally told the truth. Not every detail. Not every wound. But enough. Enough for honesty. Enough for the family to stop dancing around an unnamed fracture.

The atmosphere that evening had felt fragile from the moment everyone arrived. Rachel carried in a casserole while balancing their little boy on one hip. Emma and her new husband came straight from Dallas, still carrying the glow and exhaustion of newly married life. Nathan arrived last from graduate school, dropping his backpack by the stairs before hugging his mother a little longer than usual. Something in him already knew.

The meal itself moved carefully at first. Familiar traditions. Prayer over the food. Safe conversation. But Kate felt the weight of the secret sitting at the table with them.

Finally, Grant set down his fork. "There's something your mother and I need to share."

Silence settled instantly. Kate still remembered how steady his voice sounded despite the tension she could feel radiating beneath it. Grant didn't minimize. Didn't excuse. Didn't hide behind vague language.

He spoke honestly about the affair, the separation, the counseling, and the painful months that followed. More than once, emotion roughened his voice, but he did not retreat from the discomfort of being fully seen by his children.

Jesse went very still beside Rachel, his jaw tightening as their young son played on the living room floor completely unaware that the adults around him were learning how to become a family again. Emma cried openly. Nathan paced quietly into the kitchen and back before finally asking the question none of them had wanted to say aloud.

"So… are you staying together?"

Grant looked at Kate before answering. "We are rebuilding," he said. "And by the grace of God, I believe we're healing."

The room stayed quiet for several seconds. Then Rachel spoke softly. "Thank you for telling the truth."

Something about those words loosened the tension in the room. Not because everything was resolved. But because honesty had finally entered the house completely.

Over the months that followed, the healing extended beyond Grant and Kate. It reached into the family itself. Grant became unexpectedly transparent with his sons. The conversations were rarely dramatic. Most happened late at night by phone after long workdays and ordinary life had settled down.

One evening Jesse called after Rachel and the baby were asleep. "What happened, Dad?" he asked quietly. "Really?"

Grant leaned back in the darkness of the guest room he had occupied for months during their separation. "I stopped paying attention to the condition of my own heart," he admitted. "Pride got in quietly. So did self-pity. I justified things I should've confessed much earlier."

The silence on the other end deepened.

Finally, Grant said, "You guard your marriage long before you think it needs guarding."

Those conversations mattered.

Nathan listened differently. Thoughtfully. Graduate school had sharpened his intellect, but his father's failure softened something in him—the realization that weakness was not reserved for bad men. Sometimes it appeared in good men who stopped being honest about their emptiness.

And Kate found herself having gentler, wiser conversations with Emma after the wedding. Not fearful conversations. Intentional ones. One afternoon while unpacking gifts in Emma's apartment, Kate folded tissue paper carefully and said, "Don't just ask if he loves you. Learn how he carries stress. Learn what discourages him. Men don't always know how to say when they feel unseen or overwhelmed."

Emma looked surprised. "You wish you'd understood that earlier?"

Kate smiled sadly. "I wish I'd understood how quietly distance can grow between two good people."

Emma reached for her mother's hand. "But you found your way back."

Kate looked down at their intertwined fingers. "Yes," she said. "By the grace of God, we did."

The healing wasn't perfect. There were still tender places. Awkward moments. Questions that surfaced unexpectedly. But something new had entered their family now—humility. Not polished appearances. Not performance. Truth. And truth, Kate was learning, created stronger foundations than pretending ever could.

One evening, months later, Grant stood alone in the backyard watching his grandson chase fireflies across the grass while laughter drifted through the open kitchen windows behind him. The house sounded alive again.

Kate stepped quietly beside him, slipping her hand into his. "You, okay?" she asked.

Grant nodded, his eyes following the little boy running through the dusk. "I was just thinking about legacy."

She leaned her head lightly against his shoulder.

"For a long time, I thought legacy meant success. Reputation. Providing well." He exhaled slowly. "Now I think it may simply mean leaving behind honesty… repentance… and a family that knows grace is real."

Warm light spilled from the kitchen onto the patio stones behind them. Inside, Emma laughed at something Nathan said while Rachel carried dessert to the table.

Kate squeezed his hand gently. "Maybe the most important thing our children learned," she said quietly, "is that broken things don't have to stay broken."

Grant looked at her then. For the first time in many years, neither of them felt the need to pretend they had all the answers. They only knew this: God had met them in the ruins. And somehow, slowly, He was building something stronger from what remained.

CHAPTER 59
The Body Remembers

Austin, Texas

They were not making love yet. That mattered.

Grant lay beside her, one arm bent beneath his head, the other resting lightly over the blanket between them. Shared space. Shared warmth. But no physical expectations. Trust first and desire later.

The house was quiet. Kate shifted slightly, brushing her hand across her chest as she turned toward him. She froze. She pressed again—more deliberately. There. A small marble-sized hardness beneath the skin of her left breast. Firm and unfamiliar. Her stomach dropped.

Grant noticed immediately. “What?”

She didn’t answer at first. She was mapping the shape with her fingers.

“Katie?”

“There’s something,” she said quietly.

He sat up. “What do you mean something?”

She guided his hand to the spot. “Right there.”

He felt it. The silence that followed was different from any silence they had known before.

“It could be nothing,” she said automatically.

She was a labor and delivery nurse. She knew better than to dramatize. She also knew better than to dismiss.

"I'll call my GYN tomorrow," she said quietly.

One Week Later

The body remembers. She had told him that once. How extreme stress can surface later in strange, cruel ways. Friends who had gone through divorce and been diagnosed with cancer months later. Women who held everything together until their bodies could not.

The biopsy confirmed the mammogram. A small carcinoma. Left breast.

Grant's chest tightened when she told him. "This is my fault," he whispered.

She looked at him sharply. "No."

"I broke you."

"You did not give me cancer."

"But I—"

"Stop."

The word was firm. "This is not punishment."

His eyes filled.

Later that night they lay staring at the ceiling.

"Tomorrow, I'll call the surgeon Dr. Lange recommended," she said.

Her voice sounded professional. But beneath it something trembled.

Grant turned toward her. "What are you afraid of?"

She hesitated. "I'm afraid of what they'll take. I'm afraid I won't see our children and grandchildren through all their major milestones."

He went still.

"And" she whispered, "I'm afraid of looking in the mirror and feeling altered."

The word hung there.

Grant inhaled sharply. "Don't."

"You're not the one who might lose part of your body."

"No," he said quietly. "But I almost lost your heart."

The truth settled between them.

"And I don't care what changes," he continued. "I care that you're here."

She believed him. That was the miracle. Months ago, she would have questioned tone. Now she simply saw him. Terrified. Humbled. Devastated at the possibility of losing her.

The surgeon later gave them good news. Early-stage invasive ductal carcinoma. Less than two centimeters. HER2 positive. Treatable. Lumpectomy. Radiation likely. No chemotherapy.

Still, the word *cancer* echoed louder than the word *early.* The night before surgery they lay skin to skin.

“I don’t know what I’ll look like,” she whispered.

He pressed his forehead to hers. “You’ll look like the woman who chose covenant when it cost her.”

“Are you afraid,” she asked tentatively.

“Yes,” he replied.

“Of what?”

“Of losing you before I’ve fully earned back what I broke.”

She exhaled slowly. “You don’t earn love,” she said. “You steward it.”

He closed his eyes. “Then I will steward you.”

For the first time since the diagnosis, they were not divided by fear. They were united by surrender.

CHAPTER 60
The Open Door

Monopoli, Italy—One Year Later

The first time Paolo returned to Villa Santoro after Kate left for Texas, he almost turned his SUV around.

He had driven there with his vehicle full of supplies Claire had asked him to bring for the occasion.

The courtyard looked the same. Lanterns swayed in the breeze above the long table. Rosemary spilled from the earthen pots near the stone wall. Claire's laughter drifted faintly from the kitchen window. Everything was familiar, yet everything changed.

He sat for a long moment with both hands resting on the steering wheel. "*Piano, piano*," he murmured to himself.

A year earlier, he had stood in this same courtyard watching a wounded American woman slowly come back to life beneath the Puglian sun. He had not intended to love her. Perhaps that was why it happened so quietly.

But he had loved her. And letting her go had cost him more than he admitted to anyone except God. Still, there was peace now where ache had once lived. Not complete peace. But honest peace.

Paolo stepped from the car and walked through the courtyard gate just as Claire appeared carrying baskets of lemons.

"There you are," she called. "I was beginning to think you'd become mysterious."

"I am Italian," he replied dryly. "It is part of the contract."

Claire laughed.

Villa Santoro had changed over the past year. Not dramatically. Intentionally. The upstairs rooms now welcomed travelers from all over the world. Cooking classes filled the courtyard several evenings each week. Long dinners stretched beneath the grapevine arbor while strangers slowly became friends over handmade pasta and local wine. The villa breathed again.

"You're late," Claire informed him.

"I'm exactly on time."

"You're twenty minutes late."

"In Italy," Paolo said calmly, "that is exactly on time."

Claire rolled her eyes and pointed toward the kitchen. "Tonight's guest chef is already threatening to reorganize Rosa's pantry."

Paolo paused. "Ah. That bad?"

Claire grinned. "You'll enjoy her."

Before he could respond, the courtyard gate opened.

"Please tell me there's wine already involved," Evelyn announced as she stepped inside carrying an oversized straw tote over one shoulder.

Paolo smiled immediately. "Ev!"

Unlike her friends, Evelyn still somehow looked more athletic than travel weary, even after a transatlantic flight. Her formerly short brown hair had grown into a beachy-wave bob with golden highlights. It perfectly framed a face permanently kissed by sun from hours on the tennis court. She moved with the easy confidence of someone comfortable in both sneakers and linen dresses. Tonight, she wore white jeans, leather sandals, and a sleeveless navy top that showed off her toned arms.

Claire blinked. "You weren't supposed to arrive until tomorrow."

"I changed flights." Evelyn dropped her bag beside the courtyard wall dramatically. "I decided retirement is for weak people, but summer in Italy is not."

"You're not retired," Paolo reminded her.

"Exactly. Which is why I'm staying the entire summer before school starts again." She pointed a warning finger toward Claire. "And nobody is allowed to mention faculty meetings, standardized testing, or teenage drama for at least ten weeks."

Claire kissed her cheek. "Deal."

Evelyn turned back toward Paolo, her grin widening. "And I hear rumors your farmhouse restoration is finally finished."

Paolo lifted an eyebrow cautiously. "Claire talks too much."

"She absolutely does." Evelyn crossed her arms. "I would like a full tour at some point. I've earned it emotionally after hearing so much about stone walls and reclaimed beams."

"It still needs work," Paolo replied.

"Perfect. So do most interesting people."

Evelyn looked around the glowing courtyard, inhaling deeply. "Good grief," she said. "This place already feels better than America."

Something in Paolo relaxed hearing that. Villa Santoro still had that effect on people.

Inside the kitchen, warm light spilled across the old limestone walls. Copper pots gleamed overhead while the scent of garlic, tomatoes, and fresh bread filled the air. Standing at the long farmhouse counter arguing playfully with Zia Rosa in a gentile southern accent was a woman Paolo had never seen before.

She turned at the sound of footsteps. Early sixties perhaps. Dark curls loosely pinned up. Reading glasses resting on top of her head. Flour dusted across the front of her black linen dress which was modest but still did not hide her slim silhouette.

Her eyes met his. Warm, deep brown eyes that sparkled as a bright smile with perfect teeth lit up her face.

Claire stepped between them with obvious satisfaction. "Paolo, this is Charlotte Walker. She's a chef from Charleston. She's here for two weeks helping with the culinary program."

Charlotte wiped flour from her hands before offering one. "I've heard about you."

Paolo lifted an eyebrow. "Should I be concerned?"

"Probably," she admitted.

He chuckled softly before shaking her hand. Her grip was confident. Not fragile. Interesting.

Rosa pointed dramatically toward the stove. "He talks too much," she informed Charolotte. "You cook. He carries things."

"Ah," Paolo sighed. "My true purpose revealed."

Charlotte laughed—not politely, but genuinely—and something small shifted in the room. Not lightning or instant chemistry, just a tangible awareness.

The evening unfolded easily after that. Guests gathered beneath the courtyard lights while Charlotte guided them through handmade orecchiette with calm authority and occasional Southern expressions that delighted Rosa even when she understood only half of them.

Surveying the long table, Charlotte wiped her hands on her apron and smiled with satisfaction. “Well, y’all, if anybody leaves this table hungry, it’ll be their own fault. My mama always said feeding people is just another way of loving on them.”

Paolo found himself watching Charolotte every few minutes with heightening curiosity. The way she moved through the kitchen without performance. Claire had told him a few weeks ago that the chef from America was a widow of about five years. He observed her closely, looking for the signs of grief he’d noticed often in his own eyes when he looked in the mirror. He saw only a soft openness in her eyes, and he wanted to know more about her.

He noticed she wore her wedding ring on a chain around her neck instead of her hand. He recognized that kind of love and that kind of loss too.

Later, after dinner, the guests lingered over wine while music drifted through the courtyard. Paolo stood near the olive trees watching Charlotte laugh at something Evelyn had said.

Claire appeared beside him carrying two espresso cups. “Well?” she asked casually.

“Well, what?”

“You noticed her.”

Paolo accepted the espresso. “Claire…”

“I’m not matchmaking,” she lied immediately.

"You are absolutely matchmaking."

She smiled without shame. "You looked alive tonight."

The comment settled quietly between them.

Paolo glanced toward Charlotte again as she brushed hair from her face while listening to Rosa passionately explain why Americans ruin perfectly good tomatoes by refrigerating them. A small smile touched his mouth. Then he looked upward through the grapevine arbor where the string lights glowed against the darkening Italian sky.

For the first time since Kate left, the future no longer felt like a closed door. Not fully open yet. But open enough for light to enter.

CHAPTER 61
The Beautiful Scar

Austin, Texas—One Year Later

Not every scar is a mark of loss. Some become monuments to grace.

The house no longer felt like a place of fracture. It felt lived in. Earned. They lay tangled in white sheets, skin still warm from love. Not rushed or desperate, but slow and deeply known.

Grant rested on his side, tracing his finger along the faint crescent scar on Kate's left breast. The lumpectomy had left only a small indentation. Barely visible unless you knew where to look. He knew.

His touch was reverent.

"You're quiet," she said.

"I was thinking."

"Dangerous."

He smiled. "I remember the first night after surgery. You wouldn't let me look."

"I didn't want to see pity in your eyes."

"I wasn't thinking pity."

"What were you thinking?"

"That I almost lost you."

His finger traced the scar again. “It’s beautiful.”

She laughed self-consciously. “That is not the word most women would use.”

“It is for me.”

“Explain.”

He leaned closer. “When Jesus appeared after the resurrection … He still had His scars.”

Her breath caught.

“He could have erased them,” Grant said quietly.

“But He kept them. Why? As proof.”

Silence settled over them. “The scar didn’t mean death won,” he continued. “It meant death lost.”

Tears filled her eyes. He brushed the small curve again.

“This isn’t a reminder of what cancer tried to take.”

“What is it?”

“It’s a reminder that we survived.”

She placed her hand over his.

“Our scars don’t disqualify us from intimacy,” Grant continued.

“No,” she agreed.

“They deepen it,” he added.

“Yes,” Kate sighed contentedly. “They do.”

He kissed the scar. Not sensual, but reverent.

“I used to think you’d see it and remember how fragile I am,” she whispered.

“No, I see it and remember how strong you are.”

She let that settle.

The year had not been perfect. Radiation fatigue. Follow-up scans. Moments of fear. But also, there had been so much shared laughter and renewed desire. Hands reaching in the dark again.

Grant pulled her against him. “We’re not who we once were.”

“No,” she agreed and smiled faintly, “we’re better and more grateful.”

He kissed her hair. “We don’t get a marriage without scars.”

“No,” she said, “but we get one with resurrection.”

The room was quiet except for their breathing. Grant laced his fingers through hers. The same way he had done decades ago in parking lots. Only now the gesture carried weight.

They had almost lost everything. And instead, they had found grace.

EPILOGUE
Beyond Betrayal

Monopoli, Italy

The God who permits brokenness is also the God who patiently restores what is surrendered to Him.

Two years and three months after her first trip to Puglia, Kate stood once again in the courtyard of Villa Santoro. Only this time, she was celebrating. Today marked her thirty-eighth wedding anniversary.

The late afternoon sun warmed the pale stone walls, turning everything the color of honey. Bougainvillea cascaded over the terrace railings, and the scent of rosemary, citrus, and warm bread drifted through the air. Lanterns had already been strung across the courtyard in preparation for evening.

Marianne and Ev had flown in from Texas to celebrate what Ev insisted on calling "the miraculous anniversary."

Claire, meanwhile, was in her element, moving through the courtyard like a conductor orchestrating controlled chaos.

"Marianne, the candles!" Claire called across the courtyard. "Ev, you cannot reorganize the flowers again!"

Evelyn glanced up from the long table where she was adjusting a centerpiece of olive branches and white roses. "They needed balance."

Marianne adjusted her reading glasses with quiet patience. "You're all dramatic."

Zia Rosa appeared in the doorway, supervising the evening with sharp-eyed authority, occasionally correcting Claire's instructions in rapid Italian or shooing people away from dishes she insisted were "not yet fit for human consumption."

Tonight, she wore a soft charcoal dress with a cream shawl draped around her shoulders, her silver hair pinned neatly at the nape of her neck as lantern light softened the lines time had written across her face.

More than once, Kate caught Rosa pausing quietly to look around the courtyard with the deep satisfaction of a woman watching a once silent house breathe with robust life again.

Children's laughter echoed across the stone walls. Wine glasses clinked beneath the grapevine arbor. Three generations now gathered around the long wooden table while relaxing music drifted into the warm Italian evening.

Approaching the older woman she had come to love like family, Kate slipped her arms gently around her and kissed her cheek. "You kept the light burning for all of us," she whispered.

For once, Rosa looked momentarily speechless. Then she cupped Kate's face in both weathered hands and smiled. "No," she said quietly. "God did. I only kept opening the door."

Around the courtyard, family and close friends had begun to gather beneath the lantern lights. Claire had blocked off every upstairs room at the villa for the week, insisting that no strangers would be wandering through such a sacred celebration.

"This courtyard has hosted enough tourists," she had declared months earlier. "For one week, it belongs entirely to people we love."

Now the villa brimmed with familiar voices and overlapping conversations. Jesse stood near the stone wall talking with Nathan while Rachel helped Emma arrange small plates of desserts near the long table. Laughter drifted easily through the warm evening air as local friends, extended family, and a few cherished guests from Monopoli mingled together beneath the grapevine arbor.

The village baker, a longtime friend of Rosa, had delivered fresh bread earlier in the day. Kate had met him many times in her months in Puglia and insisted Rosa invite him to the festivities. As he arrived again that evening with his adult son, Allsesandro, he hugged Rosa and refused payment for the bread. "Some celebrations must not include payment," he had said simply.

The villa felt alive in a way Kate had never imagined that first summer. She smoothed the soft linen of the pale blue dress Claire had insisted she wear—light and elegant, perfect for the warm Italian evening. A delicate silver bracelet rested against her wrist, catching the lantern light as she moved.

Across the courtyard, Grant stood with Claire near the long table. Kate paused for a moment just to watch him. He wore a crisp white shirt with the sleeves rolled casually to his forearms, dark trousers, and the relaxed confidence of a man who had learned how to breathe again. The Mediterranean sun had left a faint bronze warmth across his face.

He looked rested. Younger somehow. Undeniably handsome. Kate felt a small flutter in her chest that surprised her—a familiar spark carrying echoes of their earliest years together. Grant glanced up and caught her watching him. The smile that crossed his face made her heart lift.

Claire leaned toward him and muttered under her breath, "You've already married her once, you know."

Grant exhaled slowly. "This feels different."

"It is," Evelyn said, appearing beside them with a knowing look. "You're choosing her without illusion this time."

Marianne approached holding a folded piece of paper. "Just in case," she said quietly, handing it to him. "These are the vows you two wrote together this morning."

Grant glanced down at the page before smiling. "I won't need them," he said. Still, he slipped the paper into his jacket pocket.

Jesse stood near the long table with his now four-year-old son while Rachel laughed beside him, her dark curls pulled loosely back from the warm Italian evening. Parenthood had softened Jesse in good ways. There was still strength in him, still ambition, but less urgency now. More presence.

Nathan leaned against the stone wall nearby, relaxed in a way Kate rarely saw during his graduate school years. Allesandro had drawn him into a conversation about architecture and restoration, and for once he wasn't overthinking every word he said.

And Emma—Kate's eyes softened as she watched her daughter move through the courtyard beside her husband. Newly married and still discovering the rhythm of life together, Emma carried herself differently now. Not merely loved. Chosen.

At one point Grant glanced across the courtyard toward Jesse and Nathan. The look that passed between the three men held something quieter than mere affection. Respect and earned honesty. Months earlier, those conversations had been painful. Awkward sometimes. But now, watching his sons laugh beneath the lantern lights, Grant understood something he once missed entirely: Transparency had not weakened his authority as a father. It had redeemed it.

Jesse's wife, Rachel appeared beside Kate carrying a tray of small lemon cakes. "I just want you to know," she said, "the boys talk differently now."

Kate tilted her head slightly. "What do you mean?"

Rachel smiled faintly. "More honestly. About marriage, stress, temptation, and faith." She glanced toward Jesse. "Our family tells the truth now. That's rare." Emotion tightened unexpectedly in Kate's chest.

Across the courtyard, Emma slipped her arm through her husband's as they listened to Claire passionately explain her newest renovation plans for the upstairs rooms.

Kate remembered the quiet conversations she and Emma had shared during the past two years. Conversations about paying attention to each other's inner world. About guarding intimacy before distance had time to grow roots. The family was not untouched by pain now. But perhaps that was what made this evening feel so sacred. Nothing here was pretending anymore. Not the marriage. Not the laughter. Not the gratitude.

Just then, the courtyard gate opened again. Kate looked up instinctively and then smiled widely.

Paolo stepped through the gate beside Charlotte, both carrying the easy warmth of people no longer haunted by the past. Charlotte wore a flowing sage-green dress, her dark curls brushed softly away from her face, while Paolo looked relaxed and deeply at peace in a lightweight linen jacket and open collar.

Something inside Kate settled at the sight of them together. A year earlier, seeing Paolo again might have stirred complicated emotions. Now it stirred only gratitude.

Charlotte embraced Kate warmly. "You look beautiful," she said sincerely.

"So do you," Kate replied.

Paolo stepped forward next. For one brief second, both seemed aware of the history they carried between them—not romantic anymore, but sacred in its own way. Then he kissed her lightly on both cheeks in the traditional Italian manner.

“Tonight is a good night,” he said, his eyes glistening.

Kate smiled. “Yes,” she answered. “It really is.”

Grant joined them naturally, extending his hand toward Paolo without hesitation.

No awkwardness. No competition. Only grace hard-earned by all of them.

“You have a beautiful family,” Paolo told him sincerely.

Emotion flickered briefly across Grant’s face. “Thank you,” he replied. “And thank you… for being kind to my wife when she needed friends around her.”

Paolo smiled warmly. “She was never difficult to care about.”

Charlotte touched Paolo's arm lightly then, drawing his attention toward Rosa calling everyone to gather before the ceremony began. As they walked away together beneath the lantern lights, Kate watched them for a moment.

She felt only joy.

God had never intended Paolo to become her future. His friendship had simply been part of her healing—a steady reminder that life and joy still existed beyond heartbreak. Some people enter our lives not to become the ending of the story, but to help carry us through the middle chapters until healing has done its work.

Kate smiled and turned back toward Grant, grateful for every step that had brought her here.

Renewed Vows

Kate approached just as the sun began its slow descent behind the olive trees. Her three dear friends and family members gathered quietly behind her. The courtyard glowed gold.

Grant waited for her to reach him and took both her hands in his. For a moment, neither spoke. Thirty-eight years of memories rested in the silence between them.

"I don't promise perfection," he said finally, his voice steady. "I promise presence."

Kate felt her eyes fill. "I don't promise fear will never whisper," she replied. "But I promise to answer it with truth."

They had written vows together that morning at the small kitchen table, but now the words came naturally, not rehearsed or memorized.

"I choose you," Grant said. "Again." He handed her a single coral rose—her favorite.

Kate smiled through tears. "And I choose you," she whispered. "Again."

When he kissed her, it was not to claim. It was to honor.

Applause rose from the gathering. Wine was poured. Laughter returned.

Later that evening, music drifted through the courtyard as twilight settled over Villa Santoro. Kate leaned into Grant's shoulder beneath the lantern lights. "It sobers me to think how close we came to losing this," she said quietly.

"Yes," he replied. "Me too."

She rested her hand lightly over her chest. "And I thank God for the scar, Grant."

He knew exactly what she meant.

"It doesn't remind me where our love failed," he offered. "It reminds me where God's grace prevailed."

Soon everyone gathered around the long wooden table they had come to love. It was a newer and longer version now; one Claire had commissioned from a village carpenter using reclaimed olive wood.

"You never know who might arrive," she had said while supervising its construction.

Tonight, the table was full. Kate ran her fingertips lightly along its edge. The wood was not perfect. The carpenter had intentionally left the grain and knots visible—marks where storms, seasons, and years had shaped the tree before it was ever cut.

She thought of the faint scar that curved across her own body now. Once she had feared it. Now she understood it. Scars were not proof that something had been destroyed. They were proof that something had survived.

Grant followed her gaze down the table where friends and strangers now sat together laughing.

"What are you thinking?" he asked.

She smiled. "That broken things can still hold a lot of life."

He squeezed her hand. "Sometimes more life than before."

Lantern light flickered across plates of roasted vegetables, bowls of pasta Zia Rosa still refused to let anyone else make properly, and baskets of warm bread from the bakery down the street.

Claire moved easily between guests, laughing in three languages while refilling glasses. Kate watched her for a moment. There was something new in Claire now. No restlessness, just passionate purpose.

"You're staring," Grant said beside her.

Kate smiled. "She's building something beautiful."

Grant followed her gaze toward the upstairs balcony rooms. "Looks like she already has."

Kate looked once more around the lantern-lit courtyard. Once, this place had been her refuge. Now it felt like something more. Healing had not come the way she once imagined. It had come much more slowly. Through truth. Through surrender. Through grace neither of them had earned.

Grant squeezed her hand. "You, okay?"

She nodded. "Yes. More than okay. Blessed beyond words."

She looked again toward Claire laughing with guests near the long table. Villa Santoro was no longer simply a place people visited. It was becoming a place where stories began again—where weary hearts found rest, where old wounds healed, and where people gathered around a table believing that grace still had more to write.

Kate rested her head lightly against Grant's shoulder. Some stories, she realized, only make sense *piano, piano.* Slowly, slowly. And sometimes the most beautiful beginnings grow from the places that once carried scars.

Not the end.

Just the beginning.

DEDICATION ... CONTINUED

To My Husband, Lew

This story was born from heartbreak, healing, and the beautiful truth that God still restores broken things.

Thank you for the courage of your surrendered heart and allowing the Lord to deepen and transform you. Thank you for choosing me and us again and again and fighting for what truly matters.

The last five years of our marriage have become some of the most meaningful and hope-filled of our lives because of your humility, faith, perseverance, and renewed love. You have become not only a godly husband, but my best friend.

What the enemy once intended for destruction, God has used to reveal His grace, redemption, and healing power in ways we never could have imagined. Your willingness and support to allow our story to inspire this fictional one is a testament to your humility and desire to be used by God.

Thank you for walking beside me with honesty, tenderness, and renewed purpose as we continue building a legacy of faith, love, forgiveness, and restoration for our family and hopefully for others who need hope that beautiful things can rise from broken places.

I love you deeply… forever and a day.

Why I Wrote Beyond Betrayal

In the fifty plus years that I've known Jesus, I've learned that he never intends for our pain or losses to be forgotten or wasted. He is a God of pursuing love that desires redemption and restoration. With him. And with each other.

While this book is a work of fiction, it was inspired by a very painful season in my life. There are many similarities between Kate and Grant's story and mine.

Sadly, "gray divorces"—couples divorcing after the age of fifty—have more than doubled since 1990. Now, over one-third of divorces involve people in this age group.

I wrote ***Beyond Betrayal*** because I faced the prospect of becoming single in my mid-sixties and was forced to face the possibilities of how my life would change on many levels.

Like Kate, I chose to address my husband's infidelity with a strong commitment to seek God's will rather than my own. Trust me when I say there were many times I wanted to run or simply close that chapter of my life. But … God.

I knew his will was for me to pursue forgiveness, restoration, and redemption. However, I could only control my side of the relationship. Through patience, prayer, godly counsel, surrender and more prayer, my husband's heart softened and he began to listen to the Holy Spirit once again.

Today, I am married to a humble, godly man who thanks God each day for our marriage and the opportunity to "finish strong" and leave a legacy of love and commitment to our sacred covenant.

Not all stories end like Kate's or mine. But I believe with forgiveness, patience, and prayer there is great hope for many marriages to be saved. I pray this book will encourage couples to seek God's will and patiently wait for his supernatural intervention.

With God—ALL THINGS are possible.

In His power alone,

Danna

P.S. Enjoy a sample chapter from my upcoming sequel novel in the pages that follow.

FAITH • HOPE • LOVE

Book Two in the Villa Santoro Series
A Story of Courage and Late-Life Romance

Sample Chapter:
The Dangerous Thing About Hope

Monopoli, Italy

The problem with Villa Santoro, Evelyn decided, was that it gave people entirely too much time to think.

Back home in Texas, life moved fast enough to outrun introspection. There were tennis practices, faculty meetings, grading papers, booster club emails, church obligations, and endless teenagers asking questions that could have been solved with basic common sense and five minutes on Google.

But here? Here people lingered. Over espresso. Over conversations. Over sunsets. Over emotions.

Which was precisely how she found herself sitting beneath the grapevine arbor at eleven thirty at night wondering why a Frenchman with tired blue eyes and a habit of asking inconveniently thoughtful questions had suddenly become such a complication.

"You're glaring at your wine again," Claire observed from across the courtyard table.

"I'm thinking."

"That's usually when trouble starts."

Evelyn ignored her and took another sip.

The courtyard was finally quiet after another full evening at Villa Santoro. Lanterns swayed gently overhead while distant music drifted from somewhere deeper in town. Most of the guests had gone upstairs an hour ago.

Most. Not all.

Near the kitchen doorway, Paolo and Charlotte were quietly clearing dessert plates together beneath the warm spill of light from the kitchen. Charlotte had become a familiar part of the villa now, returning several times each year to teach cooking classes that guests booked months in advance. Paolo always seemed lighter when she was there. He looked comfortable and very present. And yet something about them still felt guarded.

Charlotte laughed heartily at something Paolo said in Italian, her hand brushing his forearm as she moved past him toward the sink. Evelyn noticed the way his entire expression softened at the contact and the way Charlotte pulled back just slightly afterward, as though closeness still surprised her.

There was affection between them. Real affection. But also caution. Two people who had already loved deeply and understood exactly how much could be lost.

For a few years, Paolo had carried grief around like a second skin. Now he looked more alive than wounded. Still thoughtful. Still healing in places. But open again. Mostly.

Yet every now and then Evelyn caught Charlotte watching him with an expression she couldn't fully read as if she were standing near the edge of something beautiful and dangerous at the same time, uncertain whether she possessed the courage to step all the way in.

Claire followed Evelyn's gaze. "You know," she said casually, "it would be healthy for you to admit happiness is still possible after sixty."

Evelyn nearly choked on her wine. "Oh, good grief."

Claire smirked. "I'm serious."

"No, you're matchmaking."

"I'm strategic."

"Claire."

Her friend leaned back in her chair looking entirely too pleased with herself.

"You've spent thirty years taking care of everybody else while pretending you don't have your own emotional life."

"I teach high school," Evelyn deadpanned. "Of course I have an emotional life. Most of it is chaos."

"You know what I mean."

Unfortunately, she did. Evelyn stared out toward the courtyard wall where climbing jasmine spilled over the old stone. She had genuinely loved her life, mostly.

Teaching history. Coaching girls who needed confidence more than trophies. Friday night football games. Early morning tennis drills before the Texas heat became unbearable. Watching awkward freshmen slowly become capable young women.

There had been dates over the years. A few disappointments and a couple "almosts" but never love. Not the kind that rearranged your future.

And now suddenly, at sixty-four years old, she found herself staring down two enormous questions at the exact same time. Luc Moreau. And whether to leave America entirely.

Claire leaned forward. "You know the school district needs your retirement decision by August first, right?"

Evelyn sighed immediately. "Thank you for bringing that up while I'm emotionally fragile."

"You're welcome."

The truth sat heavily between them.

It was already late July. If Evelyn intended to retire and move to Italy permanently this year, she would need to resign soon. The villa business was growing faster than Claire expected. Cooking classes were booked into autumn. Retreat inquiries were arriving weekly. Travelers from three continents had already passed through Villa Santoro that summer alone.

And Claire wanted help. She needed help. She had discussed an idea with Paolo to build a couple bungalows to accommodate more guests on the property.

Yes, she needed *real* help. Not temporary help. Someone who had a deep attachment to Villa Santoro. She needed Ev.

"You'd be incredible here," Claire said encouragingly. "You know that, right?"

Evelyn looked around the courtyard instinctively. The lantern lights. The long table. The warm stone walls. The slow rhythm of evenings that stretched instead of rushed.

Part of her could suddenly imagine it. Which terrified her. Because Luc complicated everything. He wasn't a tourist passing through for two weeks. He lived in southern France near Nice, where he owned a small specialty kitchen and wine shop that had belonged to his family for years. Being self-employed gave him flexibility. He could spend weeks at a time in Italy.

But his life was still rooted there. His business. His friends. His routines. His history. And Evelyn still had an entire life waiting in Texas. A house. A career. Students expecting her return in September. A church community. Security and predictability. Meanwhile, her heart was beginning to behave like a complete idiot.

The kitchen door opened before she could continue spiraling internally.

"Please tell me there's wine left," Luc said as he stepped into the courtyard.

Tall. Lean. Slightly silver at the temples. Tonight, he wore a light blue linen shirt, sleeves rolled up elegantly like European men all seem to do. His beige, linen trousers somehow looked elegant instead of wrinkled despite the humidity. It was infuriating.

His gaze landed on Evelyn immediately. Always immediately. "There you are," he said.

Her stomach betrayed her with an entirely unnecessary flutter. "Yes, here I am," she replied.

Claire stood abruptly. "Well, look at that. I suddenly remembered I promised Rosa help inside."

"You absolutely did not," Evelyn informed her.

But Claire was already disappearing into the kitchen. Traitor.

Luc sat across from Evelyn and slid the bottle of wine toward her, nodding for approval to pour.

"You disappeared after dinner."

"I was helping clean."

"You were escaping."

Evelyn looked up sharply.

The annoying thing about Luc was that he noticed too much. As if betrayal had trained him to study people before trusting them. His ex-wife had left him for another man after twenty-six years of marriage. He rarely spoke about it directly, but the wound sat quietly beneath almost everything he did.

"You make me nervous," Evelyn admitted before she could stop herself.

Luc blinked once, surprised. Then unexpectedly, he smiled. "Good," he said. "You make me nervous too."

Well. That was deeply unhelpful.

The courtyard grew quieter around them. Somewhere upstairs, a balcony door closed softly while cicadas hummed steadily beyond the olive trees.

Luc leaned back studying her carefully. "Claire says you may move here."

Evelyn groaned. "Claire says many things."

"But is it true?"

"That's the problem," she admitted. "I don't know."

For the first time that evening, real uncertainty crossed his face. "My life is still in France," he said quietly. "I can travel more now than before, but my shop is still there. My responsibilities are there."

Evelyn nodded slowly. Nothing about this was simple. They were not twenty-five-year-olds falling recklessly into romance. They were two older adults with established lives, obligations, habits, and scars.

Luc looked down into his wine glass.

"You know what frightens me most?" he asked quietly.

She shook her head.

"That I could love someone again and still not know if either of us is willing to change our lives enough to make it possible."

There it was. The real thing beneath all the attraction and flirtation and lingering eye contact.

Risk.

Evelyn looked away immediately. "No offense," she muttered, "but French people become emotionally dangerous after ten p.m."

He chuckled as if amused. "And Americans hide behind humor whenever something matters."

"Unfortunately, true," she replied.

Claire's voice drifted faintly from inside the kitchen where she and Rosa were clearly eavesdropping.

"I can still hear you two!" Evelyn called loudly.

"Good!" Claire shouted back. "Then stop pretending you don't like each other!"

Luc laughed outright then, warm and completely unguarded. And to Evelyn's horror, she realized she was beginning to love hearing that sound. Which meant this situation had officially become dangerous.

Not because she was falling. But because for the first time in decades, she was genuinely considering changing her life for love.

DANNA DEMETRE

Danna Demetre is a Christian author, speaker, and wellness educator whose deep faith has shaped both her life and her writing. For decades, she has encouraged women to pursue emotional, spiritual, and physical wholeness through biblical truth, personal growth, and resilient hope.

She is the author of several nonfiction books, including *Eat Live Thrive Diet*, and has spoken to audiences across the country on topics ranging from healthy living and relationships to faith, identity, and finishing life strong.

Beyond Betrayal is her debut novel and the first book in the Villa Santoro Series. While fictional, the story draws inspiration from real-life experiences and the universal realities of marriage, heartbreak, forgiveness, and restoration. Through richly layered characters and the breathtaking backdrop of Southern Italy, Danna explores the transforming power of grace, authentic friendship, and second chances.

Her fiction is especially written for women in midlife and beyond—women who still long for purpose, beauty, meaningful connection, and the assurance that their best chapters may still lie ahead.

Danna lives in San Antonio, Texas, with her husband. When she's not writing, speaking, or encouraging others, she enjoys time with family, exploring new places, and nurturing her growing love affair with Italy.

She is currently at work on the next novel in the Villa Santoro Series. Enjoy the sample chapter she's included at the end of this book.

Stay in touch with Danna:

www.DannaDemetre.com

Made in the USA
Coppell, TX
30 June 2026

83310837R00252